THE LAST
HARD MAN

Other Books by Joe Hoffman:

Jordan's Angel

In Dreams Awake

Personal website: joehoffmanbooks.com

THE LAST HARD MAN

JOE HOFFMAN

ARPress
45 Dan Road Suite 36
Canton MA 02021

Hotline: 1(800) 220-7660
Fax: 1(855) 752-6001

Ordering Information:
Quantity sales. Special discounts are available on quantity purchases by corporations, associations, and others. For details, contact the publisher at the address above.

Printed in the United States of America.

ISBN-13:   Paperback   979-8-89389-693-0
                eBook   979-8-89389-694-7

Library of Congress Control Number: 2024923895

To Kathy, whose inspiration and motivation
in my life has led to an enlightened imagination
that we share with just a titch of dementia.

1

The sun peeked through the eastern window on this crisp, Thanksgiving morning in West Virginia. As Matt looked over to the other side of the bed, he noticed that Becky, his wife of five years, was still asleep. A golden opportunity to show his bride why he was the best thing that ever happened to her since sliced bread. Matt would slip out into the kitchen and make the coffee. He would then follow it up with a bedside delivery, and wait hopefully for his just reward. He would also have to hold back on the panting in anticipation. He didn't want to appear ridiculously anxious, or wake their very precocious, four-year-old daughter, Mary.

Becky was beautiful. She was even more fetching as she laid in bed, asleep and defenseless. Her blond hair glistening in the early morning sunlight that poured through the bedroom window and across her pillow.

When Matt arrived in the kitchen, he realized that his scheme had been thwarted. The coffee was nearly finished. Becky had been up and gone back to bed. Another strategy was in order as the ever-scheming Matt made his way back to bed without disturbing Becky.

"Faked you out again, my dear." Becky said with her head still on the pillow. "Today is my morning to spoil you. However, if you feel you need to do something to earn your morning dessert...cream and sugar, please."

Matt leaned over and kissed Becky on the cheek and smacked her on the butt.

"Let me have another one of those before you go to the kitchen." Becky said.

When Matt leaned over the bed for a follow up kiss, he found himself locked in Becky's arms.

"Let's have dessert first, this morning, shall we?" Becky asked.

"Whatever you ask, my dear." answered Matt. "I am merely your humble servant."

"Right now, I'm not interested in humble, I have an itch, and I don't think humble is going to scratch it," Becky returned as she assumed the position atop her humble servant.

"God, you're beautiful!" Matt said as he looked up at her in the penetrating light, now deep inside her, as the sun reflected her naked beauty. She looked back at him with an amorous smile and then closed her eyes and threw her head back with a moan.

Becky was five foot, ten inches tall with blond hair and blue eyes. She was slender, but had broad shoulders and had a muscular upper body, but she was every bit of a woman despite her physique. She made him very happy behind closed doors, and he was very proud of her. She always took care to make him feel her total love toward him. There was no doubt in their minds that they both were with the one person Almighty God had chosen for them. Becky was Matts life and there was no other place he wanted to be than where he was at this moment.

He had traveled from the flat lands of Helena, Ohio, to be with her, and he had never regretted the move to the West Virginia hill country. It was a completely new life than the one he was used to, and Becky was someone unlike anyone he had ever met before. She was kind, she was warm, and she always made him feel welcome. For the woman that Matthew was totally devoted to was a coal miner.

As he looked at Becky in the sunlight, he couldn't help but recall what she had said to him when he asked her why she wanted a bedroom with a window facing the east? She answered him saying, "so I can make love to you in the morning and you will know that you are my reason for the sunrise." That was enough for him, he never asked again. He just looked forward to every morning, and he was never disappointed.

As Becky fell onto Matt's sexual pose, he put his arms and legs around her and held her close as she trembled atop of him with a light trickle of sweat rolling down her cleavage.

Matt was a well-kept, ripped, six foot, two inches tall. He always kidded Becky that his muscles were spread over four more inches of body than hers were, as his excuse for being so slender. But whenever Becky laid on top of him while making love to him, she didn't complain. She was proud of her trim, well kept, husband.

Matt was a Lieutenant for the Fremont, Ohio, Fire Department, who like so many agencies, went to the aid of FDNY, following the 911 attacks.

While he was on a search and rescue mission at the twin towers, a large slab of concrete debris shifted, severing the nerves in his left leg, making it impossible for him to stand on a ladder and perform his duties. He became disabled from the very thing in life he loved. He worked as an Instructor for a while and even filled in as an E.M.T. Technician, but the disability was more than he bargained for, and it wasn't long until he was retired, with a paying disability, at the age of thirty.

Becky looked down at him and while kissing him on the lips, cheek, and eyes, whispered softly in his ear to roll her over.

Matt accommodated the wishes of his bride, and in an instant was lost within the grips of the moment. The realization of the sexuality of making love to Becky. They were tightly gripped together, breathing heavily in unison, and sweating lightly despite the temperature of the season. The world was okay with the both of them while they were making love. There were no others in the world but the two of them and they made love that way every day. They were one, like the Minister said at the wedding. And from that oneness they made Mary four years ago.

Mary was four going on fourteen, her grandmother would say. She had her mother's beauty and her father's Yankee stubbornness. But it was obvious that she was her daddy's girl, and Matt, being away from his natural home, had nothing but time and love for both of his ladies. And he showed it unselfishly toward both.

She was blond like her mother, but had her father's brown eyes. She was kind of quiet, if not reserved, however, she was ahead of her age in maturity. She was unselfish for a little girl, and like her father, dropped everything for her mother when she came home from work. She helped her father with the house work, the shopping, and even signed her mother's name on the checks when the monthly bills were paid. The two of them were quite a pair.

Becky would beam with pride when the three of them were together. Those two, taking such good care of her, was an envious sight for anybody. The three of them made a great life together, in the big blue house on the top of the hill, and at the time, there was no talk of a fourth member to the family. Although Becky came from a large family, and her brother's and sister's had large families, she and Matt always felt that a smaller family was a better way to go, and that is how it was for the family on the top of the hill and in the middle of the horseshoe.

Hope, West Virginia, was a typical coal mining town, except for its design. The town was built on the flatland of a mountaintop, and the mine was at the bottom of the valley. So, in essence it looked like a horseshoe. From the vantage point of 342 Greeley Street, Matt could look over the complete town from his front porch. He could see the three church's, the Baptist, the Methodist, and the Catholic church, the banks, and the restaurants. Matt and Mary could look through a telescope and see Becky come up from the mine on the work car as she headed for home. On really nice days, they would walk down to the visitor's center and meet her and they would all come home together. Otherwise, the moment they saw Becky, a hot bath was prepared, a chilled glass of wine was poured, and she was met on the back porch where her shoes were replaced with a foot massage and a pair of slippers. It was a ritual that was followed by many families. However, usually, the man was met by this kind of treatment, and not the wife.

But in this family, it didn't matter, and Matt never took the kidding serious about him being a 'mister mom'. Because Matt knew, as did most of them in town; his disability paid more than most of their jobs did.

Matt wasn't without occasional work, and often he helped out at the Fire Station. He was very instrumental in showing the mine rescue teams how to use their equipment. He would also fill in as a substitute teacher and was also licensed to drive the school bus on a fill-in basis. At times he would help the less fortunate folks with their taxes and their WIC Coupon requests. He and Mary always knew what families needed help with food and necessary living supplies. Some of the local elderly folks who couldn't afford their utilities, mysteriously found them paid from time to time. He helped several families fill out the forms to get Pell Grants for their kids to go to college. For a foreigner, with a limited history, Matt was very well respected, and was regarded as the man to go see when no one would help you. And when all else failed, he was a great baby sitter in a pinch. He and Mary took many field trips with the school children, up to the mountain for a nature hike in the spring, while the teacher's put the finishing touches on another school year. The community tended to look to Matt for the things they didn't know or couldn't do. And he was always there for them without complaint.

There was a private part of Matt, however, that no one entered. A piece of the man that was not shared with anyone else. Becky had only scratched the surface of Matt's hidden side, but she never pried and he never offered anything but his total love for his wife. That was enough for Becky.

As their breathing settled down a little and their muscles relaxed a bit, they held each other tight, neither wanting to let go. To end the moment which was so beautiful, and to go back into the world, was something they weren't ready for just yet. Mary was still asleep, so there wasn't a real reason to end the loving between them.

"How do you that for so long?"

"I practice a lot when I'm alone." Matt answered with a snicker which got him a slap on the butt. "That was nice wasn't it?"

Becky just nodded and smiled in approval.

"It still is nice. What are you doing after the festivities tonight?" Becky asked.

"Well," Matt answered, "I was hoping to meet up with my wife tonight and pick up where we left off. That is if she isn't too busy."

"What do you say I meet you here? Same place, same position, same thing?" Becky chided.

"I don't know," said Matt. "You might be all worn out carrying grandpa's moonshine up the street for any extra-curricular activity. You know how that hog wrestling always puts you in a tiff. Thanksgiving always wears you to a frazzle honey. I'm kind of worried about you."

"I didn't say I was going to do anything," Becky returned. "I just said I'll be here. Oh...keep doing that. That is nice. You needn't worry about me, my dear Matthew. Oh, that feels good! Where did you learn to do that? Never mind! Just don't stop. Damn, that's nice. No wonder I love you so much. You can't possibly practice that when you're alone."

2

A short time later, Matt and Becky, rolled out of bed. Becky broke the momentary silence by saying, "you get our coffee, I'll get the water hot."

"It's what I live for," returned Matt.

"No, honey, you just got what you live for." Becky said.

As Becky headed for the shower, Matt met Mary on the way to the kitchen.

"Good morning, sunshine." Matt greeted. "Are you hungry?"

"No, Daddy, I'm saving myself for Grandma's fried chicken." she said. "I can hardly wait."

Today was the annual Thanksgiving Day bash at grandmas. That woman could do some serious cooking. But as Matt would say, "all those hillbilly-woman can cook." And after today's festivities, was tomorrow's community Thanksgiving Day celebration at the city park. It was a good time, especially if you liked to eat. It was strange for Matt, who came from a different culture, so to speak, to see this much camaraderie in a small town. But all across these coal mining communities, the families and neighbors stayed close. Sometime almost too close, Matt thought, but nonetheless, they were all good to each other. It was a different way of life than your typical nine-to-five lifestyle. These people were in an occupation where there was no guarantee that you would always come home at the end of the day. But they accepted this, as had all the generations before them, and they went on with their lives despite the dangers involved.

In Hope, the men would tip their hats to the ladies and greet the men folk whether they knew them or not. Which in his town, that was quite rare. Where Matt came from, you walked down the street and kept to yourself, only greeting someone you had known for quite some time. But Matt was quite outgoing, so he fit right in with the crowd.

In general, all these coal towns were alike. Hope was no different. They were very outgoing and friendly, however, they weren't stupid, by any means. They could spot a foreigner a mile away, and until they were accepted, they were kept under close surveillance. They were a close-knit group of people that lived with adversity, change and on occasion, hard times. But through it all, they did it together, and the Thanksgiving celebration at the park was the day they went all out, to share a bit of hospitable prosperity together.

The family gathering was its usual good time. Becky's family was all there and they were a great bunch of people. There was never any 'inner-bickering' between them. They told it like it was, and they all picked on Matt and Ray. They couldn't get an even break, but they took it very well. They were both rewarded very well when they got home. That is how it worked, so the pain was, as they say, temporary.

The next day brought about a different set of challenges when they arrived at the town gathering.

When Matt came into contact with a certain individual, they both looked at each other admirably, but with reservation. Matt and this man, John Colb, would greet one another with the most respectful grip. Then they would look sadly at each other for a moment, shake their heads in greeting, smile broadly, and talk briefly. Becky would watch them closely as they talked.

Another person, in particular, John's father, Abner, noticed this as well. He would stare at Matt in a most inquisitive, peculiar way. Not knowing whether to trust him or figure him to be weird, and drop a dime on his Yankee ass. The stare he would give Mathew would take the shine off a new penny. John and Matt were old friends from another time, but their secret was locked up between them - for now at least.

The party went well, everybody stopping by and talking to each other. The Colbs kind of hung out by themselves. Becky explained to Matt once that everybody thought Abner Colb was a little different. She couldn't put her finger on it, but everyone thought that old Abner had inhaled too much coal dust. He would get a little rowdy at the retired union member's meeting, ranting and raving over the company's piss-poor approach to the 'black lung' issue, that faced many miners today. He was, in general, considered to be a little nuts, and wasn't taken seriously in any discussions or decisions.

Matt on the other hand had the feeling that old Abner was a little too intelligent for the place he grew up in, and probably would have been a good candidate for NASA in his younger years. Even as outgoing as Matt was, he had a hard time talking to Abner. Once Abner laid that eyeball on you, you wanted to crawl out of your skin.

These union meetings only made things worse, because Abner considered himself to have more common sense than the average bear, as did Matt. He had fallen on hard times as of late in his retirement years and he was one of those people that Matt and Mary secretly took care of. He was a friendly enough person, Matt thought, if he would stop staring. Matt would waive and nod, but the best Abner would give him was an extended stare with an occasional scowl. One of those overly studious looks. He would then look at John, who wouldn't offer any advice, and the two would go their own way. Today, John and Matt went off together and talked about the old days in Desert Storm. A secret the two of them kept between themselves. So, in sum; Matt and John kept an eye on each other and Abner kept an eye on Matt.

The day officially ended with the ceremonial desert, which by the way, won the county fair blue ribbon. That was the qualifying prerequisite. Bragging rights for the whole year.

3

Matt, Becky and Mary said their good byes and walked home from the park together. Down the sidewalk and up the hill to the house they called home. They laughed, talked and held hands all the way home. Midway home, Matt became a horse and carried Mary up the hill, but he didn't mind. He was a family man now and this was his family.

Mary was quickly asleep and it wasn't long before Becky began a conversation that took Matt by complete surprise.

"You know…, you and John Colb look at each other in a strange fashion," began Becky. "If I didn't know any better, I'd say you knew each other from some other time. You two appeared to be much more than friends today, what with that walk you two took and all. You act as if you have a blood bond, or something."

"Do you mean like a half-Indian blood brother?" Matt squirmed uncomfortably at the thought that his friendship with John Colb was that noticeable.

"You know what I mean." said Becky.

"No, I don't honey." said Matt. "I see him once a year whether I need to or not. He's the only Veteran around here I know, and that gives me something in common with someone else. I feel kind of bad for him, he looks so out of place."

"He's lived here all his life, sweetie," reminded Becky. "You're the only one that looks out of place here."

Matt looked at Becky with an insulted expression, and Becky quickly recovered.

"I'm sorry, Matt, that didn't come out right." apologized Becky. "I didn't mean it like that."

The two of them walked in silence for a while, and then Becky got her second wind and began a new angle.

"Let me just lay it on the line the way I see it." Becky continued. "Okay... follow along here. Our dear friend John Colb was a mild-mannered candy ass who never went close to the mines. We all thought he didn't want to get his hands dirty, or he was playing for the other team. I personally thought he was a pussy, but that's beside the point. Are you with me so far?

So poor old favorite son, John, goes to Officer Training School and flunks out, because he's not as sharp as his dear father thinks he is. So now, he gets put in the infantry and his candy ass is shipped over to Iraq. Stay with me now, I'm getting to the punch line here. The story goes on to say that he got his bony butt shot over there and was left behind by his squad. The story also goes on to say that some poor old slob from an Air Force Rescue and Recovery Squad goes looking for old John. It's also said that all he could remember about the man who carried his ungrateful, scrawny, ass six miles through the desert is that his name was Matt, and he was from somewhere in Ohio."

"But there are thous....," interrupted Matt.

"Don't interrupt me when I making rhetorical statements." began Becky. "Now the first time you hugged me good night, I could feel some real muscle on you. That's not the stuff you put on in the gym, that's hardened muscle that only hardened men have and not an Air Force mechanic who lived on pizza and beer. The first time we made love, I could feel more muscle and tone on you than just the obvious business end. And you never get tired from making love to me. I'm in good shape and you wear me out. And no disabled fireman could walk up and down these mountains like you can, and you're not even from around here, so don't tell me you've been doing it all your life. And you don't miss a thing, especially people's motions. You have the senses of a hyperactive eagle in a field of hunters. And I'll bet you could teach Rambo a thing or two about staying alive. Now why do I get the feeling you're not telling me everything? Now, you take all this I've just said, plus the way you two looked at each other the first time you met in the grocery store, and I say you're the poor slob that carried that candy ass six miles through the Saudi desert, and he's not the first one you ever did this for. Tell me I'm wrong; I dare you."

Matt just looked at Becky, trying to muster up some form of argument, but he couldn't. She was right. What he needed to do was find a way to change her mind into thinking she had the wrong person.

"Wake up, Mary, we're home." said Matt as he refused to lock eyes on his beloved Becky. Matt unlocked the door and let Becky in and carried Mary into her bedroom, never saying anything to Becky.

Becky was never like this before, and he couldn't figure out what brought this on, except maybe, grandpa's moonshine. As he got Mary in her pajamas, his mind raced for an explanation. Anything short of a lie would probably work. As he tucked Mary in bed, he noticed that Becky had followed him into her bedroom.

"Hell, honey, he's just a nice guy, that's all." Matt began innocently. "What's wrong with talking to him? Just because no one else does, is it a crime for me to do it?"

"It's different with you." Becky answered. "You know him. It's that obvious. I'm just asking, that's all."

"No, baby! You're accusing." Matt returned. "You're accusing me of something, and I don't know why. I've done nothing to deserve this. I'm going to bed."

And with that Matt walked away to bed, feeling alone and betrayed at the hands of the woman he loved.

"Wait a minute." Becky summoned. "Tell me about the locked foot locker in the basement."

"Rebecca, this is ridiculous!" Matt said defensively. "That's just old air force stuff that was issued to me. For God sake, honey. Listen to you!"

"Then show me!" Becky challenged.

She had just called his bluff. Matt had no interest in carrying on this charade any further.

"All right, honey." Matt surrendered. "Come on."

As the two of them went into the basement and approached the sacred corner where the double locked foot locker rested, Matt reached up for the light and grabbed the keys.

"Is there anything in there that could go off...you know...explode?" Becky asked.

"Do you want to see it or not?" Matt asked. "Yeah, probably! When the stuff gets old it gets a little temperamental. Clothes tend to explode when the air gets to them. I suppose it could happen. Especially to me, right now, I'm sure of it."

"Okay, let's forget it. I believe you." said Becky.

This had been the closest Matt had ever come to telling Becky the truth of the life he left in the desert, and a small part of him wanted to get it over with. Becky had found his Achilles heel and he knew in his heart that this would someday come back to haunt him. It was stupid to hide something as innocent as your past, but Matt clung to that innocence as if it meant his very survival.

"Come on, honey," she said. "Let's go to bed. It's been a long day."

As Becky turned and walked back up the stairs, Matt took a moment and set down on the double locked foot locker that held his secrets. How many times he wished he had left it at his mother's house, but he thought maybe someday he would need the things that were in it. Mainly rescue supplies, adrenaline, epinephrine, morphine flexpens, IV solutions and needles. A light weight, silver, thermal protective suit, ropes, harnesses and climbing hardware, an Army issue .45 caliber Colt pistol, and a K-Bar survival knife. All the necessary tools for the man who made rescues in places where angels feared to tread.

There were things in this locker that were meant to be forgotten. If there was one mistake Matt made, it was not burning this stuff when he came home. But he didn't, and now he regretted it. He wanted to show it to Becky, right now, but he feared it would end their marriage. For, he thought, how could she sleep with the man whose very daily existence depended on the people he killed to bring others out alive.

For five years Matt was able to bury what he once was, inside the love, warmth and tenderness of Becky and Mary. But now that was being threatened...by the very person he hid it from; Becky.

John Colb was like the foot locker. John was a daily reminder that he could not escape his past. Not even in Hope, West Virginia.

Matt took his time getting ready for bed in the hopes that Becky would be asleep and he could sort all this out by the time she woke up in the morning. Matt looked in on Mary once more before joining his wife in bed. As he lay next to her, she moved close to him and put her arms and legs across him.

4

"They are putting us together in teams of four starting Monday." Becky started. "We are going to the Eastern edge and hand mine that special coal that's down there. They're paying us two dollars an hour more to dig it out. That ought to firm me up a little bit, don't you think?"

Being so grateful for a different subject, Matt had to collect himself a bit to figure out what she was talking about.

"Aw, honey," Matt said. "You're beautiful, you don't need any firming up. I love you just the way you are."

"Really? You wouldn't want me to lose about ten pounds?" asked Becky admirably.

"No. You're perfect." Matt answered.

Becky scooted even closer to Matt and began kissing him. After a moment she looked up and said, "come here and make me feel perfect."

They made love well into the next morning. They would love each other and hold each other and talk about the things they both loved and what they loved about each other. Their plans for Mary as well as themselves as a family. They touched on the new mining plan that the company had, which involved Becky and about eleven other miners. They talked about going on vacation. So many families, over the years, never got out of the community to take a vacation. This was mainly due to financial issues as well as territorial considerations. The average miner never left the holler. They rarely took a vacation, and if they did, they didn't go anywhere.

Matt had changed all that for Becky. They ran all over the country. It was nothing for Matt to have a clean set of clothes on the bed for Becky when she came home from work, and the suitcases packed, only to be off on another excursion. Tonight, between lovemaking sessions, they talked about going on a cruise. Maybe even make Mary a little sister on the trip. Their plans were as broad as their imaginations and as carefree as their love for one another.

Eventually, they fell asleep wrapped in each other's arms. When the sun broke through the eastern window on Sunday morning, Becky got up and pulled the shade down and went back to sleep.

They didn't even make it to church. They just slept in for a change. There was no more talk about Matt and John Colb. The day was filled with happiness, good meals and family time together.

"I can't believe this weekend went by so fast." Becky said. "You look so forward to these holiday weekends, and they're gone before you know it. Back to work tomorrow."

"Are you excited about the new work crew?" Matt asked.

"Yeah, I am." returned Becky. "It will be a treat to get away from that big loud machine for a while."

"What's that called," asked Matt. "A continuous miner?"

"Yeah. It's a racket." answered Becky. "We're back to some down home mining, like in the olden days."

"What's so special about this stuff, that they are going after it the old fashioned way?" asked Matt.

"High sulfur content." replied Becky. "It burns hotter and they make coke out of it. And it's a seam about sixteen inches high about two feet off the floor. They used to dig it out a few years ago, but there was some sort of trouble and they closed the shaft."

"Have they dusted it yet?" Matt asked.

"I think they're only going to air it out." Becky said. "I heard the midnight shift is going to turn on the fans tonight and put in some fresh air. The rats won't know how to act with some clean air. And we're using portable carbide lights, also. That will be different."

"Are you all right with that?" Matt asked. "Doesn't higher sulfur mean more methane emission? Airing it may not be enough."

"Yeah. It'll be fine." Becky said. "They'll string some lights in a couple days."

"What's your crew? Do you know yet?" asked Matt.

"Yeah, I thought I told you." Becky replied. "Zack is the team leader. Then me, Carla Davis, and Phil. You met him yesterday. Megan's husband. Wilkerson, I think his last name is. They're all good people. We should have fun. That Carla is a riot. She's so horny all the time, just listening to her tell how she attempts to get a little from her husband is hilarious. She keeps you laughing all day long. Phil told me once he saw her drop a vibrator out of her air pack bag once."

"Really?" Matt put in.

"Yeah. She doesn't deny it either." Becky added. "The rumor is she goes back into the maintenance shack and comes out with a smile on her face."

"And you tell me there are no fringe benefits with that job." kidded Matt.

"Why don 't you pop on down some day, and I'll show what I can do with a little fringe benefit time." Becky returned.

"Little?" Matt countered.

"I meant with a little time, honey." Becky said. "Let's not take things out of context."

"Is Zach the one I met that has the big legs?" asked Matt. "He wanted to play football in Canada, wasn't it?"

"No, soccer." corrected Becky. "He's got a set of wheels on him, doesn't he? Have you ever met his wife? A total stick!"

"Well, Babe, you be sure to stick close to him in case of an accident." Matt rambled. "You may need a meal and those wheels will certainly feed you."

Becky stopped for a minute and just looked at Matt in a suspicious manner.

"What...?" mused Matt.

"Please tell me you're kidding and that you don't know that from experience." Becky said.

"Know what, honey?" Matt returned. "That reminds me that I want to put more ketchup in your lunch tomorrow. I'll throw in some salt also. Zack looks awfully tasteless to me. Some garlic toast, perhaps? A1 Sauce?"

"You're beginning to worry me, Matthew." Becky replied. "you weren't with those guys that crashed in the Andes, were you?"

"Oh, no, honey." Matt chuckled back. "But you know what I heard? This is the reason some airlines carry extra condiments on their flights."

"Let me get this straight, sweetheart." Becky returned in a serious manner. "You're saying that if I'm in a cave in, I'm expected to eat my fellow miner? How could someone possibly do that? Are you serious, Matthew? Matt, are you out of your mind? Are you horny and it's effecting your judgment?"

"What I'm saying, Becky, is that if you're ever in a cave in... don't get overwrought with ethics and starve to death. Do you see what I'm saying?"

"Is that possible?" Becky asked.

"Yes!" returned Matt as he took her in his arms. "When the shit hits the fan, survival is everything, and you must survive until I find you."

"You don't like this idea of going into this seam mining, do you?" Becky asked.

"Not really, honey." Matt replied.

"Why not?" asked Becky. "What don't you like?"

"You said that they used to mine there before, but something went wrong, and they stopped." Matt replied. "What is it that went wrong, and how do they know it won't go wrong again? Please, forgive me, honey, I don't trust those people any more than I would trust Saddam. They don't put the same value on life that you and I do."

"I see that in your eyes." Becky said. "I don't understand how you can read people the way you do, but I respect it. But we'll be all right, honey. Besides, how could anything bad happen to me when I have you here waiting for me when I get home?"

"Shit happens, Becky." Matt said, softly. "Shit just happens. Just remember, the good Lord gives us ways out of our messes. Don't ever be afraid to take advantage of them."

"Such as the advantage of having Zack for lunch, you mean? No thanks, we'll be fine, Matthew." Becky said reassuringly. "Don't worry about me. I know how to take care of myself. In the mines or in your arms. I'll be fine, sweetheart. Hey, are you up to an after dinner walk before bed?"

"Yeah, I can handle that." Matt replied. "Mary, want to go for a walk with the old folks?" Mary opted to stay in and finish watching a Walt Disney movie. This meant that she got to hold Matt's cell phone so if anything went awry, she could call them on Becky's cell phone. A little perk towards growing up. So, with that Matt and Becky donned their jackets and headed out.

5

It was seasonably crisp for the end of November. It was a beautiful autumn afternoon. Matt loved this weather, and this time of year in general. It wasn't too awfully different from Helena, except the smells were sharper and there were more pleasant odors in the air. Matt was especially fond of the smell of wood smoke. Especially if it was to smoke bacon. However, the noise level had changed from the usual quiet of a mountain town. The new fans were operating to air out the shaft that Becky would be working in tomorrow morning. The fan made an intimidating hum. There was a feeling of danger in the noise it produced. One of immense power that reminded you of a monster that you were warned about coming too close to.

They turned left on Greely street and began walking, hand in hand around the horseshoe which led around the town to the city park. There were many families walking that night, none less that Abner and Dorothy Colb. This could only happen to me, Matt thought to himself, as he prepared to extend his warmest greetings to the only family in town, he wished he wouldn't run into tonight.

It was strange that most people who passed Abner and Dorothy just nodded as they walked along. But old Abner would lean over to Dorothy's ear and give her his personal synopsis as to where they were in his book of who is and who ain't. Dorothy would just chuckle and shake her head as Abner went on with his babbling until the next family came along destined for his opinion.

Matt and Mary always held Dorothy kind of close to their heart. Matt thought what a great sense of humor she had to possess to put up with

Abner all these years. Dorothy was an elegant woman, very refined and well kept. She had the most invigorating smile and a laugh which would break an undertaker. When Abner was at her side he was as reserved as an altar boy. As if there was no bullshit that he was going to pull over anyone with her next to him. The reservation in his body language told it all. He had something to say and he knew she wouldn't let him.

Dorothy was tall, and very fit. She had the crows feet on her eyes from the wind and weather of the mountains and many bouts of laughter shared with the other wives. She reminded Matt of his mother, Theresa, who never had a bad word to say about anyone. Unlike her counterpart in marital bliss, they were lucky they did not live in a glass house.

After exchanging pleasantries with Dorothy, Matt extended his hand to Abner, whom, much to Matt's surprise, took his and returned a cordial hello.

"It's so nice to see you two again," Dorothy said. "Where is little Mary?"

"At home playing with her Chemistry set." Matt said as Becky swatted him on the shoulder.

"What is it that the neighbor girl would say at a time like this?" Dorothy hesitated. Oh, yes! Don't even go there."

The three of them let out a jovial burst of laughter. Abner being his stoic self just looked on peacefully and held his emotional expressions to himself. The four of them said good bye and Abner locked his eagle eye stare at Matt as if to remind him of who was chief cock on the block, and was soon on his way once again in search of unsuspecting prey.

"Well that went quite nicely, don't you think?" Matt asked, as he turned around to confirm his worse suspicions that Abner was watching him walk away.

Becky turned toward Matt and asked, "is he watching?"

"Yep! He's busted." Matt replied. "He was well behaved today though."

Becky began to laugh as she took Matts arm.

"You know what it is?" Becky asked. "Dorothy raped him after church this morning, I'll put money on it.

"You mean he's exhausted?" Matt asked.

"No, hell no!" Becky returned as she held Matt closer. "He's afraid if he screws up her Sunday walk, she 'll do it to him again. Hey, trust me. These mountain women have a way with their men. You'll see what happens if you get out of line."

"Discipline at its best." Matt said. "What's a good marriage without it?"

"Exactly." Becky concurred. "Now you're catching on. Walk a little faster, boy."

Matt and Becky continued their Sunday walk, and as they did, they met a lot of couples where Becky could show off her Eastern husband. The townspeople always made such a fuss over Matt when they saw him. He always had something new to say to them and always went out of his way to find a particular item on or about them to comment about. Becky just grinned with pride, whereas most woman would become jealous about their husbands flirting with all the ladies in town. But not in this case. Becky and Matt were like a Christmas card when they met people walking. Whenever they were asked where Mary was, Matt would always come up with something so off the wall that many an eyebrow was raised in concern. Becky would playfully slap Matt on the arm and say, "don't believe him."

In about an hour the Sunday evening trek was complete and they returned home to settle in for the night. Matt got Mary ready for bed and Becky got her things around for work in the morning. After that the two would settle in for a little television and a usual glass of wine before going to bed. Tonight, was no different as the two of them sat entwined in each others arm with the TV on, but not really listening to it.

It wasn't long before the holding led to kissing, which led to touching, which turned into passion. Becky turned up the volume a touch so as to hide the moment from Mary, should she still be awake.

"Damn, I love you!" Becky said between heavy breaths.

"I love you back." Matt returned.

As the loving got more intense, Matt picked Becky up, shut off the television, and carried her into the bedroom. Becky swung the door shut as Matt held her and carefully laid her in bed.

About an hour later, still wrapped in one another's arms Becky looked up at Matt and said, "the reason I'm not worried about tomorrow is that I know if anything happened to me you would come down there and get me. I am sure of it and I'm not afraid. I've never been afraid."

Matt just looked at her and smiled and said, "well, if I get delayed, don't forget Zach's leg."

6

The morning sunrise was beautiful and crisp as it broke through the mountain haze and revealed what should prove to be a beautiful day. Matt was already up and had Becky's breakfast ready when he woke her from her slumber.

Mary had also came out in a stupor in her Captain Jack Sparrow pajamas, complete with booties, and sat down at the table.

"I can see you two just aren't morning people." Matt said.

"Matthew!" Becky said seriously. "Coffee! Quick!"

Matt accommodated Becky with a cup of coffee and poured Mary a glass of milk, while patting her on the head as she let out an envious yawn, and then giggled.

"What are you two heathens up to today?" Becky asked while signaling appreciation for the coffee with a satisfying nod.

"Shopping!" they both said in unison, and then laughed out loud together.

"Yeah, we're getting our nails done, our hair done, matching tattoos, and a shot of botox under my butt checks." Matt began. "We've got quite a day planned. Hopefully our nails will dry before we pick you up from work today. It's such a drag when they smudge."

"Oh, I should think so." little Mary added without cracking a smile. "Nothing worse than smudges. So uncool!"

Becky looked across the table at the two of them and said, "God help me! You two need a job. You've got way too much time on your hands."

"Where would we find the time, honey?" Matt replied with two palms raised in a question pose.

The comical banter continued throughout breakfast until Becky excused herself to get dressed for work. Matt rose to clean up the dishes while Mary went to get dressed before they took their mother to work.

Becky emerged from the bedroom in full battle dress ready for work. She was something to see. Matt always had a funny feeling when he saw her dressed for work. Because under this facade of a steeled miner was nothing of the beautiful, sexually intimate woman he knew as his wife. She wore blue jeans, a flannel, shirt, long john underwear, steel toed boots and a handkerchief scarf around her neck. About all you could see was her face. And despite the work garb, she was still a cutie. She carried a belt that held her carbide battery for her hard-hat helmet and heavy weight gloves. There was also an emergency oxygen pack attached to her belt. And despite all this extra baggage, she could swing a pick and shovel with the best of them. And somehow, she managed to wear it in style.

When three of them left the house to take Becky to the mine, Matt commented on how crisp the morning air was. There was still a light haze burning off over the mountain.

"A might frosty this morning, I see." said Becky.

"It reminds of a pumpkin poem I once heard." said Matt.

"There's nothing your pumpkin needs to be poetic about at the moment." returned Becky.

"What does that mean?" Mary asked.

"Never mind!" Matt and Becky said in unison.

As they drove down Greely street to the employee entrance of the mine, Becky could not stop laughing. This in turn prompted Matt to ask her what was so funny.

Becky replied, "You! You and frost on the pumpkin. Where do you come up with this crap? Don't tell me you actually read a poem about frost on a pumpkin."

"Oh, hell yes!" Matt replied. "It's required reading at Gibsonburg High School, don't you know? Yeah, baby, I come from a classy neighborhood."

"That's enough, Matthew." Becky said. "Just take me to work. I can't carry around all this b.s. Today." Looking back at Mary, Becky said, "good luck, Mary. You're going to need it today."

Mary just shook her head and sighed, saying, "tell me about it."

When Matt pulled up to the employee shack at the mine, he got out and helped Becky with her belt. Holding her tight and kissing her good-bye he said, "when you get home I 'll read you some of that classic poetry if you like."

"No! No more! Stop! I have to get serious now and get to work." Becky ordered.

As they both turned and went their way, Becky stopped and asked, "what kind of classics are we talking about here, stud?"

"Only the poetry, baby!" Matt said as he waved good-bye. "Only the poetry."

As he moved the car to get out of the way, he and Mary watched Becky go into the shack as Mary crawled over the seat to sit next to Matt.

Matt and Mary had a busy morning ahead of them. They had to go to the store first, then the laundry. They were going to check on some bills that needed paying at the utility company for a new family who recently moved in. The family came up from Texas, and the father wasn't quite ready for the cooler weather. Two weeks into the mine and he caught pneumonia. They were struggling and it was getting close to the holidays. Matt and Mary were also put in charge of the food pantry, which Matt originally started, and he was also working on a *meal on wheels* program for the area's elderly. Matt would talk the Coal Company into footing the bill and then he would write the research grants for them. So, everyone made out pretty good with his projects. It kept Matt pretty busy, but he really didn't have anything else to do. He had also wanted to check out a rumor that he heard about a family who couldn't afford their grandpa's arthritis medicine. He would get that through a friend at the VA. Matt had as many angles as he had secrets.

7

The four miners met in the engineer's office before getting on the man car to go into the mine. They were told what had been done over the weekend to ready the dig site. The engineer also told them there had been some bumps recorded at the site, but so far, they had recorded a minimal seismic activity. These would be closely monitored, however, at this time they seemed to be small.

It was further explained that it could just be a shifting tectonic plate moving. He reminded Zack as team leader that he was responsible for the reporting of such activity. The engineer ended the meeting by introducing them to the project manager who would go down to the seam with them and show where they would start and the necessary survival and escape facilities in the area.

As the car began descending down to the site, Carla Davis was the first to break the silence.

"Isn't it interesting that a project manager goes down into the hole with us to show you how not to get yourself buried?" Carla began. "Wouldn't you think maybe, just maybe, someone might come up with a plan so the damn thing doesn't cave in from the get-go? I mean, like, this ain't brain surgery for Christ sake: it's a rock! And what the hell is a 'bump'? Am I missing something here? Ain't that the stuff that happened in Utah"?

"A bump is the action accompanied by a loud noise caused by the rock shelves shifting above you." Phil explained. "It sounds like the rock is splitting apart. It is as loud as a cherry bomb. Scares the living shit out of you."

"Is it dangerous?" Carla asked. "And accompanied, does that mean at the same time or some shit like that?"

"It can be, if there are a bunch together; and yes, at the same time." Phil continued. "If they have rock falling from one, it's best to pack your shit and git. I tell you, when that thing pops, you feel about one foot tall and you start heading for the door."

"Well let me tell you something." Carla added. "If I have to run out of here, you better not stop boy, because I'll run right up your ass and out your mouth."

"That was real lady like, Carla." Becky said.

"Hey, this is no time to be sexually correct." Carla returned. "My ass is outta here, baby. How do you like those apples?"

About that time, as luck would have it, a mid-level bump occurred, and everyone froze in their tracks.

"What the hell was that?" Carla quickly asked as she began an automatic stroll toward the exit.

"Everyone just hold still a minute!" ordered Zach. "Easy you guys. Everyone all right? Let's get next to the wall. Just relax. Phil, was that what you were talking about?"

"Damn straight." Phil replied.

"What do we do next?" Zach asked.

"Look for rubble coming out of the ceiling." Phil said.

Just then another bump sounded. This was twice as loud as the first and shook the wall a bit. Carla and Becky both began moving toward the exit.

"My grand-father says if there are three in a row to get the hell out." Phil added. "Everybody just be cool."

Everyone stood perfectly still and looked up at the ceiling as a submariner looks up to the surface during a depth charging.

"Just be still. It'll pass." Phil said reassuringly.

"This is not fun!" Carla said. "This is not fun at all. I say we get our sweet asses outta here right now."

"Just stay under the beam, Carla." Phil said, as he noticed Carla was attached to him with a death grip. Putting his arm around her, he said, "you'll be all right."

After what seemed to be an easy twenty minutes, Phil gave the 'all clear' and the team began moving down the shaft to where they were going to start digging.

"What the hell causes that, Phil?" Carla asked like a big sister who wanted consoled.

"I hear it's the rock plates above us moving across one another." Phil explained. "When the pressure hits the shaft here, it splits the rock plate on the ceiling and that causes the pop, or bang. Why it's called a bump, I don't really know. Damn, but that scared the shit out of me. I think they instantly make you feel helpless. If not for the grace of God, your ass is grass."

"I tell you what." said Zach. "If I never hear another one of those in my lifetime, it will be two too many."

Nodding at Phil, Zach gave him a grateful, respectful nod which said, "thanks Phil."

Having unhooked from Phil, Carla said, "all right, let's get this tour on the road. Is that a blanket laying up there? How quaint."

Carla went ahead of the team like a girl scout, and was soon upon what appeared to be a blanket laying upon the wall at a support beam. There appeared to be what was an antique lunch box and a pair of partially rotted shoes, visibly showing the rusty steel toe sticking out under a faded red and green blanket. Behind the blanket on the floor was an empty bird cage and an empty, dented jug.

Never being one to error on the side of caution, Carla leaned down and picked up the blanket, shaking the dust out of it slightly. What she saw instantly paralyzed her.

Zack, who was carefully studying the wall structure, paid no attention to Carla's catatonic state.

It was Becky first, that noticed that Carla wasn't moving. When Becky starting trotting up to her, Phil also gave chase.

"What's the matter, Carla?" Becky called.

"Carla?" Phil hollered. "What is it?"

Phil approached Carla on her right side and rubbed up against her slightly. Only then did she move, and then with a start. She took a gasping breath and just continued to stare at the blanket. When Phil took his gaze off Carla and looked down, he also stared in disbelief and said nothing. Becky took a second to realize what it was she was looking at and then muttered, "Jesus! Zach, you better get up here."

Zack, who was a cautious fellow, walked up to the three of them from the outside perimeter of the group. Zack looked first at Carla and then down at the blanket, and said nothing.

"Is he real?" asked Becky. "How did the Engineers miss him yesterday?"

Getting brave, Becky put down her gear and bent down and lifted the blanket, where Carla had dropped it, from the skeletal remains of what was a coal miner. He looked peaceful as he lay there. He looked more mummified that he did rotten. She reached down and touched his shirt-covered arm, but found there was nothing but bones under it.

"Any I.D.?" Phil asked, as he released Carla to help Becky, but Carla refused to let him go.

"As Becky reached around to his hip pocket, Carla came alive again and said, "don't break him, Becky!"

"It's empty." Becky said.

"We better leave him alone." Phil said. "Zack, you have the phone hook-up, we better call this in. Come on, you guys, let's step back."

"I don't know about you guys, but I'm taking the rest of the day off." Carla said.

"Yep, let's all get ready to get our stuff and as soon as they get here, I'm leaving too. You okay, Phil?" Becky added.

"Yeah. Carla's right." Zack replied. " This ain't no fun anymore.

Phil went over and knelt down next to the man lying there in front of them and became very somber and alone in his thoughts. Becky went to him first, repeating her last question, "are you all right, Phil?"

"Have you any idea how this man died?" Phil answered. "This poor bastard starved to death. Jesus, this could be one of us someday."

"How do you know he starved to death, anyway?" Carla asked. "He could have died instantly. You don't know that."

"Yes, I do." Phil said. "Look at him. Look at his face. Those are rat teeth marks on his boots. That's a rat foot lying on his shirt. He ate the rats before they ate him. My God, what a horrible, lonely way to go, starving to death in the dark. I think I'll just set with him for a while until they come for him."

Phil looked up at Becky with a tear forming in his eye and said, "will you set here with me? I don't think we should leave him alone."

Becky sat next to Phil and put her arm around him and held his hand. He was so beside himself, that he began to tremble. Carla also joined them as Zack called on the emergency phone. The three of them began a vigil around the old man.

"Why do you suppose he is down here alone?" Carla asked. "Didn't they do teams back then in those days? Where is the rest of his team?"

"I'll bet Abner Colb knows who he is." Becky added. "The damn rats ate off all the ends of everything. Looks at his fingers. God, I hate those damn rats!"

"He does look peaceful, though, don't he?" Carla said. "How long do you figure he's been down here?"

"They said they closed this shaft a long time ago because of a problem." Becky said. "You don't suppose this was the problem, do you?"

Phil moved closer to the man and noticed a necklace around his neck. Pulling it away from his shirt collar, he commented, "look at that, a Saint Christopher's medal."

"I don't know, you guys" said Carla, "but it don't look like it did him a hell of a lot of good."

"Shit!" Phil responded. "This man was in heaven ten minutes before the devil knew he was dead. My granddaddy always said, all miners went to heaven. That a guardian angel comes down and sets with them until they pass and then they carry them up to heaven."

"You really believe that shit, Phil?" asked Carla.

"Yeah, I do!" Phil said. "What else do I have to believe in down here?"

Carla joined hands with Phil and Becky as they sat and talked, waiting for Zack to return from the phone.

"Could you imagine setting down here, alone and afraid and an angel comes and sets down next to you." Carla said. "Talk about your shit being weak."

"Yeah, but at least you wouldn't be alone." Phil added.

"Are you afraid of dying alone?" Becky asked Phil.

"Yes!" Phil said. "I'm afraid of rotting down here just like this poor bastard did. Alone, scared, broken up and starving to death in the dark, as the rats look at you, waiting for a free meal. It's almost like a wake-up call. This is my fear, lying right in front of me. It's like the Lord is showing me what I wouldn't listen too when he told me. But I'm like this poor bastard. I don't know anything else, I've nowhere else to go. I'm afraid to leave here, and I know damn well that I will die down here, and there is nothing I can do about it."

Becky held Phil ever tighter after this, but the mood was soon broken by another loud bump down the shaft a bit, which shook the three of them out of their mourning mood.

"And this shit doesn't help any, either!" Phil claimed as Becky rubbed his back.

Zack returned from the phone and said, "there are on their way down. They said don't touch anything. They want us topside right now. I told them about the bumps. They said there was an earthquake in El Salvador this morning. The engineer thinks it could be aftershocks."

"The engineer's full of shit." Phil said. "Hasn't he ever heard that the ocean is a shock absorber? I'll bet that jackass went to Harvard."

"We've been ordered topside." Zack said.

"Screw them people!" Phil said. "Just like the jungle. I ain't leaving him alone until they get here."

"If we get off early today, I might get a quicky before the old man goes to school." Carla said as she looked at her watch.

Phil and Becky just looked at her, but in reality, Becky thought to herself, that lying with Matt, naked, would certainly take the stress away of the moment.

Zack came and stood alongside the rest of the team as they held their vigil with the old man.

"I'll bet you're right, Becky, Abner probably does know this guy." Zack surmised. "My grandfather told me that Abner and another man got trapped in here once upon a time, and Abner dug them out and he carried this guy all the way to the top. When they got to the opening, the guy was dead. He said Abner was never the same after that.

Phil reached down to the man and removed the Saint Christopher medal from around his neck despite the objections from Carla.

"We keep this alive by someone always wearing it." Phil explained, as he put it around his neck. "As long as it's worn by a living mortal, the spirit of this old man lives on. If something happens to me, one of you guys wear it."

"Well, excuse me for mentioning it, but if you take that off of him, and something happens to you, wouldn't you kind of think maybe that it's a bad luck medal?" Carla asked.

"She's got a point there, Phillip." Becky interjected.

As Phil was preparing an explanation for the non-believer's the rescue and recovery team arrived on the scene. They approached the man in a most cautious manner, which prompted Carla to comment, "he ain't gonna bite you, for Christ sake!"

The silence was broken by the emergency alert siren sounding topside.

"Come on you guys," Zack said. "we're done here for today. You guys be careful down here, the walls are talking big time."

The team of miners got into the man-car and headed for the sunshine and fresh air at the top of the mine.

"What time does your husband go to school, Carla?" asked Becky.

"Two o'clock!" replied Carla. "There's still time if he doesn't wimp out on me."

Becky just laughed even though all the while she knew her man was home waiting for her. She definitely needed him this afternoon. She was nervous and unnerved by the dead miner, and had begun to feel scared and alone. She felt sorry for Carla who just wanted to get home and get laid, but right now, that was Carla's problem to deal with it however she could. As for Becky, she just wanted Matt. He would know what to say and how to say it. Her thoughts returned to the ride to the top as the car broke through the darkness and into the daylight. Becky looked forward and noticed that Carla was holding Phil's hand.

8

Shortly after noon, Matt was awakened by a shrill sounding siren from down at the mine. That was soon accompanied by the siren of the Sheriff and the EMS vehicles that were screaming to the mine. Both Matt and Mary became immediately alert, as that was the warning that brought the mine rescue units scrambling in the event of a mine cave in, and Matt knew that Becky was deep in the mine at this time of day. The peace of a typical afternoon was quickly broken and Matt had to beware not to panic in front of Mary. This could not be good.

As Matt and Mary got off the couch, they both ran upstairs to the hallway window that faces the mine and looked through the telescope. Matt grabbed his binoculars off the shelf and they were both zeroed in on the action. There was a great deal of activity, but no smoke or fire units donning their protective suits.

"It looks more like a Police action than anything else." Matt said. "No fireman, no smoke, no air masks. That's strange, don't you think, honey?"

"There's mommy!" Mary exclaimed.

"Where?" asked Matt.

"Over by that food truck." Mary said.

As Matt looked through his binoculars, he could see Becky standing next to Zach who was consoling her. Becky was openly upset as Matt could determine looking through his glasses.

As Matt looked about, he could see that there were several onlookers starting to collect at the mine, but the Sheriff had cordoned off a section at the mine entrance with rope and had put a deputy on guard at the site.

Shortly after, a fireman went in carrying a gurney, and a man Matt ascertained, looked like the county Coroner.

This is getting worse instead of better, Matt thought to himself, as he looked for the other two members of the team. A man, who looked like a foreman came up to Zack, and after a short conversation, they all headed for the locker room.

Just then Matt's cell phone rang. It was Becky who was asking for a ride home. Matt and she talked briefly concerning the events that had just happened.

Matt closed his cell phone lid and said to Mary, "let's go get mommy. She's done for the day. My turn to drive."

When Matt arrived at the miner's pick-up point, he was surprised to see none other than Abner Colb among the onlookers. He didn't pass up the opportunity to give Matt a stare down, who briefly replied, "good afternoon Mister Colb."

Becky walked quickly across the lot and into Matt's waiting arms immediately upon seeing him. Then she then hugged Mary, and said, "let's get home."

Matt opened the door for his bride and then hooked Mary into her car seat. There wasn't a word said for a while until they were off the property and on the main road. Matt opened the conversation."Any idea who he was?"

"No," replied Becky. "He was all bones and a shirt. He had rat marks in his shoes and his fingertips. There were even little rat parts lying on his shirt. It looked like he ate them to keep from starving to death. That was horrible."

"Who found him?" Matt asked.

"Carla." Becky answered. "She walks up to him and takes the blanket off and shakes it. Then she just stood there in a trance. I'd rather not talk about it right now, okay? Let's just go home."

On the other side of the parking lot, Phil called out to Carla. "Do you need a ride home, lady?"

"I'd rather have a ride to your cottage." Carla replied.

"Climb aboard, my dear." replied Phil. "Your wish is my command."

"You know, the good Lord must be looking out for us." Carla commented.

"And why would that be?" Phil returned.

"Because, your old lady and my man both play for the other side." said Carla. "If we didn't have each other how would we ever get laid?"

When they arrived at the top of the mountain, they came upon a driveway leading to the cabin.

"Here we are my dear." Phil announced.

"Let's get inside. I have something for you for looking out for me today." said Carla. "And trust me, you're gonna like it!"

9

"**D**o you want some help with your shoes, honey?" Matt asked. "I'll start your bath water."

Becky bent down to take her shoes off and just gave up and sat down. Reaching out, she took Mary into her arms and they held each other tightly. Matt observed this through the bathroom door, and thought this is better left alone to the two of them. He closed the door as not to disturb them and continued filling the bath.

Shortly thereafter, there was a knock on the door. It was Becky asking, "are you ready for me?"

"Anytime, sweetheart." Matt replied.

Becky came in and shut the door behind her. "Stay with me, would you?" she asked Matt as she began getting undressed.

She stood in front of Matt completely naked. He was still as impressed with her beauty as he was the first time they made love. She was beautiful and trim. She had a slim waistline and beautiful rounded breasts mounted on an athletic chest. She had a muscular butt that was well rounded and with her natural blond hair, she was in every respect, the most beautiful lady Matt had ever seen.

"Just pull up a chair, Matt." Becky said. "I don't want to be alone right now."

Becky told Matt the here's and there's of their experience in the mine this morning. She was visibly upset, but the more she talked and the more Matt listened intently, the more relaxed she became. Before long they were even laughing, mainly because Matt told her how ol' Abner put the 'look' on him.

"You know, that old bastard reminds me of an eagle with a broken beak." Matt said to Becky, causing her to break out into a hysterical giggle. "He puts that evil eye on you like he's getting ready to cornhole a mouse. Can you imagine waking up to that look first thing in the morning? That definitely must be true love."

"You are crazy." Becky said as she continued to giggle." Where do you come up with this shit? And what does, 'cornhole' a mouse, mean?"

At this question, Matt started giggling. "Holy shit! I thought they taught you guys down here that in the first grade. You know, beware of your uncle- that kind of thing."

"You're sick, Matthew!" Becky accused. "You definitely need therapy. Get yourself in here."

"What?" Matt said as he looked at his wife standing naked in the bathtub.

"I said therapy." Becky explained. "You need it and I need to give you some of it. Assume the position."

It appeared that the stress of the morning had been alleviated. At least for the time being. This was, as Matt could attest, Becky's way of working off nervous tension. As Matt could tell during the therapy, she was still very tensed up.

Shortly after what was to be the most therapeutic bath in the last few years, Matt prepared dinner for the three of them and there didn't seem the need for any more talk of the experience of the morning's activities. Dinner included pot roast, red skinned potatoes, cream corn and spinach. Matt also made Beck's favorite, cherry cobbler. It was at best, quite a feast.

After the usual festivities of cleaning up the dinner dishes, Becky prepared for work the next day and spent time with Mary, as it soon became dark with the time change. Matt fired up the fireplace and the three of them stretched out in front of the fire on an artificial bear rug, that Matt told Mary he purposely went to Alaska to slay for his soon to be wife, her mother. And with that act of bravery he would win her mother over to live happily after. This, in Matt's mind, somehow corresponded to the story Becky was reading to Mary.

Becky would just give her standard comment that Matt was truly a brave soul and how much Becky honored his action of a man in regard to showing her the love that he had. With this went a look not to unlike that which Matt was usually given in the event Becky recognized a line of bullshit coming on.

Before long it was Mary's bedtime and upon putting her to bed Matt and Becky once again laid in front of the fireplace.

"I'm worried about the shaft, honey." Becky began. "We had three bumps today in a mine that they're not supposed to happen in. The one was loud and had us all scared. Did you ever hear what caused them to shut that mine in the first place? I wonder if it didn't have something to do with that man?"

"Does that still bother you?" Matt asked. "I was hoping the bathtub therapy would have helped you over that. Do you need a little more specialized treatment?"

"Well, you know, it's not something that just leaves your mind all of a sudden just because your husband screws your brains out. Close, mind you, but not totally. Phil said that one day old man Colb carried someone out of that shaft and when he got him topside, he was dead. Did you ever hear anything like that?"

"No." Matt replied.

"Zach said that Abner probably knew who this guy was. He did look like he had been there for a very long time."

"Is that section of the mine dry or damp?" Matt asked.

"Well, you know, there was dust around." Becky remembered. "So, dry, I would say. Why?"

"I was just wondering if he had been mummified by the dry air, that's all." Matt explained. "Did he stink at all?"

"No. Nothing at all. It surprised me that his clothes weren't rotten." Becky said. "How do you rot and not rot your clothes?"

"Dry air." Matt said. "I have heard that Abner has been around for a long time, he probably does know him. He is on disability, I heard, did you know that?"

"Yes." Becky said. "That's why he always shows up at those union meetings."

"Yep, got hurt in the mine." Matt returned. "However, he has no lung problems, so that's good."

"How would you know that?" Becky asked as she turned to him and put the blanket around their shoulders and took off her top.

"Because he doesn't wheeze when he talks." Matt explained. "Black lung people wheeze and hack a great deal of the time."

"Hmm. That's interesting." Becky said. "Any dessert left?"

"Out there or right here?" Matt returned as he helped her take off his shirt.

"Did you hear about the earthquake in El Salvador today?" Becky asked.

"Yeah, a pretty bad one." Matt returned.

"Could that cause 'bumps' in the mine?" Becky asked.

"I would think the ocean would have absorbed that, wouldn't you?" Matt queried. "That's a long way off. But, you know, I really don't know."

"That's what Phil said when they told us the 'bumps' were from the earthquake." Becky went on. "Do you know what else was strange today? He and Carla were holding hands when we rode up to the top today."

"Carla was probably pretty upset and needed a buddy." Matt surmised.

"I don't know." Becky continued. "It seemed to be more than a "buddy" thing. Their hands fit together quite nicely. It looked like they had done that before."

"Really. That's nice in a way." Matt replied. "You know about his wife and her husband, don't you?"

"What! They're having an affair?" Becky asked with complete surprise.

"Well." Matt said. "I kind of doubt it. He's queer and she's a lesbian."

"Shut-up!" Becky said, coming off the blanket. "How do you know all this shit?"

"Abner told me!" Matt said. "He said he's had his nose on them for quite some time now."

"Oh, bullshit! You're just saying that." Becky returned as she lay back down and scooted closer to Matt and pressed her breasts against him.

"No!" Matt said. "I'm giving you the straight skinny. Abner told me he's had his eye on those two hussies for some time now. And you know what you're in for if Abner has his beak in your direction."

"I think that if you don't quit hanging around Abner, your beak is gonna get just as big." Becky said.

"Well, that could be." returned Matt. "But you bet I'll know where to put it."

"Oh, really?" Becky mused.

The conversation was finished for the night as Becky fell fast asleep after they made love. But as Matt continued to hold her, he couldn't help but be aware of his helplessness and fear. He knew what Becky was feeling after seeing the dead miner, and also the fear of what could happen to her down in the mine, but he was coming up short of words to comfort her.

Matt was very dissatisfied with the level of concern that the management gave over the bumps, that although rare in this area were a common threat today. Tomorrow was another day and perhaps the mine would settle down a bit. That would certainly help matters as far as he was concerned, but that was selfish Matt thought, he wasn't in the mine...his wife was.

10

The next morning dawned with a gloomy, gray, overcast, wet look. When Matt woke up, he was curled up with Mary, who informed him that Becky was already up and in the shower.

Rising from the floor and stretching his bones he walked out to make coffee, only to find that is was already made. 'What a pleasant surprise,' he thought, as he looked out the window at the uninviting dawning of a new day.

The fear that accompanied him to sleep the night before, was past as he and Mary talked about starting their Christmas shopping after taking Becky to work.

When Becky came out of the bathroom, Matt met her with a kiss and a thank-you for the coffee.

Becky returned the affection and quietly said, "you've got something on your nose."

Grinning widely, Matt playfully cracked her on the butt, as she walked away.

After breakfast the Jensen household was dressed and out the door. Becky immediately noticed how heavy her lunch pail was, and commented to Matt that he was only feeding her and not the whole shift. Matt quickly began his litany of all the reasons she might need this extra food with her and how lucky she was to have a husband who looked out for her nutritional needs in the time of unexpected peril. He went to say that someday she would thank him for just this extra bite. In closing Matt reiterated that the rats need something to eat also. That was what the stale cookies were for.

Looking admirably at her husband, Becky said, "I was too easy on you last night. I had hoped to tire you into reality. Maybe tonight."

As Becky exited the car, hugs and kisses were exchanged between the three of them, and Matt and Mary were off to do their chores for today.

"Well, Mary, my dear." Matt started. "We're off to pay Abner's gas bill and then to the mall."

Matt had to make a stop first at the Adkins general store for gas. When he got out of the car, who did he run into... Abner.

"Morning Abner, lovely day in the mountains, don't you think?" Matt said.

"Yep!" Abner answered. "Every day in the mountains is a beautiful day."

"Any word on who that miner was they found yesterday?" Matt asked.

"Why?" Abner said in a course tone, putting his hand on the crook of Matt's left arm with a tight grip. "Some things are better left alone, you should remember that. That's the trouble with you Yankees, you stick your nose where it doesn't belong."

Matt looked at Abner with a surprised, defensive look in his eye. He could also see Mary setting in the car, but she was unaware of Abner's tone towards her father.

Trying to be calm, Matt said, "Abner, take it easy! What the hell's the matter with you?"

"There's too much interest in this dead miner if you ask me!" he said with a scowl. "Bury the bastard and let's get on with our lives."

"He is part of our lives," Matt returned. "much more yours than mine. People hereabouts think you might know him and I tend to believe the rumor."

"Nobody cares what you believe." Abner struck back.

"Well, think about it, Abner, you know everybody in this damn town and anyone who has come and gone for the past fifty years." Matt continued. "So, don't bullshit me. Hell, you probably put him down there."

"Who told you that shit, boy?" Abner shouted as he pushed Matt back against the car, jarring it to the attention of Mary in the front seat. "You better not be spreading any shit about me around town. Strange things happen to nosy people, you know."

Abner took another step toward Matt, but he stopped short when he noticed Matt took one toward him in a defensive gesture.

"Abner what's the hells the matter with you?" Matt asked. "Have you lost your mind. I don't believe anything about you and that miner. Hell, who gives a shit. I don't care if you knew him or not. I don't care if you killed him or not. It's none of my concern."

Several of the towns people had gather across the street by the Post Office and were watching the discussion between the two men with quite an interest.

"What do you care about this anyhow?" Matt returned to the discussion. "It's the company's problem, not yours, and I'm damn sure not going to make it mine."

"You just remember what I said to you, boy, about sticking your nose in somebody else's business." Abner said with a motion of his arm. "I'd hate to hear something happened to that pretty little daughter of yours."

With that Matt became angry. With one quick move, completely unnoticed by Abner, Matt was deep in his face, nose to nose.

"Don't make me kill you Abner." Matt threatened. "It would be so easy and they would never find you. Don't even think of fucking with me, or mine. Your life is not that valuable to me."

With that Abner backed up, turned and walked away. The conversation was over. Matt returned the gas spigot to its holder and stalling a bit before returning to the car, looked across the street to the onlookers at the Post Office who were breaking up and going on their way once again.

Upon entering the car, Mary was looking at Matt wide eyed as could be.

"What's Abner so upset about daddy?" Mary asked. "I've never seen him mad. He's weird, but never like this."

"I don 't know, honey. But he sure is mad at me about something." Matt said. "Well, honey, let's go pay his gas bill. I've got a feeling he's just frustrated about not having any money."

"Doesn't he know we'll take care of him, daddy?" Mary asked.

"No, sweetheart." Matt answered. "He doesn't know we do. He assumes someone or something takes care of him, but I don't think he knows who or what."

"Maybe we should tell him, so he's not so mean." Mary divined.

As the two continued on to the Wal-Mart store to do some Christmas shopping, Matt's mind started running a mile a minute. Maybe ol' Abner did kill that miner after all, and has some idea that I have figured it out.

But, why would Abner do that? But, why was Abner so postal over the subject that he brought up and accused me of spreading vicious rumors. I was too busy getting into my wife's pants to give a shit about poor ol' Abner, last night, Matt thought to himself. You never know. Some strange shit happens in these small towns and it stays buried for a long time. And what ever became of Abner's daughter?

"I'll be damned," Matt said aloud.

"Did you swear, daddy?" Mary asked.

"No honey, I said look at the dam." Matt corrected as they luckily drove over the bridge at the dam of the Trunk Fork river.

That does make a lot of sense, though. Matt began thinking to himself again. He remembered Becky telling him that Abner's only daughter came home pregnant one day, and the next day she went to live somewhere else. There was never any mention as to who the father was. Maybe the lucky dad was now a pile of bones down at the local mortuary. Matt looked at Mary without thinking and said, "you know, that's possible."

"What?" Mary said.

"Those new chairs your mother wanted." Matt answered. "That's an idea for you to tell Santa to get her for Christmas."

As Matt and Mary began their Christmas shopping, Matt's mind would not stop going over his intuitions and the conversation he had had with Abner a short time ago. He couldn't wait to tell Becky.

II

Becky's day began with a little less fanfare, but not with any less excitement. As they got out of the man car, there was a large bump which froze all of them in their tracks.

"I have no intention of dealing with this shit today!" Carla exclaimed. "I don't care what any of you say, this is bullshit and I am not working like this."

"Yeah, I'm with her." Becky said. "This is bullshit."

"Let's just feel it out a while." Phil said. "Let's listen awhile. Just be quiet and listen."

"For what, my dear?" Carla asked embarrassingly.

"Let's just see where it goes, honey." Phil said. "While we're waiting to see where this is going, let me be the first to tell you as a team that Carla and I are in love. For the time being, please keep it to yourselves."

"I've heard of bombs, but this takes the cake." Zack said. "But, congratulations, you two. It's been a long time coming, I've told you that before."

"What do you think, Becky?" Carla asked.

"You know me, guys." Becky replied. "Anybody in love is all right with me."

"What is that?" asked Carla nervously.

"What's what?" Becky returned. "Love?"

"No! That noise. Can't you hear that. Christ, I can feel it!" Carla screamed and ran into Phil's arms.

All four miners looked up at the ceiling as they all heard and felt something. It sounded like something dragging something over the ceiling of the mine.

"Everybody get under a brace." Phil said calmly. "Becky get over here with us."

The dragging sound grew louder and began to cause a noticeable vibration in the floor of the mine. The miners could feel its very motion as it made its way across the ceiling.

"My God in heaven!" Phil exclaimed. "Do you believe this shit? That is a bona fide tectonic plate moving through the bedrock above us. God, it must be one big slab of rock. This is the shit earthquakes are made of."

"Right, Phil, this makes me feel all bubbly inside." Carla said. "Can you get it to go away and scare the shit out of someone else?"

As the four of them continued to fix their gaze on the ceiling, Phil began to move with the vibrations. The grinding and the growling got deeper as the vibrations became increasingly violent.

"It's slowing down." Phil said." I think it's gonna stop right above us. Holy shit! Wait until my granddaddy hears about this."

Phil tried to move farther away from the pillar which support the overhead beam, but Becky and Carla had a death grip on his arm that was inescapable. All of a sudden, the growl turned into a loud screech, and stopped, making an explosive sound and projecting a large spear-like stone which hit the floor so hard, it obliterated the projectile into dust.

"Damn!" Phil exclaimed excitedly. "That is power. Did you see that shit, Carla?"

As easily as it came upon them, the noise and danger was gone, and it was as quiet as a tomb in the shaft. No more vibration was felt, and only the beating of their hearts was heard.

"Is everybody okay?" Phil asked as he broke free of the girl's grip and looked cautiously about. Zack, make sure we don't have any methane building up. Let's just hold still a minute and make sure it's gone. Anybody feel anything?"

After about a minute, Zack broke the silence when he said, "I think we're all right on gas. I think it's clear."

"Come ladies," Phil said as he offered his arms to aid the women. "Shall we take a stroll down the shaft together?"

"Becky, don't you dare put your hands on his butt!" Carla said.

"Ladies, please." Phil joked. "There's enough to go around."

As the team of miners made their way to the area where they would start digging, Phil tried very hard to make light of the situation. The more he talked, the more the others got caught up in the conversation. It wasn't long before they were on location and had their equipment set up and had began the first drill mining that had gone on there in over ten years.

"Let's put the gas meter and the seismograph on sensitive for today." Phil said to Zach. "If that rock changes direction, we'll never hear it with all the noise."

"Got it." Zach replied. "I called in the bump and they said no one else heard anything in any other shafts."

"Really?" Phil asked. "Either someone's full of shit or we're getting old. Ain't no way, no one else could not have heard that."

After about two hours of drilling and picking in the dark, save their headlamps, the light cord was turned on and the mine was quickly illuminated.

"Let there be light!" Becky shouted.

"I knew it." Carla said. "There always has to be someone coming up with that old cliché. Let there be light is so Baptist. You know what I always say?"

"I'm afraid to ask." Becky said as she grunted while removing a piece of slag from her coal dig.

"It's about time you turned the friggen lights on down here." shared Carla proudly. "Now, don't that have a ring to it?"

"You're gonna have your hands full with this one, Phil." Zach said. "Whatever happened to that little wallflower of a woman you were married to?"

"She went and got herself a girlfriend." Phil answered with a blank expression on his face.

Zack raised upright and just looked at his friend. Glancing toward Becky, she nodded her head assuring Zack that it was true. Zack walked over to Phil who had still not acknowledged Zack and extended his hand.

"Jesus, man, I didn't know that. I'm so damn sorry." Zack said.

"Don't be sorry. I should have seen it coming when that same broad was hanging around all the time with a shit eating grin on her face like she just gave an opossum a blow job." Phil said. "Didn't pay attention to the signs. I was too busy elsewhere. But I'm a lot better off where I am, that's for sure."

Shortly after that conversation a small version of a John Deere tractor came down the mine with a set of trailers to haul the coal out with. Since this was an older section of the mine, the coal was hauled to the top by mules. When they reopened this section of the mine, they never laid rails, they left the floor the same.

So, now, with three teams coming to this dig, they had to put something together quickly to handle the production. So, an old miner brought three trailers attached to a tractor down, and two pizza's and a 12 pack of beer for the lunch he was paid to deliver. Productivity was served and everybody got a free meal. The practice of an occasional adult beverage being consumed in the mine was an accepted benefit.

As Carla was the first to open a cold Bud Light she made a comment which brought a lot of blank stares. "Do you know what I like about this place? Take a gander! Beautiful trailers and a brand new John Deere tractor in front of them. What is wrong with this picture? No comment? How many engineers do you think it's gonna take to figure how in the hell they're gonna turn that tractor around in this shaft to take these trailers out? Talk about progress. Where in the hell is that stinky mule?"

"You know, I knew that didn't look right," said Zack. "But I couldn't put my finger on it. Leave it to you Carla to keep us straight. Beer please."

"Catch!" Carla exclaimed as she tossed a brew to Zach. "Here, Becky. You're not too good to drink with us po' folks, are ya?"

"Oh, hell no!" she replied." And hand me one of the fattening crusts too. You know, we drink enough beer and we'll figure out how to turn that tractor around."

"After lunch." Carla said. "Then who'll care? Where did Jack go? He dropped off our dinner and I didn't see him leave."

"He lit a smoke and took off up the shaft." Phil said. "Damn, he's been here for years, hasn't he? Doesn't he live down from you, Becky?"

"A couple of houses down, yeah. He's good people." Becky replied. "Kinda laid back, doesn't hurry much. Just kinda gets there when he gets there."

"As slow as he is, I can't figure out how he had all those kids." Phil said.

"Good things come to those who take their time." Carla said with an evil grin.

"Did you and Phil need a private break this afternoon?" Zack asked.

"What do ya think, Phil?" Carla asked. "Feel like a little lovin' after lunch?"

"I'm up for a little run around the block with you anytime, Carla, my dear." Phil replied as he passed a round of beers.

"Forget it!" Zack said.

"Speaking of lovin'," Carla said as she turned her attention to Becky. "I heard a rumor about you."

"Oh, yeah." returned Becky. "Do tell!"

"Okay, here it goes." Carla began. "I heard your man, draws you a hot bubble bath, and has you a chilled glass of wine every night when you get home from work. Tell the truth. What's said in the mine, stays in the mine."

"What can I say?" Becky returned proudly. "Guilty! And it gets better. I usually get a back rub if I want and supper is always ready by the time my bath is done. He's done that for years."

"No shit?" Carla asked.

"No shit." Becky answered.

"I've heard he's disabled." Zack said.

"Yes he is but don't tell him that." Becky said. "He cut himself while at the ground zero clean-up and he can't stand on a ladder any more. And since he was a fireman, he's a little bit screwed. So, he is now actually a house husband. He takes care of me, Mary, and does all the chores. I've got it made. It's really a nice arrangement."

"Now does this disability carry itself into the bedroom?" Carla pried.

"Oh, no." Becky beamed as her face flushed a little. "There is no problem there. We have an arrangement. He said that one thing he would always want, if he was working, was to come home to a loving wife who dropped everything for him when he walked through the door. So, that is exactly what I get. A hot bath and a cold glass of wine. After supper we hang out as a family and after Mary goes to bed, we drink some more wine and usually make love and fall asleep in one anothers arms. It is really wonderful. He's a wonderful man. He never treats me any less than a queen. He's very easy to live with and very sexually appealing as well as satisfying. I have it made and I know it. I would never do anything to change it. And no, you can't borrow him."

"Oh, you heartless, selfish bitch." mused Carla. "Share the wealth! I'm just kidding!"

"How can you guys make a living with what you make, with him on disability?" Zack asked.

"Believe it or not, his disabilities are as much as my paycheck." Becky explained. When he got hurt, he was on vacation from the fire department. He was also on his two weeks of duty with the Air Force Reserves. So, he got the double wammy, so to speak. But, it's not easy for him, he bores easily and Mary is usually the only person he has to talk too. I think he'd rather be working, and my pouring him a bath and a glass of wine."

"He was a gulf war veteran, I heard somewhere." Phil said. "Is that true?"

"Yes." Becky answered.

"Does he have any issues?" Phil added.

"I really don't know." Becky began as Carla passed her another beer and a slice of pizza. "He's different than anyone else I've ever known. He's not nuts, per se', and I don't think because he's from Ohio, but he's different. He senses trouble before it happens. And when that E.M.S. helicopter flies over the house, he gets all tensed. His muscles tense up the veins pop out of his neck, and he kinda goes into a deathlike trance. He'll get up in the night and goes to the window and tilts his head as if he was listening for something, and he's still asleep. I just take him by the hand and walk him back to bed. I swear he can sense a bird fart.

Sometimes in his sleep he will say, 'checkmate king two, this is white rook, over.' And he'll say it several times as clear and as calm as an angel. I have no idea what that means. One night he said, 'thirty plus, and I only have twenty rounds. Roger that...laying fast.'"

"Did you ever ask him about any of that?" Phil asked.

"No. Never. I leave him out there and I just help him back when he returns." Becky answered.

"And that doesn't scare you at all?" Carla said somewhat defensively.

"Not a bit." Becky said. "You should see him with Mary. He would never harm us. And you know what else? I love him and it's a different piece of our lives that we share. A lot of people don't have that."

"Why would you want too?" Carla spoke up.

"I don't know, really. It's just another part of the man I love. It makes him unique, I guess." Becky explained.

"He's unique because he's a killer?" Carla said sarcastically.

"Who said he was a killer?" Becky said. "Why would you say that?"

"My father married my mother when she was fifteen." Carla began. He went to Vietnam when he was eighteen. He was in the Air Force also. He flew jungle rescue missions. He came home from Vietnam when he was twenty-one. He got out at twenty-two. I remember him coming home as a little girl. And I tell you this: he was one spooky son of a bitch. My mother always said that if you see him at night in front of the window, and he wasn't smoking, don't touch him. He was never mean to us, but there were times when he would have a blank stare, and his eyes were black. He would look right through you. A wonderful man and a great father, but I've heard he was one nasty hombre'. We all loved him, but there was an invisible boundary around him. And I never thought that was a unique thing. I was afraid of him, but I also felt sorry for him.

Sometimes I would see my mother holding his head to her chest as he cried horribly. I always wondered what made a man as hard as he was, cry like a child. My mother told me a few years later that he had some things to work out and she would help him all she could. Crying would bring him back to the wonderful man he was. One time my brother saw a picture of him from the jungle and asked him what were those things around his neck. Do you know what he said?... Ears!

Now, understand, I'm not saying anything bad about your husband, but those Air Force rescue guys were not in that jungle to check on the tourism. They were one nasty breed of pups. And whether it was my father or your husband, I'd be careful who I slept with, if I were you."

"I think I know my husband by now, wouldn't you think?" Becky replied. "And it didn't seem to bother your mother any did it?"

"You know what?" Zack interjected. "That can be said about almost anybody over any situation. Look at old lady Guntherson. Her husband would come from the mines and beat the shit out of her. So, she gets rid of his ass, and marries poor Fred from the gas station. Fred said they were screwing like a couple of rabbits one night, and she pulls a club out from under the bed and starts wailing on his ass like a red headed stepchild. Ol'

Fred says he loves the sex, but the whoopin's he could do without. Hell, they're still sleeping together."

"Wouldn't that be a bitch?" Phil asked. "Just think, you're making love to the woman of your dreams and instead of an orgasm, she pulls out a club and knocks your dick in your watch pocket. That's got to leave a mark, don't it?".

"I think he's asking for it, Carla." Becky said.

"Hell Becky, he can't handle what he's getting now." Carla said. "What's he gonna do with a beatin' on the side? Okay, everybody, give me the crusts and I'll feed the rats. They gotta eat too. Here's one right here. Come here, fella."

Becky watched at a distance as Carla fed the rats the left over pizza crusts. It looked natural that the rats ate from her hand and seemed to have no fear of her at all, as they munched away at the well anticipated meal.

"Here, Becky." Carla said as she threw her a crust. "Give this to the little fellow next to you."

"Oh shit!" Becky exclaimed, as she turned and saw one setting alongside her. "Damn I hate those pesky little bastards. I sure as hell don't want to feed them."

Becky tossed the crust in the general direction of that pesky little rat. Taking the morsel graciously, the rat scurried away from her and went off into the darkness.

"I swear that little shit had white eyes!" Becky said. "What's up with that?"

"It's the darkness." Phil said. "They're like albinos. Their retinas lose their color at birth because of the darkness. That's why you always see them squinting in the light."

"My God," said Carla. "I'm in love with a rat expert. Get yourself over here and give me a kiss before I go back to digging rock like an underprivileged piece of poor white trailer trash."

"You're the one who has two cars jacked up in your driveway." Zack said. "And there are rumors that you tried to take the wooden paneling off that station wagon. If that ain't poor white trash, I don't know what is."

"Zachary, my dear friend." said Carla. "Would you please take your high society lips and kiss my poor white trash ass?"

"Carla you shameless hussy!" said Phil. "Already cheating on me. But honey, didn't you tell me you were stripping that paneling for Zach's living room?"

"Yeah, see how he is?" said Carla. "I think the pot is calling the kettle black here, old friend."

"All right, dear friend. Let's all get back to work." Zack replied as all the beer cans were collected and hidden along with the pizza boxes.

That ended the first luncheon celebration in the new seam. Soon everyone was back to work and trying to carry on conversations despite the clanging of the pick axes. The growling sound a shovel makes with the loud banging of the coal against the cold steel sides of the carts was especially nerve racking. Soon Carla began her routine of the air drill and a symphony of sound put everyone in synchronization with each other. This would get them through the afternoon. They would be off at four o'clock.

12

Matt and Mary finished with their shopping spree, and after a lunch at Denny's, headed for home. Matt figured he could get a nap before Becky came home and he wanted to check on Abner. He thought maybe he would call his wife and just kind of feel out the conversation. Wouldn't it be something, Matt mused to himself, if Abner really did have something to do with that dead miner? Things were different around here about ten years ago, and Abner was in the mines back then. Something caused him to go off on me, Matt thought. Oh well, it's probably cirrhosis.

Matt gave up on the phone call and laid down with Mary for a nap. After all, he didn't want Abner thinking he was getting soft. That would be construed as a weakness, and he couldn't afford that after what happened this afternoon. So, he would let Abner wallow in his anger and figure it out himself.

Matt fell fast asleep and after several hours, he awoke alarmed at the time. Becky would be getting off in ten minutes, and he didn't have her bath poured yet.

Matt rose quietly not to disturb Mary and went into the labors of afternoon love. He prepared Becky's bath and poured her a glass of Asti, which was being chilled since breakfast. Just the way she likes it, Matt thought to himself. I will make my bride happy and welcome her when she arrives home from work today.

Matt set down on the edge of the tub and noticed a nervousness about himself. He compared it to a nervousness an animal gets when a storm is brewing. It was unlike the nervousness that an approaching flashback would warn about after an extended nap. It was something he couldn't put his finger on. A fear, a premonition, a warning of things to come.

As he continued to search his inner self for an answer, Becky came through the back door. Good, he thought, her bath is ready. I'll think I'll get her naked, drunk, and jump her bones. Can't hurt me a bit, he thought as he walked to the mud room.

"Hello, beautiful lady." Matt greeted. "How was your day, today."

"Oh great, honey." she answered as she hugged and kissed him. "We had a big lunch today. Pizza and beer, compliments of Carla and Phil, who announced that they are lovers and have been for quite some time."

"Really?" Matt asked. "A little Peyton Place soap opera at the depths of the earth. Are they engaged?"

"No, just having sex." Becky answered.

"Well, that's good." Matt replied.

Why is that good?" Becky countered.

"Oh...just because. Here let me help you with your sweatshirt." Matt responded.

"So, you approve of this sort of behavior, do you?" Becky questioned.

"It's not in my place to judge, honey." Matt explained. "I believe that people shouldn't be lonely or unhappy. And knowing what those two have to go home too, I can't believe the other side of their bed is a happy one."

"How do you know this shit?" Becky asked seriously.

"I just listen, babe." Matt went on. "You learn all kinds of stuff if you just listen. I've seen those two going off together for quite some time now. I think it's neat. I'm happy for them."

Matt helped Becky get out of work clothes, catching every glance he could get, and as he was leaving Becky said, "stay here with me. Is there something on your mind? You look pre-occupied, as they say in Ohio."

"I don't know." Matt answered as he sat down on the chair next to the tub. "I woke up with this nagging intuition and I can't put my finger on it. Ran into old Abner today. That was interesting."

Becky cut Matt off in mid thought when she said, "did you hear the latest on that miner they found yesterday? Some big shot from Charleston said he was murdered. He found a cut on his ribs and says that is a knife wound scratch. Don't that blow your mind? Oh well, sorry to interrupt you, go ahead."

Matt sat on the tub as Becky handed him the wash cloth to wash her back, and his mind went a mile a minute remembering the conversation with Abner.

"What about Abner, honey? Put some muscle in that scrub, would you, slacker?" Becky asked.

"We were getting gas at the Shell station and he appears out of the blue." Matt began. "I said hi, asked him how his day was, and he just stares at me with that eagle beak of his. So, I'm thinking, what the hell is your problem. I asked if there been any word about that dead miner? This crazy sonofabitch goes off on me. He gets in my face, and he even pushed me back against the car. Hollering about that some people should keep their nose out of other people's business, and that nosy people sometimes end up face down in the creek around here if they don't keep their place. The second time he comes back at me, I had left the fuel nozzle in the spout and turned on him. He stopped, but continued to threaten and lecture me as he walked backward across the street. People at the Post Office just stared at him as he started on them. I've never seen him that nuts before. It wasn't like him. I was concerned for him, I really was. I debated on calling his wife, but thought better of it after a while. I don't know what got into the old geezer. I'm kind of worried about him. He's half nuts, I know, but he's never been violent before."

"Well, honey, the rumors at the mines are that maybe this body is the miner who left town unexpectedly about the same time Abner's daughter left to have her baby. Some think he was the father. Needless to say, Abner didn't accept him as a son -in- law. I've known Abner a long time, as has my father. He says he wouldn't put it past Abner to fix an old wound the old fashioned way." Becky explained. "This is the old fashion way of fixing wounds around here. You know, Matthew. It wouldn't surprise me a bit if he had something to do with it. He always has been a crotchety old bastard. Is Mary asleep?"

"Yes." Matt answered.

"Hand me that towel, would you?" Becky asked. Get me some more wine and let's go to the bedroom. I could use a frontal massage. I'll be quiet."

Matt poured Becky another glass of Asti, and as he neared the bedroom, Mary woke up and was walking out of her room.

"Mommy has a kink in her back, so I'm going to rub it out." Matt said. "Would you like me to put the Mermaid movie in for you."

"Yeah..." Mary said in a stupor. "Will you get my bear and my blanket?"

Matt took the glass of wine to Becky, who was already lying on the bed half asleep.

"Give me a second." Matt said. "I'll be right back."

When Matt returned to the living room with Mary's bear and blanket, she was already fast asleep. Matt tucked the bear under her arm and covered her up. It was back to the bedroom for a different kind of caring. Matt lived for this.

When Matt walked through the door he found, to his surprise, that Becky was sound asleep also. So, he covered her up, and took supper off the stove. Shortly after that chore he took a shower and he too got ready for bed.

13

After his shower, Matt stood aimlessly looking out the window into the dark night, when he noticed the strangest activity. It looked like Abner pushing someone in a wheelchair down by the corner drug store. The men had stopped moving, and Abner sat on a park bench facing the man in the chair. Abner was dancing around on that bench like he was having a fit. On the bench and off the bench, like his pants were on fire. The man in the wheel chair kept looking around as if he was worried about their conversation being overheard and waiving his hands as to calm Abner down a bit.

Lord, what I wouldn't give to have pants on to eves drop, Matt thought to himself. Matt continued to watch as the events got even stranger. Abner rolled the man in the wheelchair over to his van. The man stood up, put his chair in the back seat, opened the front door and crawled into the driver's seat.

This is too much, Matt laughed to himself. There are some strange ducks out tonight. As Matt watched for a moment longer, he saw Abner look around to see if the coast was clear and then meandered down the sidewalk toward Matt's house.

Matt tightened the cord on his bathrobe and quietly opened the front door to get a look at old Abner as he walked past the house. As he waited, Abner never came by the front of the house. This prompted Matt to take a second look out the side window. When he looked out into street, he saw Abner looking in at him from the street. Matt jumped at being startled, but couldn't tell if Abner saw him or not. Abner continued to walk around

Matt's house and look in all the windows in search for...whomever or whatever.

Matt stood perfectly still in his dark house watching Abner get ever braver as he got closer and closer to Matt's house. Finally, even to the surprise of Matt, the outside security lights, that Matt installed a year ago, turned on flooding the yard as well as Abner in total daylight. Abner, quite shocked, walked quickly around the house and back to the sidewalk and headed for home.

That sonofabitch, Matt thought. What the hell is he up to? And who is the semi-paralyzed man he was talking to. He didn't get a license plate number, only the make and model of the van. This made Matt's head spin a mile a minute. Oh, I've got to get to the bottom of this. This is too exciting to pass on. He went to the bedroom to get dressed.

Matt checked on Becky and Mary and grabbed his coat. He was out the door in a covert move that would have made Boris Bettanoff take note. As he made his way around the outer edge of the house he looked down the street towards Abner's house and noticed that he was still walking home. It was as if he had all day and was trying to keep away from his wife, since he had walked past his own house and continued meandering down the street.

As Matt neared the front of Abner's house, he caught a glimpse of the living room curtains move and saw Abner's wife looking out the window. Trying not to appear obvious, Matt stopped walking and stood alongside a big oak in a dark shadow. It was beginning to rain slightly, and much to the surprise of Matt, the van with the wheelchair bound man drove up to the corner and stopped.

Coming around the corner were two large, broad shouldered sultry looking dudes, who obviously weren't from around here. This concerned Matt, because even with the chill of the air the men had their hands free from their pockets, and their coats unbuttoned. As the men approached Abner, they separated a bit and continued to approach him.

As Matt hid in the shadows of the big oak, he could look in and see Abner's wife still staring out the window with her fingers at her mouth, obviously deeply concerned. The one man got very close to Abner and this scared Matt to the point where he began walking down the sidewalk and thinking of a reason why he was there in the first place. Just then he remembered he hadn't eaten supper. So, he thought to himself, I'm on my way to Sally's Diner for a bite to eat.

As Matt got closer, he caught the attention of the man in the van who rolled down his window and watched Matt approach the men. He could also hear voices raising the tempo, and it appeared to be at Abner's expense.

Matt didn't really want to get involved, but it was too late. He felt Abner was in trouble, and these two goons could whip Abner's ass and he wouldn't even see them move.

The last thing Matt heard was, "we know you know, old man. Don't make this hard on yourself. The next time…"

"Good evening gentleman." Matt began his performance. "I didn't think we were going to get rain until tomorrow. Hey Abner, let's go grab some supper at Sally's. I found where to get that axle part for your Model T, and I want to run the prices by you. Can I have my old friend for a while?"

"Yeah, you can have him, we're done with him." One of the men said. "Remember what we talked about, old man. This ain't over."

Matt, in an attempt to calm the situation said, " ooh, that sounds serious."

The other man approached Matt and put his hand on his chest and said, "why don't you mind you own business, hayseed?"

Matt looked down at the man's hand on his chest and said, "you really don't want to do that."

Glaring deeply in the man's eyes, Matt could see that he was an Italian. The man noticed that Matt didn't have an accent about him. The man took his hand off his chest and the two of them turned and walked away. As they did, the man in the van started his engine and left as well.

14

"How is it that there are two Waps in Hope, West Virginia, and they both know you?" Matt asked. "Abner, it's none of my business, but what in the hell have you gotten into? And stay calm, your wife is looking out the window. Don't look around! We're going to walk to Sally's. I doubt very much if these two assholes are looking out for your well-being. And when one of them calls you and old man, that is not a compliment for longevity, it's a threat. And what the hell were you doing walking around my house tonight? Does your wife know what's going on here? Don't think they won't go to her to get to you. These really aren't the kind of people you invite over for dinner, you know."

In a minute they were out of sight of Abner's wife and were walking into Sally's Diner. As Matt opened the door, he caught a glimpse in the light of Abner's face. Matt best described it as terrified. He was shaking and desperately trying to keep his composure in the diner half filled with people that he has known all his life.

A man in the far corner of the diner noticed the look on Abner's face and said, "Jesus, Abner, what the hell happened to you. You look like you just saw a ghost?"

Abner ignored the question as if he didn't hear him.

"My dear friend here just walked off the curb in front of a car and he damn near met his maker." Matt defended. "That would've scared the shit out of me too. He'll be all right, won't you? Two coffees Beth, please."

As the attention again went off Abner and onto their own issues, the place got back to normal again. Matt just set there with Abner as Beth, a very pleasantly beautiful lady, brought them two coffees.

"Do you want menus?" Beth asked.

"No thanks." Matt said. "Two bean soups and cherry pie with ice cream, will do us both proud."

As Beth returned to the kitchen to get their order, Matt sat quietly by and waited on Abner to start the conversation. But...he didn't.

"I've got to get home." Abner said. "Dorothy will be waiting for me."

"No, she won't!" Matt objected. "She came out and saw you walk in here with me. You better set here and have a bite to eat and settle down a little bit, or is Dorothy tied up in this also?"

"Who said I was tied up in anything you nosy bastard?' Abner argued." Why don't you mind your own damn business? You think you know everything! You don't know shit!"

"I know there aren't any Italians within two hundred miles of here. And I know those were Lieutenants. Do you know what a Lieutenant is, Abner? Matt asked. "Do you know what an enforcer is, a leg breaker? They came to you for one reason and one reason only. You have something they want, and I'm guessing that fake crippled fella brought them to you. I've been all over this town for the last two days, and I've never seen them before tonight. Don't you wonder why they only come out at night? It probably has something to do with that dead miner. They found a knife blade scratch on one of his ribs, you know? Stilettos are a popular weapon of choice among that class of Italian."

The mood was broken when Beth brought over the soup and cherry pie.

"Can we have one of these in a box for Dorothy?" Matt asked.

As Beth nodded, she was off again to the kitchen to get a piece of pie for Dorothy. Abner appeared to settle down somewhat and began to talk again, somewhat sarcastically at first, but talking nonetheless.

"I didn't ask for your help, why don't you just leave me alone. What makes you think you know who those people are. You're just a crippled fireman, you don't know shit." Abner said.

"I don't have to be a crippled fireman to know friends don't cause the other friend to damn near shit his pants. And why would an old prejudiced sonofabitch like you have Italian friends? That would make a damn cat laugh."

As Matt finished his soup and began eating his pie he continued saying, "Okay, you're right! I don't know shit. I wouldn't know a greasy

Italian from a rag-headed Arab. Eat your soup. I'd hate to see you get your ass beat on an empty stomach."

"I can defend myself!" Abner exclaimed. "I'm not a crippled little fireman on welfare like you are."

"Yeah, I can see that." Matt said. "You'll whip their ass like red headed step-children."

"You are goddamn right I would!" Said Abner.

"Shit!" Matt retorted. "You'd be dead before you hit the ground. You think these assholes are out collecting for the Red Cross? Do they know where you live, Abner? Does the cripple know?"

"Why?" Abner asked.

"Because houses burn with their enemies usually in them, and around here they wouldn't know what to look for." Matt replied. "Gasoline and matches are their third weapon of choice. Do they know Dorothy? Do they know your daughter, or John?"

Matt struck a nerve with the question about Abner's daughter.

"My daughters got nothing to do with this." Abner snapped back. "And who the hell ever told you I have a daughter. That's none of you damn business."

Abner was beginning to louden the conversation somewhat as he was getting the attention of the customers in the diner. As Abner looked coyly around the diner in an attempt to see who was listening, he again got another surprise when the two Italian gentlemen walked into the diner and sat down.

The two men came in and sat next to Abner and Matt and said, "beautiful night, isn't it?"

Matt got a good look at the two men.

Abner nodded at them and said to Matt, "see, they don't look too scary to me."

"Really," Matt said. "You think he got those scars roller skating at the park with his baby sister? Jesus, his gun is bulging out of his jacket. Wonderful guys, I'm sure. Here's Beth, let's get out of here."

As Beth brought the pie order out, Matt and Abner rose to leave. This prompted the one Italian with the scar to stand and extend his hand to Abner saying, "we'll be talking to you."

Abner stood there quite stunned when Matt stepped in front of Abner and said, "you can't carry a firearm in this state. You might want to tuck it closer to your body. You gentleman have a pleasant evening." At this they walked out the door and headed home the back way.

The two men walked home in total silence. Abner looked down at the sidewalk and never muttered a sound. When they arrived at Abner's house, the front door opened and there stood Dorothy.

"Hope you didn't mind I borrowed your husband for a bite to eat, Misses Colb." Matt said. However, Dorothy didn't answer him, she just looked at her husband as he walked past her and into the house. Dorothy looked back at Matt and went into the house with Abner, closing the door behind her.

Before entering his house, Matt looked around and found no one on the street. No Italians, no van, no one. He went in the house and went to bed, being careful not to wake Becky. But as he laid down next to her, she rolled over and put her head on his chest. She was fast asleep and didn't even know Matt left.

Matt closed his eyes and said a prayer for Abner. By the time he could return his thoughts to what happened tonight, he too was fast asleep.

15

Wednesday morning dawned with a slight mist and a seasonable chill in the air. Matt arose to make breakfast for them and was immediately looking out the window. Although it was still dark, Matt could see quite a way down the street. It didn't appear anyone was camping out at Abner's house.

As he began making the pancakes with ham and eggs, he also packed Becky's lunch. For a reason he could not put his finger on, he made her three sandwiches. He trusted his instincts and put twice the cookies and candy in the lunch box for Becky's meal in the mine.

"Do they have water down there for you guys, or do want me to put a bottle in your lunch?" Matt asked.

"Oh, hey." Becky answered. "We got water baby. This is a top rate outfit."

"Honey?" Matt asked kind of covertly. "Who owns your company?"

"I don't know really." Becky replied. "Zack does, I'll ask him. Some Italian guy from Philadelphia, I think. Why?"

When Matt heard that he dropped an egg on the floor and his mind began to race a mile a minute.

"I don't know." Matt said. "I was thinking about something."

"What honey?" Becky replied.

In an attempt to come up with some line that Becky would half believe, he said, "I was going to ask them for some money or a big Christmas party for the less fortunate this year. Do you think I'll get anywhere?"

"Yeah. You probably will." Becky answered as she came and kissed him. "If anybody can talk that tightwad out of his money, it's you. Matthew, how do you expect me to eat all this?"

"Well, you didn't eat supper last night. You'll be hungry about ten o'clock and you'll be thanking me for it." Matt replied with an expected reward.

"Honey, I always thank you for it." Becky said.

"Are we talking about the same thing here?" Matt said.

"Only you could find a comparison between pussy and a peanut butter sandwich." Becky said as she cracked him on the butt as she reached for her coffee cup.

As the three of them sat down to breakfast, the conversation was of the usual variety. Where were they going shopping today and would Matt help her father put in that water softener salt, because her father would try to lift it and he'd hurt his back again. Mary said that she would see to it personally.

"Oh, shoot," Becky said. "I'm getting cramps. Well, no little brother this month. Boy, you don't know how lucky you are. Have you ever tried changing a granny rag in a coal mine?"

Matt looked at Becky with a confused look on his face. Then he shook his head and said, "no honey, can't say that I have."

"Oh, you're gonna get it." Becky said.

"Not for the next couple days, I'll bet." Matt returned.

With that exchange of morning pleasantries, the three of them laughed and chided each other before getting ready to take Becky to work.

"It's gonna be a wet one today." Matt said. "I meant rain, honey."

"Just keep it up, bucko. We'll see who gets the last laugh." Becky returned.

Matt got her equipment and held the door open as she got in the front seat.

"Honey, this is way too much food. I'm just a little wallflower of a girl." Becky said.

"Aw, don't worry about it, honey." Matt said. "It might keep you from eating Zack's leg."

"Yuk, I'm not believing you said that." Becky said. "Wouldn't you have to cook that or something?"

"Yeah, just cook it like anything else." Matt said mischievously. "I hear it tastes just like chicken."

With that Matt got a punch in the shoulder as they pulled out of the driveway, saying, "somehow I believe you may know that first hand. Not accusing, mind you, just a hunch."

Looking over at Becky as the day began to break, he so wanted to tell her about last night, but he knew he couldn't. He felt like he was being unfaithful in keeping that to himself. But it was probably best that he said nothing. As they pulled into the miners drop off zone, Matt got out and got Becky's door as she kissed Mary good-bye. He hugged her, kissed her and wished her a good day. He also commented on her hair saying, "your new dew makes you look younger. You are a beautiful lady and I want you to know I love you very much."

"I know." Becky said returning another hug. "I love you too."

She walked away waiving, and met the other three and together they walked into the break room for the morning advisory meeting.

Tooting his horn for one last wave, Matt drove out of the parking lot and onto the main street.

16

"**W**here to, daddy?" said Mary.

"Let's go get grandpa his salt and then we'll go shopping for a while. What do you think?" answered Matt.

As the two com padres drove down the street it looked a little cloudy. Although Matt liked this part of the country, he always felt there was nothing more desolate looking than a coal mining town in the rain. Downright depressing at times. Matt turned the car into the hardware store parking lot and flipped open the trunk. As he and Mary got out they were met by Enos Traught. He was known as the biggest bullshitter in all of Hope, and that was a tough bill to fill considering the company he kept. He reminded you of Festus Haggin, on the Gunsmoke series. And every time he would say Matt's name, he would draw on the syllable of 'hew' and it was all Matt could do but laugh. A down to earth social character who would give you the shirt off his back, provided you fared south of the Mason-Dixon line. He did, after all, have his scruples.

"Math-ewe!" Enos started. "Where's your friend Abner?"

"I have no idea, and good morning to you also." Matt returned.

"Oh, for Christ's sake, we don't have time for pleasantries!" Enos retorted. "It's all about Abner. My God, there's a rumor that that dead miner is the one who made a winch out of his daughter, and he killed him. And this morning he went down to the creek and he's telling anyone who will listen that the silt is running again and the mine's gonna cave in. He getting some people upset around here, and I'm honestly worried about him. And he keeps hanging around with them damn Italians. You know as well as I do, there ain't no good ever came from Italy. My God, look what they did to Jesus! You-ins got to keep a closer eye on him before he ends up some where he doesn't belong."

"Where would that be?" asked Matt innocently.

"In a ditch, ya dumb bastard! In a ditch." Enos quickly corrected."

"What the hell are you talking about, you crazy sonofabitch?" Matt returned.

"You think this is a game, don't ya boy?" Enos said. "You damn Yankees don't have the brains God gave a cabbage."

"I don't know what you're talking about." replied Matt. "You keep chewing my ass, and for what? There ain't no damn silt in a creek, it comes from the Mississippi Delta, and it wasn't the Waps that killed Jesus, it was the Jews. So...once again...what in the hell are you talking about?"

About the time Matt was hoping for an explanation, something caught Enos's eye and he turned abruptly and walked into the hardware store. As Matt turned around to see Abner coming into the parking lot, a little faster than usual, with a big black Chrysler 300 looking to be in deliberate pursuit.

Matt's first thought was why would that scare Enos. It didn't surprise him that Abner was being followed. He looked over and put Mary's hand in his and slowly meandered toward the hardware store as well, while keeping an eye on Abner. His second thought was that this is something he surely didn't want to get involved in. As he neared the store his last thought was, where do they get silt in a creek...that was strange.

Matt watched Abner's actions as one of the men got out of the car. He appeared to be very nervous. Matt then heard one of the men tell Abner to get into the car and go for a ride with them. Abner kept walking forward as the car kept inching forward. Matt reached to open the store door and saw all the people inside looking out the window at Abner. Having to think quickly, he asked Misses Williamson if she would keep an eye on Mary for a moment. And telling Mary he would be right back, he turned and walked out the door in the direction of Abner.

When the man who got out of the car looked up at Matt, he seemed displeased and defensive. Matt, at first glance could see he was an Italian, and a well fed one at that.

"Abner, thank God you're here!" Matt began. Becky's old man wants me to get him salt for his softener and you told me you would help me find the right stuff."

"Yeah, Matt, it's right in here." Abner said, and began walking faster putting his arm on Matt's shoulder.

"Are you all right?" Matt asked.

"That sonofabitch has been following me around all day." Abner said. "Let's get your salt and we'll go to your place and talk."

As the two men entered the store, the man got back into the black Chrysler 300 and drove slowly away.

Everyone in the store just stared at Abner, but no one said anything.

"Looks like rain." Matt said to break the chill in the air as he took Mary's hand, thanking Misses Williamson for watching her.

"What do those people want from you, Abner?" a voice from the store said. That was followed by several 'yeahs.' "What are you bringing down on us? These people ain't from around here. We don't need no trouble hereabouts, you know. Matt, what's your business in this? Did you bring them here? Are they from up your way? Why don't you take them back and stay there with them? We'll get along okay without you. We did before, we will again."

"What are you so afraid of?" Matt asked in a disgusting tone. "This is your home, not theirs. No one comes into your home if they're not welcome. They're visitors, stranger's. Don't give them any more quarter than you would anyone else. I don't know what they want and I'm sure Abner doesn't either, but we take care of our own. It's not too hard to come up missing around here and lose your way home. So, relax. We'll let the law handle it."

"I think they're after Abner for all the shit he's spreading about the silt in the creek and the mine caving in. You know, no one wants to hear that shit. And what about that dead miner, Abner? Do you know something about that you should tell us?"

"I don't know nothing about that dead miner." Abner said in his defense. "And you know damn well what that silt's about. These bastards don't give a shit and you just set on your ass and let them get away with it."

"I saw that car follow you all morning. What do they want Abner?" someone said in the store.

"Did you call the Police?" Matt asked.

No one said a word to that question.

"I tell ya, I don't know what they want, or who they are." Abner said. "I'm just as surprised as you are. But I'm going to the Police right after we get your salt, so let's get to it."

Although an uneasiness settled about the store, it was accepted, for the time being, that Abner was telling the truth. But Matt felt that it was only accepted long enough for him to leave, and then they would rework it in their minds. They would get to the bottom of something that they really didn't want to know.

As Matt bought the salt he needed, he was more than anxious to talk with Abner, and get to the bottom of this. Even if it meant maybe protecting Abner from the men in the black car. Matt did not fear them, because he knew what they were, and he was well equipped to protect Abner if he had to. He really wasn't too confident in the local law enforcement, however. He also knew that if he killed them, if necessary, to protect Abner, they would only send more, and these would fight from a much longer range.

As the three of them loaded into Matt's SUV, Matt started the conversation first by asking Abner what was the importance of "silt" in a creek?

"It means that the water running through the mine is leaching through the cracks in the coal. That's why it washes the sand out of the crevices and flows out with the stream and builds up in the creek." Abner explained.

"Okay, I'll bite, why is that so bad?" Matt returned.

"Bad?" Abner shouted. "Because the sand holds the coal together like mortar. There's also a lot of bark and splinters down at the creek. That means that the support beams are rotting away. There's nothing to hold the coal and the beams together. It's like a rope that's about to break under a heavy load. There's more and more down there every day!"

"Wouldn't you think that the Engineer's would look into that?" Matt asked.

"I don't think they believe it, or they don't want to believe it." Abner continued. "They might not even know what it means. If you ask them, they say it could come from anywhere around these parts."

"Is that so wrong?" Matt mistakenly asked.

"Wrong?" Abner shouted again with his eyes bugging out. "The splinters and the bark are from Beach trees, sent up here from South Carolina. There aren't any Beach trees on these mountains."

"So, tell me this." Matt said. "Why don't the Engineers at least look into it? You've told them, haven't you?"

"I told them several times." Abner said sadly. "They don't give a shit. It would cost too much down time to go in and inspect the flow and the structure. I think when those damn plates shifted from that Ecuador quake, it screwed up everything."

"Well, how long before the timbers are rotten?" Matt asked.

"There already gone." Abner replied tiredly. "Once the splinters are together with the silt, the water is washing away the beams. It could go anytime. The real question is where. I think it's where your lady is working. The newer sections are shored up with I- beams. There ain't no rust in the silt, only beach trees splinters. They weren't there last week before they re-opened that shaft and that earthquake happened. My guess is the shit is about to hit the fan. Get your lady out of there. Get her on sick leave or something, just get her out of there for a while. I don't think it'll be long, now. Let me out here, will ya? Thanks."

And with that Abner walked off with his hands in his pockets and his head hanging down like the lonely lighthouse keeper in a Ben Richman painting. And with his dejection went Matt's confidence in the safety of Becky and her crew.

He would have to convince her to take some time off, because in the pit of his stomach, he believed Abner. He was, in Matt's mind, too convicted to be wrong. And he was right, there were no beech trees on this mountain and that was beech bark he had in his pocket. This was no time to brush him off as a lunatic. And, damn, he never asked him about that dead miner. Oh well, some other time. Soon... but some other time. Matt and Mary drove on to the in-laws house to service the water softener.

17

The man-cart made its final stop at a mile and a half down the shaft and at about one-hundred and sixty-five feet below the surface to let off Becky and her crew. Phil pushed the button and the cart took off once again for the surface.

"So, when's the wedding you two?" Zack asked.

"No hurry." Carla said. "I'm still using him for sex. No sense putting a label on a good thing, you know."

"Phil, what's your take on that?" Zack asked.

"Whatever the little lady wants is good with me." Phil said. "And while we're on the subject, we want you two to stand in for us. It'll just be a small ceremony. Not a lot of song and dance."

"Yeah," said Carla. "But I am getting a white dress."

"Shit!" Zack followed.

"Hey! I'm serious." Carla exclaimed. "I've got a reputation to keep here, you know. I ain't no hillbilly piece of white trailer trash. I'm a god damn lady, and ladies wear white dresses for their wedding."

"Agreed!" Zack replied. "Please excuse me madam, I meant no harm."

"Shit! You know I'm wearing blue jeans and my green WVU sweatshirt, you turkey." Carla advised. "I ain't tryin' to impress nobody. The only white I'll have on is my tennis shoes. Ain't that right sugarplum?"

"That's right baby," Phil answered. "whatever you want."

"Sounds like you've got him trained pretty good, Carla." Said Becky.

"He's coming around pretty good here lately, ain't he?" Carla said. "I've got to hand it to him. Of course, I do, but that's another subject. We're gonna make a go of it, aren't we babe?"

"Yes, we are babe." Phil answered. "Our better halves will take up with their queer better halves and that'll be all she wrote. There ain't nothin' else stoppin' us. Does it feel damp in here or is it just me?"

"You know, maybe I got my brains screwed out last night, and I ain't hearin' right, but I do declare I hear water runnin' and I feel chilled to the bone." Carla commented.

"There's no dust on the floor, either." Becky said. "It's like a mud."

"Just so it ain't silt!" Zack said.

With that everybody just stopped and stared at Zack. The word, "silt" struck a chord in their minds, since they have all heard Abner talking about it and getting a lot of people upset.

"Just kiddin'." Zack said defensively. "Don't mean nothin'."

"I'll tell ya." Becky started. "if I never hear that damn word again, it'll be too soon for me. That and "shifting tectonic plates. Damn, my old man got on that subject the other day. He and mom sounded like a couple of whacked out, drug crazed geologists setting around a shuffleboard court in a retirement home.

"What the hell is that?" Carla asked Phil.

"Looks like wood chips." Phil answered. "That's strange. "Must be a rotten brace up ahead and the rain washed in."

"Strange hell! It hasn't rained in three days, for God sake." Becky interjected with authority.

There was a slight vibration in the floor of the mine and Phil held out his hands in a soothing matter and everybody stopped walking.

"Let's go to the next brace and wait this out." Phil said. "It'll pass."

"What is it?" Carla asked.

"Feels like a plate." Phil said. "Let's just go to the next brace."

"Is that water running heavier than when we came down here?" Carla asked.

"I don't think it's getting heavier," Phil replied. "We're getting closer. Zach, would you call the car down here in case we've got to get out in a hurry?"

Zack was on the phone-radio by the time they reached the next brace. Everyone just huddled under the safety of the beam and held perfectly still.

"Zack, does that brace have a number on it?" Phil asked. "If it does, give it to them in case worse comes to worse."

"Remember that song Jimmy Dean wrote about the miner who held up the beam so the miners could escape?" Carla reminisced.

"I don't think we've come to that yet." Zack assured. "Let's wait here and see what happens."

"Where's all that cold air coming from?" Becky asked.

"Probably from Sloma's vent." Zack answered. "According to the map it should be up about a quarter mile and then the shaft goes left. That's probably where the water's coming from too."

"Who the hell is Sloma, and what the hell is a vent.? Carla asked. "You mean an air hole?"

"Yeah." Zack replied. "But this one is about three feet in diameter. When the barometric pressure changes, the mine breathes through it. it's just a big vent. A shaft. I think it runs about one hundred and sixty-five feet straight up, if I remember correctly. No reply on the radio about the car yet, guys. No marking on this beam either."

"There's a vibration in the beam!" Becky said. "You guys, put your hands on this and tell me if you feel something."

"Yeah, I feel it too." Zack said. "Phil it's like the stronger the vibration, the faster the water is dripping."

As they all huddled under the protection of the brace, a deep growling sound began overhead. Its intensity grew stronger, and the vibration of the plate moving overhead could be felt in the floor of the shaft.

"That sounds like a big one!" Phil said. "Going slow too!"

Small aggregate particles began falling from the cracks in the ceiling. Phil remarked that they were wet and to stand fast and let the plate pass overhead.

The crew stood by at the brace and soon they were holding onto each other and staring up at the ceiling in anticipation, as a crewman of a depth charged submarine might look up while praying to his God for relief. The plate began to move quicker and growled louder when suddenly there was a loud *BANG!!*

Carla let out a scream and fell to her knees. Phil reached for her and held her to keep her under the brace. About thirty feet up the shaft, a large piece of the ceiling fell to the floor followed by a large amount of smaller rocks. The plate had stopped.

Zack attempted to get the surface on the radio, but to no avail. Soon everything had quieted down to the point that even the water stopped running down the shaft.

"Okay, this is how it is." Zack started. "I'm in charge of this crew, and we're getting the hell out of here. We are gonna walk out, and we are gonna walk out now. Any feedback?"

"How far down are we?" Becky asked.

"Phil?" Zack asked for clarification?

"I'd say about one hundred fifty down, and about two miles from the door. shouldn't take more than an hour. The closer we get to the surface, the safer we are. Let's get while the gettin's good, Take all your food. The leader has the headlamp. Let's conserve everything else. Two by two. Let's move out! I'll take the lead."

With that the miners left the safety of the brace and began their trek to the surface.

"Where are the rats?" Carla asked.

"Probably went farther down." Phil remarked. "Let's not worry about them now. Just keep moving, shall we?"

18

$\mathbf{M}$att and Mary arrived at Becky's parents' house with the water softener salt, only to find the street bustling with excitement. When Matt pulled his SUV into the driveway, he could see the look of deep concern on his father-in-law's face.

"Did you feel that?" he asked.

"No. what?" Matt replied.

"Damn earthquake is what it was." He said. "Shook the coffee right out of my cup. If those damn plates are moving again, we're in a world of shit. The news said that Ecuador was having tremors again last night. They're gonna evacuate the mine. Some of the guys have already come out. Somebody said a tree fell out at Stoma's place. Fell right over for no apparent reason. Bet them Pollacks are running around like crazy at the mine today."

"Italians, honey." the wife said.

"What?" he said.

"They're Italians, honey. Not Pollacks." the wife said.

"Well, shit, honey. They're all inbred, how can you tell the difference?" he said.

Boy, if that wasn't the pot calling the kettle black, Matt thought to himself, but knew better than to say something.

People began going back into their houses after a while, and Matt suggested that they get that salt in the water softener before the world ended.

Throwing the bag over his shoulder, he said, "lead on young man," and off to the basement they went.

Matt and his father-in-law talked about many subjects as they were putting the salt into the softener. Matt had a great deal of respect for him, even though he was a quiet man. He loved his wife and never said a cross word to her. He was patient man who had worked hard all his life, and loved his Lord. He was a church going Baptist and never questioned Matt on his past or his religion. He would stare at Matt sometimes in an attempt to learn more about the man who had married his daughter, but when it came to questions, he never invaded Matt's privacy, and Matt deeply respected that.

He was a typical West Virginian, right up to the top button being closed on his shirt. Had he been of age, he would have served proudly for the Confederacy. He was a man of conviction, and those convictions sustained him throughout his life. He had no vices, no prejudices.

Matt had the salt bag nearly emptied when he commented, "that should do it, don't you think?"

His father-in-law didn't answer, he only stared blankly toward the ceiling.

"What's wrong?" Matt asked.

"It's coming back!" he replied.

"What's coming back?" Matt asked.

Becky's father never answered Matt, he only dropped the crescent wrench from his hand and took off up the steps which led to the outdoors.

19

As the four miners made their way quickly up the shaft to the surface, they hugged the wall and felt for vibrations. Phil was very good at leading them along, as he talked confidently in what they were doing. He also talked about getting to the surface soon, and had every intention of taking the rest of the day off.

Becky made every attempt to keep calm as they made the long arduous trek up the shaft. She was afraid and was very conscious of her fear rising with every uncertain step. She glanced at the wall as she placed her hand on it. And for the first time in her mining career she realized the in-humanness of the rock wall she held onto for her very life, in the hope it would lead her to safety. For all the many years she identified the mines as a work of the Almighty, she had now come to realize that it was nothing more than a slab of unforgiving, cold, gray, lifeless, guiltless hunk of nothingness, and she was right in the middle of it's unforgiving nature. She feared now of becoming its victim. She began to think of Matt and Mary, in the hopes of changing her fear to determination. And then, all of a sudden it came to her; she wasn't walking out of here today.

The vibrations pulsated like a lawn mower in the high grass. The water began to run faster down the makeshift gutter of the mine. As Zack tried desperately to get the surface on the radio, gravel, as well as larger chunks of rock began to fall from the ceiling of the mine. There was a consistent, annoying, vibrating hum overhead.

"All right," Phil said. "Watch your heads! Sing out everybody. Last man back there, talk to me!"

"I'm right behind you." Becky answered with a tone of fear in her voice.

"Let's stay together. We're gonna make it." Phil said assuredly. "Zack, any luck with that radio?"

"Nothing!" Zack answered

"I'm thinkin' of stickin' that radio up somebody's ass here shortly. You can't find them bastards when you need them. Are these damn walls moving or am I seeing things?" Carla said.

When they arrived at the next beam, they found the left support was lying on the floor, and the overhead beam was wedged into the corner of the wall and ceiling, split by the intense pressure.

"Damn thing is moving to the left." Zack said. "Does that mean anything to you Phil?"

"The only thing I can think of is we need to go down an inside shaft." Phil answered. "If we can get inside this bitch we'll move away from the plates. It might be a longer walk, but the shit will be to the left of us, instead of on top of us."

As soon as Phil stopped talking, everything got deathly quiet. The water slowed to a trickle and the cold breeze even stopped.

"Shit!" Phil said. "The pressure changed again. We need to step it up, and I do mean step it up!"

"Okay, this is what I think we should do!" Zack began. "Let's everybody collect themselves. Catch your breath and let's make a run for it. Let's pack our shit and git! Any comments?"

"If you get in my way, you slacker, you'll have boot prints on your back." Carla said, in a poor attempt to break the tension with a weak giggle.

"Alright, Phil, you take the lead, Carla, Becky and me." Zack said.

"Bullshit!" Carla said. "I want you behind me."

"It's okay, Zack!" Becky said. "I got your back. I'll be fine. Let's just get the hell out of here!"

"Let's unload our shit, here. There no sense in carrying this stuff uphill." Zack said." It'll only slow us down."

The four miners took off their backpacks and equipment packs and dropped them on the floor. For some reason, Becky picked them all up and put them against the wall, as if to protect them from damage. She also kept her air-pac strapped to her. When she looked up again the other three miners were already on a full gallop up the shaft.

"Hey, wait for me!" She cried.

"Come on Becky!" Zack said.

Becky took about a dozen steps, when the floor jerked so violently that it knocked her off her feet. She rose quickly and continued up the mine at a trot. The lights flickered several times, and then it got quiet again.

"We're doing fine! Phil said. "Everybody keep up! Can't be too far now."

The quiet was quickly replaced with what appeared to be a deep, intense, grinding, growling sound. This brought more debris and sediment falling from the ceiling. Becky could feel the vibration through her boots. It was everywhere. There was a very loud "bang," followed by two more, each more deafening than the first. Becky looked forward to Phil, and saw a huge cloud of dust, and a wall of rock consume him. It caught Carla before she could stop also. There was only a quick, interrupted scream, as if Carla never felt a thing. The next thing she saw was Zack, turning around. And in an attempt to run in the other direction, hit Becky so hard that he sent her flying through the air. When she collected herself, she saw Zack had become buried under an unforgiving pile of rock.

The air was full of dust and she found herself chocking with every breath.

"Air-pac!" she hollered to herself.

Grabbing it out of it's case, she tried desperately to put in on, but she had it upside down.

"Dammit!" she screamed. "Think!"

In the darkness it was very easy to panic, but with her experience, she knew the dangers of that. She was overcome with fear, but used her headlamp to light up the mask and got it on, and firmly in place.

Being able to breathe settled her down a bit, but only a little bit. She noticed that she was trembling as she sat up on the floor, where she had been lying, she didn't feel any pain, only terror.

The dust had begun to clear. The cool breeze was taking it up the shaft. She could hear the plates moving up the shaft, and the vibration had lessened somewhat.

This was the first time she got a look at Zack.

He was completely contorted. His left leg stuck out from the rock, but his right arm laid alongside it. She could see his right shoe next to his helmet. There was no sign of his head or his left arm.

As the rubble ceased falling, she began to gain her composure, and went to Zack's aid. Calling his name, she shook his leg, but there was no response. Zack appeared to be in a vertical, upside down position. Using her light as a guide she crawled over the rubble and went to Carla. She was lifeless, with an oblivious blank stare in her eyes. Her feet stuck straight up behind her head. She appeared to have gone quickly. When Becky tried to go to Phil, she couldn't find any trace of him, but heard popping, gurgling sounds, bone snapping, breaking noises. She called to him, but he failed to answer. She attempted to move some of the rubble off of him, when she realized she was standing on top of him. Something caught her attention, and as she looked to her right, she saw blood and fluid running out of the pile of rubble which buried Phil. She moved more stone and found his face.

Phil's jaw ran in a vertical direction and rested alongside his right ear. And the left side of his head was smashed. His eyes showed a look of terror and intense pain. His lungs continued to dispel air, and Becky could hear his ribs snapping under the weight of the rocks that held him. Blood and fluids were oozing from his mouth. One of his eyes had been knocked out due to the pressure, and white fluid was coming from his nose. The one person that everyone had depended on for direction and survival, had died a horrible death, just as he once foretold as one of his deepest fears. He didn't deserve this, Becky thought. He was in love and was going to start a new life with Carla. Now Carla laid dead next to him. But next to Phil is where Carla would have wanted to be.

Becky said a prayer over Phil and Carla, and then closed their eyes. She crawled off the pile of rubble and moved about ten feet away from Zack. She sat down and realized she was trapped, and alone, and she began to cry.

20

Becky's dad made it up the steps quickly and hollered to his wife to come outside. Matt was in hot pursuit, not exactly knowing what was going on. He did, however sense there was something very wrong by the way the two of them acted.

"This one's bad, mother!" Ransom said. "I could feel it through the basement floor."

When Matt ran out onto the sidewalk, he too could feel the rumbling in the ground. Mary let out a scream and Matt was quick to respond to her. Becky's parents immediately held each other in their arms and stared toward the entrance of the mine.

A rumbling noise, similar to that of an underground train, began to drown out their voices as well as their thoughts. As they stood in horror of the quake, Becky's father hollered out, "here it comes!" With that warning a large deafening gush of air and debris exploded from the mine entrance, spewing dirt, coal and anything in its path not tied down, one hundred feet in the air and just as far. The debris went through office windows as well as car windows. The expulsion was horrendous.

"What the hell was that?" Matt asked.

"The mine just collapsed!" Becky's father said. "And my Becky's in there!" He dropped to his knee, too emotionally weakened to stand, and wept.

Then the sirens went off.

For a moment Matt stood there like a deer caught in the headlights. And then he got it. Becky *was* in there. By his understanding of the violent reaction of the mine, that it had to be monstrous in strength to cause that kind of damage and be felt that far away. But that was one thing he didn't understand. He only weighed out in his head how a fragile human being could possibly withstand anything that overpowering.

Matt's thoughts were interrupted by Becky's dad when he said, "we better get down there! Maybe they were all out. Abner said they were gonna call them all out."

As they made their way down the street, all the emergency vehicles were making their way to the mine entrance. Most of them were volunteers who answered the mine sirens. The closer they got to the mine Matt noticed that there was no smell of smoke or the by product odor of combustion, only the putrid smell of wet dust. Some of the miners were still coming out. Some visibly injured, some just shaken up, and some just out! One miner exited the mine with no clothing on his upper body. The force of the cave -in literally ripped his clothes off. One man screamed in agony because his back looked like a pin cushion of wooden splinters. Other miners got out of the mine and into the daylight and dropped to the ground, totally exhausted. Their muted sounds barely identifiable as prayers of thanksgiving. A great deal of the miners appeared to be in shock as some of them wandered aimlessly, until an E.M.T. came to their aid. Many of them fell to their knees and tried to catch their breath. Between gasping, coughing, vomiting and hysterical wailing, there were no serious injuries. It was unbelievable how many of them were caked in mud and covered in splinters. But they all had the same look in their eyes. They had seen the devil, and the bastard damn nearly got them all.

A voice rose up from the driveway asking if there was a count. An engineer replied that the safety officer was working on that right now, although he thought that they were all out. That made Matt and Becky's parents feel a little better.

Another engineer was talking to an escaped miner and making notes on a mine map, trying to establish the location where the cave-in occurred.

The E.M.T.'s continued to treat all the injured as more of them, from Buskskin, arrived on the scene. However, with the arrival of the crews also came the arrivals of the wives, and the hysteria started all over again until an engineer got some order to the situation.

Matt and Mary got as close as they could to the mine entrance area in an attempt to find Becky, but to no avail. Matt looked down at Mary and she had a pale stupor look about her. He never realized until now, but this was no place for a child. The scene reminded Matt of a car bomb in a Baghdad marketplace. But he, as everyone else, had no intention of leaving.

The work crew leaders were taking head counts and reporting them to the safety engineer so they could establish if everyone had gotten out safely. As Matt looked around again searching for Becky, he saw Abner standing alone with his arms crossed looking back at him, as a Sheppard looking over his flock.

The ambulances began arriving now and the sirens just heightened the anxiety and tension in the whole area. The screaming and hysteria started all over again by the arrival of the ambulances and the piercing warning sirens, until the Police Chief ordered them turned off.

The Police Chief ordered fireman to clear the traffic lanes, and made a call to Buckskin, where there was a Trauma 4 Level Emergency Room. The miners were piled in to the ambulances. If they could sit, they sat, and the more infirmed went on stretchers in separate ambulances.

Lastly, a section boss emerged from the mine and said there was no one behind him. He had gone back as far as he could, and there was no one left to come out.

Matt put Mary in his arms and hurried down to the safety engineer.

"Becky! Where's Becky Jensen?' Matt asked excitedly.

"Phil! Phil! Where are you? Phil Wells! Where are you?" Phil's wife began to scream. "Where is my husband? Where is Zack, Becky, and Carla?

Matt turned around and saw a frail lady in a tattered dress and sandals standing alone. Matt recognized her as Zack's wife and immediately went to her. She stood emotionless with a blank stare about her and looked blankly into Matt's eyes. It was as if she was the only one of the crew who knew exactly what had happened, and despair quickly engulfed her. She became wobbly and swayed momentarily when Matt grabbed her in his other arm, and hollered for a medic.

It was now evident that not everyone got out of the mine.

21

The mine foreman hollered for the search and rescue teams to gear up and meet in the break room.

"Let's get a location and a plan and let's get down there. The quicker we move the better!" he said.

A medic came and quickly gave aid to Zack's wife. As Matt knelt by her side, he couldn't help but feel sorry for her. What would become of her if Zack didn't come back. Hell, he thought, what would become of any of them if their better halves didn't come back?

The mine foreman continued barking out orders for the search teams, but Matt could make no sense of them. He was beginning to shrink into his own private feelings and thoughts. He could feel fear taking control of him. In his heart, he kept looking at the mine entrance, with a strong conviction that Becky would come walking out of there, and this would all have been a bad dream. She was too strong for this. But when he didn't see anyone come out of the mine after the dust had cleared, he couldn't help but remember when the section boss said that he had gone as far back as he could, and there was no one on this side of the pile. So, where were they? On the back side of the pile or in the pile?

"Get the pipe drilling rig fired up and get it over here." the mine foreman said. "Somebody show me where they were and where we can drill an air and phone hole! Somebody call the owners! Come on people, let's move it! Somebody get the lights set up! Let's move out!"

His shouted orders gave one a sense of relief that there was definitely someone here who was taking control of the situation, and knew what he was doing.

The last of the ambulances had just pulled away with Zach's wife aboard. Matt asked Phil's wife if they had any children that needed looking after. She just looked at Matt blankly, as if this was all his fault, and walked away.

It appeared that everyone handled this in their own way. This was new to Matt, and therefore, he had no experience at this sort of thing. But it appeared to him that everyone else did, and there was an accepted way to deal with this. But Matt was in no way familiar with it.

Matt walked toward Becky's parents and saw Abner still standing on the top of the driveway entrance with his arms folded.

Before Matt could say anything, Abner said, "the next twelve hours are the most important. Let's hope they can get a hand up on something before day break tomorrow. The longer it takes, the worse it gets. Your Becky's in a strong crew, and that mine boss knows his job. His granddaddy was Louis Bova. He died about forty years ago down south a ways. He knows what it means to lose someone in a mine. He's a good man to have on this."

"Did Zack have any kids?" Matt asked Abner.

"Dorothy would know for sure, she sets up the auxiliary care units for times like this. We all take care of our own during times like this. She'll have a list of everyone and their kin."

"Did the silt cause this?" Matt asked.

"It didn't cause this," Abner said. "It only made it easier to happen."

""What happens next?" Matt asked.

"It'll be a circus." Abner said. "They'll come from everywhere. The whole thing will be a mess. I've seen it before. The damn news people get in your face and ask you how you feel. It's all you can do not to knock 'em on their ass. The Red

Cross will be here in the morning. The owners will call an information meeting The Governor will probably get involved. Everyone will start collecting in the church.

We get kind of deep in our God during times like this. Church is about the only place you can go to be alone as a community."

As Matt looked aimlessly into the late December afternoon, a feeling of hollow misery began to rip at his stomach. For the first time since he met Becky, she was apart from him in such a way that he had no clue as to how to find her. The very woman he swore at the altar to protect was in a hole somewhere below him and he was helpless to save her. He would have to trust the crews of the men who were in the rescue party, but he realized that none of their wives were in that hole, and he really doubted their dedication. He hoped he was wrong.

22

Several cars began to come on the scene. On lookers mainly by the way they were dressed, Matt surmised. Among them was a big black Chrysler which drove past the entry guard and right up to the entrance. As Matt watched, a large, well dressed man with slicked back black hair got out of the driver's seat and opened the door for another man. The man took a moment to finish reading an article in a newspaper, and with a smile on his face, disembarked the car. He was a well kept, older gentleman with snow white hair, and a facial appearance that could freeze a rock. The man glanced uncaring about the gathering crowd which were beginning to increase, as were the State Police from Charleston.

Matt thought for a moment that the older gentlemen was a little nerved by the presence of the police, but he shook off that opinion, until the older man sent word to the police to move back. This reaffirmed that he was probably a little dirty, and did not like it when a State Police Captain replied to him an empathic "no!" It was apparent that 'battle lines' may have to be drawn before any rescue attempt could be launched.

As the older gentlemen entered the office at the mine entrance, which was now ordained the command post, a man was heard at the top of the hill saying, "that's all we need down here is that asshole! Why don't that sonofabitch stay in Philadelphia where he belongs?"

Shortly after the older man's arrival, another Chrysler drove up to the mine entrance. The two men who got out of this car were the ones that were following Abner earlier that day and were also the ones in the restaurant. When Matt glanced back toward Abner, he noticed he was gone. When he returned his gaze to the mine entrance, he found Abner standing next to him.

"This is starting to stink." Abner said. "And that white haired bastard just made things worse. He'll have a damn gunfight with the law, before this is all said and done."

"Is he the owner?" Matt asked.

"Yeah, kind of." Abner answered. "More like the guy who makes sure the owner gets his cut if you know what I mean."

"No." Matt replied. "Not really."

"Believe it or not, this place is owned by a company from Salerno, Italy." Abner explained as Matt looked at him confused. "No shit! That's what I wonder. What the hell is an Italian doing owning a mine in West Virginia. And those people you saw, they're not businessman either. They take turns making sure the one doesn't stick it to the other one. Rumor is they front out as an International Gem Stone Broker. Good luck finding a ruby down here. It's not the cave in that brought the old man down here though. Those thugs come first to make the way clear, then he comes in free as a bird. There must be trouble in paradise. If this turns into a media event, you won't see ol' Angelo Carelli here for very long."

"Why not?" Matt asked.

"They can't protect him down here." Abner explained. "He's not a well liked man. Very feared by those under his authority."

"If you don't mind my asking," Matt said. "how do you know these things?"

"Things," Abner smiled. "hell, I know him. I thought there was something going on when I saw those two thugs down here."

"Yeah, Abner, but those two thugs took an interest in you." Matt said. "Doesn't that concern you at all?"

"No. Not this time." Abner said. "We'll do this some other time, but for now we've got to get your Becky back."

Abner's answer took Matt aback slightly, but his concentration was broken by Becky's dad beginning to break down about losing Becky. For Mary's sake Matt attempted, as did Becky's mother to calm him down, but he was being overcome with his worse fears; that mountain had his Becky and it wasn't giving her up.

A man with some obvious vested authority came out into the parking lot where everyone was gathered, and made an announcement. "We're going to need this area clear for some heavy equipment to come in. We've gotten permission to use the school cafeteria as a meeting area. Why don't we all go on home and let's meet at the school at, say, eight o'clock. We'll have a better idea of what we got our hands on and where we're going from here. So, please, let's break it up and meet again at the school at eight."

"Come on," said Abner. "I'll help you get him home."

Although Matt was grateful for the help, he was a little taken back by the concern that Abner had for his Becky and her father. Abner was always a distant figure to him, and never one to volunteer any kind of compassion toward anyone. Matt got a sense that Abner was soon to become his new best friend.

23

Becky sat on the mine floor, mostly terrified, as she listened to more tectonic plates move across the ceiling. Occasionally, some gravel fell from cracks in the ceiling, and she noticed that dust was coming as well. This meant that there was no danger of water seeping into the mine from cracks in the ceiling.

She had begun to collect herself somewhat as she sat there. She was using her miner's light to see with, and knew that wouldn't last too much longer. The lights were out, probably from the sharp rock cutting the power. As she looked around, she kept telling herself not to panic. That this would all be over soon. They had people who found trapped miners for a living. They would find her. All she had to do was stay alive; any way she could. Her mind locked on Matt and all the things he used to kid her about. Like eating Zack's leg. Packing a lot of food in her lunch box in case she wanted to spend the night...or two. She remembered him telling her to build a fire on the down side of the wind. Not only would that keep her warm, it would carry the smoke downwind and someone else could possibly smell it, leading them to her. She remembered Matt telling her that a warm body could think better. Stay warm, and stay fed. Protein is the best.

As Becky looked around, she noticed there was a lot of burnable wood about. Some of it was splintered quite small enough to use for kindling. She remembered that Carla as well as Zack smoked, so she went foraging for a lighter. Carla was the most visible, buried only to the chin. Becky thought she would try to free her from the rock grave she was in and then bury her again.

She remembered that part of Matt's lecture on survival was that he put matches in the lid of her lunch box. Along with these were some aspirin and a spare emergency feminine article. That Matt thinks of everything, she thought to herself. She reached in the lid of her pail and found ten Ohio Blue tip matches.

"These bad boys will light anytime, anywhere!" Matt would always say. I hope he put a map in here for me to find my way home.

She switched her miners lamp off momentarily to see if there was any light coming through anyplace. After setting in total darkness for a few minutes, she was beginning to panic, and turned the light back on. She decided that she should busy herself with making a fire. It would be easier to wait for rescue with a fire.

As she walked through the mine, she noticed a shaft leading to the left that she hadn't noticed walking past. It appeared that the shaft behind her, as well as the shaft they were walking in the direction of, was blocked. Where this shaft from the left came from she didn't know. However, when she switched off her lamp again, she could see no light from that shaft either. She continued her search for firewood, and prompted herself to stay on task.

She looked at her watch to check the time, kind of an added comfort to her, she thought. But, when she did, she noticed the whole face of the watch was broken out. Well, so much for that, she thought. She stopped in her tracks and asked herself what day it was. After thinking a minute, she realized it was December 3rd. I've got to get my butt out of here, she mused to herself. I've got a lot of Christmas shopping to do.

Gathering enough wood to last her awhile she made a cozy little fire up against the shaft wall across from her and set down on the floor with her legs crossed thinking, her I am, come and get me. And then she began to think of Matt's litany of survival, and began to cry.

She called to mind a discussion she and Matt had one day out of the clear blue sky. She was trying to get some grasp on his past when they began talking about survival in the most unforgiving places. She remembered him saying that you simply could not afford to be emotional. Emotion was a crutch, not a stepping stone. You take the task in hand, no matter how large or how small, and you just do it. That meant your survival; emotions made you weak.

She stopped crying, took off her helmet, fluffed her hair and leaned back against the rock. Talk to me Matthew. Get me out of here. She closed her eyes and began to feel the warmth of the fire and it gave her some comfort against the inherent chill of the shafts fifty-six ambient degree temperature.

It didn't take long for the rats to come to her begging for food. Although Becky hated rats, she hated them near her worse. She remembered what Carla said about them on the day she gave them those pizza crusts, and dug into her lunch pail and skimmed off some bread crusts and tossed them their way. The rat's kind of looked at Becky, wiggled their noses so their whiskers shook and went off running down the darkened shaft. After giving some more bread crust to what appeared to be a pregnant female rat, she got comfortable and fell asleep.

24

The walk back to Becky's parents' house seemed to be one of the longest Matt had ever made. Her father was completely spent by the activities at the mine. Abner walked the whole way with them. He was between Matt and Becky's father with a guiding hand on his elbow. Matt couldn't quite grasp it, but he reminded himself that this is a different kind of grief. One which although the reality of death to a loved one weighed heavily in your mind, hope was still a factor to be reckoned with. Maybe a far off factor, but maybe the only factor. He was beginning to learn that at times such as these, people hang on to the smallest glimmers of hope. He didn't condemn it, because he didn't totally understand it. But he feared that before this was over, he too would cling to the smallest thread of hope for getting his Becky back.

When they arrived at the front steps of their home, Becky's mom said, "we'll be fine from here. I'll take him inside so he can get some rest. Thank you, Abner. Give my best to Dorothy. Matthew, we'll stay in touch. Family is all we have now. Family and strength in the Lord. I'll see you tonight at six. You might as well plan on supper."

Matt and Mary walked a few doors down to their own house and went inside. Matt felt that it was the worse homecoming he had ever had. There was no sunlight, no glow of a happy home. The place had the pallor of death. There was no happiness, only sadness and gloom. They were missing their sunshine; Becky.

Matt put Mary down for a nap, and when he kissed her on the cheek, she just stared emptily into space. It was as if she had a better grasp on the situation than Matt did. She didn't even take her bear with her. Matt covered her up and she closed her eyes.

Matt himself went in and lied down as well. He wasn't tired really, he was scared and mentally drained, because he hadn't as yet come to grips with what had just happened. As he lay there, his mind kept drifting in and out on the events of the day. He finally convinced himself that the only thing that mattered the most was how they were going to get Becky's' crew back. Nothing else really mattered. What if they couldn't get her back, he thought, then he fell off to sleep.

Matt began drifting back and forth to memories of Becky in his dreams. At times she was smiling and other times she was crying. He could clearly make out her face during one of his dreams and she was screaming his name with her arm stretched out. A series of wailing sirens interrupted him, waking him to find Mary lying next to him. He heard a knock on the door. It's was Becky's mother. It was time for the meeting.

Having got Mary up, Matt really didn't know what to do with her. Should he find a babysitter or take her. However, he thought, everyone would be at the meeting, so there was no place to take her. Matt decided that she had as much right to be there as anybody else, and got her in her coat.

The people going to the meeting reminded Matt of Mass on Easter, when those people were coming in late. A large mass of people moving toward the school and not a word was uttered between them. This was a definite stress situation waiting for a place to happen. Matt attempted to get a handle on it, but he had no idea where to start. He hadn't the experience or the expertise to even make an educated guess as to what was going on. He decided that he would just listen and learn all he could.

When they entered the school cafeteria there were chairs set up just as they are for the kids at lunch. Across the front of the room there was a row of tables with some of the brass setting there. Also seated there, to Matt's surprise were those two Italian goons. The Mine Supervisor, the one who gave all the orders earlier in the day, was seated in the middle of the group. The man looked spent. It looked like he had worked hard all day and got nothing accomplished. There was also a Federal and a State Mine Inspector there as well. When the Federal Man sat next to one of the Italian goons, the goon adjusted his coat and moved his chair a few inches away for him. He looked quite uncomfortable, and it was quite noticeable by the Fed setting next to him, who appeared to be quite amused by his nervousness.

The meeting came to order. The Mine Supervisor started out with introductions and then went right on with his limited amount of information. He went to a large map, and made circles in different colors. He went on to say where they thought the mine cave in occurred by making a circle, and where it stopped. He continued by saying that the only way he thought they could find survivors was to drill several two-inch holes into the open shafts and drop sound equipment and closed circuit T.V. cameras into them. They needed some form of idea where to begin digging and at the present time he had no idea. The calls throughout the shafts intercom system were not turning up anything, but they would keep trying.

To the best of his understanding, there was no rear entry into the shaft that Beck's crew were working. And he was also quite certain there would be sufficient oxygen down there, because of the ventilation system was up and running.

He advised the townspeople that he had devised five teams of five rescuers each to work around the clock. And hopefully by the time they made all their tests and calculations they would be ready to get a fix on them and get them out. He said that there was no electricity down there, according to the meters.

He made one last last circle on the map, suggesting that this is where he thought the miners were; on the back side of the cave in.

Before he opened up the meeting to the others or took questions, he said it was too early to speculate as to the health and well being of the crew. He did, however, have all the hope in the world and the faith in his rescue crew. He assured all the folks that he would not rest until all the crew was found, and he also said that the owners said they would spare no expense in getting the crew back safely. He also gave an update on the conditions of the miners that were injured.

The answers he gave to those who asked questions were very polite and professional. Abner was right, he did seem to know his business and had a deep concern for his people.

In closing the meeting, he asked everyone for their prayers and their patience. He then said we can all meet tomorrow at noon and we'll hopefully have something by then. Misses Colb is in charge of the Auxiliary if any of the families need anything. He concluded with saying that CNN and several other news agencies would be on the scene shortly. He reminded them they did not have to talk with these people if they didn't want too. If they became annoying, such as knocking on your door or parking in your yards, call the Police Chief, and he will take care of them. Until tomorrow then.

After the inspector finished that statement about the press, one of the Italian goons stood up and said, "if you have any trouble with the news weenies, call us and we'll take care of them."

That in turn prompted the Police Chief to stand interjecting, and say, "you stay out of this! We don't need your help around here."

Roy Huddler looked as serious as a small town constable could be in the mist of the company he was keeping. He stood about six foot tall, and was in good shape for a typical West Virginia, small town police chief. He wore a tan buckskin coat and a white Stetson hat. Under his coat he carried a Colt 45 automatic pistol. He was ready physically for any confrontation, but mentally, Matt thought, was a different story. Quite capable of keeping the peace, but not in enforcing it. Not at this level, that is.

As Matt rose, he noticed Abner standing in the back corner all alone. He stood there waiting for Matt and Mary.

"This is about the way these first meetings go." Abner said.

"Have you been in a lot of them?" Matt asked.

"My share, I suppose. We'll know more by morning." He said. "Let them work through the night and see if they don't come up with something. With those mine inspectors hanging around, they'll have someone to answer to, they won't be slacking with those two here. I wonder how long the Italians are going to stick around. That fat one sure is a nervous fellow, ain't he?"

As the three of them headed for the door, Matt turned around, while holding Mary's hand, and noticed Chief Huddler and the nervous Italian concluding a discussion, that appearing by the looks on both men's faces, did not go well.

"What do you make of that, Abner?" Matt asked.

"Oh, I shouldn't worry too much about Roy." Abner said. "He'll stand tall until it gets dangerous and he'll shoot that Wap in the back, and throw him in the holler some place. He can get all the help he needs. Mountain justice is a little different than what your used too."

As the two of them left the school Abner started the conversation.

"I would've hoped they had a little more information than that. The sensors must not have been recording any activity. Unless the wires got tore up. But they figure the electricity is off all over the mine. I'm just thinking out loud. Let's wait to see what tomorrow brings. Are you hungry?" Abner concluded.

"Yes, I am," Matt said, "I slept through supper."

"Let's go to the diner," Abner said, "it's meatloaf night. I can't stay too long though, it's duty night."

"What...is duty night?" Matt ventured to ask.

"I'm a married man, I have spousal responsibilities." Abner said with a grin.

"How can you screw at a time like this?" Matt asked.

"You've got to do what you're called to do, Mathew." Abner said. "I've got to keep my Dorothy happy."

25

As the three of them made their way up the hill to the diner, Mary became luggage instead of mobile and was soon in Matt's arms. When they entered the diner, Matt and Mary caught a lot of eyes. Well-wishers that Matt didn't even know came up to him and Mary and gave their support. Both in condolences as well as prayers.

The three of them were seated in a corner table and the waitress came and took their order for the meatloaf special. Mary took a glass of chocolate milk and a cookie. She was not the night owl Matt was, and was already ready for bed.

As the three of them waited for their order the usual buzz of conversation was at a normal level. The conversation being about the cave in and what was being done about it. A couple of rescue workers came in and filled their thermos' with coffee as they were preparing to go down in the mine. They were all given a bit of enthusiasm in their search for the night, and all were wished a blessed safe journey. As they left to go to the mine, the buzzing returned to normal, and all of a sudden it stopped.

Mathew was busy feasting on the meatloaf and when he noticed the quiet about the place, he looked up at Abner who was looking at him. Very cautiously, Matt looked over his shoulder only to see Zach's wife standing next to him. Matt stood up and got her a chair asking her if she was hungry. As she answered him that she was, Matthew introduced her to Abner. "Abner, this is Zach's wife...." said Matthew. "I'm sorry.... I don't know your name."

"Melissa." she answered. "My name's Melissa."

Motioning to the waitress, Matt ordered Melissa the meatloaf special and helped her with her chair.

"It's nice to meet you, Melissa," Abner returned. "if there is anything you need my wife, Dorothy is in charge of the auxiliary. She'll get you anything you need."

"Are you feeling better?" Matt asked.

"Yes, thanks. I didn't do too well this afternoon, did I?" She asked.

"It's understandable," said Abner. "none of us do at a time like that."

"Not to worry." Matt said. "Are the kids being cared for tonight?"

"I don't have any kids." Melissa said. "We never took time for them."

Breaking from the conversation, Melissa looked casually at Abner, and recalled the conversation her and her father had about Abner and Dorothy. Melissa knew who Abner and Dorothy were long before Abner knew her.

Matt looked at Melissa trying to figure out why she came here, and what made her tick. He felt sorry for her as he stared, not so much in pity, but in the fact, she was all alone in the world. If this turned out badly, what would happen to her? She appeared so petite and so breakable in a fragile sort of way. She was, however quite a refined lady, despite her wearing the same tattered dress she was wearing this afternoon at the mine. But that didn't make the girl, Matt reminded himself of in a disciplinary sort of way. She wasn't here to be judged, she was in the same shape as the rest of us, and we all had to stick together here. She had fair skin and looked maybe in her early thirties, with hazel eyes. She had shoulder length black hair and neatly manicured fingernails. She wore a modest wedding ring, and no other noticeable jewelry. She was in essence, very well kept.

As Abner talked with her, Matt saw a parental side to Abner that surprised him totally. It was like he was making up for lost time with his daughter. He and Melissa talked like they had been friends for years. Interestingly enough, Matt thought, she and Abner weren't talking about the cave in. They were deeply involved in a conversation about her parents. Melissa's parents moved to Washington a few years earlier when her father retired. He was a shift supervisor in the mine, and got a job in a plant there as a production foreman. But, to top things off, they just left on a ten day Alaskan cruise, and wouldn't be home until Christmas. Melissa said she had sent a telegram to the ship to advise them of the cave-in and tell them about Zack. She hadn't however, heard back from them.

As they talked, people came and went announced by the overhead bell over the door. The little ding caught everyone's attention. Pleasantries were exchanged and there was a steady hum of conversation all throughout the place. All was cordial and everyone came and wished their prayers for Matt's wife and Melissa's husband. All was normal until an abrupt hush came upon the place with the ding of the bell. As Matt and Abner looked up, they met the eyes of the two Italian thugs and the frail distinguished man with white hair. Matt couldn't help but notice Abner's expression when the older man came over to the table.

As Matt looked up at him, he noticed he was five foot, ten inches tall, and couldn't weigh more than one hundred and fifty pounds soaking wet. He was impeccably dressed and had deeply set, brown eyes. His hair was as white as an iceberg. He reminded you of a President who had the security of the Secret Service on his hip. For what Matt had been told about the man's skeletons in his closet, he appeared quite calm. He took his hands out of his pocket and came over to the table. He went to Abner's chair and while extending his hand said, "hello Mister Colb, it's good to see you again. It's been a long time."

Abner stood up, to the amazement of Matt, as a bodyguard got very close to them, and shook his hand saying in return, "yes it has, Mister Carelli. You look well."

"Thank you," he returned. "I'm doing good after that cancer treatment. But they tell me that is all behind me now. Did your son make it home from that Saudi Arabia mess?"

"Yes, he did." Abner returned. "Thanks for asking."

"Thank God, that war is a dirty business, how is your lovely wife"?

"She's well, I'll tell her you asked," replied Abner.

"Yes, please do that." The old man said.

"Let me introduce you to these fine folks," Abner went on. "This is Matt Jensen and Melissa Aiden. Melissa's husband and Matt's wife are trapped in the mine."

"I'm so sorry to hear that," the old man said. "I assure you that everything is being done to find those miners and return them home to their families. I will not rest until they are found. I will share no expense to find them. I think we have good people on the teams and I am confident that we will find them all, and they will return well, and very soon. If there is anything, I can do for you fine people, please don't hesitate to ask. Anything at all."

Matt and Melissa both replied thank you, as the old man and Abner once again shook hands. As the three of them left, the one fat Italian looked threateningly at Matt. Matt held his ground and just stared back at him. In his gut Matt knew that this was not the last time he would see this goon, but he did think the old man was pleasant.

As all eyes were fixed on the table where the four of them were setting, a low buzz of conversation soon returned, as did their conversation. Matt just set there and his mind again shifted to Becky. Melissa and Abner went back to the conversation of her parents. Beth brought the dinner orders to them and Mary began wolfing down her meatloaf. Melissa hit it pretty hard as well. Zack never entered the conversation.

"He doesn't seem too bad, Abner." Matt said. "The old man."

"He's fed more fish with men than you have with worms on a hook." Abner replied. "Pleasant yes, but you wouldn't want to make an enemy of him. Not of that man. He lives on borrowed time. That's the line of work he is in."

"What does he do for a living?" Melissa asked.

"He owns this mine for one thing." Abner answered. "And many other businesses, I'm sure."

"What does that have to do with fish." Asked Melissa.

"He is the kingpin of an American mafia family, whose family is based in Salerno, Italy." Abner answered. "Their favorite way of getting rid of enemies is cement shoes in the river. It leaves no trace."

"How would a man who owned a coal mine from Italy have enemies in West Virginia?" Melissa asked. "It's a shame what happened to his family."

With that Abner, Matt, and even Mary stopped eating.

"What are you talking about?" Asked Abner.

"His wife and two daughters," Melissa continued. "They died in a boating accident. They were sailing and the boat exploded. Some fuel leak, they said."

"How do you know this?" Abner asked.

"I was at the funeral," Melissa said, my mother used to babysit for his kids. It's funny, his lawyer babysitting for his kids."

"Your mother was a lawyer?" Abner asked. "His lawyer?"

"Yeah, she was a Corporate lawyer," Melissa said. "That's how I met him and his family."

"Really," Abner said. "What did his wife do?'

"She was a Psychiatrist." Returned Melissa. "Her name was Rhianna. Neat lady."

"Where did you guys live at this time?" Abner asked.

"Philadelphia. I'm originally from Philadelphia." Melissa said. We moved here after his wife and family died."

"What did your father do?" Abner continued.

"Not much." Melissa answered. "He worked for the Government. He was gone a lot. I think he was a spy, because he could speak so many languages."

"But you guys moved here from Philadelphia so your father could be a coal miner?" Abner said.

"Yeah. Sounds like bullshit, don't it?" Melissa answered quite to Abner's surprise.

As Matt sat at the table, eating his dinner and listening to the conversation, he couldn't help but believe that he was way out of their league as far as the conversation was concerned. And yet he was surprised as to the depth that Abner was involved in the conversation. The old man and Melissa definitely had a history even though the old man did not recognize her, but then why would he? She was the daughter of the lady who was his lawyer, and had a history with the old man.

"How long did your daddy work for the coal company?" Abner asked?

"I don't think he ever did, actually." Returned Melissa. "He was just kind of there, if you know what I mean. Three years probably. Then my mother got transferred back to Philadelphia, and my father decided to retire, so they just packed up and left. I was dating Zack at the time, so I just stayed behind and we were married in a quiet ceremony without parents."

"What were his children's names?" Abner asked.

"Alexandria and Rosario." Melissa answered.

With that answer, all parties had finished their supper, and Mary was dozing in her chair. Matt motioned for Beth to bring them their bill.

"What time are we meeting tomorrow, eight a m?" Matt asked. "I've got to get my little girl home to bed before she falls asleep on the tabletop."

Standing up and helping Mary with her coat, Abner and Melissa also rose and got ready to leave.

"You remember if there's anything you need, don't hesitate to call." Abner said. "See you at eight."

"Thank you, Abner." Melissa said, "I will."

As the three of them walked out the door, they all went the same direction.

Although Abner and Matt lived on the same street, Melissa lived in the opposite direction. That was somewhat strange, Matt thought as they walked. He also thought it strange for her father to have retired, for no older than he was. And why would a man who could speak several languages and traveled about the world, go to work in a coal mine? A lot of things were strange, Matt thought, but maybe it was because of the day's activities.

As they arrived at Abner's house, they bid him good night and went toward Matt's house. And right alongside Matt and Mary was Melissa. It was then Matt noticed that she didn't even have a coat.

A few doors from Matt's house, Melissa said, "I need a place to stay for a few days until they find our crew. I don't do well alone. I won't be a burden."

She didn't wait for Matt to give her an answer, she just held the storm door open for Matt to unlock the house and then walked in behind him.

With Mary being sound asleep, Matt took her into her bedroom and got her ready for bed.

"I'll be right back," Matt said, "make yourself at home."

Matt felt a little uncomfortable while getting Mary ready for bed with their new boarder. He couldn't throw her out, but it was very uncomfortable having Melissa in Becky's house. He did have a spare bedroom in the house, so it wasn't as if he had no place to put her. And how could someone as cultured as her not do well alone. He thought she would've wanted to be alone as much as he wanted to be.

He put Mary in her bed, put her bear in bed with her, and covered her up. She was already asleep when Matt kissed her good night. When he walked out in the other room, he found Melissa sound asleep on the couch, still dressed. Matt pulled her shoes off, and covered her up with a blanket, and then went to bed himself.

Matt had hoped to lay in bed and come up with a solution to this mess which had presented itself, but he was bombarded with all the events of the day. So many things didn't make sense to him, but the only priority he had was getting Becky back. Oh, how he missed her not being in his bed. If this was a prelude to the rest of his life, he was convinced he couldn't go through it. Not without his Becky. He rolled over and set the alarm and was fast asleep.

26

Becky awoke from a would be nap without any idea what time it was. The fire had burned down to an ember, and a few of the local rat population had come by to beg for supper. Becky got out some bread crusts from her lunch box and found a note from Matt. She gave the bread to the rats, and noticed one of them was pregnant. She peeled some meat off of her sandwich and fed her. She couldn't get over how docile these creatures were. She had always heard the worse about rats, but here was one in a motherly way, eating within three feet of her.

Becky got up and put some more wood on the fire. It immediately brightened things up to the point where she could see Carla's arm sticking up and decided to borrow her watch. It made her crazy not knowing what time it was.

The best Becky could figure, it was about ten p.m. They should have a plan up there by now, she thought to herself. She desperately wanted to get out of here. She went on another scavenger hunt to collect more wood. That was one thing very plentiful here in this shaft; wood and rats. She could stay warm and not get too lonesome.

After running her errands, she decided that she had to find a suitable place to do her business. She decided on the furthermost part of the shaft where the air flow would take it out. It was then she remembered Matt's note. Taking it from her pocket, she unfolded it and read it. It said, "have a great day honey, and we'll see you tonight. If worse comes to worse, stay close to Zack until I can come and get you. Stay warm, stay calm, stay alive. Loving you always, Matt."

She walked back toward the fire thinking to herself that she hoped it wouldn't come to that, but in her mind, she knew that it was possible. As she sat down at the fire, a rat in a motherly way came up to her, and standing on two hind legs, begged her for food. She smiled slightly and tore off a piece of bread crust and tossed it to the pesky little rat. Is this what it has come too, she thought to herself. Me, living with the rats. A guest in their home.

At times as she sat there in the shaft, she thought she could hear noises. But she remembered what Matt said about conserving her energy, and chose not to holler. She listened intently for the recognition of a voice. Although she was unsure of what the noise was, and still unfamiliar with the sounds a quiet mine shaft makes, it did give her hope that someone was indeed looking for her. Leaning against the wall while listening, she fell fast asleep.

27

Six am. came awfully early Matt thought as he rolled out of bed. He was immediately reminded of Becky and his new boarder. As he looked out the east window, he noticed that there was activity down at the mine. As he was about to open the bedroom door and go make some coffee, he remembered that Melissa was asleep on the couch and returned to the closet for a robe. As he looked out the window again, he realized that the activity he heard was only shift change. There was a parked ambulance down at the entry way in the event one was needed in a hurry. One of the problems that rescuers faced was injury to rock slides on small cave ins that would trap them without notice. Even though rescuers held themselves in higher esteem over the other miners, it was a dangerous business which forgave few mistakes.

Matt exited the bedroom in his morning attire and went about the business of making coffee. It was strange not to wake Becky, and have Mary on his coat tails, but the house was very quiet. He stuck his head around the corner of the kitchen to see Melissa still asleep on the couch, in nearly the same position he covered her up.

As Matt waited for the coffee to brew, he noticed there was very little activity on the streets this morning. Obviously, the mine would be closed today, and everyone would shift their attention to the eight o'clock meeting at the school cafeteria. School was also canceled due to the accident, so there wouldn't be any school buses running. There was the new arrival of a CNN news crew truck on hand, complete with one of those big dishes. Abner was right, he thought to himself, as the coffee finished perking. There will be people coming from everywhere in no time at all.

With the coffee pot filling the house with a pleasant aroma, Melissa was prompted to wake up and come out into the kitchen.

"Cream or sugar?" Matt asked.

"Both, please." Melissa answered in a half stupor. "And good morning."

"Are you hungry?" Matt asked his new guest.

"No. I'm not much of a breakfast person." She answered.

Matt's first thought was that as skinny you are, you're not much of a food person at all.

"I do need to borrow your car, though." She announced to Matt's surprise. "I've got to get out of this dress and take a shower. I'll be back in time for the morning meeting, okay? Do you need me to pick anything up for you at the store?"

"No, I'm good thanks." Matt replied.

As she stood up waiting for the car keys, Matt asked her if she needed a "to go" cup.

"Yeah, thanks. That would be nice." She answered. "I'll be right back. Are you always like this?"

"Like what?" Matt asked.

"I don't know," Melissa frowned. "Pleasantly easy, I guess."

As Matt handed her the car keys, he went and unlocked the back door which led to the driveway. This was strange, he thought. But for the most part, Melissa was quite pleasant. Well, I'm glad I could help her out for a night. We'll get things back to normal this morning after the meeting.

Going into the bedroom to wake Mary, he found her in the same position he put her in last night, and debated waking her. He decided against it, and got a refill on his brew and settled in to his lazyboy to drink his coffee in the dark. He could think here. Sort things out and come to grips with what had happened, and say a prayer for Becky and the rest of the crew. The longer Matt sat and thought about all the things that were going through his mind, he became very aware of one major point. He knew absolutely nothing about how he could help Becky. He knew he had trained some of those rescuers in the proper use of their equipment, and to take care of and protect themselves from gas clouds and breathing in an apparatus for an extended period of time. But how to get to someone if you didn't know where they were, he had no clue.

He began to realize very quickly that he had to put his total trust in the rescue team, and he did not like that a bit. Matt was now as he had been all of his adult life, trusting in himself and his God. He found it to be very difficult to let this one go, but he had no choice.

As he arose from his chair to get another cup of coffee, he heard Mary getting up and realized it was seven o'clock. It was time to get ready.

"Good morning, sunshine." He greeted Mary. "How did you sleep?"

Mary sleepily looked up at Matt and asked, "is mommy home yet?"

"No, baby, she's not." Replied Matt. "Maybe we'll know more today."

As Matt went to the cupboard to get Mary a bowl for her Fruit Loops, he noticed that there were several news crews now parked in the church parking lot. Just like Abner said, if it wasn't for the towns bad fortune, they would've never heard of this place. It looked like a story out of Isaac Asimov's book where all the dishes are pointed up at a satellite, awaiting an invasion of an alien nation, bent on the annihilation of the planet.

As Mary ate her Fruit Loops, Matt went into the bedroom to get dressed. Just then a car pulled into his driveway, and he remembered Melissa had taken his car to go and change her clothes. When Melissa came back, she knocked in an announcing rap, and came on in the house. When Matt looked out of the bedroom, he could see that she had a full packed suitcase, and was obviously planning on staying the duration. Oh boy, Matt thought, that's all I need.

"Man this town is dead this morning." Melissa began. "The news people are here, waiting to stir up a lot of crap on every little rumor they hear. Are you taking her to a babysitter?"

"No." Matt answered. "She goes with me."

"Do you think that is any place for a little kid?" Melissa countered.

"I would assume there will be other mothers there with their children, I should be no different." Matt returned. "Besides, we'll be hard pressed to find a babysitter this time of day. We're in this together, no matter the outcome."

When Mary finished her breakfast, Matt took her in to her bedroom to get dressed.

"I'm going to call my folks while you're doing that." Melissa said. "They'll want to know."

When Matt finished dressing Mary, he put on her coat and got ready for the drive to the school for the morning meeting. Melissa was still on the phone with her parents, explaining the events of the previous day. It was then Matt became aware that her parents were unaware of the accident, and the whereabouts of Zack. When Melissa hung up the phone with her parents, she handed Matt her coffee cup and said, "would you fill that up please? Thanks. I can only call them about once a month whether I need it or not."

"Was there a problem?" Matt asked.

"Not so much a problem, Melissa said. Everything is an issue. And there is no solution but for me to leave here immediately and come home. I would be much better off staying with them and watching the news on CNN, instead of being here in the middle of this mess. I need to come home immediately. But they aren't home themselves, they're in Miami. So, what would I go home to? And besides that, I'm trying to stay away from her the best I can."

"She probably loves you, that's all." Comforted Matt.

"No, she doesn't." Returned Melissa. "She wants to control me."

As they left the driveway to go to the school, Melissa continued to update Matt on the resulting conflict between Melissa and her parents. She went on to tell Matt that she really couldn't stand her parents, and the only reason she married Zack was to be free of them. When Matt asked about her love for Zack she said, "not yet, but maybe someday."

With that Matt thought to himself, as he pulled into the parking lot of the school, there ain't no way I'm going try to fix this at a time like this. This is not happening.

28

When the three of them walked into the school cafeteria and took a seat the mine inspector, the general foreman, and the search team leader were exchanging notes. Matt could see by the red lines on the paper that they were graphs they were exchanging information about.

Someone entered the room and Matt noticed it was Abner. He also noticed that his feet were wet. Abner came in and took a seat in the corner. The large Italian man took note as to where Abner was seated and nudged the other goon next to him. The old man with the white hair, that Matt was told was the owner, was not there.

The meeting was called to order by the rescue supervisor.

"Good morning everyone. To begin with, we have not found any of the crew as yet. We have drilled eight, two-inch holes into eight different shafts, which are illustrated on this map. In each hole there is lowered a closed-circuit video camera, with a microphone to pick any and all noises. With these devices we can look into the shafts as well as listen for voices or sounds of any kind in that shaft. These are our eyes and ears, if you will. Upon discovering where our crew is, then we can put together a plan to dig them out. This can be done by either going through the shaft itself, or through the top of the mine. Now we are going to continue drilling these holes today in this sector of the mine today. Today is the blue section of the mine. Yesterday we drilled in the red section of the mine. We drill down to the shaft and lower the equipment into the holes and listen all day to them. We've had no report of any seismic activity yesterday, so we believe that the plates have settled down. That should allow the crew to dig themselves out to an open shaft, or at least to one of the sensors to make contact with us. The video feed camera has a little red light on it so the miners could see it at a distance. So, as we are drilling new holes for the sensor's, we're hoping to gain some perspective where they might be by monitoring the other sensors. That's all I have right now. I'll turn it over to the chief and then I'll take any questions you might have. The Chief of Police."

"Good morning everyone. As you can see, the news crews are here. They have been informed and warned not to be a bother to you. If they approach you, you do not have to talk to them. If you want too, you can. Just be sure you are giving them factual information. If they hassle you for any reason, call the office. Be sure you identify what news service it was and we'll talk with them about it. You will probably recognize some of them from television. Any problem at all, let us know and we'll take care of it. Thanks."

Before the Police Chef could turn the meeting back to the rescue supervisor, one of the Italians stood up and said, "we don't want any of you talking to anybody. You've got no facts to give them any information about any way, so just stay in your homes and leave this business to us. The last thing we want is a bunch of rumors and lies being spread over the evening news. So, you don't talk to anybody, and if they bother you in any way, you come to us and we'll take care of them for you."

This statement prompted the Chief to stand up, obviously irritated by the evidence of his raised voice and said, "you stay the hell out of this towns business. You have no business in this towns affairs, and we certainly don't need your expertise around here!"

Out of the audience came a question. "What are you sons of bitches doing here anyhow?"

Several of the towns people raised their approval of the question with statements like, "yeah, go home where you belong. We don't need your kind around here. Why are you sitting up there with the rest of the rescue team? You couldn't rescue a pack of bubble gum. Why are you dago bastards following Abner all over town? And stay away from our front porch." That last statement came from a female, and raised the interest of many in the audience.

With that barrage of comments, the big Italian stood up as in defense of his presence. At that nearly half of the townspeople stood up as well.

Even Melissa stood as if she was ready for a brawl. The Chief quickly stood up and came to the front of the table to quell the uprising.

"Hold it, hold it! Calm down!" The Chief said. "This isn't why we're here. Let's just settle down! We got too much at stake here to argue at these meetings. Me and Mister: what's your name? Me and Mister Bratzi will talk after this meeting. There won't be any more trouble from our guests."

"I didn't invite those dago bastards they ain't no guest of mine." Someone else said.

"Alright, enough for now!" The Chief said. "We'll have a talk and we'll take care of this. I assure you. Now let's all sit back down and we'll get on with the meeting.

With that assurance everyone sat down and the meeting was allowed to go on Matt got a strange feeling in the pit of his stomach. These people seemed more concerned about the goons than they did about the trapped miners. Even Melissa was up in arms over them being here in town. Matt knew there were things he didn't understand, but he felt they were getting off the subject. What was it that the townspeople hated about the Italian presence? And this Bratzi goon. I've heard of him somewhere.

The Chief was able to bring the meeting back to order, and after a momentary pause the inspector asked, "does anyone have any questions?"

"Has anybody looked at the silt down at the mill?"

This question caused a lot of turned heads in the direction of the back of the hall, and caused a dead silence upon the room.

After a silence that felt like an hour, the mine inspector answered, "no, Mister Colb, we haven't looked down at the mill for anything. We've been a little pre-occupied up to now. Why do you ask?"

Matt was impressed by the way the mine inspector respected Abner's question. He didn't write him off as a lunatic. He sought for an answer and gave it.

"Because the silt is the answer where the cave in ended, and a strong possibility where the miners are." Abner answered with authority.

"How is that?" The rescue foreman asked.

"There are cedar scraps in the silt trap down at the mill." Abner related. "That tells me that there is a flow of water going to the mill. And the only part of that mine that had cedar support braces is where those miners were mining. The braces chipped and shredded and were washed downstream, and into the spring. The fact that water flows tells you what shaft is open. And you just opened that shaft the other day."

"Couldn't there be cedar scraps in other parts of the mine?" The foreman asked.

"No!" Abner answered emphatically. "Me and Ramon Garza put them in when they ran out of oak, before they went to steel I-beams."

"What does the silt have to do with anything?" The mine inspector asked.

"Nothing at all, "the fat Italian said. "Let's move on, I'm don't want to listen to this old bag of wind."

The mine inspector looked at the Italian like he had some authority, and said, "does anybody have anything else?"

"Yes!" Matt interjected. "We want to hear about what silt does, and means. And Abner looks like the only guy here who has an idea where the miners are at. So, I'd love to hear what he has to say, we might learn something. And since my wife is down there, I'd especially like to hear what he has to say."

"Do you think I want him teaching me anything?" The fat Italian said with a sneer.

"You would if you had brains enough to spit." Matt said.

With that the Italian stood up and glared at Matt in an intimidating manner. Matt also stood up saying, "take a good look, asshole. I don't want you to forget." Turning to the mine rescue foreman Matt said, "now, are you going to answer my question or not?"

"Mister Colb, could you explain to us what silt has to do with our situation?" The mine inspector asked.

"The silt washed out of the cracks of the coal. It was put there when the coal seam was formed millions of years ago. It's like a filler. When it washes away, the coal loses it adhesion. The silt is like a paste, it doesn't dissolve, it gets caught in the mill filter. It carries with it, the cedar scraps as it goes downstream. The silt tells us that the seams are breaking down, and the cedar tells us where. And with these plates moving, it wouldn't take much more to shake it all loose. The cedar isn't as strong as the oak, it was just available at the time." Abner explained to a very attentive crowd.

It was obvious to Matt and Abner, that the experts had no idea what to say. So, after a moment of silence, the quieter of the two Federal Mine

Inspectors spoke up and said, "at the end of this meeting would you show us on the map where that is?"

Before Abner had a chance to answer, the rescue foreman adjourned the meeting saying, "let's meet back at six tonight and we'll see where we are, shall we? We've got work to do. And we will look into this silt and cedar business also. Thanks folks, have a good afternoon."

As everyone got up to leave Matt looked over at the fat Italian, who did not return his glance, but went out the back door with the other goon.

"Thanks for your help." Abner said. "I still don't think they believe me."

"That's because they don't know what you're talking about. You'll have to show them." Matt answered.

"Watch out for that wap, he don't like you." Abner said as he walked up to the desk to show them where the cedar was placed some twenty years ago.

Collecting Mary, and Melissa, Matt walked out the door and headed home. Being very mindful of his surroundings, he glanced to see if the waps were around as he got into the car.

"Do really think that was smart to badmouth that grease ball?" Melissa asked.

"Just setting boundaries, my dear. Just like pissing on a bush." Matt said. "They live by intimidation. He's too fat to maneuver in a fight."

29

Matt thought that he found it very easy to talk to Melissa. He even called her "my dear." He would have to stay focused on the way he talked to her in front of Mary.

"Have you ever been to the mill?" Melissa asked?

"I've driven by it, why." Matt replied.

"I've been by it several times. Zack always thought it was a neat place." Melissa said. "If you want to drive over there, I'll show you where the filters are that Abner is talking about. It's kind of a romantic place, in a funny sort of way."

Matt took that in stride, and felt bad about the fact that for a short time, he had forgotten about Becky. That bothered him to the point of feeling guilty. He hadn't had time to sort out why Melissa decided to move in with he and Mary yet. But he wanted to keep his attention focused on Becky, but he feared Melissa was trying to pull him away, and his weakness was allowing her to pull him away. That scared him, the fact that he was becoming weak in the grips of another woman. It was as if she was a buffer for the inevitable, but he had to be strong for Mary. Even though she was only five, she knew what it meant if another woman came out of her mother's bedroom.

When they arrived at the mill, Matt turned to ask Mary if she would mind staying in the car, but she was sound asleep.

"That's probably better if she sleeps." Melissa said. "She'll be fine, we'll be able to keep an eye on her. Come on, I'll show you what Abner's talking about."

As the two of them walked down the short path to the base of the mill inlet, Melissa began shivering in the mid-winter early morning haze. She pointed to a section of the inlet that had a mud-like substance and a bunch of debris that resembled cedar chips.

"See what he's talking about?" Melissa asked Matt quite innocently. "That is the mud between the coal cracks, and that debris is the cedar support beams. This proves that the mine is open where the team was working. It all flows downstream to a spring and comes up about a quarter mile from here. Somehow, it's connected to a place called Sloma's shaft. I don't know where that is, but I know it's private property."

"And you find this place romantic?" Matt asked.

"Yes, Zack and I used to make love right here where we are. The rippling of the water was erotic, according to him. I think it smells like coal dust, honestly." Melissa said.

"Are you ready to go?" Matt asked.

"Sure. Are you hungry?" Melissa asked.

"No." Matt replied. "Are you?"

"I'm always hungry." Melissa returned. "We could go down to the church, I'm sure the lady's auxiliary has put a luncheon together. Let's check it out."

"Okay." Matt said as he turned the car out to the main road.

The drive home from the church was quiet. When Matt pulled into the driveway, Mary awoke in her car seat and told Matt that she was tired.

"Time for a nap, little girl?" Melissa asked.

"Bratzi," Matt said. "Does that name mean anything to you?"

"Not that I could put a finger on," Melissa answered. "But it kind of grinds on you, don't it? I do remember a show on A&E about the Mafia, and a young Luco Bratzi was mentioned as being one of Al Capone's enforcers."

"We're talking the thirties here, grandson, maybe?" Matt asked.

"It wouldn't surprise me any. They do call it 'the family', you know. You got the internet, right? We'll go in the house and 'google' that greasy bastard. They've got nothing on us." Melissa said as she giggled.

"Did you ever see a guy in a wheelchair driving a van?" Matt asked.

"No." Melissa answered. "You saw him here?"

"Yeah, two days after that dead miner was found." Matt said. "And guess who he was talking to?"

"Probably Abner." Melissa said to Matt's surprise.

"You're right! How would you know that?"

"Abner's about the only guy around here who knows anything about everything." Melissa sad. "And it wouldn't surprise me one iota if Abner knew who that miner was, and how he got there, and who put him there. More than that, it wouldn't surprise me if it was Abner! He is one strange ranger. Did you ever see Abner just looking? And you want to ask him, what the hell he's looking at. But there he is, looking off into the sunset, and you know he's not missing a thing. Well maybe a few screws. But for the most part, he's on top of things here. That's Abner. And one more thing about Abner, he knows it was you that pulled his scrawny ass kid out of that dessert with a bullet in his butt. He told my old man about it when you started coming into town to see miss Becky. He's got your number. That could be a good thing, however."

"Damn, no wonder he looks at me funny, sometimes." Matt said.

"Yep, that's probably it. He definitely has the nose for it, doesn't he" Melissa said laughingly. "Come on, let's take Mary and put her down for a nap and get on the computer. Let stir up some dirt on our Italian friends."

30

Becky awoke with a stir against the cold rock wall that was her new, sparsly furnished bedroom. Her first vision against the faint glow the embers of the fire gave her, was a rat standing on its hind legs looking back and forth as if trying to identify a presence. Becky could feel a slight vibration under her as she attempted to get on her feet. The cold rock mattress had left her stiff, as she attempted to get blood back in her joints. She put her hand back on the wall and could feel a humming sensation in her fingertips. This humming brought a scurry among the rat population as they ran for what could only have been cover against an invasion.

Becky thought that the rats could hear what she could only feel, and as the rats moved down the shaft, so did Becky. The farther she moved away from the cave in sight, the weaker the vibration got. As she went toward the rubble where her three friends were buried, the vibration was at its strongest. The pile of rocks stopped her investigation there. Then, it just stopped.

Trying to put all her experience together she began weighing what that was. She thought it was to uniform to be tectonic plates moving, and there were no bangs following it. As she began to walk toward the dark area of the shaft, the vibration started again. Then it came to her, that wasn't the sound of tectonic plates moving, it was a drill. But it was on the wrong side of the pile.

At this point she became very excited and started moving in circles, as if her rescuers would be coming through the wall at any minute. Becky remembered what Matt had told her about survival. Be patient, be calm, and don't waste your energy reserve. She paced for a minute, put more wood on the fire and decided Matt was right. She would set here, relax, and wait for them to drill another hole in her direction. Then they would drop down a phone line. She'd order a pizza and be out of here in time for supper at home.

As she stood there and felt the intensity of the vibrations, her hopes of being rescued soared. Her mind raced a mile a minute as to what she would do to give thanks to the Almighty for her blessing of being able to go home today. As her finger tips lost the vibrations, her hopes faded as well as the drill; it had stopped. Her first thought was they were moving the drill closer to her. But as time passed, they never returned. Using Carla's watch, she tried to make estimations as to how long it was between vibrations, but the time was passing to long for her benefit. It wasn't lunch time, and certainly not shift change. The best she could figure it was a little past four, but, she thought, a.m., or p.m.? She also noticed that as time went on the pesky little rats came back toward her, no longer interested in the humming noise, only if Becky had something to feed them. Did they know something she didn't? And wouldn't the rats be used to a vibrating environment? Unless this was a new vibration that they hadn't heard before.

As she stood there staring up at the ceiling, her hopes and excitement of being rescued and going home began to dim. She could feel herself slipping into despair. She called to mind what Matt had told her on the times when they walked and talked. He said when you lose hope, you lose your will. When that happens, you fill in the void with despair, and then you will find ways to die.

As she began pulling herself together again, she noticed that the pregnant rat was lying on the floor apparently in a bit of trouble. Instinctively, she walked over and bent down to help. The rat was panting as if very hot. But, she thought, how can you be hot down here? She went over to the small trickle of water running through the mine and took some in her hand and sprinkled it on the rat and then placed her hand on its head behind her ears. The cooling sensation appeared to relax the birthing mother, and she stopped panting. She put some water on her mouth as well, and the rat looked up at her and licked the water off its lips. The mothers abdomen began to move as if having contractions, and a few moments later the first of the little ones appeared head first from the mother.

Becky put some more cool water on the mothers head and in a joking fashion she said, "okay, who's the father? We'll have no derelict fathers in my shaft. There's a new sheriff in town. Man up, whoever you are."

My God in heaven, she thought, I'm talking to rats. Let me get this straight Lord. You brought me here because she needed a mid-wife, or should I say a mid-rat? Okay, that's cool. Job is done, I'm ready to go home. Matthew, she screamed. "Get me out of here!"

31

"**Y**ou are not going to believe this!" Melissa called out. "Look who I found? There's even a picture of him. Oh, I am good. C'mon, give it up. Put them hands together."

"I'll be dipped in shit," Matt said. "our very own resident mafia goon. How did you find this?"

"FBI files, I know their website password." Melissa answered as she held out her hand to be congratulated.

"Look at that. Luciano Bratzi, Investigated for extortion, money laundering, hijacking trucks in Philadelphia. Got a "no bill" from the Grand Jury in 2007, has not been a subject of interest since." Melissa read off the screen. "Must be the fixer for that white haired guy we saw in the diner. They have a tendency to put them out to pasture to keep things quiet when they get a little notice. They are legitimate businessmen you know. God fearing Christian men who are pillars of their community. Alter boys the whole lot of them. Who else do you want to see?"

"Mister Carrelli." Matt answered.

"Well I be darn." Melissa answered. "Angelo Carrelli in the flesh. Damn, I doubt if he ever served mass at Saint Anthony's. This is one bad mo' decker. Listen to this! Believed to have shot his father and mistress in a hunting cabin in Vermont, but could never be proven. Released to the custody of his mother, and lived with her until college. An honor graduate from M.I.T., with a degree in Physics and Fossil Fuels. Went to Salerno Italy to form the family business, there's that statement again, in strip and deep Coal shaft mining. The company was very successful, but after Angelo returned to the U.S., there were labor problems at the mine, and it was closed. Later that year the State took control to avoid a power failure. It goes on to say that Italy refused old Angelo access back into the country. There appears to be a question concerning some missing engineers, and the State owns it to this day."

"Then that kind of answers the question as to how an Italian knows anything about coal mining." Matt added. "So, is he considered legitimate, or is he a criminal?"

"I think he is what the FBI calls 'a person of interest.'" Melissa said. "There seems to be a little problem with, yep, you guessed it, loading dock crane operators at the coal docks in Cleveland, Ohio. Hey, your neck of the woods! It says, that there was some ugly union vandalism to good old Angi's home and office. It goes on to say that three of the crane operators, who also instigated the union disagreements failed to show up for work on Friday, and did not go home. Angello went to their homes to make amends, but, oh, you are not going to believe this, they were found dead in a boat on the Detroit river nearly two-hundred miles away, three days later. Tell me, does that Angi know how to cover his butt, or what? He is a smooth operator. I'm beginning to like this guy."

"So how is it he's here?" Matt asked.

"Elementary, my dear Matthew." Melissa went on. "It looks like The Greater Philadelphia Coal and Energy Company purchased our mountain in nineteen seventy- nine. And, I say, 'and', under the direct supervision of Angelo Carrelli, Chief Executive Officer, and Chairman of the Board. Man, this Angelo shits in some pretty high cotton, don't he? Definitely no slacker here. No wonder he has goons with him. Did you ever notice how well behaved they were when Angi was around? That big greaser could put old Angi in his coat pocket and no one would ever see him."

"I can't figure out how Angi, as you call him, knows Abner. They're not in exactly in the same social class, would you think?" Matt questioned.

"I got the impression Abner did something for Angelo once upon a time." Melissa surmised. "They looked like two foxes in a hen house, those two did." Which brings us back to the dead miner. You never know, maybe he used to work in Cleveland as well, and wasn't one for Michigan's fishing."

"You're bad girl." Matt said.

"No Matthew, I'm a realist." She returned. "I get the impression that good old Angelo has never done anything for nothing." Melissa went on. "And I doubt if he's ever forgotten those whom he helped and those who owe him for it. He's a lot like selling your soul to the devil. When he comes calling, you will deliver, or there will be hell to pay. No mention of family here, however. They may have been killed."

"What?" Matt blurted.

"That's the standard discipline plan in the Salerno Mobs." Melissa said.

"How do you know these things?" Matt quizzed.

"My father. He taught me a lot." Melissa said. "It's kind of a long story."

"I'll pour the coffee I don't want to miss any of this." Matt said as he rose from his chair and went to the kitchen.

As he was pouring the coffee, he began to think of how intellectually interesting this coal miner's wife really was. Obviously, she wasn't from around here. There was more to her than he had the intelligence to unfold. He hoped she would confide in him, so he was at least on the same page some of the time.

Melissa closed the lid on the laptop computer and took the coffee from Matt. She looked at Matt and with a fleeing gesture of her hands said, "my father was a spy. He was a CIA operative when I was born in Italy. Yes, Salerno. My father was a plant, an informant, in the Italian Mob. He looked exactly like Chas Palmary, the actor who portrayed a lawyer in the movie *Jade;* so, it was easy for him. And of course, the FBI didn't go to Italy. So good old dad gets into the "other" Salerno Mob, run by a guy named Zamboni, like the hockey machine.

So, one day, while setting around the table eating spaghetti, ol' Zamboni says he wants Angelo wacked. Well, that's not in my dad's game plan, because he's using Angelo's friendship to get next to Zamboni. So good old dad does the only Christian thing there is to do. He gives ol' Angelo the news and spills the beans on the plan to do him on the curve down by the sea, and then basically, put him in it.

So, Ol' Angelo, not being one who wouldn't show up for his own surprise party, leaves the office a little early. However, he's not in his car, he's in a gigantic front-end loader and meets Zamboni's men on the curve, and puts "them" in the sea. So now, old Zamboni is out three goons, his driver, and his new Mercedes. It is not a good day for the home team. So now, to add insult to injury, ol' Zamboni knows he's on borrowed time and tries to make amends with Angelo. But Angelo is no where to be found. So, Zamboni hides in his house under guard for nearly five years, and there is never any word on Angelo. About that time around the five years of hiding, rumors start to surface that Angelo, God rest his holy soul, has gone to the Father after a battle with prostate cancer. This spreads like wildfire. They even have a prayer service at the church for the salvation of his mortal soul. Flowers and the whole bit. Our dear friend Zamboni figures that this is God's work and has been delivered by the lamb of God himself, and all his sins are forgiven.

So, he goes on with the plans for his daughter's wedding, and a massive town party. And as luck would have it, the ceremony will be at Saint Antonius of Saint Leon Church. I say luck, because the church got struck by lightning once and burned down. Angelo paid to have it rebuilt. So, everybody looked on it as Angelo's church. So, having no enemies, because divine intervention took the only enemy Zamboni had, he goes all out. Rich man, poor man, peasant, lord, chimney sweep, moat cleaner, honey dipper, you name it, he invited them. Not a smart move on his part. My father would always laugh hysterically when he told this part of the story. Someone crawled into the back of a hollowed-out statue and shot old Zamboni right between the eyes. Justice was served, Salerno style. Three weeks later, Angelo showed up on our front port in Bethesda, Maryland. I set on his lap all afternoon.

He is how I ended up here, my father needed a place to lay low and Angelo was too eager to help. But he didn't recognize me at the diner, or at least I don't think he did."

"So, your father didn't have black lung?" Matt asked in passing.

"Hell no!" Melissa said. My father would never get his hands dirty, let alone his lungs. Hell, he showers after sex."

"How is it he looks like an Italian? You don't." Matt asked. "What's your maiden name?"

Melissa look at Matt and began laughing. "Johnson!"

"You are too much!" Matt said. "Alright, let's see if this adds up. We got your great uncle Angelo down here for a mine cave in, but he brings all his goons with him. I still don't understand why Angelo cares about a few trapped miners."

"Right," said Melissa. "But you're forgetting a very big piece of the puzzle here. Remember our dear old friend, the mysterious dead miner. And remember, Angelo was here before the mine collapsed. He has a heavy interest in that dead miner, and I doubt seriously if he was in his wedding party. And he's kind of partial to our old friend Abner as well. I think, my friend, there are pieces here of a very large puzzle, and nobody's talking. I think whatever it is they want, that Abner either has it or knows where it is. Abner couldn't be in a more precarious position if he was carrying a sign. No wonder he's edgy. My gut feeling; Angelo could really give a shit about four trapped West Virginia coal miners, he wants what Abner knows about the one they already found."

"But Dorothy doesn't seem to be any lost for wear." Added Matt.

"No, you're right, she doesn't. She may not have a clue. She will be worth watching in the days to come." Melissa said. "Let's get Mary up and around, the meeting is about to start. Afterward, let's go to the diner and act like a mouse and listen for some dirt. God, I love a mystery, and I guarantee that Angelo will give us one."

32

Becky woke from a brief nap, unaware that she was even sleepy enough to fall asleep. She immediately began to listen for drill noises, but heard nothing. Even the pesky little rats had left her side.

She got up from her makeshift bed and began to collect more firewood for the fire. She walked aimlessly around the shaft with a burning piece of wood, looking for escape routes as she went. All she noticed was a continuous wall of gray, unforgiving rock. Trying desperately to keep from sinking into despair, she remembered the words that Matt wrote her about staying alive until he could find her. But as she thought about Matt, she also thought about Mary and depression and loneliness began to overcome her. She tried the mine phone again, but that was dead still. She had hoped for a little technological relief by now, but it was obvious that wasn't going to happen. Looking at her watch she could best figure it was close to five p.m. She knew that the rescue miners would not stop until they found her or gave up hope. The best she could ascertain, she had only been down here approximately thirty hours.

She started to take an inventory of her food supplies. Even though she had the munchies, she chose to stay disciplined on her eating. After all she had a colony of rats to feed now as well. As she thought again about what Matt used to tell her about Zack's leg, she caught a glimpse of those three buried in the pile of rubble that Zack had thrown her clear of. But the more she looked the more alone she felt.

She didn't feel hungry at this time; however, she felt the beginning of cramps come over her. What a hell of a time to be on the rag, she thought. And old Matt, true to form, packed her extra granny rags.

She sat back down on the rock floor and quickly rose again thinking, all I do is set. I've got to find a way out of here and still conserve energy.

Becky grabbed up her burning stick again and began to go for a walk. The mine shaft was certainly a lonely desolate place, littered heavily with rusted remnants of miners who passed through here a long time ago. She came to a junction in the shaft where the shaft that had become her home, ended into a wall going in each direction. To the right of her the shaft had been filled in by the cave in. To the left looked like a long black hole where danger lurked behind the shadows of a darkened environment. Becky could feel a slight breeze blowing in her face, but was a little too cautious to explore any further. Turning on her miners' lamp for only a brief moment for a glance, all she could see was a long empty shaft with no lights and no debris laying along the walls. That told her that there hadn't been anyone down here for years. In a last attempt to muster up bravery she took a few more steps and, once again thought she felt the vibrations of a drill.

She stopped walking and began concentrating on the location of the vibration. As she turned around, she saw a few of the local rat population running away. Knowing she was searching in the right direction she placed her hands on the wall next to her. The vibration was so evident that it began to drop dust from the ceiling. As she held the wall and lowered her head as to not get dust in her eyes, she could actually hear the bit clanging in the wall.

Then again, it stopped. Granite, she thought, they must have hit a seam of granite. That drill could be twenty to fifty feet from her and she could hear and feel it if it hit a seam of granite. Becky stopped where she was and waited impatiently for the drilling to resume. She decided to look for something to pound with in the hopes of making a vibration of her own. A rusty old drill bit would be nice, she thought to herself, as she went on a scavenger hunt.

She noticed as she searched that the breeze was shifting back and forth across her neck. This she knew was caused by the mine breathing. But where, she thought, was the mouth that it was breathing through? She noticed again that the rats were looking up at the ceiling and not running. Those pesky little rats were certainly confusing, she thought as she began to feel another vibration. But this one was under her feet. It was coming through the floor. It was stronger than a drill bit, and began to think it was another tremor caused by a shifting plate. She cautiously stopped and got close to the wall to wait it out. Even the vibrations gave her hope that they would reveal a way out, a way home to Matt and Mary.

Becky thought it was getting a little colder in the mine, as she zipped up her hooded sweatshirt. She tried to recall what the date might be. She remembered that she had three weeks to shop for Christmas and this all happened on a Monday morning. She slept two sessions between meals. It must be Wednesday. She also thought to herself that they would probably search for a week and give up on us. She wondered how many miners were trapped besides her, and were they searching for more than just the four of them.

She sat down on the floor close to the wall and began thinking. We were on the other side of that pile when the mine collapsed. We turned and ran about two minutes before I saw that stream of water pouring out of the ceiling. The last thing I saw was Zack knocking me on my ass. We never made it to another level or to another shaft. We were still in the same header. They should know where we are. Matt is right, just set still and they'll find you. I sure wish I could find something to make some noise with, and was just a little more confident in Matts faith in rescue teams.

I wonder what happened to all that water, Becky thought. We were going up hill, that water should be flowing down hill, but the stream is trickling up hill. That damn plate must have sealed off the stream that was falling through the ceiling. But, what does that mean for me getting out of here? And why am I getting water coming from the back of the shaft. This is all messed up, or else I am. Could we have been going down into the mine deeper when it caved in, instead of on the way out? But everybody agreed as we took off running, we couldn't have been going the wrong way.

But in the long run, Becky thought, continuing to sort things out, it really doesn't matter which way we were going, except they will be looking for us four minutes up the shaft when I am indeed two minutes down the shaft. "Matthew, where the hell are you at?" Becky screamed.

33

Coming up the shaft one of the members on the rescue team stopped dead in his tracks, and turned around.

"Did you hear that"? He asked the team leader.

The team leader looked questionably at the rescue miner as if to ask; what? "I didn't hear anything. What did you hear?" He asked his partner.

"It sounded like a scream. Some woman hollering for her kids." He said.

"Could you tell from where?" The team leader asked.

"It sounded like over and behind us." He answered while turning and touching the wall. "Let's have a look at the map and make sure someone else isn't working this area."

"Come on man, it's shift change," another member said, "let's get topside."

"Go on if you want," the team member said. "I'm going to stand and listen a bit."

"Okay, I'm out of here," the anxious member said.

"No, you're not, "the leader barked. "We go together. Shut up and listen."

"Do you feel that breeze? It could have been carried on that." The team member said.

"Yeah, I feel it, but where the hell did it come from?" the leader said, "and I doubt if we're going to hear some mother hollering at her kid from where we are. What did it sound like?"

"It sounded like someone hollering 'Matthew'." The Member said.

"We have a Becky and a Carla down here." The fourth member said. "And Becky's husband's name is Matthew."

"Holy, shit!" The team leader said as he pulled out a blunt faced hammer and began pounding on the floor and the walls. "Mark this on the map coordinates and we'll come back to it later. Maybe we can drill over to the next shaft, there shouldn't be one under us."

The team stayed ever so quietly at that spot and listened intently for at least fifteen minutes. Then the team leader said it was time to move on. He then pulled out a can of orange spray paint and marked the spot on the floor and wall where the rescue member heard the voice.

"Dammit, I don't want to leave here." The leader said. "We've got to go. Anybody game for a double shift?"

The team began to leave and go topside ever so slowly as if expecting to scare up a voice from the darkness and being afraid to miss anything.

"Good ear, kid." the leader said. "Somebody better call the cart down."

34

Matt got Mary bundled up and the three of them piled into the car for the ride to the school cafeteria. As they wound their way through the streets of Hope, they could see the signs asking for prayers for the miners and several candle lit vigils surrounding signs. One place had a picture of Becky, Zack, Carla and Phil surrounded by candles asking for prayers and support. It was very touching, Matt thought, but wasn't something Mary should see. Maybe, he thought to himself, she's not the one who shouldn't see it, maybe it's me.

As they pulled into the school parking lot they were approached by several reporters with cameras. Before Matt got out of the car, the police moved them back to a roped in area, and gave them a stern warning.

"Hey, Matt, come on over here, we want to talk to you a little." One of the reporters said.

Matt just looked at him and smiling, waved his index finger in a negative manner and got Mary out of the car seat. As they entered the hallway to the cafeteria the saw the two goons standing by the cafeteria door.

"What's this asshole's name again?" Matt asked Melissa.

"Luciano." Melissa answered.

"That right. What's the other greaser's name?" Matt asked.

"Grease ball!" Melissa answered laughing.

When they arrived at the door, the goon and Matt met eyes in what was obviously going to be a test of the level of testosterone.

"Luciano, good to see you again." greeted Matt. "Where's Angelo?

Luciano looked at Matt with a look of surprise as his eyes just got bigger.

"Small world, isn't it?" Matt chided.

"Senior Bratzi." Melissa started. "Looks like your putting on a little weight down here with this good down home mountain cooking. You had better be careful, Angie will put you on a diet."

Having walked through the doors to find a seat, Melissa turned to Matt and said, "I think the other greaser likes me."

Matt had to bite his lip on that one, as all the people looked at those two as they came in and gave them hugs and condolences, promising them their support and their prayers.

Matt noticed another pow-wow back on the stage of the cafeteria between the mine supervisor, the federal mine inspector and a crew of rescue workers. They were pointing to a location on a map. Just then Matt's attention was taken away by a well wisher who volunteered their services to babysit if Matt needed a break. Matt courteously thanked them and reminded them for now they just have each other and they like to stay together.

While Matt was talking to her the team leader pointed to a location on the map indicating where they heard the noise. After crosschecking several coordinates, the mine supervisor said, "let's keep this between us for now. This is important and well worth an intensive follow up. But I don't want to stir things up and give false hopes until we're positive. But, good job. Did you mark it?"

"Yes," the leader said. "We were thinking of a double shift and going back down there while it's fresh in our heads."

"That's okay, but don't go down there unannounced, we've heard there were quakes in Chile today. This could get worse if we're not careful, so please, no lone ranger stuff. Good job, men, good job!" He said.

"How far do you think a voice will carry down there. We think we may have caught it on a breeze of air. You can feel air moving in several different directions?" The team leader asked.

"I would think with no acoustical absorption down there, quite a ways." The federal mine inspector said. "But I doubt if what you heard was an outside mother calling for her child. Are we monitoring those sensors regularly?"

"Not like we should." The mine supervisor said. "We need more manpower down here. Can you get us some people down here who know what they're listening to. One of our geniuses said he recorded two rats screwing yesterday."

"That's interesting." The federal man said.

"Why is that interesting?" The rescue supervisor said.

"Rats don't screw in the winter." He replied most knowledgeably.

The supervisor just looked up at the federal man, and shaking his head, rubbed his eyes and said, "let's get started, shall we?"

"All right, good evening everyone," the supervisor began. "We have made a chart of all the places we drilled today, and we are going to man the sensors continuously. As of yet, they have recorded nothing, but we are still going to drill and listen. We are moving through the area where we think the miners might be, or at least the path they would have taken to seek safety when the evacuation order was given. The rescue shanties are all empty, however the phone lines have been destroyed by the rock and debris brought about by the cave in. As a point of interest, the oceanographic and atmospheric experts have concluded that our cave in was caused by the earthquake in Ecuador. The bad part of that is that there was another one in Chile today close to the same magnitude. So, we are going to be monitoring those tremors very closely. President Obama has ordered all underground mining operations halted until mother earth settles down a bit.

Folks, we're getting absolutely nothing down there. Now that doesn't mean we're stopping, not by any means. What I'm trying to say, is that it is hard going down there, and we can't even lock onto a place to begin. So, when I tell you I have nothing for you, I'm not putting you off in limbo, I mean just that; I have nothing I can tell you. We are going to send the teams out again tonight and continue on with our grid search. We'll keep that up until we completely search the whole mountain and then we'll search it again. I'll see you again in the morning about nine o'clock. Hopefully we'll have something promising to tell you then. Any questions?"

"You haven't drilled a hole where the cedar beams are yet. Why not?" Asked Abner.

"I believe that was accomplished this morning, Mister Kolb." The inspector said.

"According to your chart, you are one shaft short of where the cedar beams are placed. And the water is still flowing and the silt has chips in it." Abner returned.

"Have you tested the water that runs out of the mine?" Matt asked.

The mine inspector looked at Matt and asked why?

"Because that water will carry trace elements of blood, bodily fluids and decaying tissue. It may tell you if you are in the right place and whether you have survivors."

The inspector turned around and looked at one of his assistants and nodded. The assistant rose and putting on his coat asked if Abner would accompany him.

The mine inspector looked at Matt and said, "we'll do that right now sir. That's all I have for tonight. The news crews are in town, so I'll turn this over to the Chief of Police for any questions you have for him. Thank you all."

"Call the Bratzi Brothers!" Melissa shouted out. "They'll clean out all trespassers. But if you see Anderson Cooper, he's mine!"

"Who the hell are the Bratzi Brothers?" Someone in the crowd said.

"I'm not believing you said that." Matt said.

"Believe it," said Melissa. "Have Bratzi. Will travel."

"Hey Abner, we were thinking of maybe having dinner together at the diner?" Said Matt. "Are you in?"

"Yeah that would be nice, unless you want to go over to the church," answered Abner. "There putting on a feed for the families. Of course, it's a Baptist church, but I don't think they'd mind if someone out of the flock stopped by. My Dorothy might have a go at you. Something to think about."

"There won't be anybody at the church we want to eavesdrop on." Said Melissa quietly. "We need to go to the diner."

"Yeah, we're thinking the diner. Melissa here's a Presbyterian, that won't work." Matt said.

"Oh my God, no! Saints preserve us!" Abner said. Alright, I'll take him to get the water sample and I'll meet you there."

As the three of them exchanged their goodbyes there was the usual banter of each others opinion as to how the meeting went.

"You know, if I wasn't expected to be there, I think I'd pass." Melissa began. "I don't think they'll be to many more of those meetings. They have no answers, or ideas. They haven't as much as a record of a chipmunk fart. Now, mind you, it's a big mine, but they should know exactly where they were at the time. Were they not monitoring the locations of the crews, and getting output reports on a regular basis? Oh, hey, swing by Rite-Aid for me, would you? I've got the lunar curse. You know what I'm saying? They should have had the slacker patrol keeping an eye on them all the time."

"I don't think there was any monitoring system in that seam. Becky told me they just got electricity on Tuesday," added Matt.

"Oh, great." Returned Melissa. "So, they weren't keeping track of them, after all. That figures. Okay, Matthew, I can do this all by myself, you needn't accompany me. How's that for grammar from a poor mountain girl?"

As Melissa left the car and went into the store Matt began to feel guilty about enjoying the time he was spending with Melissa. It was obvious he couldn't help it since she had become a boarder at his house, but he had the sense that he wasn't missing Becky because of Melissa. And yet, he thought, maybe that was a good thing. She as well, had to be hurting and lonely, why couldn't they both fill the void for each other without cluttering it with guilt or the luxuries lonely adults take with each other.

He knew, if he was honest with himself, that he was beginning to become attracted to Melissa, and that was something he could not allow himself to do. Although he liked Melissa's company, he loved his wife, and still clung to the hope that she would return to him. Melissa, in a sense kept him rational. He thought he may be in shock a little since this all happened, but he should be raising hell with the mining company to find his wife, and he wasn't. He was just going day to day depending on the skills of someone else to find her.

Melissa didn't seem to be in that bad of shape over Zack being missing. She sure looked a shade different since the day she passed out at the parking lot of the mine, and Matt felt like he was adopting the same attitude with Becky as well. He felt as if he was giving up on his wife's return for someone in the same shape as he was who was right here, right now. That wasn't him, and he had to find a way to fix it.

35

Abner and the assistant got into a company pickup truck and headed for the filters at the base of the creek coming out of the mine.

"Mister Colb," the assistant said. "Jeff Borg, he said extending his hand. Do you think the silt and the debris tell the story of where the miners are?"

"Yep! The answer is in the silt." Replied Abner. "Do you remember a few years back when that mine exploded from a buildup of methane gas. It's the same principal. The water washes out the silt and in this case the coal separated. In that methane case, the gas leaked in through the cracks until it got too low to rise against its own pressure. It was only a matter of time. Here, with nothing to hold it together, that earthquake shook it loose. But the cedar chips tell where the stream is, and that stream was formed by the cracks left by the cave in. There's no oak splinters and there isn't any rust in the filters."

"Well, they're going to drill in there tonight." Jeff said. "We should know something by morning."

Abner and Jeff arrived at the filter and Jeff collected his bottles for the water sample.

"You might even get some of this silt and send it to whoever you're going to send it to. This slop holds all kinds of secrets."

As Abner showed Jeff the ropes of silt and splinters, Jeff collected his water samples as well as a plastic zip lock bag of silt and splinters. As they were working and talking a car drove in the drive and parked behind Abner and Jeff.

When Jeff turned around, he was alarmed to see it was the Bratzi brothers. "Can I help you gentleman with something? We've got this wrapped up out here."

"Why don't you go on back to the office, kid." The goon said. "We want to have a talk with our friend here."

When Jeff turned to look at Abner to make sure that was all right with him, Abner looked like he saw a ghost. Jeff immediately knew this was no good.

"No, that won't be possible right now, me and Mister Colb have some errands to run after this. The mine inspector wants to see us both back together soon." Quivered Jeff.

"Get your ass out of here kid." Said Bratzi. "There's no need for you to get hurt."

"Who said anything about getting hurt?" Jeff stuttered.

"I did! Now beat it!" Hollered Bratzi.

Melissa exited the Rite Aid store and opened the car door. When she got in, she laid her parcel on the seat. Noticing its size, Matt said, "wow the economy size."

"Stick a cork in it, Matthew." Melissa said as she laughed.

As they pulled out of the drive and back onto the main road, Melissa commented about all the cars at the filter. When Matt looked over, he couldn't believe his eyes. "That's the greaser's car!" He said.

"Are you shitting me?" Melissa said. "I don't see how this could be good. Pull a u' ey'!"

Matt turned around in the gas station and headed for the filter pond. As they were approaching the drive, they could see both the goons were out of the car. One in Jeff's face and the other headed for Abner.

"Can you take these bastards?" Melissa screamed. "I don't think they're here collecting for the red cross. Shit! I don't have my gun!"

When Matt and Melissa pulled into the driveway, they got the attention of everyone there. And it appeared at first glance that they were Abner's new best friend.

"What's our story?" Asked Melissa.

"We're getting Abner for supper." Returned Matt. "We'll be right back Mary."

As the two of them got out of the car it was obvious that Jeff and Abner were besides themselves. Jeff walked right up to Matt like he was his best friend, patted him on the shoulder, and said, "we've got our samples and we're leaving now," and got into the truck.

"What do you want?" Bratzi asked Matt.

"Just came to pick up my old friend for supper." Matt answered. "Are you guys having supper at the church tonight?"

"What's a weaselly little prick like you care about where I eat?" Asked Bratzi as he took a step toward Matt.

As Matt took a step as well toward Bratzi he said, "I was worried about you getting something to eat. They're very particular where they feed the pigs in this neck of the woods."

"Well we better get to it." Abner interjected "Foods getting cold."

As Matt turned to walk back to the car Bratzi said, "we'll see each other again soon."

"Be looking forward to it Luciano." Matt said.

As he turned away, he looked at the other goon so as to size him up. He was heaver that Luciano, and wore his tie too tight. He had enormous upper body bulk, however mostly fat. He breathed heavily like he had heart trouble. Matt figured if he had to take both of them at the same time, he'd take this one first. The trick was not to let one of them get their hands on you. They could crush your whole body.

Matt, Abner and Melissa got back in the car and let Jeff leave first. His nervousness was still evident as he swerved in the driveway and stalled the truck. As they headed back to the main road, Matt looked to see which way the goons went. They headed out of town. Interesting, he thought, where were they going. He had calmed down from the altercation, although he had a lot of questions for Abner.

"I think it would be wise if we went to the church." Said Abner. "You know what they always say about safety in numbers.

"This might be to our advantage." Matt said. "Jeff will go right to the federal boys and tell them about this. That can only mean safety for Abner. Maybe they'll even leave."

"Maybe." Melissa said. "Or replaced with two more with more manners. Are you all right back there Abner?"

"Let's eat." Matt said. "This playing hard ass builds up an appetite."

"Have you a gun in the house, Matthew?" Melissa asked.

"Yes, why?" Asked Matt.

"No reason, really," replied Melissa. "Just a passing thought. Nothing to concern yourself with."

36

It was evident by the growing number of cars in the parking lot that a great deal of people had showed up for the evening. Many more candle lit vigils were being placed on the church grounds. Signs began to adorn the area with well-wishing prayer and support for the miners and their families. It was very impressive to Matt that a community would come together so well at a time like this. To Abner it appeared to be second nature. Melissa, just being Melissa, got out of the car and commented on how good the fried chicken smelled.

Matt collected Mary and as he walked to the church entrance, he cautiously took a look around the perimeter of the church much like a sentry would on guard duty. His instincts were once again taking over for he and his daughter. He knew that in his attempt to protect Abner, he would also put Mary in jeopardy. He felt the responsibility for both. For Mary it was obvious. For Abner, he had no idea.

When Matt arrived in the church, he immediately noticed that Abner and Dorothy were deeply involved in a conversation. Did Dorothy have any knowledge of the situation that Abner was in, or were they in it together? Matt put Mary down and they walked to the serving line for supper. Everyone made a fuss over Mary and wanted to hold her and kiss her. Mary just wanted to eat. As they took their place in line Matt saw people, he didn't remember seeing at the Thanksgiving church social or the July 4th town festival. And he wasn't sure if he was getting paranoid or not, but he thought they were all staring at him.

Getting their dinner, he and Mary sat down at a spot and Melissa came and sat down next to them. Matt thought that was only fair since they were sharing the same house, it would be rude for her to set somewhere else, despite the looks of the local womanhood present at the gathering. What is your problem, he said to himself? As he and Mary were eating, a lady came and sat down with them, expressing her deepest hope and prayers for the return of Becky. She asked Matt to introduce her to his sister.

"This is Melissa Aiden," Matt said. "Zack's wife."

"Oh, I'm so sorry, I don't think we've ever met." I'm Pastor Smiths wife, Denise.

"How do you do, I'm Melissa." She answered. "Very nice to meet you."

"I hope you know our prayers are out there for Zack as well." Denise said." Are the other two spouses here?"

"I don't think I ever met them," answered Matt. "Do you know them Melissa?"

"I hear they had left town to be with their families until this gets straightened out." Melissa answered "I don't know where their families live though. Where's Pastor Smith at, Denise?"

As they were eating their dinner and trying to sort out the Abner escapade, Pastor Smith came out and began a prayer service just as Matt had a chicken leg in his mouth.

"Jesus Christ," Melissa moaned. "Do you think I could finish my mashed potatoes first?"

"Just a quick prayer for our families and our miners and then we'll get back to eating." Pastor Smith began. In a moment he was finished and everyone seemed to be at peace with everyone else. All of a sudden Matt noticed that Becky's parents weren't here, and he didn't recall seeing them at the meeting either. Matt took out his cell phone and called them. He felt bad because he got all caught up with Abner and the Italians and he forgot all about them.

When Becky's mother answered the phone, she told Matt that she was sorry that she wasn't looking after his needs, but that Becky's father wasn't doing too well and she hadn't been out of the house with caring for him. Matt promised that he and Mary would stop and see if they needed anything in the morning. He bid them good night and then Mary talked to her grandmother and hung up the phone.

"Getting pulled a little thin, are we Mathew?" Melissa asked.

"Yes, without noticing." He answered.

"I think we both need the same thing." Melissa said. "Some sleep, some answers and some fun. When's the last time you really had fun?"

"The last time I saw Becky." Matt said. "Everything went to shit after that."

Matt and Melissa sat there and talked like old school friends with each other and with every well wisher that stopped by. The concern was very genuine and the love these people had for each other was unbelievable. It showed so easily and without measure. Complete strangers coming up and offering everything they had and in every way to help them get over this hard time. Matt looked at many of those people and knew they didn't have anything more than what they were wearing, but they would gladly share it with him, Mary and Melissa. He made a commitment that when this was all over, he was going to do more for these people. He would find the way and the means, but first he had to get his Becky back.

Melissa went and talked with Dorothy momentarily and asked her if she wanted her and Matt to take Abner home. She said she was going to keep Abner with her to help her clean up a little after the old fogy's finished playing cards.

She said good night to Dorothy and Abner and returned to the table to get Matt and Mary and head for the house. Matt was holding Mary who was already sound asleep in his arms, as he walked over to say good night to Abner and Dorothy before leaving.

"See you at the Nine o'clock meeting Abner?" Matt said. "Did Jeff say how long it would take to get those water samples back?"

"No, he didn't." Abner replied. "See you tomorrow folks. Thanks for the ride."

"Anytime." Melissa answered. "We country folks have to look out for one another nowadays."

As they left the church, Melissa helped him put Mary in her car seat.

"Swing by my house, would you, please?" Melissa asked. "I'm sorry to ask you to run me all over, but I have something there I need."

"Sure, no problem." Matt replied. "We country folks have to look out for one another nowadays."

"Do you think that was a bit much?" Melissa asked laughing. " You ain't heard nothin' yet. I'm just getting warmed up."

Matt turned into Melissa's driveway and waited while she went into the house. As he turned around to check on Mary, he noticed she was awake.

"I thought you were asleep, honey." Said Matt.

"Why did that church have mommy's picture outside by the trees?" Asked Mary.

"Well, they're all praying for her and the others, so putting a picture outside makes it more personal," replied Matt in a way that would maybe be easier for her to understand.

"Why don't you just go down and get her?" Mary asked.

"Well, I can't right now, honey," returned Matt. "There are people looking for her that do that. It's their job."

"Mommy said you taught those men how to find people." Mary said, in an innocent tone. "Why haven't they found mommy yet?"

"I don't know, honey." Matt whispered. "I don't know."

Matt turned around in his seat, somewhat at a loss for words. He really had no idea of the pain within Mary's heart over the loss of her mother, but by the conversation he could still tell she expected her mother to come back. Her only misunderstanding was when, and exactly where she was. He felt he needed to do more for Mary at this time. Like Becky's parents, he had somewhat abandoned Mary as well for the sake of Abner's well being, but Abner wasn't his problem, that's what they have police for. He needed to get his priorities straight, but he knew the events were set against his control. Mary was right, he probably could get Becky out of there if he had the first clue as to where she was. One person probably knew where she was; good old Abner. Maybe that was the reason he felt compelled to keep him alive.

He knew he needed to talk with Abner to get some straight answers about why these goons were so interested in a small mountain town resident. Interesting, Matt thought to himself, Melissa said her dad needed a place to hide once, maybe Abner did as well. It is amazing what you can hide down here if you put your mind to it. Maybe that's why Abner and Angelo are such close friends.

Matt's thoughts were interrupted by Melissa closing and locking her front door. She got in the car with what appeared to be a leather pouch type case.

"What have you got there kid?" Matt asked.

Melissa opened the case and produced a handgun saying, " sixteen shot, double action, nine millimeter, Baretta semi-automatic pistol. Never, I repeat, never leave home without one. Especially designed for those friends on the Mediterranean side of the world.

"Nice," commented Matt.

"My dad," returned Melissa.

"What?" Asked Matt.

"My dad. He gave it to me for a graduation present." Said Melissa. "What did you get for graduation?"

"Drafted!" Replied Matt.

"Genuine CIA issue weaponry. Untraceable." Melissa continued. "So, if you need to ice someone, this is the baby to do the job."

"I had a thought," began Matt, "and then I'm getting off this subject. Do you remember when you said you came here because your father needed a place to hide for awhile? Well, do you think Abner came here to hide?"

"No," answered Melissa. "I think Abner has always been here. But I do believe he was the go-to man if the owners needed anything. That's probably how he knows Angelo so well. And there has always been the dirty little secret about Abner's daughter who left town strangely in a rumored motherly way. And although the police haven't come straight out and accused Abner, I'll bet they're thinking Abner is a prime suspect in the case of that dead miner. He definitely has something they want, I just don't know how long we can protect him. I wish my dad were here, he could find Abner's daughter, and probably have a goon or two of his own stop in and vacation here awhile."

"How did Zack get along with your father?" Matt asked.

Melissa started laughing before she could answer the question. "Zack was scared to death of him. He thought my father was an exiled James Bond standing by at the ready to put chaos and mayhem on mankind for queen and country. And of course, my father ate that stuff up. He never let him think anything different. That crazy bastard!"

"Do you want to take a cruise through downtown?" Matt asked.

"Yes, of course," answered Melissa. "Let's go find us some greasers."

37

After taking a pass through the metropolis of Hope, they both decided that the town had rolled up the sidewalks and was closing up for the night. No signs of any Italians roaming about. They were heading home. As they passed Abner's house, they were just shutting off the lights and calling it a day themselves. It amazed Matt that things were so peaceful despite what was happening all around them. He asked Melissa's opinion on it.

"These are mountain people. They put their love in each other and their faith in their God. They've done it this way for years. And if for some reason it doesn't work, they get their rifles and meet on the street and discuss it in a different way." Melissa answered. "These people take care of their own and their God takes care of them. They're good people, but some think they're stupid and try to take advantage of them. Nothing could be farther from the truth. If something was to happen to the Bratzi's, the judge would probably bring the shovel, and the prosecutor would hold the light. Mountain justice has no red tape."

As they rounded the last corner before pulling into Matt's drive, he could see the police car parked down by the post office, in direct view of Abner's house. Jeff must have put the word out about the visit at the filter earlier this evening. That was good, Matt thought. Maybe we could all get some much needed rest.

Once at home, Matt inconspicuously checked the perimeter of his yard. He knew in his heart that he hadn't heard the last of the Bratzi brothers. He thought of how good of an idea it was to carry his own pistol. Taking Mary out of the car seat, he noticed she was sound asleep after a busy day.

"Do you need some help with her?" Melissa said.

"No, I'm good, thanks." Returned Matt

"I'll put us on some tea then after I get into my pajamas." Melissa said.

Matt tucked Mary in and went out to the living room and started a fire. His mind wandered as he thought of all the times, he and Becky would lie next to the fireplace and make love. All the talks they had, all the plans they made. The things they had together that made them so glad they had each other. This absence wasn't planned on, and it was beginning to hit Matt very hard now. Knowing that he was cold, could only mean Becky was probably cold. But she had a coat, he packed her plenty of food, and gave her a crash course in survival. As Matt stood there looking at the flames, he knew in his heart that his God would not take away the greatest gift He ever gave him. He knew Becky was still alive. And the longer she was gone, the more he knew he'd have to go get her. But how in the hell could he find her and where? Abner would know, Abner knew everything.

Matt sat down on the couch trapped by his thoughts and a rising despair and was soon fast asleep. Melissa came from her bedroom in her pajamas, and gave up on the tea idea. Putting a blanket on Matt, she herself crawled under the blanket and fell fast asleep next to Matt.

38

Becky was having a sleepless night, but one of hope as she listened to the drills endlessly pounding above her head. But none of them ever came through the ceiling. The dust and gravel would fall from the ceiling and a great deal was covering Zack. But why, she thought, were they not breaking through.

After listening intently to every attempt, she came to realize the reason why they couldn't drill through the ceiling. The very ceiling that was protecting her from the mountain from falling in, was also preventing anyone from getting to her. She was under a protective, tectonic plate of granite.

The drilling would stop for a while and then would resume a few feet away, only to stop there as well after only a few minutes. The rescue teams were using portable air drills, and were probably exhausting themselves quickly. They had to clear a path through the shaft, depending on how much debris there was in the shaft, and then bring their heavy drills into place and drill. It was tedious, tiring work. And without finding any evidence of life through the audio/visual equipment they put down the two-inch holes, they moved steadily through the mine.

As Becky and her little rat friends looked hopefully at the ceiling, the shaft started to vibrate again. It appeared to be like a tremor, coming and going in a timed succession. She knew that this would bring a halt to all drilling as the shift supervisor would call them out of the mine immediately. The last thing they needed was two rescue projects.

Becky returned to her little spot on the mine floor hoping against all hope that they would resume drilling again, but she knew that wasn't going to happen. Since they couldn't get through the shaft floor, they wouldn't return here again. They would write it off as 'cleared', and move on to the next part of the grid. Without their drilling in this area, she didn't have a hope of being rescued.

Her mind drifted off to Matt and wondered if he was coming, when was he coming and how was he going to find her when the rescue teams couldn't? She knew that the only chance she had now was to dig herself out, which she knew she would tire easily and didn't have the food to sustain her. If she did try to dig herself out, she would have to complete it within a day or two before she ran out of food, or lost her water supply.

She remembered all the times Matt would tell her to set tight, that they would find her. If not, then at least stay alive until he could find her. How, now, she thought, was he going to do that? Setting there for a few more minutes, she decided to give it another day and see what happened. She added wood to the fire and ate a half of a ham sandwich, and listened nervously to the tremors.

With the warmth of the fire and the filling meal, she soon fell asleep, amidst the movement of the mountain above her.

The rescue team came out of the mine in a hurry after the last shift of the plates. On member of the drill team said that the plate had literally sheared off his drill bit. The team left drills and all in the shaft and got out of there quickly.

They reported to the rescue supervisor the positions on the grid where they had drilled. After they were done briefing the supervisor, one of the rescue members said that they were not drilling into open shafts. And at times their drill bit struck an impenetrable rock shelf. At times the bit didn't go five feet. The mine supervisor looked angry for awhile and then relaxed a bit saying, "we may have to go back there. Show me once again exactly where you ran into the shelf."

After the rescue team leader showed him on the map, he said, "this is exactly where Abner thinks they might be. Is this the place where the bit wouldn't go through the plate? It does make sense really, if they were still in there and alive, this is one place where they could hide. There was electricity down there, but I'm not sure about the ventilation. I doubt if there any fans down there. Did you hear any water running?"

"It's too noisy to hear anything down there." One of the drillers said. "I don't understand what all this crap is about wood splinters in the water. What does that have to do with us, right now, right here?"

"Because the shaft that you are hopefully drilling into is the one where Abner says the cedar posts are at. Those are cedar splinters getting caught up in the filter. That means that the shaft is at least open to that section. Since there are splinters in the filter, that means we have a continuous flow of water. So according to Abner's calculations, that is the only standing shaft in this whole vein where they could be and survive. And unfortunately, it's the only vein we can't get into."

"How do we know they were mining in this area in the first place?" A driller asked.

"We know they were in that vein when the plates started shifting, because a call on the phone came from that area. I'm hoping they headed out to the opening when the plates started moving. We know they didn't get to far, because they were never sighted by the other teams. We got through the ceiling twenty feet before the cedar posts, because we have video of a rubble pile where the shaft caved in. I figure if they're in there at all, they are on the other side of that pile. That is what I hoped your video would've shown. But since you didn't get in there, we will have to come up with another way to get a video feed into that vein. Do you know how far that plate is?"

"We only drilled it about ten feet," one of the men said. "then after it sheared off the bit, we got the hell out of there. The damn ceiling moves. Call me delirious and send me home an idiot, I don't give a shit, I tell you that damn ceiling is moving!"

"I believe you." The foreman said. "We got a report of a sink hole behind the school. The ground looks like it was torn."

"Can we get in through there?" Someone asked. "Lower my skinny ass down from a crane. Maybe we can get into the shaft from there."

"I don't understand." The foreman said.

"If the ground tore, it might be because the shaft tore as well and left a gigantic hole where we can get in. If it did tear that deep, maybe the shaft is open and hasn't filled up with dirt. It might just be a back door. How deep do we have to go to get into this shaft with the cedar logs?"

"I figure three hundred and fifty feet, give or take a few. They're not so deep, it's just that we can't be sure where they are, if we did go through all those plates. I know we've got to try, but how long can they survive down there if they are alive? This drilling through plates, especially granite ones, is a drug out affair. The other problem is that if you went down that crack and it decided to seal, we'd be talking about you in the past tense. I'm very reluctant to send anyone down there until this mountain settles down."

"How much faith do you put in the Abner fellow?" The team leader asked. "I've heard nothing too stable about him since I moved here. There was talk at the diner last night that he probably killed that miner. They say he knocked up his daughter. And them damn Italians follow him everywhere. There's something very strange about that guy. What's your take on this?"

"I've always felt that Abner was a little too smart to mine coal. My daddy thought the same thing. But he was a hard worker, or should I say a smart worker.

My daddy said he never broke a sweat, but had just as much tonnage as anyone else. He got sick one day and never came into the mine after that. He had enough seniority to work topside. To answer your question, nobody knows those shafts or those veins like Abner. If he tells me there are miners stuck down there by the cedar supports, I figure he knows what he's talking about. I went to school with his daughter. For a hillbilly she was beautiful. It was sad when she left. Even worse when she didn't come back. Her and my sister were close. Why the Italians have a burr up their ass over him, I have no idea. But I will say this. If it comes between those waps and Abner, the Bratzi brothers are going down. I'm sure we have enough burial space down there for two more. So, yes, I trust Abner's advice. It is amazing how he knows so much about the water runoff and what's in it. He's a pretty smart feller."

"The mountain's moving again." The rescue leader said. "The seismograph is jumping right off the paper."

"Let's go outside and check it out," the supervisor said. "Did anybody smell gas or get a reading while you were down there? My God in heaven, you can feel the plates move through your boots. If this mountain doesn't settle down soon, we're all screwed. Jack, call your wife and see if anyone's having an earthquake somewhere."

39

Melissa woke Matt from a deep sleep.

"Wake up, there's trouble at Abner's." Melissa said.

Matt unlocked the front door and stepped out on the sidewalk. He noticed he was still dressed. In a few moments Melissa, in her pajama's and bathrobe was behind him and hiding her gun behind his back.

It appeared that the on-duty police officer and two deputies were talking to someone on Abner's porch. As they took a few steps down the walk, it became clear that they were the Bratzi brothers.

"What are they bothering him about at this hour?" Matt asked

"It's an old trick." Melissa said. "Keep them tired, on their toes and scared. But why involve Dorothy in this? This is too far, even for them."

As the two of them listened, the conversation began to heat up on Abner's porch. One deputy was heard saying, "you touch me, you go to jail! If you don't leave now, you go to jail! If you come back here ever again, you go to jail!"

A few moments later the Bratzi brothers turned to leave. Before Luciano got into his car, he stopped and glared at Matt and Melissa, giving some kind of hand signal.

"I'll be damned, Matthew." Melissa said. "We've just been challenged. Are you up for a good fight, you old city slicker?"

Before Matt could answer Melissa, the deputy hollered over to them that the show was over. "Everything is all right here. Go back to your homes and get some sleep."

Matt and Melissa turned and went back into the house.

"Better get your shooting iron son, it looks like war with the Bratzi's." Melissa said.

"I'd just as soon keep away from a shootout if I could." Matt returned. "I don't think the local constable would look to highly on a gunfight in his fair city. Besides, if I was Bratzi, and I wanted to get to me, I'd take my kid."

"So, are you saying you'd let it come to that, before you did anything about it?" Melissa asked.

"What are you getting at, Melissa?" Matt said in a most concerned way.

"I say, let's get the Bratzi's before they get us. Not here, but out of town. Bait them and take them for a ride. We could stick them in one of those empty house trailers by the river bottom." Melissa explained.

"You sound like you've given this a lot of thought." Matt said. "Do you really want to go this far this soon? They'll just send someone else if the Bratzi's don't come home."

"I'm sure there is room in those rusty trailers for more than one mobster. Besides, they took their battle to Dorothy on her doorstep, we are just a side item to them now. Something to spend an afternoon doing. It would be fun. And I know just how I would do it too." Melissa added.

"Why don't we let them come to us?" Matt asked.

"Because we'd probably get it in the back. These people are not honorable. You should know that. You used to deal with some unscrupulous people yourself. Did you ever care about the honor of those people you zeroed in on at a thousand yards half buried in a sand dune? Would they care if it was you on the other end of that bullet path? We're all the same here. The one advantage we have over the Bratzi's brothers is that we're not afraid of them. By the time they figure that out, it'll be too late. Then we can get back to finding your wife."

"What about your husband?" Matt returned.

"Becky will fight her way out, Zack won't. I doubt if Zack will ever come out of there alive. I knew that every time he went down there."

"Then why did you look so shocked when I saw you on the knoll at the mine entrance that day?" Matt asked.

"I always hoped I'd be wrong. It was like a premonition. I felt it in my bones." Melissa explained. "I tried to get him to stay home in the hopes that the feeling would pass, but he was hell bent on going to work. I hate these premonitions, they always have a way of coming true. I have one about us too. But first, we have work to do. I'm going to bed. See you in the morning."

Matt also headed to bed after checking on Mary. So much had happened today. And in sum, it wasn't a bad day, but it was sure full of surprises. As he thought of the events of the day, he recalled what Melissa had said about the premonition about him that she had. He certainly didn't want to go there right now. He could feel himself becoming attracted to her, but he refused to take his mind off Becky. He knew he was getting lonely, and Melissa was certainly attractive with a great sense of humor. At times he felt himself wanting more from her than just friendship, but he quickly expelled that from his mind. But every day it got a little harder. Because, he thought, every day Melissa got a little more fetching, a little freer, and a little more flirtatious. And deep inside his heart, he knew he was weak toward the sexual advances of her at this juncture of his life. In his heart, Melissa insinuated to him that his Becky was gone. Every day with her, lessened his hope of getting Becky back. Every day he felt she made him weaker. Maybe, he thought, maybe getting Becky home would be his salvation from all this.

He began to feel angry at his God for putting him into this situation, but he remembered it was also his God who promised to deliver him from all this. He rolled over in bed and closed his eyes. He didn't want to think anymore.

Tomorrow he would get his gun out of the foot locker. That Melissa is quite feisty, he thought. If I was a Bratzi, I'd be scared. He cleared his mind and was soon asleep.

40

The mountain settled after a few minutes. The workers who stood outside at the opening of the mine, and felt the plates move, all agreed that their time was very limited to find those four miners.

Jacks wife told him over the phone that there had been another earthquake in Chile. Early reports were it was not so bad, but very long in duration. She also said that President Obama issued a statement requesting that all mining operations in America are halted until these tremors stop. She also said there were other mine cave ins, but no one was in them at the time.

"I'm afraid this is going to get worse before it gets better." The mine supervisor said. "Let's call it a day here, men. Go on home, be with your families. What time is the meeting, eleven? See you tomorrow. Good job, everyone."

As Jack and his drilling partner, Ray, were walking to the car, Ray said to Jack, "it was weird when he asked if any of us smelled gas. I swear I smelled smoke."

Becky woke up after her nap and listened for the plates to be moving, but they were quiet. She noticed that the drillers had left as well. The fire needed stoked up a little and as she moved to get some more wood, she noticed that she was having cramps. Oh, I'll bet my dear Matthew even packed me some of those, knowing good and well I might need them some time soon.

As she got more wood from her pile she noticed that the rats were on a begging spree. Even though it was quite humorous to see them come up to her and stretch on their hind legs to stand taller, she noticed how skinny they were. Some of them had lost the shine to their fur, that the fire cast on them. They looked like they were starving.

Becky opened her lunch box, and although she noticed that her supplies were becoming limited by now, she broke off some bread crusts, and peeled some of an orange to feed all those who came calling. It always puzzled her why they never ate in front of her, but scurried away with the feast in their mouths and ran into the dark part of the shaft.

As she watched her dinner guest scurry off, she decided to take a walk and headed down the shaft. She felt very insecure the farther away from her fire that she got. She also noticed that she was stiff and sore, and didn't feel she had the strength she had a couple of days before. She did a few deep knee exercises to warm herself a little, and that seemed to help. Could I be getting that weak because I sit all the time, she thought to herself? She began to walk back and forth in the shaft, and the exercise felt good. Her mind was playing tricks on her as she was beginning to think that she had to stay strong in case she needed to aid in her own rescue. If there was even the slimmest possibility that she could find a way out of her timely grave, she needed all the strength she could muster.

Her mind began to wander to Matt and Mary. She began to become unbearably depressed, but thinking of them gave her a sense of hope. Albeit, maybe false hope, but hope nonetheless. She began thinking of what if they gave up the search, but her mind interjected her with rallies that Matt would come to her rescue in the end and bring her safely out of this tomb.

But then, reality re-entered the game and she thought, how in the hell is he ever going to get in here? If they can't find me how will he know where to look? But she knew in her heart that if Matt could get in this mine, that he would find her. She didn't know how he would find her, but she knew he would. With that reality fix, she continued on her short laps around her little corner of the world with a little less stress, and just thought of how she could make herself comfortable until somebody came for her. The sooner the better.

She went back to her spot on the floor and grabbed her miners light. She took it down the shaft with her, but found nothing in the way of escape. As she shinned it on the walls, she began to feel the unforgiving lifelessness of the cold gray-black walls which surrounded her. What a horrible place to die she thought, alone in the dark.

As she made her way back to the spot, she was visited by a few more pesky rats in need of a meal. She removed some more of an orange peel. The rats had seemed to find a taste for the peel. As she bent down to sit down, the bodies of her three friends made some gurgling sounds followed by the snapping of bones which were succumbing to the weight of the rocks which had claimed their lives. Becky looked fearfully at Zack's' leg, trying not to remember what Matt had said about it if she ever needed a meal.

She thought that she should bury all of Zack. His leg sticking out of the rubble was a terrible depressant, and that was the last thing she needed was another reminder of what may be awaiting her.

She put the notion of the burial behind her and went about the task of gathering more wood to get her through the night. Although she had no idea what time it was, she didn't want the fire to go out. She did notice however, that she had to go on a wood gathering hunt, as the supply of wood was starting to wane somewhat. She was more concerned about her dwindling food supply. She had plenty of water, but her food supply was becoming scarce, and she dreaded the alternative.

As she listened intently for more drilling, she couldn't keep her mind from wandering back to the thought of where did the rats take the food she gave them. They would pick it up in their mouth and run off into the dark area of the mine. She wondered how far back the shaft actually went, since she did not have the resources to see down the shaft.

After her wood gathering expedition, she sat back down at her spot and began thinking of Matt and Mary, and the day when he would come and take her home. She had noticed lately that if she kept positive thoughts, she could better fight off depression. If I only had Matthews deep faith, she thought to herself. Then I could will myself out of here and go home on my own.

As she relaxed after her wood hunt and her dinner, she closed her eyes, deep in her thoughts, and drifted off to sleep.

41

$\mathbf{M}$att, Melissa and Mary all woke at the same time. Matt was surprised to find Mary in bed with him. He was, however, very happy it wasn't Melissa. As Matt began making breakfast, Melissa reminded him that he needed to see his in-laws today. Meanwhile, she would mingle around town and pick up all the dope she could about Abner and the Bratzi brothers. During the morning's conversation, Melissa brought up a different scenario.

"Did you ever notice that although the Bratzi brothers are brothers, they don't look anything alike? That was never more noticeable as it was last night when the quiet one stood in the light of Abner's porch."

"What are you thinking?" Asked Matt.

"West German." Melissa returned. "Did you get a look at his cheekbones? They're high. Much higher, and deeper set than his brother. I knew there was something different about him, and all of a sudden last night it was obvious. I'll bet that's why he doesn't say much. His English is probably terrible."

"That is scary, you know." Said Matt. "Guess who else has high, deep set cheekbones?"

Melissa looked questionably at Matt, but did not offer a guess for a moment. Staring blindly out the window, she paused, looked toward Matt, and said, "shit!"

"The fog is starting to lift a little now." Said Matt. "But, still, what does that have to do with that dead miner? Unless of course he wasn't a miner after all. And maybe Abner wasn't one either. Maybe, just maybe, these two chaps found themselves after many years. Maybe they're a couple of spies who never came in from the cold, they just turned down the heat and went into hover mode. The fat one is carrying a grudge, if you ask me. And maybe he's just riding on the coat tails of Luciano. Luciano could be a bona-fide wap working for Angelo, in the coal mining business and the other one is on his own mission. That mission has to do with Abner. It always struck me as funny as to what would a couple of Italian gentleman who came into a coal mining town, before the cave-in, I might add, go and seek out Abner. But when that miner was found, that changed everything. They're not only seeking out Abner, they are dead on his ass. And the cops still don't know who that guy is. He must not be of interest to the U.S., otherwise the State Department would be all over the place like white on rice. Melissa, I think you've got something here. You know that one wap never says much. He just studies and sizes you up. He's a lot like Abner. Before this stuff started Abner never said anything either. He just stared at you with that nose of his like an eagle looking to sodomize a mouse. And, speaking of Angelo, where has he been all this week? You're right, girl, you've got some work to do today."

As the three of them sat down for breakfast, they were all kind of caught up in their own thoughts. Matt was first to break the silence. "What if that miner wasn't the father of Abner's daughters' baby? Maybe it was the quiet one? Or maybe the dead miner was one of the original partners? I heard they thought that he was killed after work hours. Something about he left work the day before, but didn't report for work in the morning, and was never seen again. Maybe he was the quiet one's partner and he's here to avenge his partner death, and it took him this long to find old Abner. Hell, Jason Bourne would never let that ride. There'd be hell to pay."

"My, what an active imagination you have, Matthew." Melissa said. "Besides, I think this is more on the line of the Maltese Falcon, or the early days of James Bond. These people are in a different league than Jason Bourne."

"Are they just as deadly?" Asked Matt.

"Yeah, kind of. They just go about it in a different way. And if they are, or should I say, were spies, they're unemployed now and have nothing but a vendetta to keep them going. It would surprise you how well these people can blend in. You wouldn't believe some of the stories my father told me about those Russian spies who were called back to Russia after the cold war ended. Most of them stayed here and just went into the woodwork.

Now they call them sleeper cells. It's very possible that Abner, the quiet one, and the dead miner were, at one time, a working team of spies. And what better place to hide than right here in the mountains. It also stands to reason as far as money is concerned. Abner doesn't have a pot to piss in. And if they were unemployed spies, they'd have to start from scratch finding a job. Maybe the quiet one works with Angelo, and has for years. Maybe Abner and Dorothy were partners. Why else would they go to his house with her there. They are a strange bunch of people, those Russians. And ironically enough, Abner and Dorothy do fit the mold. I'll see what I can find out today while you're next door. It'll be fun."

"Where would you go to look for that kind of information?" Matt asked.

"My father, the spy hunter." Melissa answered.

"How is it you think Abner and Dorothy fit a mold?" Matt asked. "They are different as night and day."

"A pair of Russian spies posing as husband wife are doing just that. They are posing. I doubt if those two are married, or ever have been." Returned Melissa. "Abner fits the mold because he is so intelligent. Those Russians didn't recruit idiots. I think Abner's problem is that he let these people here know how intelligent he was because they wouldn't listen to him. Needless to say, somehow his wisdom about that silt in the filter got some one's attention. And rightly so. What the hell would a hillbilly coal miner know about the flow of silt, uphill I might add, in boon dock West Virginia? He attracted someone's attention with his grandstanding, and they put the quiet one on a fast train to nowhere to find out the story. Dorothy on the other hand is just as smart as Abner, just a little lower on the level of excitability. She'll do a wonderful job on the church auxiliary, at the same time she'll be working on a way to get an American scientist over to the motherland. Did you ever notice how physically fit she is? She may not be active presently, but she damn sure hasn't put her camera away. Did you notice, she wasn't hiding behind Abner on the front porch last night either. I'm thinking she was in kick ass mode. That deputy didn't save Dorothy and Abner, he saved the Bratzi brothers."

"Are you telling me you got all this off the line of someone's cheek bones?" Asked Matt.

"Yeah, kind of." Replied Malissa. "All of a sudden, it makes a lot of sense. My father used to say that you can search for years, and then someday the damnest thing jumps out in front of you and explains the whole thing. All of a sudden, things are making sense. All right, you get to your in-laws, and I'll see you at the meeting today. I've got to go home and pay some bills. Bye Mary!"

With that Melissa grabbed her coat, her car keys, and her graduation present and was out the door. After cleaning up the kitchen, Matt grabbed Mary's coat and his, and was out the door as well. He dreaded going to Becky's parents house. Her dad was so depressed, Matt knew he would drag him down as well. Matt felt pretty lucky that he was, in his personal opinion, keeping it pretty well together lately. But he never felt comfortable with Becky's dad. He never knew what to say to him, and now he was hurting and needed a friend, and Matt wasn't sure how to do that for him. But he would go over there today and see what he could do. Who knows, he may be just what Matt needed to feel alive and hopeful again. After all, Becky had been gone a week already.

42

When the two partners walked out the door, Matt couldn't help but remark to Mary what a beautiful day it was. Mary said, "you need to get Mommy home Daddy so we can go Christmas shopping." As the two of them walked down the street they could hear Christmas music coming from the Methodist church. And all of a sudden, the loneliness hit him like a train. He felt so guilty about getting caught up with the Abner saga, that he hadn't taken time to feel bad about Becky. But he thought to himself, what can I do now? Worrying is not going to get me anywhere. And he still had a daughter to take care of. His mind began spinning as he looked out over the town.

It sure was peaceful out here today, he thought to himself. Who would ever think they had four lost miners in that mine. Were they losing hope of ever finding them again. There were more earthquakes last night in South America. That was bound to take its toll on going down there to search. That could be the whole problem, they weren't going far enough down. Matt understood the drilling, the drop cameras and audio equipment, but maybe the crew was lower down. Maybe when the cave in began they went down to get away from the rocks, hoping to find another way out. And why in the hell can't they get to the cedar supports? That made no sense at all. These are questions he would ask at today's meeting. He, as well as everyone else, was getting tired of the lack of information.

When they got to the steps of Becky's parents house they were met there by her mother. "Hello, you two, I haven't seen you in an age." Becky's mother said.

"Hi Mom, I brought you someone to play with." Matt replied.

"Well good." Becky's mom said. "I'm thinking about baking pies today, and I could sure use a hand. Ransom is in the other room."

As Matt walked into the other room he wondered where he ever got that name. They were religious, so maybe it meant the ransom Christ paid for our sins. That made a lot of sense.

"How are today, dad?" Matt asked.

"Not too good, Matthew." Ransom answered. "My Becky is still in that hole. When are you going to get her out of there? What in God's name are you waiting for, boy?"

"What am I waiting for? How the hell do you expect me to get her out?" Matt fired back. "That's what they got those damn rescue workers for. If they can't find her, how am I supposed to? You think I don't want her back? You think I'm just setting around with my thumb up my ass? If I knew where she was, I'd be the first sonofabitch down there. Do you think you're the only person who has lost the woman you love? Damn you dad for saying that!"

About that time Ruth stuck her head around the door and cleared her throat, reminding the two men that there was a little girl out here.

"Abner knows where she is." Ransom said.

"Abner don't know shit!" Exploded Matt. "About the only thing he knows is how to attract attention. I wouldn't get to close to him if I were you, you'll have those damn Italians on your front porch next. Then what the hell and I supposed to do?"

"Abner's coming over later after the noon meeting." Ransom said. "And then the three of us are going over to his house to talk."

"About what?" Asked Matt.

"All I'm asking is that you listen to him. Here what he has to say. What have we to lose? He's not asking much in return." Ransom said.

"In return for what?" Matt asked.

"Becky!" Ransom said.

"Becky? What the hell does he have to do with Becky?" Matt stormed. "She's in a hole in the middle of a goddamn mountain! How does Abner have anything to give us that'll help my Becky."

"He says he knows where she is and how to get her out." Ransom said.

"Horse shit! He tells me where she is and how to get her out, I'll kiss his ass in the court house square!" Matt hollered.

"He's the only chance we've got, Matthew." Ruth said entering the room from around the corner. "The only chance any of us have in getting our children back. I believe him. Just hear him out, please, that's all we ask."

"How would he know more than the rescue teams that are down there looking for her?" Matt asked. "He's no smarter than they are. He's got no crystal ball! I agree he has a good argument for the silt theory, but that still doesn't tell us where she is. I don't think anyone knows where she is."

"If he tells you where he thinks she is, and how to get to her, would you go?" Ruth asked.

"Yes, in a heartbeat! But what is this return business? Is he selling you this theory of his?"

"No, it has nothing to do with payment." Ransom said.

"Then what?" Matt returned.

Ransom looked at Ruth, who was wiping her hands on her apron, as she walked across the floor to be next to him. She sat down on the arm of the chair her husband was setting in. Looking Matt in the eyes she said, "let him tell you that when you talk this afternoon. It's not what you think. And please Matt, leave Zack's wife out of this."

"Why?" Matt asked. "She's harmless."

"Maybe! But her father asks too many questions." Ruth answered. "Questions that the answers to are a long time past."

"Maybe he should! We could all use some answers around here." Matt said.

"To these questions, there are no answers, Matthew." Ruth added. "Please leave Melissa out of this. I wish to God we didn't have to involve you, but I'm afraid it can't be helped. We'll talk after the meeting." Having said this, Ruth walked back out into the kitchen.

Matt looked over at Ransom, who appeared to be in a coma. He just stared straight ahead.

After the tension died down a little, Matt rose to leave saying, "Mary, honey, are you ready to go?"

"I thought she'd stay with me this afternoon." Ruth said. "You have a lot on your plate today."

"This should have never happened!" Ransom said to Matt's surprised. "We guarded against this. Who would've have ever thought?"

"Who'd ever thought what? Mine cave-ins happen?" Replied Matt.

"I'm not talking about the mine, Matthew." Ransom replied.

Matt walked to the door in a complete state of confusion and anger and left without even saying good bye. He would go home where he could sort out the very meaning of what just went on there. What, he thought to himself, was Ransom talking about? And how could Ruth be so calm about it? Was there something he didn't know? Obviously, these people were in a different league than he was. What was all this crap about Abner not asking much? And why not tell Melissa about the meeting? She was the only sane one around here. This was too much. This had to be a bad dream. How could Abner know where the crew was when the rescue team had no idea? This just didn't seem kosher in Matt's book.

What choice did he have, but to let it play out? In the end he had nothing to lose. If it led him to Becky, then it would all be worth it. But what a strange way to run a railroad.

43

Matt went to the rescue meeting at the school as he had done twice a day for a week. The meeting was called to order, but there was no news at all.

The mine inspector started the conversation the same as he always had: "we've been down to the lowest level of the mine where we think the miners could have been, but found nothing. He went through the ritual of running his finger, "swiftly" across the map showing where the drilling took place. Matt was close enough this time to see they had yet not penetrated the area of the cedar supports which were still plugging the silt filters. They had however, passed it. He also noticed that the Italian goons were not there either. Nor was Abner.

"What's the story where the cedar supports are?" Asked Matt. "It looks like you still haven't gotten in there yet."

"We haven't been able to drill through the tectonic plate that has come to rest over that spot as yet." The inspector answered quite wearily.

"So then, wouldn't it be feasible to drill a rescue shaft on this side of the plate and dig through the debris to get to them?" Matt asked. "Obviously there is still a lot of silt running through there and they are obviously protected by the plate. Doesn't that make sense to you?"

"It's quite a gamble, sir." The inspector said.

"So, what else do you have to spend your money on? What do have to lose?" Shouted Matt. "You've done no digging at all for two days. This is the only place they could be and be protected. It you can't go through it, go around it." Matt turned to the crowd and shouted, "what do you think, does that make sense or not?"

The crowd, quite to the support of Matt, joined right in and started giving their opinions.

"We've got a shaft drill and a yellow capsule over at Buckskin just waiting to get in there. What the hell are you waiting for? Get off your ass and drill some big holes for a change. Quit pussy footing around, for God sakes. Abner told you where they were, what the hell are you afraid of? Go down and get them!" Several miners chanted in.

"I say we find someone who knows what the hell they're doing!" Shouted Matt. "You sonsabitches are pissing us off!"

"We have to be patient, sir, for safety sake." The inspector said.

"Bullshit!" Matt retorted. "If you were worried about safety, this would have never happened. Those supports could have withstood a plate moving across them, if they weren't rotten. They are running out of food by now. If they're hurt, they are suffering worse as the days go by. You know as well as anyone what rocks do to bones. We're running out of time, and you have absolutely nothing to give us hope. You are as empty as your promises. Did you, sir, go home to your wife and kids last night?"

The mine inspector just stared blankly at Matt, somewhat lost for words. "Yes," he answered.

"There is a hole where my wife sleeps. That hole is in the bottom of that mine. You told us we could depend on you, and you have lied to us. You sing us an empty song every damned day. You are no stronger than the rotted timber that my wife's crew depended on for protection." Matt shouted. "Now you, sir, are hiding under those rotten supports! And your time is running out as well!"

Matt turned and walked out the door as the crown cheered and clapped for him. He was beyond himself. He had let himself become angry and that made him vulnerable. He remembered the words of his commanding officer when he went out on a mission. "remember.... you simply cannot afford to become emotional." He was beyond that now, and with that awareness, everything changed. And just then he recalled his conversation with the mine inspector when he said, "Abner told you where they were!" That's the same thing Ransom had just told him. How does Abner know where they are?

44

Matt left the meeting angry, frustrated, and becoming short of hope for the love of his life. He was, in fact, too angry to drive. He thought a walk would do him good and clear his head from the confusion of not only the meeting, but the things Ransom and Ruth had said earlier this afternoon. He would walk home and then go over to Abner's house to see what all this other business was about.

As Matt cut across the town through an alley, which took you over to the rear of the school, he noticed a figure he knew to be Abner. Matt having about fifty yards to catch up to Abner began to increase his gait to cut him off at the back of the building over by the dumpsters. As Matt was trotting through the alley, he caught a glimpse out of the corner of his eye of movement at those very dumpsters. It was the quiet Bratzi brother. As Matt continued gaining on Abner, he could see that the Italian thug was definitely going to ambush Abner at the dumpsters. Matt quickly got out of the line of sight of Bratzi and sped full speed to Abner, catching him at the end of the building.

Matt made a motion to Abner to be very quiet, and whispered to him that one of the Bratzi brothers was waiting for him at the end of the building by the dumpsters. He and Abner made a quick plan. Abner would walk close by the building and Matt would walk on the inside of him and one step ahead. Bratzi would most likely pounce on him there, using the dumpsters for cover. But when he jumped out, he would come in contact with Matt instead. That would even out the field a little better. What to do with the body was something they would deal with later.

About three feet from the corner of the building Matt caught up the one step with Abner and put his hand on his arm, while moving one step ahead of him. Just then Bratzi lunged out from behind the dumpster with a raised stiletto in his right hand. As he continued the downward plunge with the knife. Matt blocked the knife wielding arm with one quick move, and drove a fatal strike into Bratzi's throat with his right hand. It made a horrific crunching noise. Matt still held Bratzi's right arm against his body until the weight of Bratzi forced Matt to let him fall to the ground, dropping the knife alongside him.

Bratzi laid there clutching his throat in terror as he gasped for a breath that couldn't get through his fractured wind pipe. After further gasping and several convulsions Bratzi slumped to the pavement that he lay on. His eyes appearing to be in shock and confusing surprise.

Matt and Abner stood in momentary silence when Matt broke the silence saying, "let's throw his fat ass in the dumpster. If anyone ever does find him, they'll never figure out who did this. Give me his knife."

Taking Bratzi's knife from Abner, Matt wiped it off with his handkerchief and lifting the lid of the dumpster, threw it in.

"Okay Abner, let's put him where he belongs," Matt said as they made a few futile attempts to lift him. With several tries they got him in the dumpster and covered him with some trash from the school.

"Christ, that pork chop was heavy. Are you all right, Abner?" Matt asked.

"What did you just do?" Abner asked. "You done that like someone who has done that before. You saved my life. Why did you do that, you could have been hurt!"

"Ruth tells me you are going to tell me how to save Becky's life, I was just returning the favor, in advance."

"Dorothy!" Abner said. "If they came for me, they'll come for her. We must hurry!"

With the slamming of the dumpster lid the two men were off at a gallop to Abner's house.

45

Melissa had finished her chores and was heading back to Matt's house when she came behind a garbage truck. In an attempt to avoid any delays, she took a quick right down an alley and took another right at the next intersection. Soon she was in the alley behind Abner's house when she saw who appeared to be Luciano Bratzi sneak into the back door of Abner and Dorothy's house. Stopping her SUV by Abner's garage, she took off to the house at a dead run. She didn't bother knocking. However, when she entered the house, she was greeted by the thudding sound of Luciano's head hitting the sink. When she looked again, she saw Dorothy with Luciano's head in a death grip. With one quick twist, she broke his neck and he fell helplessly limp to the kitchen floor. Dorothy then defensively turned her attention to Melissa, who put up her hands and screamed, "no, wait!"

Dorothy relaxed her stance and said to Melissa, "my lands, what brings you here, dear?"

Melissa, who was trying to desperately regain her composure, and catch her breath, just looked wide eyed and fearful at Dorothy and said, "I saw him walk into your house and I thought I'd see if I could help."

"Well, that was nice of you dear," Dorothy said. "Well, what shall we do with him now?"

"Is he dead?" Melissa asked.

"Oh, most assuredly, I should think." Dorothy answered. "Oh, shoot, there goes the garbage truck. Where is my Abner when I have a chore for him?"

"Are you all right, Dorothy?" Asked Melissa. "He's so big, and you're so ...smallish. Are you sure you're all right?"

"Oh yes, my dear." Returned Dorothy as she went to the sink to wash her hands.

"I was just going to make a peach pie for the church support group dinner tonight, when I saw him sneaking across my back stoop. He should have known better than to come back here again."

"What do you mean by again?" Melissa asked.

"Some other time dear." Dorothy said. "We're going to have to find a place to dump him. Let's wait for dark, shall we, dear? Let's set a moment and have a nice hot cup of tea, shall we. Where is that man of mine?"

"I think there was an afternoon meeting." Melissa remembered. "Matt was going to go."

46

"**H**ere," Matt said as he held Abner his cell phone, " call your wife.

"How the hell do you use one of these damn things? Here, you do it," surrendered Abner.

Taking the phone from Abner, who gave him his home phone number, Matt dialed the number and was quite relieved when Dorothy answered.

"Hello? Yes, Matthew. Have you seen my man Abner?" she asked.

"Yes, Dorothy," Matt answered, "he's here with me. Is everything alright at your house?

"Oh yes, Matthew, everything is fine." Dorothy returned. "I had some company, but it's all fine here now."

"It wasn't one of the Bratzi brothers, was it?"

"Oh yes, that'll be fine Matthew." Dorothy said.

Matt suspecting something amiss, asked if Dorothy had company, she answered, "yes, that sweet little Melissa stopped over for tea, dear. Are you boys coming home soon?"

"Yes, we're on our way now. See you soon." Matt said as he hung up. "She had company from Bratzi," Matt said, "but by the sounds of it, he left.

"Yeah, right, this earth, maybe." Abner said soundly. "No way in hell is he getting out of her kitchen alive."

"We're talking about Dorothy here." Matt reminded Abner. "Your Dorothy, little frail Dorothy."

"There's nothing frail about my Dorothy, believe me. Let's get home!" Abner interjected.

The two men made their way across the schoolyard and down the alley. About ten minutes later they were walking up the back porch steps when

Melissa was running there to greet them. Her eyes told Matt the story. It was now only a matter of hearing it from Dorothy.

"Are you all right, honey?" Abner asked as he planted a juicy kiss on her.

"Oh, yes dear, I'm fine." Dorothy replied. "Kind of got the juices flowing again, if you know what I mean."

"I understand what you mean honey. We had a little excitement ourselves. It has been awhile, hasn't it? Tell me what happened." Said Abner.

"Well as I was telling Melissa here," Dorothy went on, "I was making a pie for the church support group, when I saw this 'bump' coming up to my door. Before I could get my Walther, he had forced himself right on in. So, we had the usual idle chit chat, you know, like what the hell are you doing in my house? He just gave me that shit eating grin of his and reached for my arm. I guess I didn't need my Walther after all honey."

"No, you certainly didn't honey." Replied Abner. "He must not have had any idea who you were, did he?"

"Wait a minute!" Interjected Matt. "Are you trying to tell us that you killed him?

He's three times your size Dorothy. And why would you have a Walther, may I see it?"

"No, you may not see it." Returned Dorothy excitingly. "And don't forget that you are a guest here young man. Don't make me turn you over my knee like a red headed stepchild!"

"I apologize, Dorothy," Matt returned, "but this just doesn't make sense. And what did you mean Abner about his obviously not knowing who she was?"

Abner and Dorothy looked at each other for a moment as to gain each other's permission, and then walked into the parlor for a discussion, excusing themselves.

47

"What happened down at the school?" Melissa asked. "Dorothy said you and Abner were down there doing something with the other Bratz."

"I came out of the meeting and saw Abner walking across the grounds to the back of school." Matt continued, "The other Bratzi, that one, pointing to the body on Dorothy's kitchen floor, dropped the other one off. I saw him walking along the trees toward the dumpster where Abner would come out. So, I caught up with Abner, and when we got to the dumpster, Bratzi came at him wielding a stiletto."

"Abner cleaned his clock, too?" Melissa asked?

"No", said Matt. "I was between them. I would've got the knife. I killed Bratzi.

We threw him in the dumpster, and came right here."

"Damn, this is getting good." Said Melissa. "I'm getting wet. I'm sure Dorothy did too when that lump of shit hit the floor. Man did she ever lay that fat bastard out. Damn!"

A few moments later Abner and Dorothy returned to the kitchen.

"Well, where should we take him, Matthew?" Abner asked.

"We?" Matt answered.

"Yes, we!" Abner said. "I helped you get rid of that other sonofabitch. You can help me get rid of this one."

"Sounds fair." Added Melissa.

Matt could only cast a gaze in Melissa direction before he was cut off again by her.

"Throw his fat ass in one of those trailers down the holler." Said Melissa.

"He might stink dear." Added Dorothy. "Let's take him to the landfill after our meeting at your in-laws tonight, Matt. His brother will be right along on garbage day."

"You guys sound like you've done this before." Said Matt.

"Well, Matt, we never had the luxury of a nearby land fill when we were younger." Dorothy said as she winked at Abner, and he began to blush. We made due with what we had. Don't believe what anybody tells you, Vodka is fattening! Thank God for Gorky Park."

"Dorothy, please don't be offended, but what the hell are you talking about, isn't Gorky Park in Moscow? Matt asked.

"Nothing gets past him." Dorothy said as she nudged Abner. "He reminds me of you years ago."

Abner just chuckled as he swatted Dorothy on the butt.

"Uhh!" she said. "That's nice!"

"Why don't I put on some tea, and we'll have ourselves a little talk." Dorothy suggested. "Melissa you might as well hear this too. When the men go talk, we'll go ditch Igor here. We're going to be great friends, now that we know we can trust you. You're not upset are you, dear?"

Melissa looked at Matt like a kid on Christmas. Full of anticipation for explanations she had been waiting years for. Her father had only ever told her bits and pieces of her neighbors and the senior citizens who lived here and called this place home. She adjusted her Beretta in her blue jean's waist band, and went to sit down in the parlor saying, "no, not at all."

Melissa had never been this far in Dorothy's house. It was quite decoratively furnished, she thought to herself as she looked around the room. There was art of Van Gogh and Monet. A lot of old German flair to the place and some nude art as well. Dorothy had kept quite a charismatic flair about. Not exactly what she would expect to find in a coal miner's home. One thing she had learned as a child, was that nothing in Hope was exactly as it seemed.

She walked into the dining room to find a highly polished table and six chairs around the dinner table, as well as a crystal chandelier hanging above it. She noticed a photograph of Abner and another man. The other man looked vaguely familiar. As Melissa stared at it, Dorothy entered the room.

"Abner's great day in his career." Dorothy said. "Leonid Brezhnev awarding him the Lenin Cross for Meritorious Service to the Motherland.

He was a little younger then and as you can see, he had more meat on his bones then also."

He's a Russian, isn't he, Melissa thought to herself. What is Abner doing with a Roosky, and in the motherland? "Excuse me, Dorothy," Melissa said, "I'm a little confused."

"That's understandable, dear." We'll make sense of it shortly, I assure you. Abner honey, are you two boys coming?"

As Dorothy placed the tea cups around the table, Melissa continued to look at the paintings and the memorabilia. There was no further artistic mention of Russia.

Abner took Matt's arm as they walked into the dining room saying, "we'll talk privately, later at Ransom's house. It's best if we don't talk about our arrangement in front of the lady."

We don't have an arrangement, you crazy bastard, Matt thought to himself. What's going on here?

Dorothy poured the tea into the cups as the guests took their places. Ironically,

Abner set at the head, then Dorothy at his right. Matt and Melissa sat side by side.

"Well, where should we start dear?" Dorothy said while looking anxiously at Abner.

"A table wide swearing to secrecy, I think would be a good place." Replied Abner.

"Is this one of those, you could tell us and then you'd have to kill us, scenarios?"

Melissa mused.

"Oh no dear, nothing that covert." Dorothy answered. "You watch too much television."

Matt sat there intently listening when a thought came to his mind. Where the hell would an old lady living in the mountains ever hear of and use the word 'covert'?

"I guess we should start out with our real names." Dorothy started.

This certainly put the conversation in a 'covert' mode, especially with this extremely large corpse still laying on the kitchen floor, next to the oven, where a peach pie was being prepared for the church social. A church where a great deal of 'love your neighbor' is preached. Something didn't add up. Now your real names aren't Abner and Dorothy? This, Matt thought to himself is a good time to shut up and listen. This could only get better, and he still wondered what this has to do with getting his Becky back. And what arrangement was Abner, or whatever his name was, had to do with him.

"Well, you see," started Dorothy, "my name isn't Dorothy. It's Anastasia Andronovich. And this handsome man is Yuri Chevronatski. Although we have been together for about 30 years, he is not my husband. We have lived together, quite faithfully, for a long time, and I might add, in sin. It's not a pre-requisite with the KGB to be married. Actually, it's frowned upon. We are both from Russia. Abner here is from Murmansk. You may have heard of it Matt, it's a major submarine base for the Russian navy. I'm from Sochi, a small fishing village off the coast of the Black sea. The winter- Olympics were there a couple years back.

We were recruited shortly after college, and we were introduced socially at the Moscow School of Scientific and Nuclear Studies. You guys call it Quantico. I was, or should I say am, an Economist who can speak five languages, and my beau here is a Doctor of Nuclear Physics. The safety protocol that the Russian government puts in their nuclear program was Abner's design. Unfortunately, it was not initiated in Chernobyl. We all know how that turned out, don't we?

After a little paperwork additions to our files, Abner had a diploma from MIT and I was the proud shinning Economist from Harvard School of Business. And after a little correspondence course as to who our friends and our professors were, we were on our way to saving the western world from the threat of Communism. It always amazed us how easy it was to get documents in this country.

So, there we are. Abner working at the Submarine Assembly Plant in Groton, Connecticut, in the Nuclear Research Propulsion Lab, and meek little me watch dogging major stock exchanges to keep them honest. How am I doing, honey? Did you want to break in here?"

"No, honey, you're doing fine." Replied Abner.

That statement struck a chord in Matt's head. The way he said it, the clarity of the words, and the confidence which he spoke, made it clear that Abner, or Yuri, was not the town idiot. That's how he knew about silt and cedar support timbers. That eagle beak facade was really a cover for a highly developed mind. He wondered how he missed the Bratzi brother at the school dumpster? Or did he?

"Did you catch any crooked stock brokers?" Melissa asked.

"Oh, my goodness yes!" Chuckled Dorothy. "You American's are as immoral as we are."

"Did you throw them in jail?" Melissa continued.

"Oh no, dear. They were much to valuable skimming off the profits."

"What did you do with them then?" Melissa queried.

"Well," Dorothy explained," when I saw what they were up to, I got a list of all the woman in the greater Groton area, and believe me there were a lot of them, who had children, rent, and no providing husband. So, I maneuvered the excess stock earnings to an anonymous donor, which I controlled, to these women who didn't have enough. It got so lucrative, I had to add the greater New Haven and Bridgeport area. It was my gift to humanity. Abner called me the Robin Hood of Groton. He even went as far as naming the anonymous donor as Sherwood Forestry Enterprises. Eventually I had to throw some Federal Agent a bone and report one or more, but I always kept what I needed for the ladies. Oh, by the way, did I mention there was an extra bonus on Christmas. Those were the good old days, weren't they honey? We felt so good about life and we were so much in love. We'd come home after work and have dinner. Then we'd take our Vodka in the living room and laugh about the business of the day. Then we'd make love well into the night. We were Russians living the American dream. It didn't get any better than that. And to add just a little for retirement, we put a great deal in our own Forestry fund as well."

"Do you still have it?" Melissa asked.

"Oh yes, dear," Dorothy said, but it's not too easily accessible right now."

"Tell me about the photo of Abner and Lenny?" Melissa inquired.

"While I was working at Groton," Abner began, "I was working on a reactor's ability to over perform itself without increased heat. I designed a way to put an additional twenty-six percent on a submarine's reactor drive train and not labor the system. That made the Typhoon Class submarine out of reach of American attack submarines. It merely outran the competition. To this day, I am told an American submarine cannot catch us on the open sea. I was awarded the nation's highest honor for bravery, believe it or not. But it ended my job there, and Dorothy and I were happy there."

"How did you end up here?" Melissa asked.

"Well dearie, your father was responsible for that." Dorothy answered. "There was this most vial of all men: Aldrich Avery. He worked for the CIA, and soon found a few spies who weren't too careful, and as we say in the business, and turned them. He made a whole network of double agents. He would use them to sell American secrets to the Soviets, and then have them pay him for the luxury of staying out of prison. He would sell anything secret to anybody. He sold East German military secrets to Israel. And Israeli secrets to Egypt. Then he would sell the countermeasures of defense to both of them. And when he wasn't busy, he was recruiting more young KGB agents and selling their identity to our enemies. Somehow that sleazy rodent found the whereabouts of two Nazi's and sold them to Israel, then sold an escape plan to the ODESA in Portugal. By the time the cat and mouse game ended, they were too old to bring to trial. They both died before they could hang.

But the worst thing that bastard did was sell the names of the Russian agents he had turned. Not all at once, mind you, just a few at a time. As he needed money for only God knows what, he would drop a few more names. So, in order for Moscow to get them back to the motherland, the KGB told them they were to be promoted for highest service to their countrymen. There would be celebrations, their families would be there, they would spend time with their wives. The highest recognition you could give a spy. When they arrived, they were executed in the tunnel leading to the KGB headquarters. Their wives and kids were never heard from again. Probably Siberia at a work camp. All because that bastard needed money to buy his wife something. We knew of him, we just never met him.

So, one day, Abner and I are setting on the front porch, sipping iced tea, wasn't it dear, when this pleasant young man walked up on the porch and introduced himself. We're living in Palo Alto now, because Abner is working at the Jet Propulsion Laboratory. Your father was the most pleasant person we had seen in a long time. And he has no problem telling us how proud he was to be an FBI agent assigned to Counter Intelligence.Well, this front porch relationship went on for years. We had Christmas dinners together, we were there when you were baptized, and we became very close friends. But we always wondered what was on his mind, if anything, in relationship to us. We didn't know if he was grooming us for the gas chamber, or if he just didn't know. We were careful. There were a couple of spies living down the street from us, and they came over for canasta on Tuesdays. When we were alone the subject never came up. The man, Alger, once asked Abner if he could supply him with some information on fission reaction. Abner just looked at him and said, "what the hell is that?" He never asked again, and they started to find other friends.

So, what happens, this Avery bastard learns of us and our whereabouts, from whom we don't have any idea. We really think the source is dead now because a chain of events ended abruptly when this guy, who worked with Abner at Groton, and asked way too many questions, jumped out in front of a truck. We were out for an evening stroll, and neither me nor Abner had the urge to jump in front of that truck, but he saw it as his sworn duty. Go figure.

So anyhow, one day this rodent came right to the house, alone, walks up on the porch and starts telling us we are going to give him all the information there is about nuclear fission and how it relates to submarine propulsion. And we are also going to put it in a portfolio, and in our native tongue. This guy's got balls of steel, right? So, not to be led down to the den of iniquity I tell him his best bet is to go to his broker and look through the stock portfolios and see if there is anything that looks good to him. It's all in our native tongue, English. Abner gives him a dumb look and he leaves. But this worm comes back, and he has pictures of all our personal history. He says, He'll be back in a week, and he is very good friends with Moscow. He'll expect some results by then, or they will be told. Abner would have killed him on the spot, but there was a little league baseball game at the park, and we didn't want to attract any attention. So, the weasel walked."

"Damn little league. But not for long," added Abner. "Go on honey, I forgot about all this. But I'll never forget the look on that maggot's face when you told him to go to a stock broker for a nuclear fission portfolio. I damn near soiled myself."

"You were a Nuclear Physicist and you had a gun, and knowledge of the martial arts?" Asked Melissa.

"Oh yes, it wasn't safe out there for a couple away from home and on their own in our line of work." Replied Abner. "You just never knew. You trusted no one except each other. We backed each other up. We took turns doing what had to be done. But as Dorothy will tell you, there came a time when we had to put our very freedom in one man's hands."

48

"**A**bner, you said that Bratzi didn't know who Dorothy was, what did you mean by that, and knowing what you know now, who were the Bratzis?"

"Sweepers," Answered Abner "I knew Angelo Carelli saw me at the mine that day they brought up that dead miner. I was all over the news."

"What does Carelli have to do with this?" Matt asked.

"He took over the interests for the Italian mob. He was our handler. He also is a defected KGB spy, but he's in it for the money" Abner explained. "Carelli doesn't care about the Motherland, only himself."

"Will we have to take care of him as well?" Matt asked.

"Yeah, sooner than later." Abner said solemnly. "He'll be back when his goons come up missing. We'll work something out then."

"Are there other ones here besides you and Dorothy?" Matt asked, now a little more confused.

"Yeah, but let's not get into that right now." Said Abner. "Secrecy must be maintained for now. As far as the Bratzis not knowing who Dorothy was, I figure they weren't told who she was, or what she was, by Carelli. They probably thought she was an everyday housewife."

"Did you see Bratzi coming around the dumpsters at the school?" Asked Matt.

"No, I didn't." replied Abner. "But I heard the car door shut and saw the other brother drive away. With it being a through street, I thought it was strange that he stopped. The dumpster was the most logical place for him to be."

"How would you have defended yourself against him, he's three times your size?"

Matt continued.

Abner made a smirking noise through his nose, and reached down into his outside pants leg. With one easy motion, he returned with a large switchblade and activated the blade, and said, "I never leave home without it."

Dorothy let out a chuckle and said, "my Abner could skewer Robin Hood with that thing."

"Damn," Melissa said in amazement. "So, tell us more about the person you put all your trust in. Did he help you or did he betray you?"

"Oh, he was a godsend, my dear." Replied Dorothy while looking at Abner for agreement to speak.

"That's a good way to put it, darling." Abner replied.

"So, one day, a lovely gentleman comes over to the yard," Dorothy begins, "while me and Abner were playing in the garden. And I do mean playing, my Abner had a fetish about making love in the middle of the squash patch. And, may I add, not necessarily in the dark."

"You're getting off the subject, my love." Abner interjected.

"Oh, sorry." Dorothy said as she collected her thoughts. "I still get all flustered when I think about those days, Abner. I tell you, my Abner, the leader in his field of nuclear physics, and with a green thumb to boot, was a walking erection. I'm sorry, I'm getting off the subject again. Anyway, we're out in the garden, you see, and this dashing FBI agent strolls up, obviously exhausted and extremely thirsty, and literally plops down on my garden bench, tosses his hat, and loosens his tie, and goes on to tell us about the most disgusting man in the Federal employ. What's worse, he is in his sector, and he is responsible for capturing him. He goes on to tell the story of how this man is exploiting Russian spies and infiltrating American interests and security systems and selling all the information to the highest bidder. Abner and I are looking at each other and thinking, this could work in our favor. So, I ask him, what does he look like? He says he has no idea, but he has been told he looks like a rat. Well Abner damn near gets whiplash looking at me, and I can tell he's thinking. So, we give the man another glass of lemonade and talked about an hour more, oh, that man could talk. We invited him over later that evening for a special cup of tea, making some lame excuse for the present time.

So now, Abner and I are alone, and I can tell his mind is going a mile a minute, and it's not about getting my skirt up in the squash patch, which is not to say, it wasn't a beautiful day for it!"

"Ahem!" Abner interrupted clearing his throat.

"Yes, right," Dorothy said coming back to reality, lightly shaking her head. "So, we concocted a quick plan that would work in our favor. We would give the FBI Aldrich Avery, and if necessary, down the road, they would give us asylum. And if the FBI double crossed us, which they were known to do at times, we would kill this wonderful young man, and move into hiding. Of course, you couldn't fault them for their lack of integrity, we were spies, you know. We weren't someone you would want to see teaching your children ethics class."

"And all this time, no one was none the wiser about you?" Matt asked.

"They didn't have a clue." Dorothy said. "We were good, hard working kids that went to worship on Sundays, and kept to ourselves. I don't think anybody even knew our names until that nosy neighbor called the cops one night when me and Abner were playing a little loud in the squash patch. I thought that cop was going to ask Abner for directions. He kept shinning his flashlight and cocking his head. The only thing he could say with those big eyes of his bugging out was, 'could you move it inside, please?' That was a classic. Oh yes, we moved it inside all right, didn't we dear?"

Dorothy took a minute away from the conversation to get everybody more tea.

When she returned and poured everyone another cup, she kissed Abner and said, "we definitely need to get that lump of shit out of my kitchen, my pie is nearly finished. God, those West German's are big. They nurse on the tit until they're sixteen, you know. Okay, where were we?"

Dorothy went on to tell of the events of that night, when that polite FBI agent came to the house for tea. "Before he arrived, he called, as a common courtesy, to see if they needed anything. Abner told him he was having a problem and maybe he should bring a few of his friends.

When they arrived, Abner filled them in on the problem we were having. I thought he was going to wet himself. His eyes got big, his trigger finger was twitching, and he had a hard time setting still, checking his watch every few minutes. We contrived a plan where we would set at the table, and even had a notebook for reference. The agents would position themselves in the other rooms well within earshot and gun range. It was a matter of moving the car down the road and waiting for our trap to spring.

As sure as clockwork that arrogant little rodent slithered up on our porch, and just opened up the door and walked in. He starts out with his usual banter of how he is feared throughout the intelligence community, and that he has sent more people to their executions and prison than anybody else in the network. So, if we wanted to stay on this side of the wall, we better have what he said he wanted. Well, not to let that sleazy bastard get one up on us, I asked him if he found the Stock Broker that he was hunting for to help him with his portfolio. Because we didn't care who he was, and what affiliation he had with the prison system, we are not brokers.

About that time, he had reached his limit. He scowled some form of foreign verbiage and stood up and raised a hand toward me. My Abner jumped up and smartly cracked him on the bridge of the nose with his Luger. Sexy little weapon, that Luger. About that time your father, Missy, came from out of the bedroom and arrested that smug rodent looking eel, and dragged him away. I hear they will be piping sunshine into him for the rest of his life. Your father, God bless him was so excited that he made section chief over this, it took him a few years to figure out who we actually were. But one day he did figure it out and came knocking on our door.

When he did, he didn't come in threatening us with forever in some moldy pit on that dreadful California island, he merely said, 'let's talk.' He just said that there were several of us in the area who had worked for the Motherland, and he had offered them all the same deal. We promised to quit spying, and he would relocate us in a nice little cozy country town and would protect us from those who would harm us. And that is how we ended up here. The poverty issue is a front, or at least it was for awhile, but that is a story for another day. Matthew, you and my Abner will talk about that later. Okay, --- I say we get this road kill out of my kitchen. Abner, if you bring your pickup truck to the back stoop, we'll all take a hold of him and put him in it. Me and Melissa here will deposit him after dark. Melissa, do you think we should mix up a batch of whipped cream for the pie, dearie?"

"I'd like a piece of that pie too, dear." Abner said as he swatted Dorothy playfully on the butt.

"You' re going to get more pie than you will be able to handle after the meeting tonight." Dorothy answered. "And, yes, I'll save some whipped cream."

Melissa looked at Matt and kind of grinned as if she got an erotic idea. Matt tried not to let his eyes meet with Melissa's, but it was too late, she had caught him looking. Melissa definitely had that look in her eye.

"Dorothy." Matt began, "whatever became of your daughter, if it's not too painful to ask."

"Oh no," Dorothy replied. "she lives in a quaint little house in Maine, by the ocean. Alone, I'm told."

"Why? Was she pregnant like the rumors?" Matt added.

"Oh, no." Dorothy said. "The Kremlin launched a project to recruit our children for operatives in the sixty's. We wanted no part of that, so we concocted a story that she got pregnant after a football game and we sent her away. I guess a lot of people around here do that, so there was no question. Of course, the hounds were sniffing her tail, or should I say trail for years. They finally gave up. But we don't have the means to get her back here or support any family, if she has any. But we can work that out after you men talk tonight also."

Abner brought the truck around and they loaded the last of the Bratzi brothers in the back of it for his final resting place. Obviously, the location was not disclosed. As Matt flipped the tailgate into place, he wondered if there would be more of them to come. He also knew that someday soon, they would have to deal with Angelo Carelli. He hoped they would all go away, but in his heart he knew better. He had hoped he could quit fighting, once and for all. But he feared there would be more to come before this was all over with. He turned and looked at Abner saying, "let's get over to Ransom's house and see what this is all about."

He and Abner said goodbye to the girls and headed down the street.

49

$\mathbf{B}$ecky woke up in the late afternoon, without any idea what time it was or what day it was. The longer she tried to figure it out the lonelier she became, and with the loneliness came the hunger. With that came the ever increasing voice in her mind of Matt telling her to stay close to Zack. You can't think if you're hungry. Stay fed any way you could until I find you. But that was about the only option she had left. She put wood on the fire in the hopes of increasing her core temperature. The cold rock floor had caused her discomfort in her hips, and it was becoming very difficult to get comfortable in any position. Putting all these maladies she was experiencing together just made things worse.

The crackling fire made her feel somewhat better as she was getting a little warmer, however, she couldn't get her mind off of Zack. She reached into her pocket and pulled out her pocket knife and opened the blade. She looked at Zack, and contemplated how she would do it. How would she prepare something like raw flesh, if she indeed went in that direction.

Remembering the graphic and upsetting movie she and Matt watched about the soccer team in the Andie's, she surmised that she would cut strips of meat, like thick bacon and dangle it over the fire long enough to make it edible. She began to get nauseous the longer she thought about it, but at the same time her stomach was growling again, and she was becoming noticeably weaker. She could no longer hop up from a setting position, she had to roll over to her knees like an old lady trying to get out of the bathtub. 'This was not good', she thought. She folded her knife closed and put it back in her pocket.

As she looked into the fire, the reminder of her hunger returned with a vengeance, as did her fear and depression. As she sat, leaning against the cool, lifeless, gray rock, the mother rat came over for a visit, and jumped up on her leg. She sat there for a few minutes and then turned and scampered away. "I don't have anything for you today." Becky said aloud, as if the rat really understood her.

Her mind quickly returned to her depressing state, and she began drifting away blankly gazing down the open shaft and let her mind drift away to her time with Matt before Mary was born. Life was beautiful, and it was a never ending dream come true of the courtship of a gentleman, followed by respect, and finally a beautifully memorable marriage. Not like the norm was around here nowadays, where the girl goes to a square dance and then for a ride in a pickup truck and is quickly screwed, and her life is set. If she is really lucky, her beau has a job, and is a decent guy. And maybe, just maybe, they might be in love.

It was different with us, Becky thought to herself, Matt had a job when she met him, and he didn't even own a pickup truck. We dated and got to know each other that summer where she met him at the county fair. They were able to spend about six weeks together, while Becky visited her sister that summer. What a wonderful summer it was with Matt. Trips to the lake several times a week. Picnics, ferry rides to the islands, and Matt's special place: Lakeside. The walks we took, the romantic talks about us and the things that made up 'us.' I never thought it could get any better, but it certainly did. We were apart most of the fall. In that time Matt tried everything he could do to rehab his leg, but he finally had to give it up. I still remember the night he called. His tone had a sense of apprehension in it, as if there was something horrible he didn't want to tell me. It was the worse discussion we ever had. It was then I realized how deeply I loved him. When he knew that he couldn't go on without me physically, and I knew I couldn't get along without him passionately.

Becky recalled the time Matt came down to see her for Christmas. He came the second week of December and got a big room at the Holiday Inn. He came for dinner the following Sunday after church to meet her parents. It was funny watching him in our Baptist church. It was like he was a fish out of water. When we were having dinner, my father asked him if he ever had gone to church before. Matt said yes, but he was a practicing Catholic.

About that time my father was taking a sip of coffee and I thought he was going to choke to death. Of course, Matt couldn't let a good thing go, he mentioned to my father that most people have that reaction when they are slapped on the back by the Holy Spirit in the presence of a Catholic. My father and mother loved him from that day forward. He was no longer Ed and Theresa's baby boy, he was their Matt. However, there would remain in their eyes, a diligent attempt at conversion to the Baptist faith. Matt could count on that.

Recalling old memories of her and Matt brought a smile to her face, as well as a glimmer of hope. Matt wouldn't dare leave her down here after all the things they shared together. Like Matt always said, "we're just getting started."

Becky recalled the first time her and Matt made love. It was a typical spring mountain morning, as there was a fog over the entire valley. It was a down day at the mine, so she and Matt had planned to go for a ride through the countryside, and check out the hollers, collect some wildflowers, and enjoy a picnic lunch in the meadow. Becky came through on her end of the bargain by bringing the cooler and the blanket, and Matt got the food from the local deli. By the time Becky met him at the Holiday Inn, it was windy and raining something fierce. So Matt spread the blanket out on the floor, lit some candles and pulled out a surprise bottle of wine. They had their picnic right then and there in the room. After several sandwiches and glasses of wine, the two love birds got a little sleepy and decided to take a nap. And that's when it happened.

It was the most beautiful time, to date, that she and Matt ever spent. The togetherness that making love brought, and the trust it produced was something new to Becky. She didn't understand all the logistics of it, but she knew she liked it, and it would always be a wanted, as well as needed, pleasure. She was surprised by the tenderness of this man she loved. She learned a new side of Matt she never knew existed. She made up her mind that day, that Matt was her life, her soul mate, her best friend, and now her lover. Despite the weather outside, it was a beautiful day inside. One she would never forget.

As she sat on the cold, unforgiving, stone floor, she was warmed by the memories of the life and love she had at home. The trick was getting home to enjoy it. The other trick was what to do about the cramps that were now forming in her lower abdomen. One thing was for certain, she wasn't pregnant.

Reminded now of a different discomfort she had to deal with, the pangs of her hunger returned once again. As Becky began to feel sorry for herself, momma rat returned, and scampering upon her lap, brought her a grape. It was a little shriveled and dried up, but it was something to eat, nonetheless. Becky held out her hand, and as the rat dropped the grape into it, she looked up at her, turned, and scampered away. You have got to be kidding me, she thought to herself. There is something wrong here. She was getting dizzy and felt weak.

She recalled the story Matt told her about Saint Rocco on one of their days in the park. The story is about the carpenter who had severely injured himself while on the job. It so happened that Saint Rocco would daily feed all the stray dogs in his village. Since he was a bachelor, he lived alone, and was laid up to the point that he couldn't even get out of bed to feed himself. When he was close to starving himself, all the stray dogs that Saint Rocco had cared for, brought him food and licked his wound on his leg, allowing him to maintain his strength while he recuperated. That story always amazed Becky, and the fact that she had recalled it now gave her hope of survival. She watched the mama rat scamper off into the shadows of the shaft and softly said, "thank you."

She took one last look at Zack, took out her knife, and got off the floor.

50

Matt and Abner were met at the door by Ruth, who had the most intriguing smile on her face. "Hello, gentlemen," she said. "Come on in, Ransom is in the parlor waiting. I'll bring you some tea. Mary is still napping, Mathew. I told her you would be coming to get her when she woke up."

"Thank you, Ruth." Matt said as he headed into the parlor behind Abner.

The setting was one of those mystery and intrigue movie types where all these maps are laid out on the table. The shades were drawn and it appeared there was a need for a great deal of secrecy. It reminded him of the story of Mary Surratt's parlor the evening John Wilkes Booth came over and discussed the assassination of President Lincoln. Maps, schedules, river crossings, livery stables all adorned the table. It looked however, that Ransom skipped the livery stables for this mission. Jesus, Matt thought to himself, they hung Mary Surratt. What was I getting into?

Ransom started out the meeting. "Well, I think it's obvious why we're here. I assume you talked in detail with Abner here. It's not easy to put your trust in someone with the secrets that he and Dorothy hold. Especially to someone who is a near stranger that hasn't proved himself as far as trust is concerned."

"Is this a damn job interview, dad?" Matt said with an unsettling air of annoyance. "What the hell does trust have to do with where my Becky is?"

"Don't be offended, Matt, there is quite a bit at stake here." Ransom continued.

"What does trust have to do with it," Matt interjected. "I thought we were talking about how to get Becky back."

"We are," said Ransom calmly. "But what we are going to tell you is going to lead to a lot of questions, and the answers must never be revealed. We will be perfectly honest with you, but you must promise that this never leaves this room. Abner's life, as well as mine, depend on it. Yes, son, Abner and I used to run in the same circles in a different life. That secret must never be revealed."

"No shit!" Matt exclaimed. "You and Ruth were in the same business as Abner and Dorothy? I'll be damn. Does Becky know this."

"No, and she must never find out!" Ransom answered. "Nothing that we tell you here tonight can ever leave this room. You must promise me this. So many lives hang in the balance. Even yours, since I understand that you killed a man tonight. So, secrecy is important to you as well. Did Abner tell you who the Bratzi brothers probably were?"

"Yes, scrubbers I think he said." Matt answered. "Do you think they were looking for you?"

"I think Carelli knows we are somewhere at large, and we think he recognized Abner from that news report." Ransom answered.

"Carelli and the Bratzi's were here long before that news report aired on TV." Matt reminded Ransom. "Are you sure he wasn't here on mine business and just happened to notice a couple of old friends in the crowd? Have you ever seen those thugs before this?"

"No, these look like retired operatives to me." Abner added.

"I think Carelli had an interest in that dead miner, and that's why he beat feet to get here so quick." Matt said. "But how did he know where he was at last, and who he was? He did take the remains for burial, you know. Was that miner part of your social circle? Was Carelli your handler?"

"Yes! Both!" Ransom said sadly as he looked away from Matt and down at the floor. "Both things are true. How do you know these things?"

"I watch television." Matt answered. "I've learned more on the 'Americans' than I ever have from books."

Ransom was quiet after that. He just looked out into space waiting for Abner to say something, but Matt kept the conversation going.

"How many scrubbers are there around here?" Matt asked. "How long has your band of spies been disbanded?"

"I don't know, why?" Abner asked.

"Would you know one if you saw them alone on the street?" Matt replied. "Are they all West Germans like Bratzi? Those goons were pretty hard to miss."

"I think I could identify one by sight." Abner replied.

"Why did they come to your house? Why did they follow you around town that day? Did they know you personally, or did they just happen on you?"

"No, they know me." Replied Abner.

"Do you remember when they first came after the explosion and got out of their car?" Matt continued the questions. "They were working the crowd. They were hunting for someone specific. And you were standing atop of the rise like the Pope. You would've been hard to miss. Igor knew Dorothy well enough to come right into her kitchen. That asshole came in there to make it personal. Otherwise he could just have easily sniped her through the window. It amazes me that they come to your house publicly. Are they attempting to debrief you Abner, or are they here to kill you?"

"Probably both." Replied Abner.

"Did they ever come here Ransom? Was Ruth an active agent like Dorothy was?" Matt asked.

"No." Ransom answered. "But Dorothy knew Igor in training at the center in Moscow. Why all the damn questions?"

"Well, dad, you told me I'd have questions." Matt replied. "And after I get Becky back, I may have to spend the rest of the winter trying to keep you guys alive. Confucius say, the more you know about your enemy, the easier he is to deal with. So, let me ask you guys this. If Carelli wasn't around, would any scrubbers be able to recognize you?"

"I doubt it," Abner said. "We're the last of his agents, I think. Why?"

"Are there any more of your graduating class living around here?" Matt asked.

"Probably a dozen or so." Abner confided.

"Damn!" Matt exclaimed. "Well, they've got to live somewhere, I guess."

"What are you thinking, Matthew?" Ransom asked.

"I say we kill Carelli, and put a stop to this bullshit before they can regroup." Matt said very soberly. "Before he can point you out to someone else. Your secret dies with him."

"How are you going to do that?" Ransom asked. "You can't just kill him."

"Yeah you can." Matt returned. "He's an old man, they have heart attacks in this altitude all the time."

"You make it sound like a walk in the park!" Ransom said.

"Yeah, good point. The park would be a very good place for it." Matt said. "Do they want to kill you, Abner?"

"I think so." Abner said. "We all have too many skeletons in the closet."

"But they don't know about you and Ruth at this point, dad?" Matt asked. "Is that right?"

"No. Not yet." Ransom said.

"How does it happen they know Abner, but don't know you?"

"We worked different countries." Ransom said.

"Oh, that makes a lot of sense. This is what I think." Matt went on. "I think Carelli will be back here to look for his boys, but I doubt if he'll come alone. The question is when. That alone will confirm his suspicions that you guys are indeed here. We might have to make a plan. They are all strangers here, so they won't be missed. Is Carelli still active in the KGB, or is he working with unemployed goons?"

"No, he left to pursue other interests that paid more." Abner said. "Shortly after the wall fell."

"if this is true what interest does that spooky bastard have in you this late in the game?" Matt asked. "And do all these bastards look like they fell out of a hearse? They look like malnourished Nazi's."

"Well, we're going to get to that here in a minute." Ransom said, as he cast a glance to Abner.

"Okay, sounds good." Matt replied. "I'll be damned, all this time I thought you two were a couple of old coal miners with an awful lot of class. You sons a bitches. Okay, in the meantime Abner, where's my wife, exactly?

51

Becky paced the floor for a minute or so in an attempt to delay the inevitable, but her stomach wouldn't let her. She collected more firewood, and surmised the best way to prepare her meal. Matt did put plastic ware in her lunch box, but it wouldn't sustain the necessary heat needed to cook the meal. She then concluded that her lunch box was suitable for a frying pan. There was no more putting it off.

She stood in front of Zack, or what there was visible to her, and remembered the good times they had working together, and all the fun they had together at the company picnics and the towns Thanksgiving get-togethers. She thought about his wife Melissa, and how she must be coping with this. She always appeared so frail, Becky thought, and hoped Matt would look after her. Of course, not too good a looking after, but enough to help her over the rough spots.

For some reason Becky remembered the talk her and Matt had about Alfred Packer, the man accused of cannibalism in 1874 in the Colorado mountains. For the first time in her life, she understood what compelled Alfred Packer to do what he did while guiding people through the San Juan Mountains. The rage of crippling hunger can make you do strange things, and although she was being filled with guilt as she stood in front of Zack, she had no choice. She was starving to death and she knew it.

She made the first cut on his right leg to the left of the knee where the quadriceps muscle joined the knee. She was surprised there was no blood, only the pale pink color of the muscle tissue. She cut a piece about five inched long and two inches wide. It was also one inch deep. Due to the nature of Zack's muscle structure, there was no fat build up under the skin. The incised piece of meat was odorless, morbidly cool and slightly stiff.

She held the meat in her fingers, trying to come to grips with what she had done, and was about to do, but she felt no further remorse, only the anticipation of ending the excruciating pain in her mid section was the only thing on her mind. She turned and put the meat in her lunch box and put it on the fire. Within minutes, it started to sizzle, but the aroma was anything but inviting. She adopted a mind set that this may never taste good, but it would keep her alive, hopefully until Matt would come and get her. As she let the meat cook a few minutes longer, the thought of her being rescued, by Matt or any of the crews, was beginning to be a broken dream. She felt she would most likely starve to death down here, and now she was only prolonging the inevitable conclusion. Although her hopes were waning, hope was all she had. The hope that the man she loved would come and find her ending this nightmare. She took a small bite out of the first hot meal she had had in seven days.

When her tongue came in contact with the flesh, her saliva began drenching her mouth. The mental aspect of what she was eating caused her to wretch violently. However, they were only the dry heaves, she thought, since there was nothing in her stomach. She took another bite and chewed slowly and ever so carefully, until the morsel was total chewed. She then swallowed the first piece of digestible protein she had had in days. She ate the last piece that she had cut and set back to feel the effects, if any it was having.

A few minutes after the first piece settled in her stomach, the pain of starvation eased a bit, only to be replaced by a stronger anticipating feeling of more. She knew that the small piece she had just eaten would not sustain her for long, and she returned to Zack's leg. She cut off a piece a little deeper this time getting more muscle, and quite a bit bigger. She realized she was automatically doing what Matt had told her to do, without thinking, as if he was right here with her. She was very comforted that in a small way she felt Matt's presence in the mine with her, taking care of her. She put the piece in the lunch bucket to cook. In the harrowing view of watching one of her best friends being cooked, she had a strange feeling of satisfaction about her. The pain in her stomach was gone, temporarily perhaps, but gone nonetheless. She let the piece cook a few more minutes and then took it out.

She was surprised that it went down so well, and even had a taste that she could relate to other meals. She remained somewhat self-conscious, and skeptical, but she was feeling satisfied, and she felt that no way in hell was she ever going to explain why she did what she did. She was beginning to feel alive again, and that was a welcome change no matter what her situation.

She had done what Matt told her to do, now it was up to him to keep his end of the bargain and get her out of here. As she leaned back against the wall of the mine, she began to relax, although she had an uncomfortable feeling of a presence about her, she soon fell comfortably asleep.

52

Ruth brought the three men a fresh pot of tea as Abner unrolled a large map which looked like a honeycomb directory for a bee hive. He covered it with another map which was more readable. Abner went on to say that this was a topographical map as we stood on the grass and looked out over the field. The first was a depth map, which would be used to show where Becky was at in regard to how deep she was. The two together were beginning to make a lot of sense. However, Matt thought, it is still a picture of many holes in the ground.

Abner then arranged the maps so they were in order, and drew a line from a grassy knoll to a hole in the honeycomb. There was a hole drilled in the rock and it ended about 150 feet down the top of the mine. From that point Abner drew a horizontal line a short distance through the honeycomb to a spot where a shaft joined it. He then drew his line to the right of that shaft, and stopped a short way down the shaft.

"I think your Becky is here." Abner said. Using a tip of a pen, Abner went on to show on the honeycomb map that this is where the cedar support beams are at. "This is what washes up as silt in the creek. This is the one place the rescue teams have not been able to get through. Notice that there is no shaft above this spot. We could never blast our way any further due to an impenetrable tectonic plate. The same plate which the rescue teams can't drill through, is what is protecting your Becky, and that is where the cedar shoring braces are. The plate is probably sixty feet long, but ends on the other side of the cedar beams. With cedar chips in the creek, I'm assuming that the explosion caved the mine in on the other side of the plate, but for now it's a ceiling to them. Hopefully, there won't be any more shifting before you can get down there. If that plate were to move sideways, the whole section of the mine would fall into itself."

"How do I get down there?" Matt asked.

"This shaft you see here," Abner said as he pointed his pointer on the top map, "is a drilled ventilation shaft. It's known as Sloma's vent. It is about forty inches in diameter and 150 feet deep. It is on Sloma's property, and he does not allow any entry to it. It is actually fenced in with cyclone fencing about six foot high. But as long as he does not hinder the ventilation of the shafts, he can legally protect what he owns. There is, as you can surmise, bad blood between the owners and Mister Sloma. Rumors are that he has shot at anybody he catches around there."

"Are the rescuers aware of it?" Matt asked.

"They should be," Abner said. "But since they have been told they aren't down there, they haven't even considered going there. Now remember that this shaft is going to end at the ceiling of that other shaft, so you'll have about a seven-foot drop to the floor. Once you're on the floor go to the right. There's only one direction you can go, that shaft ends about ten feet down. That will take you to the shaft where I think they are at. Go right again, and they should be about forty to sixty feet down that shaft. I figure if they did not pass the protection of the plate, they should be alive and well."

"What makes you think they didn't?" Matt asked.

"The methane probes and the bloodhounds," Abner said. "They would have smelled them by now."

"Damn!" Matt whispered.

"I think the vent is the best way to go." Abner said. "But how you do it is up to you. Go at night under the cover of darkness. I doubt if anybody will see you, let alone bother you."

Matt sat down on a chair next to the table and put his head in his hands. Standing up shortly thereafter, he said, "damn sure looks easy enough, Abner."

"Have you got a plan in mind?" Abner said.

"I'll rappel down the shaft, find her, and bring her back up." Matt answered confidently. "It would be no different than lifting a climber off a mountain face. Weather would be a lot better, and I doubt if Becky is very heavy anymore, and we're only talking 150 feet. I think we can do it. I'll have to take supplies to mend any broken bones, food, water and I should take a protective suit to cover them against hypothermia on the way back to town. We could walk directly to the church and meet the ambulance there. I could call you on a cell phone when I'm going down and coming out and heading home. I'll get Becky first and let the rescue workers get the rest."

"How do you secure your equipment at the vent opening?" Ransom asked. "And how are you going to get that equipment down a forty-inch hole with you in it also?

"With stakes, like they secure tents, and the equipment will dangle below, going down first." Matt answered.

"What if old man Sloma sees you there, and causes you problems?" Ransom said excitedly as if he was afraid of the plan.

"Then, I'm afraid he'll have an accident." Matt replied in a matter of fact tone. "I think this will work Abner. Hell, what have we got to lose?"

"Do you have this kind of equipment just laying around?" Ransom asked.

"Yeah. Yeah dad, I do." Matt answered with his mind going a mile a minute.

Matt recalled the conversation he and Becky had when she wanted Matt to open that foot locker in the basement one day not so very long ago. Smiling, he said to Ransom," I've got all I need and then some. Okay, I'll put a plan together and work out the fine print. Now, Abner, what is it you said you needed from me?"

53

Angelo Carelli sat at his dining room table, at his New York penthouse, a converted warehouse on the upper east side, and drank his morning coffee. Although his mind was not on the taste of the coffee, nor on the fact that his breakfast was getting cold in front of him. He was lost in his own thoughts.

He felt older today, and much stiffer that the weeks before this West Virginia business had started. He wasn't the spry cougar about to strike on his hapless prey that he once was. He feared that the strange turn of events which led to the finding of Carlos in that mine, was going to cause his demise. How in the hell did he end up there? He had been his handler for fifteen years and he thought Carlos was in Paraguay. What in the hell was he doing in West Virginia? It did however answer one question that had plagued him for years; where was he, and what became of him?

His concern also became more intense when he was told by his secretary that she had not received any word from the Bratzi brothers since yesterday morning, when they shared their plan about talking with Yuri once again. What could possibly had happened to those two? He felt his control of the situation slipping out of his hands. He knew he could not lose the Bratzi brothers, because they were the only ones who could lead him to Yuri Chevronatski. Maybe he underestimated that old man, but still, nobody was a match for his men. But Yuri had somehow managed to survive in a business that didn't forgive mistakes. He knew in his own heart he needed to go back down there and see what the problem was, but who would he take with him?

He knew that the local law enforcement was slow down there inasmuch as they still had no idea who Carlos was. They didn't even find the sensor device he had sewn in his pants hem. Once they brought his remains out of the mine, the satellite picked up his whereabouts, and Angelo knew exactly where his beloved servant was. I guess he never went to Paraguay after all, Angelo said to himself smirking.

Although Angelo wasn't positive, he figured Yuri must have killed him to cover up the secret. But, Angelo thought, what was Yuri doing living down there, and how did Carlos find him? None of this made any sense, Angelo thought. Yuri must have needed some kind of help to get down in the coal mine country, because he was definitely a northern kind of guy. But could he have done that all by himself? And how did he talk his wife into it? Albeit she wasn't his wife, but they would never have parted company. And if they did, where did she go?

He could not believe how he had managed to lose contact with one the best operatives he ever had. The diamonds that Yuri had were worth millions on the black market. All those loose nukes that the Soviet Union lost when the Berlin Wall fell were useless without the codes that Yuri had. And it was Yuri who built those codes into the nukes so they couldn't be used by some tyrannical dictator or a terrorist organization out to get Israel. Yuri sensed the moods of the radicals before anyone even conceived of such a thing, and protected the world from them. The intellect of that man was second to none.

Angelo wondered if he could convince him, as an old friend and colleague, to give him the codes in return for his freedom. But Angelo knew in his heart that Yuri was the only free one of the bunch, and he knew he was capable of maintaining that.

Angelo decided he would give the Bratzi brothers one more day to surface, and then he would go down there personally to talk with Yuri. However, without the Bratzi's, he had no physical protection. Things will be better, he thought, when the Bratzi's surface. Having agreed with himself he finished his breakfast.

54

Abner got up from his chair, took a sip of tea, and began to pace the living room floor. He did his best thinking on his feet, and he knew he had to put the deal of his lifetime to Matt so they could all live happily ever after. It wasn't that he feared Matt's acceptance of his proposal, but that would the secret always be safe with him. Although Abner spent a lot of time sizing Matt up over the years, he still couldn't get in his head. He offered Matt a deal he couldn't find anywhere else in his life, but he did fear the fact that Matt might find Becky dead and the whole deal would be off.

Abner went to the table and put a map in the center and motioned Matt to come over and look at it with him. He pointed to the shaft where Matt could go down and moved his finger a short distance to the left. He began his pitch.

"When you go down the shaft, you will turn right to go to Becky and her crew. Do that first, by all means. But remember when you are standing on the floor of the shaft, and the shaft is above you, I need you to go to the left. That shaft is only a few meters long. Where the shaft ends, I need you to put your hands on the wall, shoulder high, and again look to the left. You will see a rectangular rock placed in the wall; again, this is also shoulder high. The rock will appear stuck, but with a small screwdriver it will come out. There will be a hole in which this rock hides. I need you to take the contents of that hole out and bring it back with you."

Matt looked intently at Abner as he went on.

"In that hole are two small address type black books, and a black leather bag about the size of a small cosmetic case. What is in them is something you must swear your secrecy too. I respect you enough to tell you what is in those books and the case. But I need you to swear to me that you will never divulge the contents, or that you even knew anything about it."

The two men looked at each other with an air of trust, which neither wanted to release. Abner needed the contents of those items, and actually, Matt didn't really care, he just wanted Becky back.

"Should I know what's in them?" Matt asked.

"It's not necessary." Abner said. "Just a lot of numbers which would raise your interests."

"Okay. We have an agreement." Matt returned. "What else do I need to know.

"I'll keep you updated on the movement of the plates." Abner said as he pointed again to the shaft map. "But I think the quicker you do this the better. That mine is on borrowed time."

"Okay then," Matt said. "I have work to do. I'll see you two gentlemen later."

"What about Carelli? Ransom said.

Matt looked momentarily at Abner, who was in turn looking at him, as if they were both looking for help answering the question.

"I doubt if Carelli will get to concerned until tomorrow about not hearing from the Bratzi's." Matt answered. "He'll either pop down here again himself, or send more goons. Do you know how many scrubbers there are who might know you two?"

"I'm not sure." Abner said. "It's been a long time. And they do die off. It's a shitty way to make a living, you know. I honestly don't think anyone else would know us, except for facial structure, and they don't have an updated photo."

"Well, if he comes down here, we should be able to tell if he's the only one who knows what you look like. I doubt if he'll come alone. We can keep an eye on him. If we have to, we'll do what we have to do." Matt said.

"What do you mean by that?" Ransom asked. "If he's the only one who know what he looks likes. How will you know that?"

"If Carelli comes and walks around, or drives around in the car with his goons trying to spot Abner and point him out, that's how we'll know." Matt answered Ransom. "You know what? If he does come back, we'll sic

Melissa on his ass, and she can keep an eye on him. You guys stay covered this time."

"Melissa is just a little girl," argued Ransom. "You can't get her involved in this!

"No, dad, you're wrong there." Matt countered. "She is definitely not a little girl. She's the one who told me that Carelli claimed the body of that dead miner."

"How would she know that?" Ruth interjected coming in from the kitchen with Mary.

"I assume her father told her." Matt said. "I assume he keeps close tabs on you guys while he's gone. Especially now that you've told me you're not the only ones in town. It's getting late guys, let's call it a night. An awful lot of info to digest. Abner, can I take those maps with me?"

"Sure." Abner answered. "We'll see you folks tomorrow, then. Thanks for the hospitality."

Then in an apparent Russian dialect, Abner said good night to Ruth and Ransom, and walked out the door with Matt and Mary.

"Come on Abner, we'll walk you home."

"Okay, that will be nice," Abner said.

"I need to ask you something Abner." Matt began. "If just for my own curiosity, how did you know that miner, and what was his name?"

"His name was Carlos Mendoza." Abner said. "He was one of Carelli's men. A gopher, if you will. He was sent here to buy what is in the mine. He followed me from the Groton naval yards. It took him a long time to find me. I don't know if he reported to Carelli where I was when he found me, or not. I doubt it, because he tried to rip me off. Melissa's father leaked it that I was given asylum in Portugal, but instead he brought us all here. I met him one night to sell what I had, but instead he tried to kill me and keep the payoff for himself. There was so much commotion in the mine that night, that I had to hide everything in that hole in the wall. I buried him the best I could and walked out of that damn mine in the dark. The very next day, they sealed that section off, and until the day your Becky's crew reopened the shaft, I've been a poverty-stricken millionaire."

"What's down there?" Matt asked. "Diamonds?"

"Yes! Millions worth." Abner said.

Matt lost a step in his gait, and nearly tripped over Mary when Abner told him that. "Jesus!" He said.

"Yeah, I thought you'd get a rise on that one." Abner said as the front porch light came on at Abner house. As Abner averted his attention from Matt, he saw his lovely bride standing in the threshold in a lovely lavender evening gown.

"Well, this is where I say good night, Matthew." Abner said. "Thanks for your help out at the school today, and coming over to Ransom's house tonight. I'm pretty sure that is where your Becky is. Anything I can do to help you with it, count me in. I can't begin to tell you what it means to have those items in my hands again. It'll be so nice to give my Dorothy the life she deserves again. We'll talk again tomorrow, old friend."

And with that he went up the steps in a fashion of that of the football captain taking the prom queen on a late night drive.

Matt picked Mary back up in his arms and headed to his house. When he walked in the back door, Melissa had supper going and had made a pie as well.

"Hello, my worldly travelers, are you hungry?" Melissa said. "How was the meeting? Did you learn some spy tricks? I just can't wrap my head around those two. Can you believe it? I tell you, after seeing Dorothy take out Bratzi today, I'd believe anything. Come on you two, set down before it gets cold. After supper, you have to tell me all about it."

Matt was beginning to wonder if she would come up for air when she said, "come on, Matt, sit down."

As the three of them sat down to dinner, Matt got the strangest feeling in his heart, and he began to long for Becky. What Abner said today made a lot of sense as to where she might be. But in his mind he knew time was running out for her. Matt ate his supper deep in thought of how he would go about Becky's rescue. He would occasionally look up and acknowledge Melissa's comments, but other than that he was in his own world. He would have to find a way to work this out. And Melissa, why would she cook them supper? This was getting stranger by the minute. Was that cleavage he saw? I'll be damn, he thought to himself, she's not as flat as I thought.

During supper Matt and Melissa talked about the meeting the best they could with Mary setting there. He told her about Abner's idea where he thought, 'you know who' actually was, and the apparent ease of going down to get her. There was never any mention of what he was to do while he was down there. Abner had asked him for his silence, and Matt respected his request.

"Do you have all the equipment you need for this little field trip?" Melissa asked while she gave Mary more potatoes.

"Yeah, Matt answered. "Need some medical supplies in case anyone needs treatment, but I should be good."

"How do you plan for an operation like this?" Melissa asked. "what if they're all busted up?"

"I'll take enough supplies for four, and hope I get lucky," he answered. "If we really get lucky, I'll bring them all up and have you call an ambulance."

"How high a chance is that?" Melissa continued.

"Not as high as I'd like." Matt concluded. "The odds are not in their favor. Even Abner thought it was a long shot, but even he, who has had experience in these things thought it was at least worth a try."

"Where do you get the medical supplies?" Melissa asked.

"I'll take them from the fire department, and order replacements." Matt answered.

"It's not like I stole them, I bought them in the first place."

"Is there anything I can do to help?" Melissa said.

"You can be a great help in helping me put all this together." Matt asked as if begging. "And watch what's going on in town. And keep an eye on old man Sloma. Abner said if I had any trouble at all it would be him."

"What if he sees you and tries to stop you?" Melissa asked. "Do you want me to go with you?"

"I don't know about that yet," Matt said. "If he tries to stop me, I'll have to take him out and bury him down the shaft. And I plan on going tomorrow night, I think. It's supposed to rain, so there won't be many onlookers. There's not a lot to plan. I know where the vent is, and I'll memorize the shaft configuration. Abner figures they are about two, fifty-foot shaft lengths from the vent. And I have all the ropes and pitons I need in the basement."

"What's a piton?" Melissa asked.

"It's a large metal spike that you pound into rock to secure a rope or foothold."

Matt said. "I figure I'll have to put them in a thermal suit and pull them up, like a bundle of potatoes. Pull them up one at a time about ten feet. Hook them to a piton and climb about ten more feet and pull some more. They should be reasonably light weight by now."

"Sounds like you've given this quite a bit of thought." Melissa commented.

"Ever since Abner talked about a long shaft accessible from the surface, that has been all that has been on my mind." Matt answered.

"So, you're planning on tomorrow night then," Melissa asked with a break in her voice.

"I think so," Matt said. "Are you going to be all right with that while I'm gone?"

Melissa looked Matt right in the eye. He could see her eyes were welling up with tears.

"What is it, Melissa." Matt asked. "Are you afraid Zack may be dead? That is something we both have to prepare for, you know."

"No, Matt," Melissa answered. "I'm afraid Becky will be alive, and I will lose you."

That took Matt directly off guard. He glanced over to Mary who was looking at him as if she was expecting an answer.

"Maybe later tonight is a better time to talk about this." Matt replied. "After the little one is in bed."

"Okay," Melissa said.

55

$\mathbf{B}$ecky awoke with a start, as if she could sense a presence in the mine. She looked over against the far wall and could see what appeared to be a presence of another person.

"Sorry to wake you," the lady said. "I'm sure you have questions, they all have questions, especially at this stage in their life. You've been down here, what, thirteen days? You've done well for yourself. Having a little problem with food I see, but, don't worry. Whatever it takes to stay alive. I've been there, I know what it's like. So, your name is Becky, right.? It's a damn fine mess you got yourself into this time, isn't it? Coal mining isn't for a woman. I remember as a younger woman, watching the Gentiles and the poor Samaritan women, mostly widows, working in the granite and marble mines. Ghastly work. They should be home warming their husbands' bed. Of course, the widows didn't have a husband. Not me! My father made sure I was a lady and married me into royalty. Kind of a spineless bastard, my husband. Had a love for other people's blood, as long as he didn't get his hands dirty, he couldn't get enough." But that carpenters' kid from Nazareth, that was his undoing. Lucky, he had me or he would have fallen on his sword back then. However, if he had listened to me, he would have never had the problems he had in the first place."

"Are you real?" Becky asked. "Who are you and where did you come from? How did you get in here? Did you bring anything to eat?"

"All good questions, my dear. They will be answered in their proper time. Here, has some bread." The lady said.

Taking what appeared to be bread from the lady's hand, Becky took a very cautious bite. Becky became instantly satisfied. She handed a finger full of the morsel to the mother rat, who took it and ran away at twice the pace as she came to Beck's side. Becky noticed that the lady appeared to be Italian, and was well kept. She had beads on that Becky had never seen, and a golden bracelet that shimmered, even in the weak light of the mine. She smelled of expensive perfume. Not heavy, but clean. The lady was in the bottom of a coal mine, and she was elegant. And she was not bothered by the rats. That surprised her, she appeared to have no fear.   "Thank you," Becky said. "Who are you?"

"I am Claudia Percolus," the lady said.

Becky gave an inquisitive wrinkle in her forehead, that the lady picked up on.

"You must be a Christian," she said. "You've heard the name, but just can't place it. At least you accept it. The Jews won't even do that. Need a clue? I am the wife of Pontius Pilate. I'm the one who begged him to set Jesus free, but he was so afraid of those Jewish high priests. 'You are no friend of Caesar, they would scream'! He should have put that Anis character on the cross instead. That would have put an end to all this jealousy. I had horrible dreams the night before, and my stomach ached as if I my bowels were being eviscerated. I had no idea who this Nazarene was, but he touched me in such a way that I couldn't stand by and do nothing. A brilliant career with the highest favor in Rome and he threw it away over the accusations of a spineless temple priest.

I became a Christian shortly after that. Luckily, we were called back to Rome and my once glorious husband was condemned and exiled to Gaul. This was not before he managed to overthrow an uprising in Jerusalem by crucifying half the region. Some spineless Jew complained to Caesar, and we were brought back in shame. He had been warned before about his lust for blood. So, you really can't say it wasn't his fault. I never saw him after that. I was told by a messenger that sometime later that he committed suicide."

The lady handed her more bread as if she had a whole loaf of it, but Becky couldn't see where she got it from.

"They died right away?" She said, looking at Zack, Carla and Phil "I doubt if they suffered."

"What are you doing here?" Becky asked.

"I've been sent here to sit with you awhile. I think you call it, keep you company." She said. "It's part of my saintly duties as an angel to visit those in peril, and lighten their burden. And since you are a Christian, you get special attention."

"How long have you been doing this?" Becky asked. "Can I touch you? Are you real?"

"I died in seventy-six A.D., so ever since then. And you can touch me, but we are not of the same worldly composition. I'm afraid you would feel nothing at all. But it's your faith that sees me, and talks with me. It is your faith that has sustained you these thirteen days."

"What day is it? What time is it?" Becky asked.

"We don't deal in time really. I do know it is the twenty-second of December." She said.

She handed Becky some more bread, and dropped some on the floor for the rats.

"Pesky little creatures, aren't they? You should have seen them in France." She said.

"Are you going to stay with me until I die?" Beck asked sadly.

"No. No. I'm not kind of angel." Claudia answered. "I'll stay with you awhile, and after I'm gone you will never be positive I was ever here with you, but you won't be hungry, and your faith will give you a burning memory of a supernatural visit you had with a lovely lady when you were in need. You will always *think* this happened, but you will never be positive. But there is not a day that will go by that you won't thank the Father for this *thing* that comes to your mind occasionally. That will be your gratitude."

"So, I'm going to survive this?" Becky asked, eagerly awaiting the answer. "I'm not going to die here?"

"Oh, no, my dear." She said. "You have many years of life left with children to raise and grandchildren to experience. Not to mention a good husband to take care of."

"Well, how am I going to get out of here?" Becky asked. "They are going to give up the search soon. Then what?"

"Your husband will come and get you, just like he said he would." She explained. "And when he does, take very care good of him. He has pain in his life that only you can take away. He has issues that no man should have to deal with at a time like this. Love and cherish that man, because he is a gift from the father. You will always be reminded of this, even though you will never openly be told by him."

"Do you know my husband?" Becky asked.

"Only what I need to know for this visit with you. I liked what I saw when I sat on the edge of his bed the other night as he slept." She said.

"You have seen Jesus, haven't you?" Becky asked excitedly.

"Yes." She answered. "But it wasn't his best day."

"When did you realize He was the son of God?" Becky questioned.

"The day I saw him in the praetorian something happened to me. I felt a burning in my soul. Like this moment in life was special and it should be cherished, even considering his condition." She said. "But then he died and the storm came. It wasn't like any other storm. It was horrible. The winds blew the camels over and the Centurions off their horses. The curtain tore in half in the temple. But when the dead rose from their graves and began moving about, I knew this was no ordinary man. I have been in grace ever since. His resurrection was something to be remembered for all ages."

"Do you come and do this often?" Becky asked, nervously looking for ways to keep the conversation open.

"Only to those who are Christians in despair, and have prayed to the Father for his help. He knows who they are. Spent a lot of time with Mother Theresa in her days. Great lady. Ghastly place, Calcutta. And the Nazi's: That was a different subject altogether"

As Becky sat there, she began to be very tired. Although she fought to stay awake, she had no control over her stupor.

Claudia rose and took Becky's hand. In doing so she awakened Becky slightly.

"I will be going now," Claudia said. "Remember in your heart what we talked about today. Always be grateful for this and those you love and love you. Your faith has saved you. Sleep well, my child. You'll be just fine. Raise Mary in the faith, and never let her waiver."

Becky looked toward the voice she was hearing in her stupor, but then she realized Claudia was gone, and Becky fell deeply asleep.

56

Dorothy closed the door behind Abner as he entered the house and affectionately placed her hand on his back. "Here, honey," let me take your coat, she said. "How did the meeting go?"

"Good, darling. I think he will do it." Abner said. "At least he sounded convincing."

Taking his coat she walked toward the closet in clear view of Abner's searching eyes.

"You haven't worn that outfit in quite a long time, my dear." Abner commented. "I've always found it to be so fetching. It compliments your figure so well. You are as beautiful as the day I met you."

Dorothy smiled softly and said, "I wore it just for you, my darling. I know it's your favorite."

Walking over to Abner, she put her arms around him and kissed him passionately on the lips.

"It's like the old days, isn't it, honey. We'd both come home from the office and we'd be in one anothers arms making love well into the evening. It's ironic in a way, the cold war ended and we seemed to have lost the need for our private warmth and protection. It's like the fear of capture was over and we didn't need the security of our physical love and touch. I have missed those days so much. But just talking about it today with Mathew and Melissa, lit the fire inside of me again, and I must admit I became quite damp. It's like we're working again and we are both just coming home from the office. And I so desperately need your love to make me feel protected, because the war is so cold and lonely, and I can't get through another day without your touch."

Abner never said a word, he just smiled at his bride, and taking her hand, led her into the bedroom.

With that nasty mess of the Bratzi's behind them, and Matt going into the mine to retrieve their life savings, maybe she and Abner could get back to the business of enjoying each other sexually without the burdens associated with the life of a couple of spies in hiding. And maybe, just maybe, they could get Anastasia back. The very prospect of returning to the passion of that life excited her erotically. That was the last thought she had before the bedroom door closed.

Abner was like a younger man all of a sudden. In a single swift move of his hand, he had switched off the light and firmly planted his hand on Dorothy's butt, prompting a satisfactory moan. He moved his hand to her throat, and keeping her firmly in hand, reached up and pulled her nightgown free of her body exposing her firm breasts and round buttocks to the invading winters night moonlight, that now poured into the room illuminating his brides amber glow.

Abner examined his lady in the moonlight as he became more and more erect. He kissed Dorothy's mouth deep as he massaged her breasts before dropping to his knee to a position which made Dorothy moan and shiver with orgasmic pleasure. With one fluid passion filled motion, he picked up his bride and laid her flat on her back. Continuing his oral foreplay, he could not help but become aroused by the gratifying moans of his satisfied wife. He then moved on top of Dorothy, and as the moonlight continued to flood the room, he entered her inviting womanhood while she let out the deepest groan accompanied by a most intense orgasm.

Their love making went on well into the night, as they recalled their sexual encounters from years gone by, while preparing for their next session.

Eventually they were both spent, and agreeing to pick up where they left off in the morning, they held each other in their passionate nakedness and fell asleep.

57

Matt put Mary down to bed and sat on her bedside and talked for a few minutes.

"Daddy, why can't you just go down and get mommy. Uncle Abner knows where she is." asked Mary innocently.

"I think I will baby," Matt said. "It may be the only way to find her."

"Is mommy still alive?" Mary said.

"I think she is, baby." Matt replied. "I had a dream last night and a woman told me mommy was waiting for me to come and get her."

"Who was she daddy?" Mary asked.

"I don't know who she was. It was a very strange dream. I felt awake all the time." Matt replied.

"When will you go daddy?" Mary asked.

"Tomorrow, I think, honey." Matt said. "We'll keep an eye on the weather. You better get some sleep now, baby", Matt said. As Matt bent down to kiss her goodnight, she was already fast asleep.

"Do you put everyone asleep that easily?" Melissa asked jokingly.

"I've lost my charm, I'm afraid." Matt said.

"We'll see about that." Melissa said.

With a half halfhearted laugh, Matt made his way to the kitchen to get a beer. As he walked through the living room, he asked Melissa if she wanted anything.

"A glass of wine would be nice," she said. "I'm feeling romantic tonight. I'll light the fireplace."

That lit a spark of cautious curiosity in Matts mind. What is she thinking of now, Matt thought as he got out a wine glass? This was an event that was always reserved for he and Becky. After the supper dishes were cleaned up and Becky put Mary to bed, she and Matt would set down, light the fireplace, and drink a glass of wine. Then they would go to bed and make love until late in the early morning. Even opening a bottle of wine left Matt feeling very awkward, and he wasn't sure what to do about it. He was actually afraid he would be enticed by Melissa's advances.

They were both in a state of sexual depravity, and although reasonably young, they were old enough to know what a pleasure and therapeutic effect it would have on both of them if they were to make love. Pouring the glass of wine, and grabbing himself a beer, he went into the living room and sat next to Melissa.

She was setting there quite comfortably. She had let her hair down and unbuttoned the top button her flannel shirt. Although she was not endowed like the average mountain girl, she did, however, sport a noticeable, and inviting cleavage.

Matt felt his pulse quicken as Melissa took the glass of wine from his hand and said, "thank you." The touch of her hand was very warm and soft. Her eyes had a magnetic sparkle to them as Matt fought against himself not to be caught up in her gaze. She took a sip of wine and licking her lips, she looked at Matt and said, "this is good. Would you like a taste?"

She scooted closer to Matt, and while extending her shoeless feet with her argyle socks, exclaimed, "the fire is nice. Why don't you get comfortable and relax? You've had a trying day. Let this wash over you. Let your hair down a little."

Then she put her head on Matts shoulder saying, "I think when this is all over, you and I are going to be all alone. I think we have to accept that. Personally, I have. I think you should too."

With that point she placed her hand on Matts leg, and kissed him on the cheek.

"We get along good with each other," she continued. "There's no reason we couldn't be together."

"In all the years I've known you and Zack, you have never talked to me." Matt exclaimed. "At the town festivals you would never even wave when I waved to you. You ignored my hellos at the post office, you just looked the other way. I've always felt you hated me for some reason. The day of the explosion when I saw you standing on the hill at the mine, I felt so sorry for you, because I knew you were afraid, but I knew you wouldn't let me do anything to help you. So, excuse me if I act a little confused by all this. I don't know where this is coming from."

"I was afraid that day Matt, but I'm not afraid anymore," Melissa said. "I'm ready to move on."

"Haven't you any hope that they are still alive?" Matt asked.

"No. None." Melissa said with an emptiness in her voice. "When they couldn't find them by the second day, I knew he was dead."

"It's a life he chose for himself, despite all my efforts to dissuade him verbally, and sexually, and yet, it came back and bit him in the ass. He could have done better if he wanted too. But he is just like all the men here, they don't want to leave, despite the dangers involved in their pre-determined occupation. And you, who had better a better life, came here to stay. It makes no sense to me. Why would you stay here if you didn't have to?"

"I came here for Becky, and the peaceful life that I was offered." Matt answered.

"And did you find it?" Melissa queried.

"Yes. Much more than I had ever imagined." Matt said.

"And if Becky doesn't come back, are you willing to stay here for that peace and quiet?" Melissa asked.

"I'll face that when the time comes, but probably." Matt said.

"Have you got something better somewhere else?" Melissa asked.

"No," Matt said. "My life is here now. Weren't you happy with Zack?"

"I feel I gave him my best years at the time. But I also believe I have many more romantic, sensual years ahead of me, and I don't intend to waste them on a memory. I've said my good byes. I'm at peace with it now. And you can't blame me for being attracted to you, you've taken me in since day one, despite how I treated you in the past. I have leaned on you, and you have taught me security and what it means to be cared for and looked after. I've never had that feeling before, and I don't intend to give that up." Melissa said.

"What exactly are you saying, Melissa?" Matt asked.

"I don't want to be alone in that house. So, I'm saying that I want to be with you and Mary in this house. I'm saying that I am falling in love with you Matthew."

Melissa took another sip of wine, and looking at Matt said, "I'll take very good care of the two of you."

After saying that she put her wine glass down on the table and reached up and put her arm around Matt as she came closer to kiss him.

Just then the phone rang. Matt excused himself in a quick, cowardly, fashion and got up to answer the phone as Melissa got up and went into the bedroom.

"Do you want some more wine?" Matt asked without thinking as he rose from the couch.

"Yes, please," was her answer. "I'll be right out, I'm going to get comfortable."

I dodged the bullet on that one, Matt thought as he got to the phone before the machine picked it up.

Seeing his reflection in the coffee pot, he thought to himself, you are in a world of shit this time. She looked awfully comfortable to me as she was setting on the couch. What am I going to do?

Matt was relieved to find it was the rescue supervisor, explaining to Matt that the days search had taken them back over the cedar support area that Abner raised all the commotion over. He went on to say they still couldn't drill through the plates. He added that the mine was very unstable, by safety standards, and there was a great concern as to the safety of the rescue workers. He feared they may halt the search. They would have more news in the morning, after the midnight shift monitored seismic readings through the night. But he feared that they may have to give up the search due to the shifting and shaking of the mine floors. He apologized for the bad news, but at the same time he was asking for Matts understanding of the dangers involved in searching an unsafe mine. They talked cordially for a few more minutes over the shortage issues of food and water, and then bid each other a good night.

Matt left the kitchen and detoured to his bedroom. He needed time to think. As yet he hadn't heard Melissa come out of her bedroom. He stood there by the bed that he and Becky had spent so many years and passionate nights together in, and tried to put together what was happening to him. He admitted to himself that he was attracted to Melissa, If not for her beauty, then at least her very sensual presence. He was all too aware of his needs and feelings, it was obvious Melissa had the same needs and desires, but not as afraid to express them as he was.

Matt also felt that Melissa had a good point about their spouses being rescued. It had been twelve days, and absolutely no word or hope was coming out of that shaft to liberate their hearts, or put their minds at ease. Matt was no longer positive that Becky was still alive. He had held onto that hope only because he had nothing else to hold on to. And now, Melissa stood before him with the same feelings he had, but more at ease with accepting what was in their future.

Although Matt had a plan to attempt to find Becky, and hopefully bring her home, that was far more than Melissa had going for her. He felt angry for being put in this situation. How could he ever face Becky, he thought, if he became weak tonight, and his hopes of tomorrow came true.

As his mind raced a mile a minute, he noticed that the living room lights had gone out, and candles had been lit.

He was alone, and lonely. He didn't know what else to do. He cautiously made his way to the living room.

"Who was on the phone?" Melissa asked as Matt went to lock the back door.

"The rescue team supervisor." Matt answered. "They might call off the search. The mine is in a bad way."

Going back to the kitchen counter to re fill Melissa's glass, he noticed that she had changed her clothes. He could also smell perfume. Walking to the front of the couch, he came in full view of Melissa as he handed her the wine.

She was absolutely stunning! She wore a white oxford shirt, sensually unbuttoned at the top, and somewhat oversized. It probably belonged to Zack. She had her hair in a loose bun, and a light shade of lipstick. She smelled of jasmine, as was very seductive.

"Set down next to me Matt," she said.

When he sat down, he caught a glimpse of her bare legs as she moved closer to him. He could see the side view of her breasts and her erect nipples as she turned toward him placing her arm on the back of the couch.

She was like a scene from a Hollywood movie, where the temptress seduces her prey in an act of passion. Where all the helpless prey can do to defend himself is to surrender to the desires of the temptress. Matt had always dreamed of this, but until now, he had never experienced it. And he was, indeed helpless. Matt looked into her eyes and felt her lips touch his.

58

The next morning dawned early and wearily for Matt. Just as the weather man had promised, it would be a rainy Christmas eve. Although that is what Matt wanted, it was still depressing to look out the window, where he and Becky had made love so many times, in view of the rising West Virginia sunrise.

Melissa knocked lightly on the bedroom door, telling Matt that breakfast was ready and that Mary was waiting for Santa. Although he was excited about the day, and the hopes that it brought, he was still skeptical about what the events of the previous night would bring.

Matt swung himself out of bed, and made a decision right then and there. What will happen, will happen. First and foremost, he wanted his Becky back, and today was the day he was going after her.

He had a good plan, he thought, based on the information he had gotten from Abner, and previous research of the mine's layout. It was the lesser of work, the shortest distance down, and the easiest extraction point to bring Becky home, albeit one hundred and fifty feet straight up.

He took into consideration that Becky may be injured, therefore medical supplies were included, including an IV bag with adrenaline doses and protein doses. He anticipated that he may have to carry her out of the shaft. A spare Swiss climbing seat would work for that. And he had one thermal suit for bringing someone out in the winter's air. And several food packets left in his foot locker in the basement.

He also remembered that there were four of them. He would secure the most ambulatory members of the team and bring them up, and send them to the fire station for help. But he also knew they had been down there for thirteen long days and they were probably too weak to walk. It was really a wait and see operation. He would go from there, but he would prepare for all four miners needing help. But deep inside he had to accept that all four may be dead, and worse, not where Abner said they were. But one thing Matt felt for certain. By the end of the day he would know one way or the other if his Becky was alive. He got up and went out to breakfast.

59

Abner and his bride Dorothy woke early on this Christmas eve, with a new found spring in their step. Not only had they re-found the coital fountain of youth the night before, but had managed to re-kindle the fire in the early morning hours as well. And also, a special gift should soon come their way in the form of one half million dollars' worth of uncut diamonds, which had been locked in that mine shaft for many impoverish years.

Also, with the diamonds would be a small black book of nuclear launch codes which were probably only important to a terrorist who had stolen the warheads when the Berlin wall fell. Abner never figured in their value, because he had no idea who had the warheads, and wasn't interested in looking them up. No, to Abner and Dorothy, the diamonds were their life's comfort, the little black book was just disposable baggage.

After breakfast, he and Dorothy would walk uptown and casually stop by the library to read the newspaper. Abner would set clueless in front of an internet computer and e-mail a contact in France, who would answer him tomorrow with all the particulars and the price. Although Abner and Dorothy were somewhat retired as agents of the KGB, they were by no means behind on the latest technological advantages afforded them by the library. They were, in the words of Melissa's father, quite sufficient in their role as retired senior citizens.

Abner helped Dorothy with her coat, and playfully swatting her on the butt, they were off to the library. There was much to be done today.

60

$\mathbf{B}$ecky woke up this Christmas eve morning, on the same cold, hard rock floor that she had for nearly two weeks, with no idea as to what day it was, or how long she had been there. All she could think of was that for the first time in a long time, she was not ravaged with hunger.

That brought her to the second thought she had this day; who was that woman, and was she really here or was it her imagination playing tricks on her. She wasn't sure, but she knew she wasn't hungry, and mother rat looked satisfied as well. What was that? She could however, remember the conversation they had. That woman said that Matt was coming for her, and to not lose hope.

How would she know Matt? She said she saw him. I'm sure that's what she said. But the words that held strongly in Becky's memory was that she said Matt was coming to get her soon.

Becky was more than ready to get out of here. The ground kept moving, and every time a tremor came, it would shake the floor and cause the bones to snap, and air to leave their dead lungs in groans in her three deceased colleagues. Coupled with that hideous sound effect, the stream of water running along the wall was getting swifter and beginning to pool. Although she cherished the fresh water, that could become a problem. She was out of hope, and she was becoming more and more discouraged with the prognosis for survival. The lady, Claudia, was her only hope. Maybe, she thought, Claudia told Matt where to find her.

She got up off the cold floor and went to where her three friends were entombed in the rock. She had an unexplainable urge to say good bye to them. She sat down next to them and began to pray.

61

After breakfast, Matt bid Melissa good bye, and taking Mary in tow, headed out the door. There was a great deal to be done this morning, and the weather was perfect for it. The chilled, rainy drizzle kept well-wishers at bay, with no more than a wave as Matt went first to the Fire Station to pick up an IV bag. The weather would also make it very difficult for anyone to see him at the fenced in area of Sloma's vent. He didn't want to attract any attention there.

The next stop on the mornings errands was a track phone for Mary. Matt thought that when he found Becky alive, she could call Mary on a phone that couldn't be tied up with another call. That was the best way he could include Mary in the rescue of her mother. Of course, Matt had to face what he was going to do in the event she was dead. But he thought it was best not to think that way. Of all the blessings in his life, the Lord had always cleared a path for him.

Matt was excited and confident that this weather was going to be the path to getting Becky back home. After those errands were done, Matt and Mary returned home for an inventory of his climbing gear.

It was Matts plan to rappel down Sloma's shaft, placing a piton every ten feet. This would allow him to pick up any and all survivors, climbing up to the next piton and pulling them up ten feet and securing them as he climbed up another ten feet. The task seemed tedious, but he only had to do it fifteen times. He had the strength and all night to do it. It would work, he thought, just like taking injured climbers off the face of a mountain. And by this time the survivors would be pretty light in weight, following their ordeal. It was a good plan. It had to be.

After finishing his inventory and preparing all he would need tonight, he and Mary went over to Abner and Dorothy's for one last meeting before he left. It was now three p.m. Matt planned on leaving around six. It would be dark and the church festivities would be starting about that time. He should be well hidden.

62

Abner and Dorothy arrived at the library in their usual manner. Abner, the quiet, sky, introverted self, and Dorothy, the bubbly, outgoing, mountain wife, just full of the vibrancy that mountain living gives one.

Abner sat down at a computer keyboard and Dorothy picked up a copy of Woman's Health magazine. Setting next to Abner, she pointed out an article on the gifts and techniques of senior love making. Getting a pleasant and interested nod from Abner, while he waited for the computer to boot up, she began reading.

Within a minute, the computer booted up and he had his French contact, Jacques Villenuve, on line.

> *Good Morning, my old friend. I have good news. The property that has been buried for so long, will be in my possession in the morning. There is no reason to believe that it has been tampered with. I hope to contact you in the afternoon, tomorrow to discuss trading.*
>
> *A.K."*

Abner turned his attention back to Dorothy who was turning the magazine in all different contorted directions, studying a photo of a new position in the magazine.

"What do you think, honey? We could add this to our repertoire tonight." Dorothy said while showing Abner the photo.

"My back hurts just looking at it," Abner replied.

As Dorothy and Abner mused over the article, the computer pinged Abner back into the business at hand.

Ahhh, and a pleasant morning to you as well, my old friend. I am so happy that, once again, we can do business after such a long time. I am most happy to pass on to you that while your property was held in safe keeping, the value has tripled. The original value of 1 plus Mil, has dramatically increased three-fold. Please, for reasons of security, do the math. I think you will pleasantly surprised. Looking forward to talking with you soon. Have a Merry Christmas.

Yours Jacques."

Abner sat back in his chair in a state of disbelief and shock. He began running his hands through his hair. Looking at Dorothy with a distant stare, catching her attention, he could only point to the screen.

"Jesus, Mary, and Joseph," was all she could say as she gripped Abner's arm. "We could get Katrianna back home and be a family again."

Saying this they both began to cry.

As Dorothy and Abner left the library, there was a new-found spring in their step, following the good news from France. Dorothy said to Abner, "is this what the Americans call 'their ship coming in'?"

Before Abner could answer, two Sheriffs cars and an EMS truck roared down the street, lights flashing and sirens blaring.

"I wonder what that's all about?" asked Abner. "Maybe old man Dunfee's wife is reading the same magazine you were."

About the time the two lovers turned the corner to the main thoroughfare of town, none other than old man Dunfee came walking out of his drug store to watch the commotion unfold.

"Did you guys hear about that? They found some stranger in a dumpster over by the school." Dunfee reported. "It just makes you wonder what the dumb son of a bitch was doing in there in the first place. Them easterners are sure some strange rangers."

"You meet all kinds, don't you Sam? Dorothy asked.

"I'll tell you. And more of them every day, that's for sure." Dunfee said. "Well, you folks have a nice day, I've got to get back to work. It's Friday, and the misses gets upset if I'm late for supper."

As they sauntered down the street, Dorothy commented on the fact that the lovely gentleman they found in the dumpster will be connected to the Sheriff's visit to our house the other night. And then she laughed, saying, "I'll be damned! She does read the same magazine."

"Let's hope they don't think that a couple of mild mannered elderly retirees could have anything to do with the demise of that gentleman. Where did you put the other one?" Abner asked.

"Out at the old rusty trailer park." Dorothy said. "He's at peace with his kind of people."

Shortly after noon, Dorothy and Abner were back in their house, and for the first time in years talked about going Christmas shopping later in the day. Helping Dorothy with her coat, Abner said, "I've got all I want to unwrap right here. But we must hurry, Matt will be here soon."

63

Matts errands were interrupted when the alert siren went off beckoning the fire and EMS personnel to a call. Standing in the store room with two IV bags in his hands was a little suspicious he thought, so he quickly went out the door, only to run into a fire auxiliary member.

"What's up Chad?" Matt asked.

Chad turned to Matt hastily and said, "Misses Hurley is having chest pains. I got to go, Matt. I'll talk to you later."

Matt continued on with his errands with his colleague, Mary and was soon home.

Matt went down to the basement and packed the last of the supplies he would need for tonight's mission. As he opened the foot locker, he recalled when he and Becky had the argument about his double locked personal safe, that she was not allowed to view the contents of. So much of his past life was buried in that chest. As he pulled out the rappelling gear, he noticed it still had sand on it from Saudi Arabia. He recalled the mission that was his last of his tour. It was a search and destroy mission. But instead of a building or equipment, it was a man. The then leader of the Al Qaeda, Fared Mohammod Zacharra. A diligent and skilled leader, that had eluded hunters, and drones from all over the Army corp. Matt was called in to do what had to be done at any cost.

After tracking Zacharra by the cover of darkness for three days, and living in a sand based foxhole during the day, trying desperately to keep the sand flees out of his inner orifices, he finally caught up with his prey and had him in his cross hairs at eight-hundred yards, when for some unknown reason, the mission was called off. What added insult to injury was that Matt needed the assassination of his target to cover his get away, through the commotion. Now he was a sitting duck to any one who came across his path. He knew it would not be good to have a gun fight here.

Fortunately, the visit of the Al Queda leader led to a great celebration, and the whole town was involved in food, drink, and all the other pleasures which come from a Presidential visit. When darkness fell, Matt left for the safety of his extraction point. With all the successful missions he had been on, this was the most important target, and he was called off. The same day, Zacharra was killed by another sniper while attending a meeting in some town in the east. All his training came down to one mission and it was canceled. How would he have known then that all his training would come down to this last mission.

He put the rappelling harness in his backpack, along with his .45 Colt pistol, which had been a long time companion during those days of his Saudi service. He kept the IV's in the refrigerator for the time being, and insured he had the necessary needles, shunts and tape to do the job. He had adrenaline if he needed it, and some Vitamin B-12 syringes also on hand. The last thing he packed was a thermal suit. He would put them in the suit to bring them up prior to giving them over to EMS techs. It would make them lighter and warmer when they hit the open air.

Matt was confident that he had all he needed for the most important mission of his life. His last hope was that Abner was right in his calculations. He was ready. He took Mary in his arms, and they went to Abner's house where Ransom and Ruth were already waiting.

64

Angelo Carelli sat in his New York Apartment, feeling his arthritic inflammation, and his frustration at not being able to contact his two enforcers in Hope. The cell phone calls repeatedly came back, "no longer in service." He had changed his morning beverage from coffee to Irish Whiskey when his phone rang.

Much to his dismay, it wasn't one of the Bratzi brothers, but the City of Hope Chief of Police reporting to Angelo that either of his employees had been found yet in their fair burg. The Chief advised Angelo that no one had seen either one of them anywhere about, but the search was ongoing.

Angelo thanked the Chief, and hanging up his phone, hollers at his other trusty enforcer, Rico.

Rico wasn't any old and trained enforcer, he was like family to Angelo. Or one might say, the remnants of collateral damage, as part of doing business. Angelo did business with Rico's father when he was very young. The time in a child's life when he doesn't remember anything. So, when the business arrangement went bad, Angelo took Rico to live in his home, and raise. After all, he couldn't just leave him alone in the car parked at the bottom of a stone quarry.

Rico came in and set down.

"I need you to go to Hope and check out what happened to the Bratzi brothers. They can't find them anywhere." Angelo said. "I think someone's killed them."

"Maybe there is more than just one man." Rico commented. "It would be hard for one man to kill either of them, but two, or more could maybe do it if they got the drop on them."

With that, Angelo looked strangely at Rico for a few moments.

"What?" Rico said.

"I never thought of that." Angelo said. "I lost the whole team about ten years ago. My God, what if the whole damn bunch of them lived there? I wouldn't put it past that FBI agent. He was a crafty dude."

Angelo showed Rico a photo of Abner, telling him to just look around and see what he's doing. Don't get involved with the sheriff, and be careful at night. Anything you need, get it from the police chief. Grease his palm, and he'll tell you anything.

"Someone killed the Bratzi's," Angelo said, "I'm sure of it now. Abner couldn't have done it alone, although he is an expert with his switchblade, he could clean a dropped fish before it hit the ground. Just observe. Don't mess with those mountain people. They've got no sense of humor, and they protect their own. Just be present, hang out, and listen. Go to church. Go to the support groups. Just listen. I don't want to find you dead in a shaft, son. I want you to come back home."

"There's someone else I'd like you to see," Angelo went on. "His name is Matt. His wife is trapped in the mine. He's not from Hope, he's from Ohio. He was a fire man and got disabled at the 9/11 cleanup. He was a special forces killer. Not only a sniper, but a close contact killer. Just get a look at him so you know who he is. He'll probably be with Yuri or his little girl. Don't let him see you. Leave no memory of you in his mind. He saw me at the mine, and looked right through me. Avoid him, he is evil. He is death."

Angelo rose from his seat, and going to his safe took out a thousand dollars and gave it to Rico. He hugged his son and looked gratefully in his eyes saying, "Find out what you can and report back to me daily. Be careful. If you get suspicious, stay in the next town. Be safe my son."

65

Matt and Mary arrived at Abner's house just as it was beginning to rain. Looking toward the heavens, he thanked his Creator for giving him the rain that he desperately needed for cover later that night.

Answering the door was the ever bubbly Dorothy. She was so elegant and well kept that it was hard to imagine that she was once a ruthless killer whose skills were still very much alive. They greeted cordially and went to the parlor.

Matt, Mary and Dorothy entered the parlor to Abner, Ransom and Ruth seated around the table with maps out, diagrams with numbers on display, and hope written all over their faces. Although Ransom looked a little disparaged, he was indeed glad to see Matt enter the room. He had been waiting thirteen days for word of his daughter, and although he had come to the realization that his beloved Becky may be dead, he was reignited with hope knowing that Matt was going to get her. One way or another, he thought, he would get his Becky back. Today he would live in hope, he would take tomorrow when it came. In all his fears of what his past could bring to haunt him, he never dreamed it could be the life of his only child. Even though it was an accident, Ransom blamed himself.

Abner began with a diagram of the Sloma's vent, and the direction Matt should take from that point.

"The vent is one hundred fifty-one foot deep. It is four feet wide, When you reach the floor of the shaft, face the wall and go to the right." Abner said with authority. "Get your bearings. Smell the air. It will tell you everything you need to know. You can smell death, smoke, personal odors. Get a sense for the movement of the air. And all this time, adjust to the dark, listen to what the mine is telling you, and listen for running water. These signs should tell you where they are. The first shaft is fifty feet on your right, but it is not dug through. Fifty feet more is where they were working. The granite tectonic plates are there overhead, and so are the cedar support beams. The water should run through there as well. They should all be there."

Matt looked over the map as if it were a trail into the bowels of hell. No one in the room said anything to break his concentration. He studied, and committed everything to memory. After a few minutes he turned to Abner and said, "and what you need is right here, to the left of the shaft?"

When Matt asked that, Dorothy made a slight gasp and put her fingers to her mouth. It was the first time Matt realized the importance of what 'else' was down there, and the part it played in their lives.

"Yes," replied Abner. "There is a different stone stuffed in a hole. Everything should be there about thirty feet along the wall at floor level."

"Does Melissa know anything about this?" Ransom asked.

"Only that I'm going down to get them." Matt answered. "She knows nothing more. She's more interested in the Bratzi's and Angelo."

"I don't think her father would see the humor in the fact that those he delivered from a spy's death are living high-on-the-hog on a mountainside in West Virginia." Ruth said.

"I don't think we have to lecture Matt on the importance of secrecy." Dorothy added. "Just be careful. How will we know if and when you found something?"

"I've bought a trac-phone for Mary," Matt said handing it to Ruth. "When I come out of the shaft, I'll call. Hopefully I'll have some news. If I need and ambulance, you can call then. If we're lucky, we can all walk down the hill together. However, if we are lucky, we will unfortunately have media coverage beyond our expectations. You guys, especially you Abner, must be careful about that. You can bet Angelo and any new associates will be watching CNN once word gets out that night."

"Associates," snickered Ruth. "That's a good one. We have more empty dumpsters in town, don't we dear?"

"Amen to that!" Dorothy replied humorously.

"When are you leaving?" Ransom asked "And what about old man Sloma, he doesn't miss much?"

"I figure it'll be dark by six. It's cold, raining, gloomy, and Christmas Eve. I'm thinking Mister Sloma will be getting ready for church with Misses Sloma, and he'll be too busy to notice me. Besides, I'll be able to see what I'm doing without any light. I don't think he'll see anything." Matt said. "If I'm wrong...., well let's hope he's getting ready for church."

"How are you going to get her up that shaft?" Ransom asked.

"The shaft is one hundred and fifty feet down. I'll drive an anchor into the wall of the shaft every fifteen feet." Matt explained while drawing an imaginary line on the map of the shaft. "I'll put a harness on her and pull her up to the anchors, one by one. She should be pretty light by now. If not, I'll winch her up. Shouldn't be a problem. Before we leave the shaft, I'll put her in a thermal suit. That will make her even lighter, and protect her from the outside elements. They should all come up pretty easy. And if they are alive, and I need help, we can always call the fire department."

"And if they're not?" Ransom asked in a defeated manner.

"I'll bring Becky home in any shape, and send the rescue people down for the rest." Matt answered. "We should know by midnight."

"Well, I think it's time for an early supper, don't you Ruth?" Dorothy asked. "Matthew, you're going to need a good meal for your journey."

As the maps were cleared, and the table set, Matt couldn't help but feel touched by their hospitality towards him. He understood that it was part of his family, and his descent into the mine to retrieve their life savings would indeed change their lives, but Abner and Dorothy didn't have a lot. But what they had, they were sharing with him and Mary. Matt saw a love there that he never experienced before in his life. He was grateful for having had the privilege of knowing and being part of their lives. He sat down at the table for supper next to Ransom, who exchanged the most pleading of gazes on him. It troubled Matt that a man of Ransoms stature had become so broken by these last thirteen days. Matt wondered if he didn't have a great deal to learn from his elders about the tragedies of life that he had always escaped.

Supper went on with the usual jovial fanfare of telling old war stories of the good old' days of the cold war. Dorothy had to get into detail again of when her and Abner were caught naked in their own garden by that young police office. She laughed hysterically when she recalled the words of the policeman, "can you take this inside, ma'am?"

However, this time she would be outdone by the passionate exploits of Ruth telling her story of getting stuck at night with Ransom on the ski lift in Austria. Although Ransom was not at all participating in the monolog, Ruth went on with great enthusiasm.

"It was our last week in Austria before getting relocated in Cairo for the remainder of the winter. We decided to have a child, and this was the perfect time of the month to do it. So, what better place to get down to the nitty gritty than a ski resort." Ruth went on while adjusting herself in her chair. "So, we're planning on a couple trips in the powder and then we are going back to our room for an evening together. Well, we get nuzzled against the wind in a large pine grove and the lift stops. So after about twenty minutes of setting there, I'm thinking we are going to be there awhile. So, we decided not to wait to get back to the room, because we didn't know how long we would be stuck up there. So, we made some adjustments in position and made wonderful love on that ski lift. We could see people coming up the slopes to rescue us, so we thought we should get decent. When I retook my seat, a gust of wind came down the slope and I swear I had ice crystals forming on my coochie. Ransom is holding on to me for dear life while I'm trying to pull my pants up, with the ski patrol holding a flashlight so we could get off the lift. It was most embarrassing; however the experience was amazing. Nine months later we're in Cairo having Becky. What a wonderful time in our lives back then. The cold war could have lasted forever in my opinion. We lived and loved every day as if it were our last, but every day was full of purpose.

I look back on those days, Dorothy, and wonder how did we ever get so old? I can still remember how paranoid we would get when a black Ford would round the corner when we were walking down the street, and how many times two men in hats would look our way. Ransom had a photographic memory in those days. If we saw them twice in the same week, we took the steps to guarantee our safety.

Prague was the worse. I never saw so many black cars in my life. The damn place was still full of Nazi's in 1960. The strangest characters hung out there on the streets at night. But you know Matthew, I'd go back to that life in a heartbeat. The excitement of being alive, to serve a cause bigger than life itself. We would live more of a life in one day than most people live in a month. I think we all did."

"Wait a minute!" Matt said. "You too? You're one of them too! Why didn't you tell me?"

"You are a good man, Matthew," Ruth said. "But you're in no way ready for the secrets of our lives, or those that are held within them. Maybe someday, but not today. You've got enough on your plate right now as it is."

Matt could only stare aimlessly at Ruth after that statement. "Are you kidding me?" Matt asked Ruth. Turning his head, he noticed Dorothy looking at him with a most humorously devilish look.

"We'll talk, young man." Dorothy said. "After you get back, we'll talk."

Shortly after that exchange of pleasantries, supper was over and Matt and Dorothy helped Ruth clear up the dishes. Matt did his part as quickly as possible. He went in and spent a few minutes with Mary, telling her it as important to get some rest because Santa Claus was coming tonight.

"I don't want Santa to come if mommy isn't here too, daddy." Mary said half asleep. "Can you go and get her while I'm sleeping?"

"I'll do my best baby." Matt said. "I promise. I'm leaving shortly."

With that Matt tucked Mary into bed, as she was already asleep. What a wonderful gift, he thought, bringing her mother home alive for Christmas. But what a major responsibility he held telling Mary he would try. The possibility of her being dead always plagued him every moment, and especially now as he said good bye to Ransom and Ruth. Looking into his father-in-law's eyes was the loneliest gaze he had ever shared. But everyone had done all they could do. It was up to the Lord now. It was time to prepare for the descent into the mine.

66

He started with the foot locker, that had for years intrigued Becky so much. Although many times he wanted to burn it, how would he ever know the value of it on this very night. In it was a silver, thermal pair of coveralls. Four flexpens of adrenaline, four of vitamin V-12. Some old K-rations, a K-Bar combat knife, a container of matches and a Colt 45 Army issue pistol, and 36 rounds of ammunition.

On the wall of the basement was five-hundred feet of three-hundred-pound test mountain climbing rope, a belt of pitons and accompanying D rings, and a hammer. That, Matt thought, should get them out of the mine shaft.

In the refrigerator were all the IV's he would need. He checked the batteries in his flashlight and grabbed a bag of glow sticks. He was ready. Putting all his equipment in his backpack, he grabbed his cell phone, and shut off all the lights in the house.

Matt sat peacefully looking out the window to insure himself that there was no movement outside. All he needed was a nosy church goer to ask him where he's going at six pm at night with a backpack. These people may not be the be the most city wise bunch, but even Matt knew that telling them he was playing Santa Claus would be a bit of a stretch. He sent Melissa a text on his phone and was out the door.

The weather was perfect, Matt thought. It was raining steadily but not an Ark floating deluge. He hopped in the car, threw his gear in the back and quietly closed the door. He went out through the alley and took the long way to the church parking lot. It was remarkably quiet everywhere he drove. Soon, he was at the back of the church, and tucked himself back by the church bus where no one would see him.

From here he could walk the shadows up the hill past the Sloma house, cut through the fence and the shaft was right in front of him. He looked toward the Sloma's, who just happened to be getting into their car for church, and at the same time saw their trusty dog, Sam, in the house for the night. This was going exactly according to plan.

As he walked ever closer to the shaft his eyes were acclimating to the dark.

When he got to the cyclone fence around the shaft, Matt cut through the master lock, and drove in three large steel stakes into the ground close to the support poles. One was the down rope, one was the up rope, and the third was to hold Becky as Matt climbed higher up the shaft. Once all the ropes were secure, he threw them down the shaft. It was such a dark, unrelenting hole that promised no comforts or quarter to those who entered. It appeared to be the mouth of a mighty monster, fearful in appearance.

Matt put on his climbing belt, secured a D ring to it, and stepped to the entrance of the downward shaft. Prior to dropping through the opening, he broke five glow sticks, and dropping them into the whole, watched them spiral down to the floor. He now had his first view of the mine floor. He began his descent.

The trip down the shaft was much easier than Matt anticipated. He was able to securely drive the pitons into the coal wall. This in itself took out the worry about the pitons holding the weight of Becky, or any and all of the team.

The first thing to make it to the floor of the mine was the backpack that was attached to a ten-foot leading line. Matt noticed that it hit the floor without making a sound.

Driving in the last of the pitons at the bottom of the shaft, he was at the opening of a small dome seven foot above the floor of the mine. With one more release of the rope on the D ring, his feet touched the floor of the mine. He had made it with cautious ease, he thought, quietly thinking to himself, that it was too easy.

67

The mine was every bit of the nothingness that Abner said it would be as he stood very quietly on the floor. Darkness was the only sound he heard. He turned off his lanterns and stood in the blackness momentarily, taking the advice of Abner as to get the total sense of what the mine was telling him. He could hear nothing, see nothing, but he could smell the odor of wet sand and age-old rock, and the smell that coal gives off. He smelled deeply for any sign of death or odors. He did notice however, that the wind was at his back, coming from the vent shaft he had just climbed down.

Getting his bearings after the five minutes he stood there, he unhooked himself from his harness and turned on his lantern. He put on his backpack, secured the ropes, and looked behind him for the off colored rock Abner said was where the diamonds were hidden. By directing a mag light flashlight to the wall, he noticed it easily.

Matt began the walk in the direction that Abner directed down the shaft looking for a dead shaft fifty foot in front of him. It didn't take long before he found it, exactly where Abner told him it would be. Becky, he thought, should be right in front of him. Casting a glance along the wall he saw three rats munching on what appeared to be bread, in a nook at the wall. Strange, Matt thought, where would they get that, and then he noticed the rats didn't even appear to be alarmed he was down there. The sight of the rats eating gave Matt a surge of hope as he continued down the shaft.

It was then that his senses picked up the first sign of something more than rock. He swore he heard a light cough, and then the wind shifted, and the breeze was in his face. He definitely could smell the aroma of smoke. He picked up his pace, and was soon at the next shaft.

He stood still for a moment, and just stared down the shaft at what looked like a small fire, and what appeared to be a body lying on the floor by the wall, in the yellow reflection. The fire was nearly out and the person by the wall was motionless as if they were sleeping. They were even covered up by a large jacket. There was an actual brook of water running down the shaft past a large wooden cedar support, and into the rock pile that sealed the shaft, exactly the way Abner described it.

Matt walked slowly up the shaft in fear of startling whomever it was lying there. He shinned his mag-lite on the boot heels of the person lying there, and to his surprise he thought they were definitely Becky's boots. He walked closer to the person and began to flick his flashlight beam over their eyes to wake them up. Taking a moment to lock the beam on the face of the person, he could see it was Becky, and he began to cry out of gratitude.

He wanted to go to her and take his bride in his arms, but he thought the shock would be devastating for her mental status. He wasn't sure how weak she may have become, and he was afraid of scaring her.

"Becky! Becky!" Matt called out in a normal voice. Becky! Wake up honey. Wake up honey."

In a moment Becky began to rustle on the floor, lifting her head and moving her legs, she lifted herself up on one arm.

"Becky, it's Matt, honey. Don't be afraid. You're all right. It's me honey." Matt said repeatedly.

Becky adjusted herself to a setting position, and just stared at Matt.

"Matt, is that you?" Becky asked. "Is that really you or am I dead?"

Staring at Matt for what seemed like an eternity, she held out her hand and said, "touch my hand if that's you Matt."

Matt walked slowly over to Becky, and reaching out, put her hand in his and said, "it's me honey. I've come to take you home."

"I'm cold Matthew," Becky said. "hold me."

Stepping back from her Matt put more wood on the fire, and it quickly lit the place up to where Becky could easily see Matt.

"Oh Matthew," said Becky. "Where the hell have you been? Hold me. I'm cold, I'm cold to my bones."

Matt came up and sat down next to her, putting his arms around her.

"Do you have any idea how long I have waited for you? How long have I been here?" Becky asked, still trying to discern if this was really happening or if she was hallucinating.

"Thirteen days, honey" Matt answered. "Honey, where are the others?"

"They're dead Matthew." Becky answered. "They were killed right away. They didn't suffer. They're on the other side of that pile over there. But stay here and hold me. I have to know this is real."

Matt sat there with his bride, holding her tightly and just softly talking to her about nothing of importance. He put his face again hers, rubbed her right shoulder and continued to tell her that everything was going to be alright. They sat there, in the firelight for several minutes, until Becky became more aware that this was really happening.

Becky finally looked up at Matt and said, "it's really you isn't it? You came for me just like you said you would. I am safe now, and I'm no longer afraid. Will you take me home? Will you take me to see my daughter? Will you please get me out of here Matthew?"

"Yes, honey," said Matt. "We're going to take you home. It's Christmas you know? Everyone is waiting for you to come home. We won't disappoint them."

As they sat there talking, a vibration and growling sound could be heard farther down the shaft.

"We should probably get out of here Becky, but there are several things we need to do first." Matt said. "Are you hungry?"

"Oh, God yes!" Becky said. "Did you bring me something to eat?"

"For sure, my love. Steak, baked potatoes and your favorite wine. All wrapped up in this clear plastic bag." Matt answered.

"How do you expect me to eat that?" Becky said.

"It's an IV honey, it'll feed you." Matt answered. "You need some strength for our trip out of here."

"How the heck did you ever get in here?" Becky asked.

"I came down Sloma's vent."

"And we're going out that way?" Becky asked.

"Yes." Matt replied.

"How are you going to get the others out? We can't leave them down here." Becky asked.

"I can't get them out honey in the state they're in." Matt explained. "But when we get out, we'll tell the recovery team where to find them. They have the equipment to do it. My primary interest is you."

"We must do something about Zack." Becky began. "I took your advice and I ate most of his leg. We must hide that or they will think I'm a monster and lock me up."

"Let's deal with that when the time comes, honey." Matt said as he hugged her again, and softly kissed her. "I'll take a look while you're eating supper."

Matt got up and pulled Becky to a setting position and hugging her, told her all would be well. Moving her closer to the fire he helped her remove her jacket so he could insert the IV. He sat her back down along the wall, and began the IV, and fed her some high protein nutrition bars.

"You might get a little nauseous from these honeys, but it'll only last a second. Your body will absorb the protein first." Matt explained. "Just relax and I'll go check on the others. I'll be right over there."

"Matt, is it really you?" Becky asked.

"In the flesh, honey." Matt returned. "Close your eyes and relax now. I'll be right back."

"I knew you would come for me, but I was so scared and alone." Becky added. "I thought I would die here in this damn pit. Claudia told me you were coming, and to be strong, but I was beginning to lose hope in her also. She even fed me."

"Whose Claudia?" Matt asked.

Becky never answered that question. She just leaned her head back against the cold gray stone wall and dozed off. Matt began to wonder if she wasn't hallucinating, but it was normal after all she had been through. He went to the other side of the pile to tend to the others.

68

Dorothy kissed Abner good bye, and headed to the Christmas Eve services at the church. Since she was in charge of the auxiliary, it seemed wise for her to make an appearance, even on a night like this. Abner stayed back with Ransom and Ruth.

"How long has he been gone?" Ransom asked Abner.

"A little over an hour," replied Abner. "He should be there by now. Hopefully he has found them. Damn it would be nice if he could bring them all back alive."

"How is he going to get them out?" Ransom asked.

"He's got it all worked out, he's knows what he's doing." Abner said.

"What makes you so sure?" Ransom asked impatiently. "How do you know he knows a damn thing?"

"I got a copy of his service report from a friend at the embassy last week." Abner answered.

"You did what?" Ruth asked excitedly. "What did it say, for crying out loud.?"

"It said your son-in-law isn't the candy ass we thought he was!" Abner answered. "He's been in the shit a lot of times, and has come out of it bloodied, seasoned and smelling like it, but he's always come home. He'll bring them home if they're alive. And God help anyone who gets in his way. You know he's the one who brought John out of that damn Arab desert on his shoulders. I've never told anyone, but I've known it ever since he arrived here. That, and John told me."

"I'll be damned! Your John?" Said Ransom.

"Yeah, and not only that," continued Abner. "you remember when somebody kept paying my gas and electric? It was him. I seen it right away. I was just too damn proud to thank him for it. So, I'm hoping this one thing will show him my gratitude. I haven't been very nice to him."

"It wasn't only you, Abner," Ransom said. "He was one of them damn Yankees who were too good to be true when he came down here to marry my Becky. I always hoped he would wake up and go back home, but the damn fool never did. Now I like the sonofabitch. I didn't know about John though. Damn! I was certainly wrong about that boy."

"He killed that Bratzi pig like he did it every day before breakfast." Abner said. "He saved my ass, that's for sure. There was a part in his file about an assignment to kill some Al-Queda chief. It said he tracked him, found him and waited for the go-ahead for two days when some Washington Politician pulled the plug on the operation. It said he had to fight his way back six miles to the safety of the base. It was unknown the number of bodies he left on his retreat, but the report said the enemy suffered heavy causalities. It probably wasn't in their best interest to follow him. The damn kid tried to kill the whole damn bunch of them, damn near did too."

"Are you talking about the same man that holds my granddaughter in his arms above his head?" Ruth asked anxiously.

"Not to worry Mother, Ransom said. "She's safer with Matt that she is with God! Have you got any of that Christmas Brandy left over, my friend? How long has he been gone now?"

69

Matt walked around the mound of stone and dirt where the other three were buried. He first sighted Zack, a man of strength and stamina, diminished to a figure of broken bones, shattered dreams and the very things he stood for as a man. He would tell Melissa that he had found him quite peaceful in death. She didn't need to know the particulars. The cuts on his legs were obvious where he, in death, tended to the life of Becky. Phil and Carla were very ironically buried side by side, however in the standing position. Their deformed and intertwined bodies told the tale of a quick painless death. Their eyes, still open, were locked in the loving view of one another's. They died as they had lived, in love to the end, with promises of better days ahead. They would find solitude together for eternity now, where the days would certainly be better.

As Matt stood there, the floor began to shake and move. Dust began coming from the pores in the rock overhead, and some water began to drip thru the ceiling. Matt's plans for a decent burial were quickly abandoned. He had borrowed all the time he was allowed. It was time to go.

He returned to where Becky was sleeping, and noticed that the IV bag was empty. Becky appeared to be sleeping peacefully as he removed the IV needle, and the contents of his backpack to prepare her for the arduous trip to the top.

As he unpacked the necessary items he needed, to take his bride home, Becky stirred and sat straight up with a start. "Good morning darling," Matt said. "That IV will make you a little jumpy. How are you feeling? I hope you're about strong enough to get out of here, because this bad boy is about ready to come down."

"Claudia woke me up and said it was time to go." Becky said as she looked nervously around. "So, yeah, let's get the hell out of here."

"Whose Claudia?" Matt asked.

"She's an elderly biblical lady." Becky said. "She told me who she was married to, but I forgot."

"Just so it wasn't Pontius Pilate." Matt remarked.

"Yeah, that's him, Becky said. "she fed me and said you were coming."

"When?" Matt asked.

"Yesterday, I think." Becky answered.

"Okay, honey, we've got to get all your clothes off. Shoes as well." Matt ordered.

"But honey, I'm a mess. I stink, I've had my period, I can't go out like this." Becky pleaded.

"We have to change baby, I can't carry you with all this weight." Matt explained. Put this on."

Matt handed her a silver pair of coveralls, which appeared to be tin foil long johns, a pair of light weight tennis shoes, a pair of brown jersey gloves, and a pair of goggles. He then held in front of her a harness, which went over the silver jump suit.

As Becky began disrobing, Matt was quite taken aback by the amount of weight she had lost. But he knew with his care and the proper nutrition, he would have her back to her playing weight in no time. He gave her an exam of sorts to check for any broken bones or muscle strains. Looking Becky in the eye and shaking his head, he appeared he was satisfied. He took a syringe, and an alcohol swab and rubbed a clean spot on her buttocks. After doing that he injected with the contents of the syringe.

"Ouch!" Becky said. "What was that? Did you bring a pharmacy with you?"

"Vitamin B-12." Matt answered. "It will get you all the way home. It will give you added strength for the walk down the hill. The ambulance will meet us at the church. That is...if all goes according to plan. Let me suit you up. Put your hands on my shoulders and put your leg in here."

"Do we have time to bim-bam first?" Becky asked. "It's been awhile Matthew, and a girl does have her needs."

Matt held the suit bottom open so Becky could step into it. Just then another tremor and a loud bang was heard over their heads. Becky was somewhat pushed backward by the movement of the floor. As Matt reached out and grabbed her, she began screaming hysterically. Matt had to physically subdue her to get her to calm down so he could dress her.

"It's going to be okay honey," Matt said in a soothing tone. "But we have got to pack our shit and get! Now put your leg in here, baby."

"It's alright, we'll bim now and bam later." Becky said. Besides, look at my hair."

Despite the growling and vibration of the floor and ceiling, Becky was able to put her feet in the suit. Matt put her shoulders in the suit and helped her zip it up. He then helped her get in the harness.

"What is this?" Becky asked.

"This is how we get you out." Matt answered, securing the tension on the straps.

"Were you planning on sharing this with me, or is it like when we went Snipe hunting, and I learned as I went?" Becky said with a chuckle.

"Oh, jokes," Matt said. "humor is good here. This is what happens, Becky my dear. I'm going up the hole first. And then every thirty feet, I'm going to pull you up via this harness and then tie you off to the wall while I go up another thirty. And so on, and so on, until we come out on top of Sloma's vent. When we get there, you can call your baby girl and tell her that your safe. Abner will start ringing the church bells and Ransom will get the ambulance to the church. Just a walk in the park."

"I don't need no ambulance!" Becky said in a defensive manner. Just take me home."

"Honey, they'd throw my ass in jail if I took you out of here and went home. You need checked out. Then I'll take you home. Then the media storm starts. But it's going to have to wait until after Christmas dinner."

"Matt," what day is it?" Becky asked in a confused manner.

"It's Christmas eve, Baby." Matt said as he hugged and kissed her. I promised our daughter I would bring you home for Christmas."

"I knew you would baby, I always knew you would. I bet my life on it. Whatever happened to the rescue crews?" Becky asked, as they both walked hand in hand to the shaft opening.

"They quit yesterday!" Matt said.

"Them limey bastards." Becky hollered. "They spent two days on top of me. I built a bigger fire and even hollered at them so they would hear me. I'll be damn."

"Honey, where did the rats get all this bread?" Matt asked most interestingly.

"Claudia brought it." Becky answered.

"Straight up?" Matt asked.

"Yeah." Becky said. "Go figure."

When they came to the opening of the shaft, Matt insured all ropes were secure and nothing had been touched. It was still raining, but everything was perfect for the extraction. It was as if the Almighty coordinated all their efforts.

Matt took the red rope and tied a mountaineering knot to Becky's harness. At the top of the knot, Matt fastened a D ring and checked its security.

"Okay, I think we're good," Matt said "just one more thing."

Leaving Becky's side, Matt took the flashlight and walked to the area where the discolored rock was wedged in the wall. Removing the stone, Matt reached into a nook and pulled out two black bags and a small book. Matt felt the bags and recognized the feel that stones would make in a small bag. Like a little mineral bag at the county fair. He put the bags and the book in his pocket.

Walking back to Becky he said, "that's it baby. One hundred and fifty feet and we're home. As I pull you up you will see hooks every thirty feet. Use your hands to push away from the wall so you don't get the hook in the face. It should be a walk in the park."

"What did you just put in your pocket?" Becky asked.

"Something that belongs to Abner and your father." Matt answered.

"What could be down here that belongs to them?" Becky asked.

Just as Matt was about to say how surprised she was going to be, the floor began to shake and a rumble was present in the ceiling.

"Come on baby, we've got to go." Matt said. "Me first."

As Matt took his rope and began his assent out of the mine, he was quickly out of Becky's line of sight, and she got kind of nervous.

"Where are you!?" Becky screamed.

"Right here baby!" Matt hollered down. "Thirty feet above you."

"I don't like this dark stuff." Becky said. "You're scaring me."

"Sorry baby," Matt said, "I'll leave you a flashlight on the first hook. You're going to have to guide yourself into the shaft. Ready?"

"Yes!" Becky answered. "More than ready."

"Okay, here we go." Matt said. "Remember to look down so you don't get dirt in your eye."

The task seemed to go pretty smoothly. Becky got herself up through the shaft and it wasn't long until he had her on the first hook. The shaft began to shake as the mine began acting up. Matt began working faster, and the sections seemed to go by quicker. Matt looked up and could see the moonlight, even on this overcast night.

"I can see the stars above honey." Matt reassured Becky. "It won't be long now.

After about twenty-five minutes of climbing, Matt crawled out of the top of Sloma's vent. He took a quick look around to insure there was no activity in the area. Everybody was still at church, which could be clearly seen from Matt's vantage point. He knew he had one more major task before he could relax and take his bride home. He reached down to the rope and pulled her up the final thirty feet, setting her on the grass, and holding her tightly.

"Welcome home, baby.' Matt said. "Good job."

"I want to pinch myself," Becky said. "but I'm afraid I'll wake up down there again."

"It's not a dream, honey." Matt said. "You're home. Take a look around, while I put my gear away."

"Can I call Mary?" Becky asked.

"Of course, you can honey," Matt said as he handed the phone to her. "it's ringing.

70

Ruth got Mary out of bed and dressed for church as the other two old friends drank Russian Brandy and constantly checked their watches. Ransom was getting very nervous as Ruth just tended to the duties at hand, careful not to show the tension in every fiber of her being as well. Mary would ask if mommy was home yet, and that was about all Ransom could take. He got out of his chair and began to stare out the window.

"What time is it, Abner?" Ransom asked.

"It's been three hours." Abner answered. "We should know soon enough."

"Can I have my telephone, Grandma for when mommy calls." Mary asked.

"Of course, you can, dear." Ruth answered as she handed the phone to Mary who promptly set down and put the phone on her lap.

Ransom continued to pace and check the time on his watch. He was about to set back in his chair, when the most bizarre chime set them all in freeze mode. It was the track phone Matt bought Mary.

Mary answered the phone like a teenager, saying, "hello."

All was quiet for a moment as if all time just stopped. And then as if an eagle shrieked came the words," Baby...Baby, it's me baby, it's mommy!

Mary followed with her own shriek when she screamed, "mommy! mommy!

Ruth became a little wobbly in the knees as she grabbed the edge of the chair Mary was setting in to steady herself. Ransom was spent. After the whole long ordeal, he merely slid down to the floor and leaned against the wall, weeping openly. Abner came to his aid and sat next to him, and cradled his old friend and colleague in his arms. Soon Ruth had regained herself and went to Ransoms side as well and cried out of gratitude and excitement. Abner casually looked up at the ceiling and said a quiet "thank you."

After a few minutes all had a chance to talk to Becky. When Abner finished, he headed to the church to ring the bells and tell Dorothy, who would then alert the church congregation. Ransom was next to call 911 to get the ambulance moving, and then Ransom, Ruth and Mary took off for the church where Matt would bring Becky, down the hill from Sloma's vent.

Matt collected all his gear as Becky talked with everyone for the first time in thirteen days. When she finished, Matt helper her to her feet and held her tightly in his arms.

"Merry Christmas, darling." Matt said.

"Merry Christmas, my love," Becky said, "and thank you. Thank you for the rest of my life."

"Thank you." Matt returned. "Thank you for holding on and giving us the chance to live the rest of our lives. What do you say we get out of here? Can you walk?"

"You bet I can." Becky said energetically.

Flashing a very wide smile at Matt, she took his hand and together they began walking down the hill to the church. It didn't take long and they could see from a distance that there was a great deal of activity going on, despite the chill in the air and the light snow. The church bells began ringing, and off to the right of the town, an ambulance began yelping down the street toward the church in hot pursuit of what exactly, the driver didn't know.

"The air smells like freedom." Becky said. "I've never noticed it before, but I'll never forget it. Matt, what do we tell the other families?"

"Nothing about Zacks leg. Just that they all died instantly. That Zack pushed you out of the way of the rock. That Phil and Carla were leading the way up the shaft when the cave in occurred. I covered Zacks leg. I don't think they will ever figure it out by looking at it. It was quick and they did not suffer. They all helped in saving your life. That should give them peace. They never made a sound, nor felt a thing. If you are pressed into how you didn't starve to death, you might have to tell them about Claudia. The church membership will love that, and that should satisfy them. A normal human can't fathom starving to death, they fear asking questions about things they really can't face the answer too. I don't think you are going to get any questions that you aren't smart enough to answer. You may have to talk to the mine safety people, but other than that, you don't owe anyone any kind of explanation. Remember, you were down there because of their fault, not yours. You'll be fine, and I'll be right here with you." Matt replied with the best explanation he could."

"I feel like an animal." Becky confessed. "How could someone actually do that? I realize I am alive today because of it, but you are going to have to help me come to grips with it. It's not natural. What happens to me when I've had time to think about it?"

"Time starts now, with us and with our daughter. It's not like it's never happened before. The sinking of the Essex whaling ship prompted the men to eat the flesh of their dead sailors to survive the ordeal of nearly ninety day adrift in the Pacific Ocean. The airplane crash in the Andes mountains caused the survivors to consume each other until help could arrive. And of course, you remember me telling you of Alfred Packer, who found a taste for human flesh while stranded in the Sierra Nevada's back in the 1800's. So please, don't think yourself a monster. It happens. You were fortunate you weren't down there alone. You probably would've starved to death. It's over now baby, it's behind you."

"So, what's been going on while I've been away?" Becky asked to change the subject.

"Honey, you have no idea the shit storm that has hit since you've been gone." Matt answered. "I've learned more things that have set my head spinning, that you would never believe. I realized quickly that I wasn't in Kansas anymore. Our neighbors are not what we thought they were, or are our parents either as far as that goes. I learned you were conceived on a ski lift in Austria. Strange people are hanging around. It's a little too much to get into now, but I promise I will get you up to speed. But I don't think you'll believe me. That dead miner caused more stink than you could ever imagine."

"Will things be alright?" Beck asked.

"I don't know, baby." Matt said. "I just don't know. Things are such a mess right now. You are going to be headline news when they get a hold of you. The experts listed you as dead yesterday morning. This is going to get very interesting."

As the two of them approached the bottom of the hill, Abner could be seen with Dorothy in front of his old Ford pickup truck with the headlights on in front of the church, which was filling with spectators. Becky spotted her father's car pull up, and for the first time in nearly two weeks she saw Mary running around in circles straining to see her mother. She could see Ruth pointing into the darkness in Becky's direction, but as yet could not be seen. The ambulance and police chief were the last to arrive. It was to be the greatest homecoming in the mining towns history. For the mine had given back one of their children.

72

As Matt and Becky approached the bottom of the hill, and Becky's final steps to her journey home, the lights from the church lit them up for all the crowd to see. A robust round of applause erupted as Becky waved to everyone as Mary, Ruth and Ransom broke free of the human barrier and rushed to her. Becky took Mary in her arms with a flourish of hugs, kisses and tears. Ruth put her arms around the both of them and Ransom went around all three of them. It was a beautiful sight to see. They all four fell to their knees in a grip of love and gratitude for the return of their lost loved one. Matt stood by and was quite taken aback by the display of love that he had never experienced before.

Ruth was the first to rise, and taking Matt in her arms said with tears in her eyes, " thank you, my son."

Ruth had never called me her son before, Matt thought.

Ransom was next, and looking at Matt nodded a thank you, which men understood between themselves.

Becky had to put Mary down after a few minutes, still being weak from her ordeal. Soon the EMT's were at her side giving her a quick examination prior to going to the hospital.

The homecoming prompted the mine inspector to the scene in search of answers to many questions. Matt was asked to make a statement. He only stated that the other three miners were dead. It was apparent that they died instantly. That Zack pushed Becky backwards before being buried himself. He also stated that the four miners were exactly where Abner Colb said they would be. He went on to say that there was a great deal of vibration in the shaft and stability was definitely a question. When asked how he got down there, and how he knew where to look, Matt calmly answered, "I went down Sloma's vent. Right where Abner said they were and where I could find them."

"We may pursue charges for trespassing!" The mine inspector threatened.

"It's not your property!" Came a rough voice from the crowd.

Emerging from the crowd was a large man who stood over six foot tall with a lady by his side.

"Who, sir, might you be?" The mine inspector asked.

"I am Mister Sloma," he said, "Clarence Sloma to my friends, and that is my mountain, not yours. You would do well to remember that."

Mister Sloma said nothing more. He just took his wife's hand and walked back into church. Most of the congregation followed them, and the Christmas services continued.

"I'm going to pursue incompetence and negligence!" Matt answered. "See you in court! We're all done here."

It was difficult for Matt to keep his anger intact toward the mine inspector. He had put Becky's survival in his hands and quickly learned he was merely a bureaucrat filling a slot in the process of a cover-up. He wanted to hit him, but he knew this wasn't the place or the time. His time would come. His number would be called. He would get his pound of flesh. But for now, albeit temporarily, it was a time for forgiveness and gratitude.

As Matt walked with Becky toward the ambulance and the congregation of welcoming church goers, a stranger stood in their midst. Angelo's grandson, Rico had driven down from Buckskin to see what he could see this Christmas eve. He was not disappointed. He found not one, but all the players his grandfather was interested in. He would make him proud this time. He would move to the next in line of the family leadership.

As the crowd broke up, Rico as well left and drove into town with them to get a feel for the layout of where Abner and Matt lived, before beginning the ride back to Buckskin. He had a lot to report to his grandfather. Although, as yet, he didn't know the whereabouts of the Bratzi brothers, he knew his grandfather would be pleased with what he did find out. He noticed that the diner was closed. He would have to wait for supper until later.

73

When they all arrived at the hospital there were a few reporters hanging around with their lights and satellite links. When they started with their questions, the police chief politely told them to get out of the way, He went on to say there would be a full statement in a short time.

Interesting, Matt thought. he has no answers. He walked past several reporters with microphones and quickly divined that they had no idea who he was.

They all entered the hospital and were met by a skeleton trauma team.

A nurse grabbed Matt's arm and said, "you and the girl are not allowed in her. Go to the waiting room!"

Matt casually said in reply," I'm her guardian, and She's paying the bill."

The ER Doctor saw Matt and said," Matt, come on in. What's your blood type, while I've got you here," as he slid the curtain closed. Becky's exam was thorough and quick. Blood was drawn to check for parasites and anything foreign she may have picked up underground. The doctor commented that she didn't appear to be starving and had no signs of dehydration. Her lungs appeared clear, and her eyes weren't bothered by the dark. He did however, give her a tetanus shot. After he was finished with his examination, she was taken to the shower room, because as the good doctor put it, "you are a might odoriferous, young lady, and a good scrubbing will certainly take care of that problem."

As Becky was taking her shower, Matt called Melissa and told her the situation. He told Melissa that Zack felt absolutely nothing. That he had a look on his face of peace. Prior to dying he pushed Becky backwards, and by doing so had saved her life. Matt finished by saying, "his life was not taken in vain. He had saved his fellow worker and friend."

"What will you do now, Melissa?" Matt asked.

"I think I'll go back east and start over, unless you want me to stick around." She said. "What are your plans?"

"I'm going back home and pick up where I left off. Put this behind me and nurse my wife back to health." Matt replied. "Will you be alright?"

"I'll be fine, thank you," she answered. "I think I'll take the insurance money and go on a long cruise. Thank you for everything, hanging out with you and Mary was the best time I'd had in a long time. Give Mary my love. Good bye my friend."

And then they were on their way home.

74

Everyone went back to Ransom and Ruth's house for some late night soup and to privately celebrate Becky's homecoming. Abner and Ransom put the eagle eye on Matt, accompanied by a piercing raised eyebrow. Had it not been for Matt knowing what was on Abner's mind, he may have gotten paranoid. He was however, still unsure of Ransom's part of this puzzle.

With the four women huddled in the corner getting caught up, Matt decided to take in the evening mountain air. He was quickly joined by Ransom and Abner who couldn't wait to see what their Christmas present looked like.

Matt reached into his side pocket of his cargo pants and removed a pouch with a similarity of a sow's ear, and a small black book about the size of a cell phone and handed them to Abner.

"I think this is what you asked for, my friend." Matt said. "It, as my Becky, were exactly where you said they would be. How can I ever thank you?"

"You just have." Replied Abner. "I am reborn. We have waited so long. So very long. I saw the rest of us this afternoon and told them to come to church tonight. If you came down the hill, we could all breathe again."

Ransom put his hand on Matt's shoulder and simply said, "thank you, son, for bringing this and my Becky home."

"The rest of us?" Queried Matt.

"There are a lot more players in this than I've ever let on." Replied Abner. "Did you ever notice that not everyone in this town is a hillbilly? We'll talk in a few days after the loose ends are tied up, we owe you that. But for now, let's just enjoy this day. We have all got a great deal to celebrate. And I think I'll do a little nuptial celebrating with my bride tonight. We should go on a cruise, Ransom. It'd be good for us old codgers to get out and stretch our legs. You know, breathe a little ocean air from somewhere other than the deck of a submarine. You're going to have to tell me more about that ski-lift, my friend."

Just then the door opened and Becky was standing there with a sleeping Mary in her arms and said, "Matthew, it's time to go home. Your ladies are getting tired."

Matt agreed with his lady, and going back indoors to get his coat, bid everyone a good night. Everyone made plans for the annual Christmas Hog Wrestle at one pm. the following day. It would be a wonderful celebration this year, indeed.

Opening the door to their home Matt got his girls inside. He took Becky's coat, and took Mary off her hands.

"I'm going to crawl in bed," Becky said. "don't be long."

Matt nodded okay, and took Mary into her bedroom. With Ruth already having her in her pajamas, it was an easy task to cover her, grab her bear and give her a kiss on the cheek. Shutting off the lights, Matt himself went into his bedroom only to find Becky sound asleep with the quilt pulled up tight to her neck.

Matt lay there with her for a while, just looking at what he had been given. He put his arm around her and began to cry. He had hoped and prayed for this day, but deep inside he doubted he would ever see Becky alive again. And now his every prayer had been answered, and the realization of that made him weep. How, he thought, could a human being love another human being so much. He had to rise from the bed for fear of waking Becky with his sobbing. Which really, wouldn't be a bad thing.

After several minutes, he was reminded that it was Christmas, and he had duties of Santa Claus to perform. Getting slowly out of bed he went and got the gifts out of the basement and began putting them under the tree. The job didn't take long, and he was surprised that he had carried on with the Christmas holiday arrangements despite the issues with Becky. He realized then, deep down, that his God would always bring her back home.

After he was finished with the gift placement, he grabbed a beer and went out to set on the porch. It was seasonably pleasant Matt thought although the evening had a slight chill in the air, but warm for this time of the year. Gazing out into the evening air his mind began to wander. He knew eventually they would find the two Bratzi brothers. What, Matt thought would be next? Would they send more here like them, or just let the whole mess go? Having looked in the sow's ear purse, he estimated that there had to be in excess of two million dollars' worth of jewels in that bag. He didn't think Carelli would let that go unchecked. The Bratzi's always acted like Abner had something that belonged to them, and Matt got the impression that they would pursue it to the end. The end had come for them, but what steps would Angelo take next. Matt knew he was fit for a fight, but it would have to be one of his choosing. However, he wasn't that keen on fighting battles for someone else. Matt knew he definitely needed some answers to make all the puzzle parts fit. And he was certain Abner had those answers. But did he really want to know. He just wanted to live out his life with his family.

His thoughts were distracted by a person walking down the sidewalk. He soon recognized the familiar face of Melissa. She came up on the step and sat down next to him looking off in the darkness.

"I'm sorry you had to hear about Zack this way." Matt said.

"Not to worry, I'm not surprised." Answered Melissa. "I'm just grateful that Becky made it out. You too were the only ones who had something going. I realized that last week. I would never win you to my bed with Becky still alive. But I am so glad you went down there. Now we all know the truth. Did they suffer?"

"Not by the looks of them," Matt answered. "They all looked surprised and unassuming. What are your plans? Are you going to stick around here for a while?'

"No, I don't think that would be good for either one of us. Especially me." Melissa answered and took Matts arm. "I think I'll wait until the funeral, get the insurance money, sell the house, and go on a cruise. I hear Costa Rica is beautiful this time of year, and they're always looking for young slender chicks to brighten up the landscape. I might just go down there and green up the place a bit. I think I'll stick around here a while though and see what ol' Angelo does. Who knows, maybe I'll shoot his ass. It would be a much better fate than letting Dorothy get her hands on him. Damn! That's one bad bitch!"

"When are your parents coming home?" Matt asked.

"Tuesday." Melissa answered depressingly." That's why Costa Rica looks so good."

Saying this Melissa got up, brushed off her pants and bent down and kissed Matt on the cheek.

"Thanks for everything Matthew." She said. "Another time, another place, and you and I would be doing the happy moon dance daily. Good bye, my friend."

Melissa turned and walked toward her house, never looking back. Matts eyes followed her out of sight, and with a sadness in his heart he said silently, "good bye, my friend."

As he sat there hashing all this in his head, a car drove up in front of Abner's house. Matt immediately got a sick feeling in the pit of his stomach. As he sat in the cover of darkness, he saw John get out of the car with his suitcase and walk toward the house. He was home for Christmas. Now Becky would certainly have some more questions about their friendship. He thought to himself that after this little rescue operation there was no more hiding his past. He would only be careful how he let it out.

It was time for Matt to go to bed as well. It had been a long and exerting day for him. As he rose up from the step, he felt a small tremor. Smiling to himself he thought, it would cover a multitude of sin. He thought how blessed he was. How blessed we all were. Life could go on now. But, Matt wondered, what would be the price for living?

75

Christmas morning dawned overcast and hazy, but with the promise of sunshine in the mist. Mary was up early, as was Becky, albeit a little groggy. The coffee pot was on the drip and the two girls were as skittish as a couple of grade-school girls at fall football practice.

Matt came out of his bedroom to a flourish of hugs and kisses. Some of those were quite intimate. As the girls circled the Christmas tree looking, shaking, uuhing and ahhing at the awaiting prizes under the tree Matt could only gloat at the feast he had served up for his ladies. There were even gifts under there for Abner and Dorothy. And thanks to Mary, they remembered to get one for John. The celebration was set. The only thing left was the silent gratitude for having Becky back home with them.

Matt went to the kitchen to get he and Becky a cup of coffee when the doorbell rang. Quite to his surprise Abner and Dorothy were there, and let themselves in well before the greetings were exchanged and Merry Christmas was sounded all through the house. Abner approached Matt and said quietly, "the damn library is closed today. Let me use your computer."

Being very surprised that Abner knew how to operate a computer, he agreed and led Abner to the desk and turned it on. Standing by, Abner turned to him and said, "okay, thanks Matt. I've got this!"

Matt smiled to himself and thought, this is going to be one of those days. He went in to drink his coffee offering Dorothy a cup.

The four of them exchanged pleasantries, and spoke briefly of Becky's ordeal. Matt couldn't help but notice how vibrant Dorothy was this morning. Of course, she credited it to having John home for the holidays.

The way Abner had walked into the house this morning, Matt thought there were different attributes for her sparkling demeanor this morning.

As they talked and had a second cup of coffee and more apple fritters, Matt noticed that Abner had been in the computer room for at least fifteen minutes. Mentioning it to Dorothy, and asking her if he should check on him, she merely said in passing, "no, he's fine. Just a few year end issues to clear up. He's so busy this time of year."

That was strange, Matt thought. Abner hadn't been busy in thirty years.

Just then there was another knock on the door. Matt answered it to find Ruth and Ransom there, wishing all a merry Christmas. Matt got them a cup of coffee, but when he returned to the living room, Ransom wasn't there.

"Where's dad?" Matt asked.

"Oh, he's in with Abner, finishing up some year end issues." Ruth answered.

That made even Becky suspicious, who gave Matt a quaint look and a wink and went back to the conversation with Dorothy.

About ten minutes later Ransom came back into the living room and sat next to Ruth. He affectionately rubbed her back and smiled. Becky looked at her parents and said, "what's going on here? You two are acting like you just won the lottery?"

Before Ransom could answer, Abner entered the room with an excited smile painted on a pale face that looked like he had just fallen out of a hearse. He casually sat down next to Dorothy who had her gaze locked on him.

"Tell us, dear," Dorothy said. "Is this going to be a merry Christmas?"

Abner sat like a third grader in the principal's office. He was fidgeting, with his hands between his knees with a shit eating grin on his face from ear to ear. Finally, he said nervously," between three point seven, and four million." And then he just giggled. Happiness overtook all four of them. It was the most intense thing Matt had ever seen.

Becky had no clue was all this meant. So, she finally said, "what is going on here?"

Matt got up off his chair and said to Becky, "why don't we go into the kitchen and make some more coffee, let them talk for a minute?"

Matt took Becky by the hand and walked to the kitchen.

When they arrived, Matt shut the door and started making coffee. When he turned around Becky was right there in front of him and said," come on, what's going on?"

Matt and Becky sat down at the kitchen table. Matt looked into Becky's eyes and took her hand saying, "honey, a lot has happened around here while you've been gone. I really don't know where to start. But this much I can tell you. Their days of poverty are over. But it is a long story. I promise I will tell you all about it. But for now, please be patient and don't ask a lot of questions. They will tell us all of it, and believe me when I tell you that it will blow your mind!"

76

Everybody broke up and went their own way that Christmas morning. A big dinner bash was planned at Ruth's and Ransom's house for one pm. And it was obvious that Abner had a coital gift for Dorothy he wanted to deliver before John woke up.

Finally, the Jensen family had some alone time and plenty to celebrate on this holiday season.

As Matt sat under the tree with Mary and Becky, he couldn't help but be swept over with emotion. It had been a rough thirteen days, and he knew he wasn't solely responsible for getting his Becky back. As he silently thanked a higher power, he thought he'd have to find out more about who Claudia was. The best he could derive, is that she had to have been here sometime as well.

As Mary and her mother opened up the gifts under the tree, all seemed to have been forgiven. Becky was home. Mary was happy, and all he needed to do was go along for the ride. For the time being that was.

Shortly after the gifts were opened and Becky and Mary had some bonding time once again, Matt got up and started breakfast.

"I'll get it together by tomorrow, Matt," Becky said.

"Not to worry, my dear." Matt returned. "Mary and I are here to take care of you as long as you want."

"Yeah mom," Mary said. "And we're good at it."

"I'll just bet you are." Becky said giving her two caregivers a kiss. "What do you say we get back to living? Let's get this holiday over and start some proper rehab and R and R. We've all earned it. Tonight, I'm taking a hot bath. Did I mention to you that you're washing my back? And tomorrow I'll get your Christmas gifts from Santa. Come on you two. Let's shake a leg and get over to dinner.

77

On the upper end of the county, by the Tug Fork river, in downtown Buckshin, another person was about to celebrate Christmas. However, he was going to spend it alone, and twenty miles down the road in Hope. Kind of a working holiday. Rico Carletti was about his grandfather's business. He would scope out the town of Hope and find out about some residents while he was at it. He might even run into his grandfather's lieutenants. The Bratzi brothers had to be somewhere in town.

Rico went down to Rosie's, the local diner for breakfast. It didn't take him long to recognize the fact that everyone looked at him like the stranger he was. He had to snicker to himself as he thought of the phrase, "you're not in Kansas anymore." Rosie's was buzzing with activity as Rico took an empty seat at the counter. The gossip about the daring mine rescue the evening before was the main topic of discussion among the townsfolk. It was indeed, the talk of the town. Not being oblivious to the events that took place, Rico drank his morning coffee, and just lent an ear to what was being said. The stories were that the husband of one of one of the miners went down a hole drilled in the ground, on a rope, and found his wife and brought her to the surface. All the other miners were dead. Rumor was that and old man named Abner Kolb, told the husband where his wife probably was. He arrived at this because of silt deposits down at the filter in the river on the edge of town. And sure enough, there she was!

The story also went on to say, that the rescue team was suspending their search at the end of the night. After thirteen days, there was no way anyone could still be alive down there. The only thing they could recollect about the husband was that he was originally from Ohio, and had served in the Gulf war. Some people even commented on the fact that he was crippled, and wondered how he could even get down a mine shaft, let alone come back out of it. And of course, there were those who asked how she survived down there that long.

It was the biggest thing that ever happened around these parts since the cave in itself. What the towns people didn't know, they learned from the Sheriff and CNN news coverage. To a town of Baptist believers, it was the Lord's work. And it happened on Christmas eve to boot. Imagine that.

Rico finished his breakfast, and catching up on the last gossip, paid his bill and headed out toward Hope in his rented Toyota.

The landscape wasn't what he was used to in New York. There were no freeways, and on several occasions, he had to leave the roadway to let a large piece of drilling equipment pass. He was really uncomfortable with this drive.

After what appeared to be half an hour, he arrived in Hope. The place was dead. Some news crews were clearing out and heading home. There were the sound of church bells in the background, and some pedestrians walking down the light speckled streets. All in all, he thought it was a pretty nice town. But he recalled what his grandfather had told him about their love for Yankees. So, he thought better of talking to any passers by.

He drove past what he understood to be Abner Kolb's house. He went down to the corner by the post office and parked his car. He thought that he'd just have a look around a little and then report back to his grandfather. His first real job in the family business. He would make his grandfather proud.

78

The annual Christmas dinner at Ruth and Ransoms house was well underway. The mood was a great deal different than it had been in previous years. No one was talking about how they were going to get by on a meager social security pension when things were so high priced in the area. This year, the subject was prosperity, abundance, and a new way of life that they had all deserved.

Matt looked at Dorothy, but knowing she was a financial genius, employed by the Soviet Union to disembowel opposing countries treasuries, could not accept the fact that they had no money. Maybe that was what was in the little black book.

Becky just looked around at everybody trying to keep up with the conversation. How did they all get so rich all of a sudden. After the third toast to the honor of Matt, Becky broke in and asked, "all right, all right. What the hell is going on here? Will someone please bring me up to speed here? I've decided as soon as the dinner table is cleared up, we are going to have a cup of tea and talk this out. There is something awfully wrong here. I'm happy about it, but confused."

Looking at Matt, Becky said, "you had better have some good answers if you know what's good for you."

Mary looked up at Matt and raised her eyebrows, and put her hand on her butt as if he was in deep trouble.

Before Matt could answer, Abner spoke up in Matt's behalf. "We'll talk it all through with you Becky. It's just a long story that will take several pots of tea. But this is your day, and we're here to celebrate your return. But it is time you learned some history."

"History!" Becky shouted. "what the hell does history have to do with it?"

"We all agreed that we will sit down and talk this out." Ransom cautioned his daughter. "Simmer down young lady! This is a little deeper than you can ever imagine."

Matt looked across the table at John who was just setting there in peace and quiet with no reaction whatsoever, staring out the window. His glare was locked on an object of some kind. And then it dawned on Matt that John had known all along who his parents were. Jesus, what a secret to carry around with you all those years. Matt gained a new perspective about John that day. He wasn't the young raw recruit, with a bullet in his butt, that he carried two miles through the dessert that muggy November night. He was more of a man than Matt have ever imagined. It began to make more sense to the question that Matt always wondered," what the hell was he even doing out there in the middle of the dessert, in the dark, alone, in the first place?" He decided that by the end of the day he would ask him.

79

After the dinner table was cleared off, and the dishes were done, the tea pot was put on the stove. The dining room chairs were put in a circle and the time for discussion was upon them.

Matt had put Mary down for nap in Ruth's guest room. As the adults sat down, John asked Matt if he was up for a walk.

"Let's get out of here and go to Willy's for a beer. We don't need to hear this again." John said.

"Again?" Matt asked. I've just gotten bits and pieces of it."

"I'll tell you all you need to know. Besides, there is a new face walking around town, and I think we should check him out." John went on. "I heard about the Bratzi brothers, and it won't be long until Angelo sends a replacement. If you get the chance, you should kill this replacement and then Angelo. Our parents will never be safe until they are gone. And we can't have mom cleaning up the neighborhood all by herself. And dumpsters are not the best place to hide the leftovers. Empty cemetery plots are the best for that."

"How would you know that?" Matt asked.

John just looked at Matt and grinned. "Let's go!"

Grabbing their coats Matt and John excused themselves and headed outdoors.

The outside mountain air was brisk, but pleasant on this Christmas afternoon. As the two men walked down the street in the direction of Willy's, John put on his gloves, then stuffed his hands in his pocket.

"Did you find what dad wanted you to retrieve from the mine?" John asked.

Matt replied. "Do you know about this? I mean, like everything?"

"Yes." John answered.

"How long have you known?" Matt quizzed.

"Since high school." John replied. "I came home early from school one afternoon, and found mom mopping the kitchen floor. I didn't think anything of it until I looked in the bucket and noticed the water was red. Blood red. I've always loved my mother. She was my best friend. She was always up front with me, and never had time for lies or beating around the bush like my father did. She never had anything to hide. So, I asked her what happened, and who was the body setting by the back door. She began to tell me a story of a life that I only thought James Bond lived. I'll bet we talked for several hours. After it became dark, her and I took the poor bastard out to the Cemetery, found an empty plot, threw his decrepit ass in it, threw some dirt over him and came home and fixed dinner. In those days, dad worked in the mines, so he wasn't home until about eight o'clock. So, as we fixed dinner, we talked some more. When dad came home, she went over it with him. It never even came to his mind that I was setting there. He just said, "thanks baby." After dinner she drew him a hot bath, and by the sounds of it later on that night, she raped him. She was like that. Some things got her all fired up sexually, and she took it out on poor ol' dad. Lucky bastard! So, I then went about my daily routine with a different appreciation of my parents, and an overall respect for my mother."

"Damn!" Matt said.

"Yeah, tell me about it." John replied. "There's that squirrely kid I saw walking around during dinner. Black hoodie, Yankees ball cap. Walks like his parents deserted him at the zoo. Let's walk over that way and see if we can make him nervous.

As the two friends crossed the street, the kid in the hoodie turned to look at them, but they weren't there. As Rico didn't want to call attention to himself gawking like a tourist, he continued on his trek. Much to his surprise, Matt and John came around the corner fifty feet in front of him and straight toward him.

Knowing he was made, Rico reached in his pocket to feel his gun, which was his courage if he needed it. As he walked closer to Matt and John, he felt a very uneasy presence when the two men looked him in the eye and stopped walking.

"There's nothing open today, except for the diner, young feller." John said. "You look a little lost."

"No, I'm here with the news, and I'm headed out this afternoon." Rico answered. "I thought I'd take a look around before I go home."

"New York is a long drive from here." John said. "Be careful on the drive home."

"Who said I was from New York?" Rico asked with an attitude.

"You did!" John answered pointing to his hat. "And remember it's illegal to conceal a firearm in West Virginia."

John and Matt passed by Rico on either side of him, and gave him a passing glance over their shoulder to make sure Rico didn't do anything stupid. After being satisfied that Rico was again on his way the two men continued on their way to Matt's house.

"Let's go to your house and look him up on the NARCO website. If he's as dumb as he acts, he probably has a record." John said.

"How do we do that?" Matt asked.

"We run his picture through the data base, and see what it coughs up." John said.

"You have a picture?" Matt asked.

"Yep!" John said. "You didn't think I wanted to really talk to that greasy bastard, did you? You're dealing with a professional here, you know."

Matt just looked admirably at John, not wanting to give away his inexperience as to not knowing how John took a picture of Rico, and knew he was palming a gun in his right coat pocket. So, he thought it might be better to change the subject.

"Okay, John, I have to ask you." Matt began. "What the hell were you doing in that damn dessert all alone, the same night I was in that damn dessert all alone? And how did we cross paths?"

"Well Matthew," John started. "It's a long story. And to hear that you are supplying the beer, well, your house, great scout, lead on.

When Rico was sure the two men had gone on their merry way he chanced a look over his shoulder. His mind was going a mile a minute as he saw the coast was clear. And he thought it would be best if he cleared out as well.

He hopped into his rental and headed back to Buckskin to figure out how quickly he was made. He was certain that one of them was Matt

Jensen, but he had no idea who that other guy was. He was a damn genius. He read me like a paperback.

As Rico drove out of town, he had an epiphany that was so shocking, he had to pull off the road to give it his full attention. That had to be Abner's son. He was a god damned spy, just like his old man. Holy shit! That's how he made me. He makes everybody. And it's Christmas, he came home to see mom and dad. Grandpa is going to think I brought him the Holy Grail this time. He had to get back to the hotel and tell grandpa what he had learned. It would be a wonderful Christmas after all. He didn't know what to tell him about not finding the Bratzi brothers, however. But he thought to himself that there was no one in that hick town capable of killing those two. They had to be somewhere around, he'd look again tomorrow.

He pulled back on the main drag and headed to town.

80

As the two made their way to Matt's house, John asked where the computer was. Pointing into a side bedroom, John followed the direction while Matt got him a beer.

John put the picture from his cell phone on to Matt's scanner and sent the picture to the federal criminal identification center. Within one minute, good old Rico Carelli was front and center on Matt's computer screen.

"I'll be god damned!" John said humorously. "That little weaselly prick is Angelo's grandson. Isn't that a kick in the pants? He must be out of goons to do his looking for him, so he sent his grandson. I didn't think employment opportunities were that slim in the mob. He must know the Bratzis aren't coming home for the annual Christmas party, I'll bet he makes the trip down here himself before long. Did you ever hear who that dead miner was?"

"Anything of interest?" Matt asked.

"Nothing to write home about," John remarked. "A few little larceny projects to learn the trade, but that's it." Did six months on a B&E in Attica prison. Why would they send him to that dump for a little B&E? No bigger than he is, I'm surprised he's still alive. Angelo probably bought him protection. Other than that, nothing. I've learned that some of those dummies find that they'll do time for the boss only once, and then that's enough. I remember all those fools that did twenty-year stints for bosses like Constelano, and Gotty, while they roamed free, getting fat on spaghetti and pussy. They wake up eventually. Nope, our boy is probably still a virgin."

"So," John started. "I would also like to know what you were doing out there in that dessert, all alone, in the middle of the night? Well, let me help you with that. You went out to hit Al Jaharri, am I right? And what, you set there about three damn days, with sand fleas crawling up your ass, and other places? And they aborted your mission. You probably had that rag head in your scope too, I'll bet.

Well, your man was a plant. A double. And HQ figured that out about an hour before I had the real Al Jaharri in my sights. I got my man while you crawled away from the flees under the cover of darkness. Unfortunately, I failed to check my six, and got shot in the butt. Not one of my proudest moments. It is not on my resume'. Please don't tell my mother this. So, I made it out into the dessert okay, but I had lost so much blood that I knew I'd never make it back to camp. So, I found out where you were, and basically, just waited for you to come by. That's about all there is to it. I'm sure grateful to you for coming by. I'd been dead by now if you hadn't come along. It sure is ironic that you ended up down here, isn't it? Just think, we can be buddies for life now. I'll teach you how to make moonshine. It's cheaper than Bud Lite."

Becky called Matt on his cell phone telling him it was time for desert and to get his bony butt over here pronto. As the two men closed up the computer, John said, "you'll have to keep a close watch on dad now. With you getting Becky back, Carelli will know that Abner has everything he thinks is his. He'll move heaven and earth now to get them. He'll take no prisoners. You can't either. Kill him and the wannabe grandson and dump them like you did the Bratzis, preferably in a cemetery plot. I'll cover you through the CIA if you need it. These bastards are a cancer. They must be cleared up. Come on, let's get some pie."

81

When the two of them entered the house, Becky met Matt with a stern, questionable look. As Matt walked through the door after kissing his bride, Becky gave him a firm swat on the butt.

"I don't know whether to love you or hate you. You've been a very busy little husband while I've been gone, haven't you?"

"I had to do something honey, my wife was away, and I had to occupy my time somehow." Matt answered. "You know you don't like me playing video games."

"Well I'm home now, and I guarantee you I'll find things to occupy your time." Becky answered with authority.

"Uhm. Looks like someone is going to get lucky." John interjected. After looking at Becky he changed his tune saying, "or not!"

The two families sat together eating pie and laughing, and enjoying everyone's company. Dorothy was the first to break the silence of their fortune when she said, "it has been a long road to walk, but the Almighty has shined his blessings down upon us today. I've prayed and prayed for this day, and now it is here. And so are our friends who were part of the events which led up to today. We are truly blessed, and I intend to give Abner's share to the church in thanksgiving."

Abner just sat there saying "amen" with the rest of them when he jerked his head up realizing what Dorothy had just said.

"Well, not exactly," Abner said. "We must be careful mother, as to not draw attention here. I love tithing as much as the next guy, but let's not be too hasty here."

That brought out a laugh from everybody. Even Becky found humor in it, and as she looked at Matt it was clear that he was indeed her blessing. They had so much to talk about tonight. So much to catch up on and so much to share about the last thirteen days. Becky had no idea how to tell Matt about Claudia. She wasn't sure how to explain it to herself for that matter. But in her heart, she knew that he would understand and be as grateful to her as she was. This day was going to turn out to be the best day in their lives. They would share it together, and everything would turn out fine. They were a family again, and there was a lot of living to catch up on. The walk back to the house was one of peace. Mary was exhausted, and Becky didn't have all her strength back as yet. So, the main theme in Becky's mind was a nap. And of course, Matt just went along with what his two ladies wanted.

By the time Matt carried Mary in the door, she was asleep. So, lying her down on the couch, he helped Becky with her coat and then carried Mary into bed.

"What a nice party, huh?" Becky said.

"Yes," said Matt. "Everybody had some celebrating to do today. It couldn't have come at a better time."

"So, the way I see it, Matthew," Becky said. "You have two choices. You can spill your guts about the extra-curricular activities of our parents' past lives, or you can take me to bed and give me the Christmas present I need."

"Should I light the tree, honey?" Matt asked.

"I'll show you what needs lit, young man!" Becky replied while taking off her clothes. "Just put down a pillow."

Matt locked the front door and followed his bride into the bedroom, only to meet her coming out and heading toward the tree.

"You haven't forgotten our age old tradition, have you?" Becky asked. "Come to bed Santa. I'll hear your confession tomorrow!"

Matt crawled under the afghan and held his bride tightly, for what seemed to be an eternity. He couldn't help noticing how light she felt in his arms. Like a massive weight loss had taken place. He knew he would have to take special care of Becky, until he could get her back in shape. Caressing, kissing and whispering in each other's ear. They made love well into the morning that Christmas night. They both gave all they had for each other, and swore they would never be separated like this again.

82

The sun rose beautifully the next morning in Hope. It's aura of welcome warmth brought a promise of peace and a prosperous blessing to all those who lived there. The town was happy again, it was alive. Yes, it had some mourning to do, but it had one of their daughters back alive and well. In a culture of small celebrations, this would be a magnificent feast.

The morning dawned very brightly for Matt and Becky as well. It was as if the very Lord himself made their morning coffee, and welcomed them to a new lease on life. And they had both fervently agreed they would definitely live it, and be grateful for it every day of the rest of their lives.

A meeting was scheduled at the mine regarding the recovery of Zack, Phil and Carla. The management made amends with Mister Sloma, and he gave them permission to use the vent access to retrieve them. There was some caution mentioned, because the mine was still vibrating from the aftershocks of the other quakes. There was a definite fear that the mine could experience another cave in. So, there would be no hasty assault on the mine. There was also talk about asking Matt to escort them to where the bodies were. But Becky would put an instant halt to any of that planning.

Other than that, it was shaping up to be a normal day in Hope. As Matt and Becky were standing on the front porch smelling the mountain air, Abner also came out on the porch. They all raised a toast to each other just as a garbage truck rolled by. Both Matt and Abner looked at the truck and then looked back at themselves. Matt threw his hands up in a 'beats me' expression and went back in the house.

"If that rescue team goes into that shaft and finds Zack, there are going to be a lot of questions," Becky said.

"Let's deal with it when we have to." Matt answered. "I'm thinking our recovery crew would just as soon say a prayer over them and leave them there. I'm not that impressed with their dedication to put themselves in harm's way for three dead people. Remember, I saw them in action the last two weeks. I think they are willing to let well enough alone."

"I'd like to tell you about Claudia, but I don't know how to begin, how did you know she was Pilates wife?" Becky asked.

"I've read that several people in hopeless situations reported seeing an elegant lady dressed in colorful robes and sashes, talking with them and assuring them that they would be safe. On expert divined that it had to be her, since she stood up for Jesus, he had rewarded her with a life hereafter, tending to the needs of Christians in peril. It's really neat that she helped you. I think she sat on the edge of the bed and told me I had to move now, that you were presently alive, but I needed to go get you; Now! I set up in bed, startled, and although I didn't see anyone, my heart and mind were at peace, and any further decisions had been made. I knew then, without question what I had to do."

"How did you know where I was"? Becky asked.

"Abner told me." Matt said. "He told everybody, but no one believed him. He concluded that the silt and the cedar chips of wood down at the filter proved where the water was coming from and the only place you guys could be. He put in the cedar supports years ago, and knew that they were weak. So, the cave in would stop there and that is where you would be if you were still alive."

"Why didn't they believe him?" Becky wondered.

"He's not very well liked here, honey." Matt informed her.

"How did you know how to get to me"? Becky asked.

"Maps and charts." Matt answered flatly. "He showed me where you were probably at and the path to find you."

"Explain to me again how your rescuing me, made them all rich." Becky ordered. "And explain it to me as if I was a third grader, because it makes no sense why it took you and not him to deposit the money. Was it down in the mine?"

"Yes." Matt replied shaking his head. "See, until you guys went down to mine that new vein, that section was closed off. But he had hid them down there, nearly ten years before. That was his financial life line, and he couldn't get to it."

"What do you mean, he hid 'them'. What is them?" Becky continued.

"Diamonds." Matt said. "Diamonds and a black book."

"Are you shitting me?" Becky said surprised. "And my parents were part of this scheme? What was in the book?"

"The book held account numbers of money that Dorothy skimmed off the government job she held." Matt explained.

"You mean Dorothy is a spy too?" Becky asked excitedly. And Abner? And it looks like my parents were also. Where does it end?"

"It goes a long way through this town." Matt said. "These old town folks aren't town folk, there are retired spies."

"Bullshit!" Becky hollered while getting off her chair grabbing Matt's coffee cup, and headed to the kitchen. "Go on, this is getting interesting. Wait a minute! Stop! How did all these spies end up in this town? Answer me that one Mister Bond!"

"Melissa's father." Matt said.

"Melissa?" Becky thought. "You mean Zacks wife? Her father brought them here? How the hell did he just 'bring' them here, on a Greyhound bus overnight?

"Yeah, you could say that! He was and FBI agent in charge of Counter-Espionage." Matt explained. "They helped him out and he paid them back by hiding them here after the cold war."

"Shut-up!" Becky said. "He's part of this diamond and little book caper too?"

"No, honey, he doesn't know anything about that, or can he ever find out." Matt said as he held Becky's hand in a most serious manner. "What is said here today can never leave this room. Their lives would be in danger. Your parents, Abner and Dorothy, and a great deal of people in this town. If this gets out, they will be hunted down and killed. There have been some very nasty people hanging around since you guys found that dead miner."

"Did he have a part in all this too?" Becky asked trying to put the puzzle of events together that Matt was explaining.

"Yes." Matt said. "In the black book, there was some valuable information that Abner had for sale. The dead miner was sent here to buy it from Abner, instead he tried to kill Abner. Abner had different plans and left him at the base of that section where Carla found him."

"You mean that our friend Abner killed that guy and left him down there. Our Abner. He couldn't hurt a fly." Becky stated.

"You'd be surprised." Matt said. "And his wife is worse. That Dorothy is a bad hombre'!"

"All right. Let me get this straight. My parents raised me thinking they were coal miners, when actually they were: what kind of spies?" Becky asked with a raised eyebrow.

"East German." Matt answered.

"East German!" Becky screamed. "Get out of here. That is bullshit, she said hesitating a moment. "But it could be worse...they could have been Russian. Holy Shit! East German's are Russians! Oh my God, I'll never be the same. Tell me my name is really Becky? All right, tell me this. What is a Bratzi? I've heard that name thrown around a lot yesterday."

"The Bratzi's are two brothers who work for the old handler who sent the dead miner here to buy Abner's goods ten years ago." Matt answered, hoping Becky wouldn't ask too much about the Bratzi's.

"Are they here in town?" Becky asked innocently.

"Yeah, kind of, I guess." Matt answered cowardly.

"What kind of chicken shit answer is that?" Becky demanded. Are they, or aren't they? Did they go back to East Germany?"

"Yes, honey, I'm sure that's where they went." Matt answered looking into his coffee cup.

"You are a lying sack of shit, and what's worse is that you're no good at it. You couldn't lie your way out of a Catholic bingo game." Becky hollered.

"No swearing in the house mommy." Mary directed from the kitchen.

"Sorry baby! Where are they. Straight up, no more bullshit!" Becky ordered. Are they alive?

"Here, and no." Matt answered.

"Here, as in this house, or in town?" Becky grilled.

"Town." Matt said.

"I see. And what part did you play in all of this?" Becky asked in a tone that was neither supportive nor condemning."

"Dorothy killed one, and I killed the other." Matt confessed.

"Holy shit! What happened?" Becky asked bluntly.

"The one came into Dorothy's kitchen and tried to kill her." Matt went on. "The other one came after Abner and I was with him at the time."

Becky rose from the chair and walked over to the front window. After a moment she grabbed her binoculars off the fireplace mantle and stepped out on the front porch as the police and EMS drove down the street in full lights and siren toward the school. After a few minutes she stepped back in the house.

"You didn't, by chance or poor planning, throw him in a dumpster, did you?" Becky asked.

"Yes, as a matter of fact, why?" Matt asked.

"Because the police and fire department are standing next to a dumpster which appears to have someone hanging out of it." Becky said with authority. "Would you care to elaborate on that?"

"Imagine that." Matt said as Becky handed him the binoculars.

83

Before Matt could get a clear look at the action down at the school, Abner's eagle-eyed beak came into Matt's view.

"I need a moment, Matthew," Abner said.

Walking into the front door, Abner saw Becky standing there with a stern look in her eye, that stopped him dead in his tracks. "Good morning missy." Abner said. "I need to talk with your husband a moment if I could. In private."

"No! We're going to talk together from now on." Becky ordered. "Can you shed some light on that poor bastard hanging out of the dumpster? And why are your pants unbuttoned?"

About this time Dorothy walked through the front door in her bathrobe and slippers, carrying an empty bread basket wrapped in a dish towel. Matt looked at Dorothy as she set the empty basket down on the coffee table and thought to himself, oh, you're good!

"Good morning Dorothy", Becky said. "What brings you here in hot pursuit of your husband?"

"Good morning Becky." Dorothy said. "How are you feeling this morning?"

"I was good until I looked out the window and saw someone hanging out of a dumpster at the schoolhouse." Becky replied. "It's interesting that it brought you two out of the house on this cold December morning without a coat on.

"Why don't we set down and have a cup of coffee. Are there sweet rolls in the basket Dorothy?" Matt asked.

"No, I came out of the house in such a hurry, I forgot to put some in there." Dorothy explained lightly. "So, let's figure this out, shall we?"

"I'd like someone to tell me how he got in there and what he has to do with my family!" Becky spoke authoritatively. "And you're going to tell me everything I want to know."

"I'm afraid that's not how this works, young lady." Dorothy scolded. "These are events which happened while you were, shall we say, away. They will be handled within the three of us. Turning her attention to Matt, Dorothy asked, how exactly did you sanction him?"

"Sanction?" Becky gasped.

"I crushed his windpipe!" Matt answered.

"Alright, good job. They'll never figure that out." Dorothy surmised.

"Where is his little brother, Salvatore?" Matt asked.

"Buried on the ceiling of an overturned house trailer with a carpet over his reposed hide."

Dorothy answered. "The rats will find him before the police do."

"They'll ship his fat ass back to New York, and old Angelo will be back in no time." Abner said. "Let's set him up. He's arrogant, and foolishly impatient. It should be easy. We'll put him in the compost grinder down at the grain store. The dumpster is too easy to trace. They'll be looking in all of them, now."

"John and I saw his grandson yesterday, outside dad's." Matt divulged. We followed him downtown and approached him. He'll be back. He looks like a squirrel, so he'll be easy to spot."

"Excuse me," Becky added "please, "when she saw Dorothy's stare. "You're talking about taking the lives of two innocent people here, am I right?"

Dorothy spoke up first when she put it plain, straight, and fearlessly frank, as she put up her hand, palm forward to get the total attention of Becky. "These people are not innocent. They are hardened state sanctioned killers who think nothing of who they kill or the pain they leave behind. They are rats, and need to be exterminated. They will stop at nothing to get what they want. And I personally will stop at nothing to see that's exactly what they get. Nothing!

These are not "people", as you refer to people who live in our town. These are left over from a time when anything was allowed and they came and went, gave and took as they pleased. You may be able to relate them in comparison to Nazi's. And until Abner's friend showed up in the mine, we were rid of them. Now they will have to be dealt with once and for all. Swiftly, quietly and without a trace. If his grandson was here, Angelo must be short of help. This might be the end of him and his family.

The police will be hanging around us for a couple of days. You remember they were at the house the night they were on our porch. So, except for the fact that we are old fragile retired coal miners, we will be the prime suspects. But you say you left no weapons or marks on him, so I think we're all right. I don't think the locals will ever figure it out. And you Becky were gone during all of this, so you don't know anything. I think we're good. Let's see what they do and we'll go from there. Any idea where Melissa is?"

"I think she's getting ready to take a cruise to Costa Rica." Matt replied. "She said as soon as she got the insurance money she was leaving."

"She's not one for mourning, is she?" Dorothy commented. "Isn't there going to be a memorial service? Matt, why don't you check on her today. See if she needs anything. Let's act naturally. We'll keep in touch. It'll probably take Angelo a couple of days to get down here. The first sign of anyone strange, holler. Go about your business. We can always mention to the cops that the Union probably killed the Bratzi's. Hell, that's even feasible. They won't even ask any questions. Alright Abner, let's go finish what we started. We've got to meet the others tonight at the hardware store to set up the accounts. We'll be in touch."

With that exchange Dorothy and Abner left, hand in hand, and headed back to their house. Matt felt relieved that Dorothy had this situation well in control. Now to convince Becky not to worry. That was going to be the trick. Matt had hoped Dorothy was correct in thinking that Angelo was out of people to fight his battles for him. But in his heart, he was unsure of that comfort. But he thought to himself, like she said, let's see what happens and go from there.

84

The eastern morning sun shown brightly through Angelo's Manhattan apartment as Rico and his grandfather drank coffee after breakfast. Rico had driven all night to get back to report to his grandfather what he had found on his mission to Hope. He was excited to tell him how he found Matt's house and had watched him come out of another house with a man whom he did not recognize.

He told him, proudly, of his encounter with the two men on the street corner. Although he was surprised they could tell he had a gun in his pocket, he mentioned that there was nothing notable about either of them, and that he had held his own against the two men's questions.

"I had hoped you didn't have contact with them," Angelo scolded his grandson.

"It wasn't intentional, grandfather," Rico defended, "I was walking and they were just there in front of me."

"Yes, but they knew who you were, and now they know who you are." Angelo advised. "There's something about Matt. He's not from there. He's a different breed of problem. He will not be easy to eliminate. What did the other man look like?"

"Big nose. Square jaw. Tall. Stocky. Piercing eyes. A lot of German in him." Rico answered.

"Abner's son may have come home for the holidays." Angelo said in a depressed mood. "That's not good. We have to act fast, but carefully. We need to get the diamonds before Abner can fence them. He's not as fragile or stupid as he looks. How the hell did he ever end up there in the first place, of all places? And how did Enrico know where he was? Something just doesn't add up. He sold me out years ago, and I never figured it out."

The two men sat at the table and talked at great length about their plans for the Hope situation, making makeshift plans and throwing some ideas around, when the phone rang. Angelo listened intently to the voice on the other end and when the conversation ended, he merely hung up and stared out the window.

"They just found Luciano in a dumpster with his neck broken." Angelo said. "This will change everything. If they got to Luciano, they probably have killed Salvatore as well. This requires a deeper, more refined plan. It's just you and me now, Rico."

"Who is they, grandfather?" Rico asked.

"I wish I knew, Rico." Angelo answered. "I wish I knew."

"We can handle them Grandfather." Rico said.

"I'm not so sure, Rico." Angelo answered in a defeated tone. "They play by a different set of rules than we do, and they are very familiar with their battlefield. Let's you and me take a ride down there and see what we can come up with. You better get some sleep, Rico, we'll talk later."

85

As the front door closed, Becky picked up her coffee cup and walked heavily out to the kitchen.

"What the hell is the matter with you?" Demanded Becky. "You killed a man for those two fools. What the hell are you thinking. It's obvious to me that you are not capable of rational thinking anymore, so I am in charge of this damn mess from now on."

As Becky was loading up for another barrage to fire at her husband, Matt strongly said, "Rebecca, it's time you learned something! And the only way you can do that is to set down, shut your mouth and listen."

Becky sat down under protest, crossed her arms, and put a frown on her face.

"While you were gone," Matt began patiently and subdued, "a royal shitstorm descended on this place by the name of Angelo Carelli. The day of the cave-in, Abner was standing on the knoll, and this Carelli and his goons, caught sight of Abner. Carelli thought Abner lived in Paraguay after the wall fell. However, Melissa's father brought them and a fair number of their colleagues here to live. Carelli would have no knowledge of the other's, but he has a keen interest in Abner. And now, he knows I am a friend of Abner's, and I stand in the way of him getting what he wants. We don't think he knows who Dorothy is, which is good, because she is more than capable of taking care of more than herself.

You're parents had a different handler, so Carelli is not interested in them, or the rest of the group, which I have no idea how many of them there are. The problem is that Abner has the purse strings for all of them, and he must get that distributed before Carelli comes back. But if and

287

when he comes back, he will have to be dealt with. He is, as Dorothy said a bad man, a cancer. If he has more Lieutenant's with him the next time he comes here, they will have to be dealt with also. This town, and all those dear to us are not safe as long as Carelli is alive. He will not come in peace. And he can't leave alive. He, and every mother's son of him must be eliminated. I am sorry I got involved, but they would have killed Abner had I not been with him. And to me, that means they would've tried to kill me as well. And did I mention that Abner was the only soul who knew where you were. So, we personally owe him.

Dorothy and Abner know what they're doing. They've dealt with these people all their adult lives. I trust them, and I put my family's' safety in their hands. But I am standing by to tie up any loose ends. You and Mary are still my top priority. Once this is over, we will be on easy street for the rest of our lives. But this has to stop, and you've got to stay out of it. Don't be making demands of, or shouting orders at Dorothy. She is a wonderful lady, but she does not take lightly to someone telling her what needs to be done. She knows more about this business than I ever hope to know.

I'm sorry to have to put this so bluntly, but sometimes you are very hardheaded. Stay out of it, honey. We'll be fine."

"What if we turn them into the F.B.I.?" Becky said. "That would be the right thing to do."

"Your parents would go to prison also, as well as a lot of these people in this town." Matt answered. "Melissa's father also. So many lives would be thrown in turmoil just because of one selfish killer. The stakes in this are very much higher than you can imagine. These people have lived a very peaceful existence since they were brought here. I think if the idea of rotting away in prison was brought to the table, I don't think they would leave many witnesses. We have to protect them, your parents, Abner, Dorothy, and all the others. And I feel that because they gave me you in the bargain, I'm open to help all I can and any way I can. Even if it did give them their financial lives back, I still owe them."

"I think what I am so mad about is that all my life has been a lie." Becky said, with a tear in her eye. "I can't believe that my parents were cold war spies. I don't know whether to be mad or be so damn proud of them I can't see straight. I'm confused, scared and don't know what to do. When I get like this, I get a little mean. I think it would be best to talk more with my parents about this. I certainly wouldn't want anything to happen to them. I've just to get my head wrapped around this."

"Your life isn't a lie, honey," Matt said, "the history was just changed a bit to protect you. They're still wonderful people who love you very much. I have no doubt that they would give their lives to protect you. When your mother and Dorothy were telling their stories about those days, the love just oozed from their hearts. I became jealous of the life they shared, and the sacrifices they made for what they believed in. If I could have just a day of that depth of living with you, I'd cherish it forever. I've always thought my life had some adventure in it, but when I listen to them, I realize I haven't even gotten out of my pajamas yet. I think you should talk with your parents. Make no demands, just listen, and I think you'll come away with a much deeper love and appreciation for them. I would like to say that don't be too surprised if you find their real names are not Ruth and Ransom."

"Oh, my God!" Said Becky. "I'm not ready for this am I?"

"You'll be alright. Just take it slow." Matt replied

Becky came over and sat on Matt's lap. She looked admirably into his eyes and said, "all this time, it was all about me. I had no idea what you went through. I guess what sent me into a tizzy was when Dorothy, Abner and you talked so casually about throwing someone into a compost grinder. I thought to myself, what the hell is going on, you can't make this shit up. I've been stuck in a coal mine for two weeks, give me some damn attention. I had no idea what was going on outside my little world. Just my luck their names will be Boris and Natasha Bentanoff.

With that the two lovers hugged and laughed and just made up for the time they had lost. The time together was now, and they had a life to live. She would leave this other business to Matt and get on with their lives together. She trusted her life to Matt and he came through. She had no reason that this would be any different.

86

Abner rose early that morning very spry and anxious to begin his day. After he took care of his morning husbandly responsibilities, and did some domestic chores around the house, he dressed for his trip to the library to get the particulars from Jacques on the transfer of the diamonds.

Upon arriving at the library, he was very happy to see that it was nearly empty. He was very concerned about the privacy involved in an electronic transfer of the information concerning the amount of money that was being transferred.

He connected with Jacques in a matter of minutes, and awaited his directions. Jacques informed Abner that at 3:15 p.m., a man will come to his door selling pool insurance. He will be a white male, brown hair, with a black sock and a blue one. He will wear his watch on his belt, which will be a blue military issue belt. He will be wearing a plain black suit with a red tie on a blue oxford shirt with the right collar button undone. His name is Altazar White. He has no children, but he loves them deeply anyway. He will shake your left hand complaining of poison ivy on his right. He will have a lap top computer, a scale, and a calculator. He will contact me by e-mail with all the sizes and weights. He will then transfer the funds to the National Federal Bank in Frankfort to be distributed to the banks in America, with the accounts that he will supply to you. He will show you the complete transaction, so as not to have the problems you had years ago. Tentatively, the items are worth 3.85 million. He will make the final assessment. If you agree, sign the form of agreement, and our business will be concluded. When he leaves, he will wish you the happiest of Easters this fall. Jacques concluded by saying he wished Abner well throughout the years, and was proud to call him his friend.

And that was that. The years of living in obscure poverty were over. He and Dorothy could live again. The life that he once led, although he was proud of it, was behind him now. Today was definitely the best day yet.

Dorothy and Abner arrived at the hardware store and were quite surprised to see that everyone was already there. Dorothy called the makeshift meeting to order by announcing that the diamonds were worth 3.85 Million dollars on the open market today, and that Abner had met with the 'Jeweler' earlier today and the necessary transactions had been made.

"You will each get $320,833.30, and it has been placed in an account for you." Dorothy said. "I will go over each and every one of your accounts personally with you, at which time I will give you your account number, and a bank card in which all your transactions are done. Some of you will draw from a bank account in Seattle, some from Boston, Charleston and Columbus. Everything you do will be done by a credit card, so as not to leave a lingering paper trail. Do not, I repeat, do not take it all out and put it in a local bank. I assure you it will be in the government's hands by close of business. Your bank card works as a credit/debit card, and it will be your protection. Be mindful of how you use it. For example, don't go out and buy a new car tomorrow. Upgrade carefully and casually. And I also suggest you do not use your German name. We are all unknown here. It's best to keep it that way. Any questions?"

"When can I see the money, can I put it in my hands?" Mister Bower asked.

"No sir, I'm sorry. You will never hold this in your hand." Answered Dorothy. "But I think you will be very impressed with how the new system of banking is nowadays.

"Can we get monthly payments sent to our account as in a retirement plan?" Mister Bronson asked.

"You can, but if you do that you will be responsible for taxes." Dorothy explained. "It's easier and better to go the ATM and take out what you need, within reason, when you need it. Let me say this: there are still many spies working and living in America. The F.B.I. uses all kinds of ingenious tricks to reveal them and take them into custody. Their best trick is watching the flow of money. Especially as it relates to people who haven't had any in the past. Make no mistake, you will be on their radar. Use your American names, and don't get careless. It's possible that if one of us is caught, we may all be caught. Taxes are a red line directly to you. And please, don't give out your card number for automatic payments, very dangerous."

"Can we move back to Germany, and use this money to do it?" Asked Wilbur Holt.

"You could, but I don't know why you would." Dorothy replied.

"My heart is still there, Dorothy." Wilbur answered.

"I understand Wilbur," Dorothy returned. "If you decide to do that, stop over and I'll help you transfer back to the Bank in Germany."

With that all the families began getting their accounts set up and prepared for a new life. They were all very grateful to Dorothy and Abner for the gift of financial security they were given. They knew they could never re-pay them, and also knew that it was really Abner's money, and he didn't have to share any of it.

87

Angelo woke up on Tuesday after a restless night of sleep, and decided it was time to put an end to this mess altogether. He summoned Rico and met him at the breakfast table. Together, over breakfast, Angelo began by saying he thought he thought it would be best if the two of them went down there together this morning, and just had a talk with Yuri, and maybe some kind of deal could be made.

"Maybe we could work out a split. Say fifty-fifty. That would be reasonable." Angelo explained. "After all, I did pay for them years ago, and I need that money to keep going. We have a lot of recruiting to do to fill the vacancies left by the Bratzi's. You and I are all that's left now."

"What if he is not interested, grandfather?" Asked Rico. "Do we convince him otherwise?"

"Well if we kill him, we'll never get the diamonds. And without the Bratzi's, we can't beat it out of him." Angelo explained. "We may just have to be careful here. Maybe we can meet him privately and convince him our plan is good for all involved. Let's pack some clothes and head down there."

As Rico went to him room to get some clothes, he thought to himself, 'why are we treating this old man with kid gloves?' Luciano told me if you want to get the truth out of someone, shoot them in the knee caps, and tell you anything you want to know. And he was confident that an old man was no match for him. He was going to be running this outfit soon, and he wasn't planning on learning the art of negotiation for anyone. That old sonofabitch would tell him where the diamonds were, or he'd have a hard time standing. And then after he told him what he needed to know, he would kill him anyway. Grandfather would just have to get onboard with it. He grabbed his Ruger 9mm, and zipped up hi suitcase.

A new leader was about to take over the family business, and he would be a man to reckoned with.

88

Matt, Becky, and Mary decided that after breakfast it would be a good day to take a walk. They hadn't been out for a family stroll since before Thanksgiving. By now all the news coverage and interviews were over with, and Becky was getting back into her routine of everyday life.

As they strolled happily down the boulevard the subject of Zack came up again. It weighed heavily on Becky mind, and the fear of having to explain it was becoming a fear to be dealt with.

Her and Matt talked about the chances that if anyone was to go down and retrieve the bodies, she felt it would be quite obvious what those cuts were.

Matt tried his best to relay to her that he seriously doubted if anyone would go down there any time soon. And if this mountain didn't stop shaking, he doubted if they would ever go back there if they didn't have to.

After talking further, Becky began to relax her fears on the subject, and was very cordial to other passersby as they walked along on their jaunt.

Suddenly Becky stopped walking and just looked at Matt. "Did you feel that?" She asked.

Matt stood momentarily as if concentrating and then replied "no honey, I didn't feel anything."

About that time Mary let out a shriek screaming, "mommy, the sidewalk is moving!"

Matt could sense the fear of his two ladies, and bending down to pick up Mary, nearly lost his balance when the second tremor came through. The second tremor was strong enough to shake the glass shades on the street lamps. Several car alarms were sounding off, and the majority of towns people out for a walk stopped in their tracks. A few ran for the safety of roofs and awnings. Just as soon as it came, it was gone.

As everyone looked hopelessly about, wondering fearfully when the next one would come, all became mysteriously calm. After a few minutes, everyone began moving again commenting openly about the tremors. Matt, Mary and Becky continued on their walk when Becky commented to Matt, "look at the birds honey, they're all flying in circles."

As Matt and Mary looked up, a vibration could be felt in the sidewalk itself. It didn't feel as if the sidewalk was moving, but as if the ground under the sidewalk was moving purposely. A low rumbling noise, resembling a train could be heard as the vibrations increased. Several towns people fell to their butts on the ground out of fear and protection. Prayers could be heard among those lying on the sidewalks and circled around trees. The sirens went off at the mine, although it was closed.

As things settled down again, the people got up and began to scurry for their homes, but it was a short lived reprieve. The rumbling became very pronounced, and several windows on the upper floors of the older buildings shattered raining glass down on the sidewalks below. A very loud belching sound was heard in the direction of the mine. As the onlookers looked that way, they could see an explosion of dirt, water and muddy debris violently erupting out of Sloma's vent and rising easily one-hundred feet in the air. The natural violence of that explosion sent people running hysterically away from the mine in all directions. Matt grabbed Becky, and with Mary in his arms crouched down and shielded the girls with his body, while watching the show at the mine. The unbridled violence was there to be seen, as the helplessness it left in its wake would never be forgotten.

After about five minutes there were a few aftershocks, which appeared to the imagination as a whale slowing moving through the ocean and the wake it left. The screaming and the terror subsided after a few minutes as the people walked hurriedly to the safety of their homes. Some people remained standing there and looked at the cloud of debris, and didn't move, as they too had seen the devil, and they had been spared. Most of them hugged their families and with unsaid words committed to a love and a life lived differently from this day forward. They saw it as a sign of redemption, and would learn from its lesson.

Matt, Mary and Becky rose as well, and looking at the cloud prompted Matt to say, "I don't want to sound insensitive honey, but I don't think we have a Zack problem anymore. No one will ever go down there again."

No one appeared to be injured by the looks of things as the three of them made their way home.

The cloud was ever present, as it appeared to be pulsating up and down as the mine continued to breathe. But the dust was not rising. It just hung there, like an unyielding force eager for more victims to feed its inner rage.

The odor of rock dust and coal filled the air and soon engulfed the whole town. Many onlookers who were not outside at the time of the quake were all over the street trying to absorb all they could of what had just happened.

When the family returned home, they were met by Abner and Ransom. "I think she's finished now." Greeted Abner. "Thank you again, Matt; for everything."

"I think I should be thanking you." Matt returned. "I've gotten the most out of this."

"I think we did everyone involved very proudly" Added Ransom.

As they parted ways, Matt said to Becky, "your father looks a lot better today. He's getting his color back, and he's not so stooped over. He was a mess while you were away. That's very good to see."

89

Angelo and Rico had driven all morning and well into the afternoon when they saw the turnoff to Hope. Their cold December drive had ended, as they were taking a slow cruise through the streets of the town when they saw all the police tape surrounding the mine entrance. They could also see the amount of damage from the tremor the day before.

As they approached the center of towns' historic four way stop, Angelo couldn't believe his eyes. As he looked out his passenger side window, there stood Yuri, big as life, staring right back at him. Angelo rolled down his window and said to Yuri, "let's talk, old friend."

"I'm not your friend, young or old. What are you doing here?" Replied Abner.

"I've come to get what's mine." Angelo replied. "One way or the other."

"Grandfather has been more than patient with you." Rico added. "We're not leaving without those diamonds!"

"Who is this weaselly prick?" Abner asked. "Are you employing children now?"

"This is my grandson Rico, he'll be taking over the family business soon." Answered Angelo."

"I do things differently than my grandfather." Rico said. "I don't barter with old washed up fools like you, I bury them."

"I see you're just as stupid as he is." Abner replied. "Why don't you two go home, there's nothing for you here. Take a look around, do you see any friends here? And take your other two friends' home with you."

"I bought those diamonds and those launch codes from you a long time ago," argued Angelo. "They are mine!"

"Unfortunately, your gopher came with no money. Only a vendetta to kill me and rob you. At least he got half way there." Informed Abner. "All those you trusted and thought were loyal to you, had only one interest, to rip you off and move to the French Riviera. They have all been milking you for years, and you were too dumb to see it. Have you ever wondered why you have only this kid to work with? You're old, you're tired, and you're broke. Go home. Go home while you still can."

"I don't think you understand who you're dealing with, grandpa." Rico interjected.

"Absolutely no one!" Abner replied. "Not for some time now."

"I'll give you one hundred thousand for the launch codes." Angelo interrupted.

"And what in the hell are you going to do with them?" Abner asked. "Have you stooped so low as to deal with terrorists? Those nukes will end up in your city. You'll be killing yourself. Think about it. Those people will not care where you live. There is no place you can go to be safe. And I doubt seriously if customs will let you in another country, you're not exactly unknown to the federal law enforcement officials, you know, hell they probably followed you down here."

"Why don't you let me worry about that?" Angelo said. "One hundred thousand, tomorrow morning at seven a.m. down at the filter. It's quiet down there. Come alone. We'll do business and then I'll be out of your hair forever. Oh yes, the diamonds, you owe me at least half of them. Don't be late, and don't be stupid. They are mine, and I want them!"

With that the two men drove away. They had things to talk about.

"How are you planning to do this Grandfather?" Rico asked. "Did you bring the money?"

"Hell no," Angelo said. "We're going to get the codes and the diamonds, and then we're going to kill him and throw him in the creek. He'll wash away to the bottom of the holler and won't be found until spring. That's probably where the Bratzi's are. We'll get what's ours and get the hell of this desolate place. This will get us some room to work in for a while. We can build from there. You did bring your gun, didn't you?"

90

Abner left the makeshift meeting, and headed home. When he arrived at Matt's house, he was relieved to find Matt in his garage. After setting with him and telling him of his run-in with Angelo, a momentary silence settled over them.

"We can see the filter pond from the bell tower at the old church, can't we?" Matt asked.

"That's what I was thinking." Abner said.

"Jesus, Abner, this is damn near too easy." Matt pondered. "Seven a.m. should be very quiet. The mine is still closed, so there will be no passers' by. The schools aren't open yet, so no buses. And I think they're burying the Herdy's at two p.m. Hell, Abner, let's shoot those two bastards and put them in the Herdy's grave. No one will be any the wiser, and we will be done with those sonsabitches once and for all. We'll get the car keys and ditch the car down at the trailer dump. I'm sure someone will find a good use for it. The view will be from the North, so there will be no scope glare. Jesus, Abner. How did we get so lucky?"

Abner listened intently to Matt without interrupting him. He knew he was making a plan which would bring an end to this crap once and for all. Even though Abner and Dorothy were financially independent now, there would be no peace as long as Angelo was alive.

"That'll work," began Matt. "I'll get to the tower by six-thirty and set up. You go to the pond about six forty-five. You need to face the East, so I can have the sides of them. They will probably approach you and start their spiel. The kid will have the gun. Hopefully he stands on the right side of Angelo. One shot should take them both out. If not, I'll take Angelo out next. You tidy up the best you can, and I'll get there quickly and help you clean up the mess. Hell, if you can, throw their knarly hides in their trunk, so they're not out in open. They're both skinny, so you should be able to handle them. Throw a shovel in your pick-up to cover them with. The mortician won't put the vault in until it warms up a bit. We should be good, Abner. This should end this."

"What all do you have to do?" Abner asked.

"I think I'll take my weapon over to the church tonight by the cover of darkness." Matt surmised. "And then go get it tomorrow night. Other than that, I'll just wait until morning. I think we've got a good plan. There's no sense in overthinking it. Do we need to tell the other's?"

"I think this is a classic example of what they don't know can't hurt them." Abner said.

"Yeah, you're right Abner." Matt agreed. "That's smart."

With that Becky called to Matt that his dinner was ready. The two men shook hands, and looking into each other's eyes, said nothing. They just nodded to each other and went their own way.

91

The early morning dawned beautifully, as it did every West Virginia morning. There was a slight frost on the grass and there was a slight overcasting haze to the air. Matt rose from his warm bed and dressed for his morning. All throughout his morning preparations he was hounded by the words of his commanding officer, remembering the things he would say to Matt before going out on a mission. The last pep talk bore deeply into Matts head. Matt had so hoped that those memories would fade, and he would be free of that life forever. By so far, he had very little relief.

As Matt left the comforts of his home, the visions and sound of days gone by were ever so present in his head. He was soon at the church after a short lonely walk, right on schedule. He entered through the boarded up basement entrance being ever so quiet as he made his way through the sanctuary and up to the choir loft. From there it was only a short climb to the tower.

As he got into position and set up his weapon, he could see an unobstructed view to the filter pond, and the position where Abner would stand to set up his target. Setting the scope range finder and achieving the necessary clarity through the eyepiece, he was ready. He mounted the silencer, and he loaded the British .308 caliber rifle with five rounds, and chambered the first bullet.

Matt watched as Abner arrived, also quite promptly and took up the perfect position to allow Matt a clear shot. As he sighted in Abner in his scope the voices again started in Matts head. The last words his commander said as he prepared for his last mission were loud and clear in his head. He could not understand that after all this time, how he could hold on to that. It was as if he was incapable of releasing it. Incapable of freeing himself from the monkey on his back. As Matt tried to clear his head from those demons, Angelo Carelli, and his grandson arrived at the filter. Matt followed them in his scope and put Rico in his crosshairs. He flipped off the safety.

The voice of his commander drowned out every other sound. "Do you know why I've chosen you for this mission? Because you are the last of a breed. The last of hardened killers who can do this job without a blink and without a miss. You want absolution for your sins, your tally of the lives that stood in the way of freedom that you have given to so many for so long. I will give it to you, today." Matt watched as Rico got closer to Abner. He could see there was a heated discussion going on. He watched Rico very close, putting the crosshairs of the scope on the center of his ear as the voice continued. "You are the last of them! Men who are called to do the work no one else is capable of. Now go kill this bastard, and I will absolve you of your sins, and you can go home. You, and only you can do this. Do you know why? Because you're a natural. You are hard. You are the last hard man."

The voice ended there and as Matt watched his target, he saw Rico draw a gun from his waistband. He cocked the gun and was moving it toward Abner's head. "You are the last hard man," he heard one last time as he squeezed the trigger. The recoil of the rifle and the ppfffttt of the bullet as it left the barrel brought Matt back to the reality of the moment. The bullet entered Rico's head directly through the center of his ear, spraying Angelo with blood and gray matter. The bullet did not hit Angelo as Matt had hoped.

Matt chambered a second round into the rifle, and as he watched Angelo, he could actually read his lips through his expression of panic. "What have you done?" Angelo mouthed. "What have you done?

As Angelo stepped toward Abner, Matt could see a twitch of Abner's right arm. In the blink of an eye, Abner drew from his pocket, a stiletto, opened the knife, and slashed the razor edged blade across Angelo's throat. Angelo just looked at him in horror as his life poured out of him and onto the ground. His face turned chalky white, and he fell lifelessly to the ground.

Abner looked momentarily at Angelo and Rico, and turned towards the church. He raised his arm to Matt, and nodded his head. It was finished so quickly, as if it were a bad dream that you had just awakened from.

Matt secured his weapon and left the bell tower. On the way down the aged, rickety steps he felt a sense of relief. Had his commander actually absolved him? Was he as free as he felt? He would savor the feeling as he made his way home and out to help Abner. It would never be thought of again.

92

Wilbur and Helen Heady had been married for sixty-eight years. They were life-long locals. They went to school here, attended worship at the same church, and were married in the spring. They never had any children.

One day the towns people noticed that they hadn't been seen for a while, so they asked the local police chief to make a courtesy visit. When Chief Hudler arrived there, he noticed the door was locked and the house was dark. After no one answered the door, he forced open the entrance and entered the home calling out for them, but to no avail. Upon walking up the steps to the upstairs, the chief found them both in bed, side by side, dead. They died as they lived. Together, in peace, and in love.

Today was their funeral. Matt and Abner planned to add a little Italian spice to their final resting place. Taking the bodies of Angelo and Rico, and placing them, albeit roughly and with no circumstance, or parting prayer in the bottom of the grave. They took turns covering the two with loose dirt prior to the placement of the vault. It was a good burial, probably better than they deserved, but Matt and Abner were feeling generous today and figured only the best for an old friend.

The little job went by smoothly and without incident. The next job was to donate the car to some lucky dump visitor. As they drove out of town, they saw a few people, but no one seemed to notice them driving a car well above their pay grade.

After the car was dropped the two compadres decided it was time for breakfast. So off to Rosie's diner they went. It was time to celebrate over ham and eggs and pancakes. Abner was buying.

"Dorothy is going to the funeral." Abner said. "She'll let us know if anything suspicious happens. Damn Matt. Do you really think this is finally over?"

"I do," replied Matt. "I think we can all get back to living, the way we were made too. Are you thinking of finally getting married?"

"Hell no," Abner said. "Why buy the cow, when the milk is free? And if you repeat that to Dorothy, I'll deny it"

The two men laughed openly as they hadn't done in a long time.

"Did you see the fileting job I did on that old sonofabitch? I done good."

93

Things had gotten pretty well back to normal in the coming days. Once the dust settled, and the tremors were gone, the people returned to living their dream in the remote mountain town.

A memorial service had been arranged by the coal company, and a marker had been made to commemorate the sacrifice the three miners made. Mister Sloma even agreed to have the stone placed on the very summit of Sloma's vent.

The service was scheduled to start at ten o'clock sharp. A large amount of townspeople came out in new dresses and suit coats. Prosperity had begun to flourish on the mountain town, and even the positive attitudes of the people showed. They had a spring in their step, and a smile on their face, even though it was a tad chipper out there this morning.

There were songs to sing, speeches given and all around praises to shout, as you would have in a good Christian mining town church service. Becky was asked to give a recap of working with her friends for the years they worked together as a team. She shared the good times and the fun they had, and the closeness they all felt as a team.

The service was hurried somewhat, when the smells of good cooking began to rise from the basement, since there was still the dedication service to come. It was quite obvious that the men folk were more interested in eating than they were in praying.

After the service there was to be a dedication service of the monument on top of Sloma's vent. Although it was a good idea, it was a little cold with a brisk wind, which prompted most of the people to suggest that they would look at the monument in the spring. Among those people who went up to bid their final respects, were Phil's wife, and Carla's husband. Melissa was nowhere to be found. Rumor was she went south for the warmer weather.

Becky couldn't help but feel bad for Phil and Carla's significant other. She doubted that they had any idea that Phil and Carla's heart belonged to each other and not them. Becky would comment to them that all they talked about was getting home to their spouses at the end of the day. How they had found the love of their lives, and were blessed to be married to them. It seemed to put their mind as ease.

"You laid it on pretty thick, didn't you?" Matt asked,

"Yes." Replied Becky. "But that was a good lie for a good cause. And you can dress them up as much as you want as long as it helps in the long run."

As the three of them left church, Becky handed Matt a bookbag to carry as she told Matt that the company offered her an office position as overseer of safety and health. It would pay the same, but she would not go into the mines to mine coal, only to observe that all safety regulations were being adhered to.

As Matt, Becky and Mary made their way up the hill, Becky became emotional when she thought that just last week, she and Matt were walking down the hill, alive and grateful for the gift she had been given. Now as she once again stood on the crest of Sloma's vent, she was overcome with grief. Matt and Mary both took her in hand and in minutes she was back to normal. The end of her ordeal was officially over this day as she said good bye to Zack, Phil and Carla.

After the prayers, dedication and thanksgiving were over with, the people began meandering back down the hill toward the church and lunch, leaving the three of them alone.

As soon as everyone was gone, Becky took the bookbag, opened it, and pulled out three gallon size plastic bags full of corn. Everyone took a bag and began sprinkling corn down the vent.

"What are we doing mommie?" Mary asked.

"We're feeding the rats honey." Becky answered.

"The rats?" Mary persisted. "Really?"

"Yes dear, the rats." Becky answered. "Those pesky little rats."

The End